W9-AAB-069

JUST DREAMING

THE SILVER TRILOGY

BOOK THREE

JUST DREAMING

KERSTIN GIER

Translated from the German
by Anthea Bell

HENRY HOLT AND COMPANY

NEW YORK

Henry Holt and Company
Publishers since 1866
175 Fifth Avenue
New York, New York 10010
fiercereads.com

First published in the United States in 2017 by Henry Holt and Company.
Originally published in Germany in 2015 by Fischer Verlag GmbH under the title
Das dritte Buch der Träume.

Library of Congress Cataloging-in-Publication Data is available.
ISBN 978-1-62779-080-2

Our books may be purchased in bulk for promotional, educational, or business use.
Please contact your local bookseller or the Macmillan Corporate and Premium
Sales Department at (800) 221-7945 ext. 5442 or by e-mail at
MacmillanSpecialMarkets@macmillan.com.

First American Edition—2017 / Designed by April Ward and Liz Dresner

Printed in the United States of America

1 3 5 7 9 10 8 6 4 2

For all you dreamers out there

All that we see or seem
Is but a dream within a dream.

EDGAR ALLAN POE

"SO LET'S TALK about your demon. Have you heard his voice this week?" He leaned back, folded his hands over his stomach, and looked expectantly at her. She peered back at him out of those unusual turquoise-colored eyes that had captivated him from the first. Like everything about her, as it happened. Without a doubt, Anabel Scott was the most attractive patient he had ever treated, but that wasn't what fascinated him so much. It was the fact that even after so many hours of therapy, he still couldn't figure her out. She always managed to surprise him, to get him to drop his guard, and he hated it. Every time she made him feel he was inferior to her, he was upset—after all, he was the qualified psychotherapist, and she was only eighteen years old, and severely disturbed.

But it was going well today. Today he was in control.

"He's not *my* demon," she replied, looking down. Her eyelashes were so long that they cast shadows on her cheeks. "And no, I haven't heard anything. Or sensed anything."

"Then that makes it—let's see—sixteen weeks since you

saw or heard the demon, or sensed his presence, am I right?" He intentionally let his voice sound a little superior, knowing that he was provoking her that way.

"Yes," she said.

He liked her meek tone of voice and allowed himself a small smile. "So why do you think your hallucinations have gone away?"

"I guess it could be . . ." She bit her lower lip.

"Yes? Speak up."

She sighed and put a strand of her gleaming golden hair back from her forehead. "I guess it could be the pills," she admitted.

"Very good." He leaned forward to scribble a note: *ak, d.s., v., hr, vk.* They were nonsense abbreviations; he was just making them up as he went along. Because he knew that she was reading them upside down and trying to work out what on earth they meant. With difficulty, he suppressed a triumphant grin. Yes, she had certainly aroused a sadistic streak in him, and yes, he had given up the proper professional approach to treating her long ago. But that didn't matter to him. Anabel was no ordinary patient. He wanted her to acknowledge his authority at long last. He was Dr. Otto Anderson, and one day he would be medical director of this psychiatric hospital. The institution where she was presumably going to spend the rest of her life. "Pills are essential in the treatment of a case of polymorphous psychotic disorder like yours," he went on as he leaned back again, relishing the expression on her face. "Therapeutically, however, we have done much more than that. We have identified your childhood traumas and analyzed the causes of your false memories." That was a great exaggeration. He knew from the girl's father that she had spent her first three years of life with a dubious sect that performed rites of black magic, but Anabel herself couldn't remember anything. And his attempts to find out more by means of hypnotism—which he had used even though it wasn't really allowed—had not been successful either. In fact, they knew no more than they had at the beginning of her treatment. He wasn't even sure whether the causes of Anabel's psychotic disturbance really did lie in her childhood; he wasn't sure of anything about her. But never mind—what mattered was that she saw him as the experienced psychiatrist who could read her mind, the man to whom she owed all her insights. "So at last you are ready to accept that your demon existed only in your imagination."

"Stop calling him my demon." She pushed her chair back and stood up.

"Anabel!" he said sternly. And it had been going so well. "Our session isn't over yet."

"Oh, yes it is, dear doctor," she replied. "My alarm clock will go off any moment now. I have a date to see a course adviser about my studies, and I mustn't oversleep and miss it. You'll laugh, but I want to study medicine so that I can specialize in forensic psychiatry later."

"Don't talk nonsense, Anabel!" A strange feeling came over him. Something was wrong. With her. With him. With this room. And why was the air full of the scent of his mother's lily-of-the-valley perfume all of a sudden? He nervously reached for his pen. A date to see a course adviser about her studies? Ridiculous. They were in the closed department of the hospital, and Anabel couldn't go anywhere without his permission, not even out onto the grounds. "Sit down again at once. You know the rules. Only I can end our sessions."

Anabel smiled pityingly. "You poor thing. Don't you realize yet that your rules mean no more here than—what did you call them?—false memories?"

He felt his heart miss a beat. There was something buried deep inside him, a thought or a recollection, information that he must bring to the surface. That was urgent because it was important. A matter of life or death. But somehow he couldn't get at it.

"Don't look so shocked." Anabel was already at the door, laughing quietly. "I really must go, but I'll come and see you again next week. That's a promise. So until then, sweet dreams."

Before he could say any more, she had closed the door behind her, and he heard her steps going away down the corridor. The little monster knew perfectly well that he wasn't going to give himself away by running after her, thus showing everyone that he couldn't control his patient. But this was the last time she'd act up with him that way. She wouldn't end the session against his will again. Next time he'd enlist the support of some of the male nurses. Maybe he'd have her strapped down—there were a number of methods that he hadn't exhausted yet.

When he closed Anabel's file and put it back in the drawer, he still had that faint lily-of-the-valley perfume in his nostrils, the scent that reminded him of his mother. And for a split second, he thought he even heard his mother sobbing as she called his name.

But then the voice and the perfume both went away, and everything was the same as usual.

DESSERT WAS TAPIOCA pudding, which would have taken my appetite right away if the Rasmus problem hadn't done it already.

"Aren't you going to eat that, Liv?" Grayson pointed to my tapioca, pale, translucent, and wobbly in its glass dish in front of me. He'd already wolfed down his own helping of lumpy slime with pineapple jam.

I pushed the dish his way. "No, you're welcome to it. One more British tradition that hasn't swept me off my feet yet."

"Ignoramus," said Grayson with his mouth full, and Henry laughed.

It was a Tuesday at the beginning of March, and the sun shone in through the tall, poorly cleaned windows of the school cafeteria. It cast a delicate striped pattern on walls and faces, bathing everything in warm light. I even imagined I could catch the smell of spring in the air, but maybe that was just the large bunch of daffodils lying on the teachers' table, where my French teacher, Mrs. Lawrence, had just sat down. She looked as if she'd slept even worse than me.

So there was spring in the air; Grayson, Henry, and I had grabbed our favorite table in the sunny corner near the exit; and I'd heard a little while ago that there wouldn't be a history test tomorrow after all. In short, everything would have been just wonderful, if I hadn't had the aforesaid Rasmus problem on my mind.

"Sometimes tapioca pudding can be delicious." Henry, who had sensibly skipped dessert, smiled at me, and for a few seconds, I forgot our troubles and smiled back. Maybe things would turn out all right. What did Lottie always say? *There are no such things as problems, only challenges.*

Exactly. Think how boring life would be without any challenges. Not that it had been absolutely necessary to add an extra challenge to the pile of them already facing me, anyway. Unfortunately that was the very thing I'd done.

It had happened on the evening of the day before yesterday, and I still had no idea how I was going to wriggle out of it.

Henry and Grayson had been studying for a math test at our house, and when they'd finished, Henry had taken a little detour to my room to say good night to me on his way to the front door. It was late, and the house had been quiet for some time. Even Grayson thought Henry had already left for home.

I was genuinely surprised to see Henry, not just because it was the middle of the night, but also because we still hadn't gotten around to officially changing our relationship status from "unhappily separated" to "happily reconciled." Over the last few weeks, we had silently gone back to holding hands, and we'd also kissed a couple of times, so you could have thought everything was back to the same as before, or at least well on the way there—but that wasn't it. The experiences of recent months, and things that Grayson had told me about Henry's love life before I came on the scene, had left their mark on me in the form of a persistent inferiority complex about my sexual inexperience (or "being so backward," as my mother put it).

If I hadn't been so happy that we were close to each other again, maybe I'd have taken the trouble to analyze the feelings smoldering under my happy infatuation more closely, and if I'd done that, maybe I wouldn't have thought up Rasmus in the first place.

But as it was, I'd put my foot in it.

When Henry had looked around the door, I was just putting in the new mouth guard for my teeth. My dentist, a.k.a. Charles Spencer, had discovered that I obviously ground my teeth in my sleep (and I immediately believed him), so the mouth guard was to keep me from wearing the enamel of my teeth away at night. I couldn't tell whether it was working; mainly it seemed to make my mouth water a lot, so I thought of it as my silly drooling thingy.

At the sight of Henry, I immediately tucked it between the mattress and the bedstead, without letting him notice. It was bad enough that my pajama top and bottoms didn't match, and didn't suit me all that well either, although Henry said he thought checked flannel was amazingly sexy. Which led to me kissing him, kind of as a reward for the nice compliment, and that kiss led to the next one, which lasted rather longer, and finally (by now I'd lost some of my sense of time and place) we were lying on my bed whispering things that sounded like lines from soppy song lyrics, although right at that moment they didn't seem to me soppy at all.

So our relationship status was clearly heading for "happily in love," and I was inclined to believe that Henry really did think I looked sexy in checked flannel.

But then he stopped in the middle of what he was doing, pushed a strand of my hair back from my forehead, and said I didn't need to be afraid.

"Afraid of what?" I asked, still feeling a bit dazed from all the kissing. It took me a couple of seconds to realize that it had just happened in real life, and not, as usual, in a dream where no one could disturb us. Which was probably why it felt so much more intense than usual too.

Henry propped himself on his elbows. "You know what. Afraid it might all happen too quickly. Or I might expect too much from you. Or want you to do something before you're ready for it. We truly do have as long as you like before your first time."

And then it happened. Now, in the bright light of the school cafeteria on a fine spring day, I couldn't explain it to myself . . . well, I could explain it, sure, but unfortunately that made things no better. Anyway, Henry's choice of words was to blame. That infuriating *your first time*.

It was the cue that brought my inferiority complex into play, and it also dragged its friend, my injured pride, along with it. They were both firmly convinced that Henry was somehow sorry for me because of my inexperience, or at least the expression on his face sometimes very much resembled pity.

Like at that exact moment, for instance.

"Oh. So you think I've never . . . never slept with a boy?" I sat up and wrapped the bedspread more tightly around me. "I see what you mean now." I laughed a little. "You took that

virginity stuff seriously when you and the others were playing your demon game, did you?"

"Er, yes." Henry sat up as well.

"But I only said I was a virgin so that I could play the game
with you." My injured pride was making me say things that
surprised me as much as they surprised Henry. Meanwhile,
my inferiority complex was applauding enthusiastically.

I really liked the confusion on Henry's face, and the way
he raised one eyebrow. Not a trace of pity now.

"We never really talked about it before," I babbled, almost
forgetting that I was telling downright lies, my voice sounded
so convincing. "Of course I didn't have as many boyfriends
as you've had girlfriends, but well, there was . . . this boy that
I went out with. In Pretoria."

Since Henry didn't respond but just looked at me expectantly, I went on. "It wasn't a great love or anything like that,
and we only went out for three months, but sex with him
was . . ." At this point, my injured pride suddenly switched
off (damn it), and I was on my own again.

And hating myself horribly. Why had I done it? Instead
of using the opportunity for a genuine conversation, I was
simply making everything worse. I instantly went bright red
in the face because I saw no way of ending the sentence I'd
just begun. *Sex with him was . . .* hello? Only now did I notice
how intently Henry was looking into my eyes all this time.
"Was . . . okay," I muttered with the last of my strength.

"Okay," repeated Henry slowly. "And . . . what was this
guy's name?"

Yes, you stupid injured pride, what was it? I ought to have
thought of that before. The longer you hesitate before telling
a lie, the less convincing it is. Any child knows that.

So I said, quickly, "Rasmus." Because it was the first name to occur to me when I thought of South Africa. And because I actually was a pretty good liar.

Rasmus had been the name of our neighbor's asthmatic chow. I used to dog-sit him, and for a hundred rands an hour, I took him and a pug called Sir Barksalot for walks with our own dog, Buttercup.

"Rasmus," repeated Henry, and I nodded, relieved. It sounded good. There could be worse names for imaginary ex-boyfriends. Sir Barksalot, for instance.

To my surprise, Henry changed the subject at this point, although I'd already prepared myself for an interrogation. Or to be precise, he didn't actually change the subject, he began kissing me again. As if he wanted to prove that he was better at it than Rasmus. It wouldn't have made any difference if Rasmus had been real—no Rasmus in the world could kiss better than Henry.

All that was two days ago now, and since then we hadn't mentioned my imaginary ex-boyfriend again. Okay, so my inferiority complex had enjoyed its one tiny moment of triumph, but in the long run, the Rasmus lie was not good therapy. And that was why I had to contend with a sinking feeling in my stomach, even without eating tapioca pudding, and even though Henry was smiling at me.

By now Grayson had vacuumed up my dessert and was looking hungrily around the cafeteria as if he expected to see a good fairy flying over to our table to hand out more dishes of tapioca.

Instead of the good fairy, however, Emily swept past us, casting Grayson a glance for which she certainly ought to have had a firearms license. She'd have run down poor

Mr. Vanhagen if he hadn't saved himself by swerving toward the teachers' table, while Emily went on her way to the counter where they served lunch, and where Grayson's twin sister, Florence, was waiting for her.

For several weeks now, Emily had been Grayson's ex-girlfriend, and she had problems with that little syllable *ex*. I admired Grayson for his calm stoicism when he crossed Emily's path. Even now he was just grinning. "I thought I'd had my day's quota of scornful looks in English class."

"I think she's upped the dosage." Henry leaned forward to get a better view of Emily and Florence. "I'm no professional lip-reader, of course, but I'm just about sure she's been telling your sister what you dreamed about last night. Wait a moment . . . the bunny-rabbit dream? Really?"

Because winding Grayson up was always fun, and it also took my mind off my own problems, I went along with Henry at once. "You mean the dream about the fluffy toy rabbit? Do you think Emily will give you away?"

Grayson put his spoon back in the dish and favored us with a mild smile. "How often do I have to tell you two that you're wrong? Emily doesn't know anything about the dream corridor. Apart from which she'd never go poking about in other people's dreams. She's far too sensible and realistic for that."

Unimaginative was more like it, but I couldn't say so because Grayson had more to say. "I don't know why the pair of you are always going on about it. I mean, nothing at all has happened for weeks now. That stuff is over and done with."

As always when he said that—and he said it fairly often, to convince himself that it was true—a part of me (the trusting part that liked a quiet life) hoped he was right. In fact, it was true that peace and calm had reigned in the dream corridors for weeks.

"Arthur has learned his lesson. He'll leave us alone now," said Grayson firmly, and the trusting part of me that liked a quiet life immediately played the same tune: *Right, we don't always have to assume the worst! And people change. There's some good in everyone. Even Arthur.*

"Yes, sure, Grayson." Henry frowned mockingly. "And of course he forgave you, ages ago, for breaking into his house while he was asleep and punching his nose. Very nice of him."

Arthur was sitting not far away from us, right behind the teachers' table, where Mr. Vanhagen was talking excitedly to Mrs. Cook, the headmistress, while Mrs. Lawrence, her eyes drooping, seemed about to lower her head into her soup bowl. Arthur was laughing at something that Gabriel had said, and showing his perfect teeth. There was no sign now of the injuries inflicted on him by Grayson; his face was as angelic as ever. He seemed relaxed and self-confident. I immediately regretted looking his way. The sight of him always made me furious all over again, and so did the fact that the others had no idea what kind of person was really sharing a table with them.

"Well, he may still be angry with me," Grayson conceded. "But he's bright enough to know when he has to give up." He energetically collected his assorted empty plates and dishes. "No one would give it another thought if you two would stop going through dream doors that shouldn't really exist." The doubtful expression on our faces obviously annoyed him because he looked away, but he added, thrusting out his chin defiantly, "Everything's just fine."

The trusting part of me that liked a quiet life had finally fallen silent.

"Sure, it's fine and dandy." My eyes flashed at Grayson. "Aside from a few minor details, like the fact that Arthur swore he'd get his revenge on us after he failed to murder my little sister. Or the fact that bloodthirsty Anabel has put her psychiatrist into some horrible kind of coma while she's on the loose again. Or that your supersensible, morally impeccable ex-girlfriend slinks into your dreams by night. But like I said, those are only minor details. Everything is just fine."

"That's not true." Although I had mentioned only a fraction of our problems in my list, Grayson picked on only the comparatively harmless bit about his ex-girlfriend. "Even if it was really Emily that you two saw in the dream corridor, which isn't likely, it will have been a one-off incident." He slammed a used spoon down on the pile of dishes on his tray. "Never mind the fact that she's guaranteed to take no interest in my dreams—she could never get past my new security precautions. Nor could you," he added in a grim undertone.

"Oh, is Frightful Freddy going to make people spell *tapioca pudding* backward?" I was about to ask, but I got no farther than *Freddy* because at that moment Mrs. Lawrence jumped up and climbed on the teachers' table.

And we were soon to discover that we'd been like people having a comfortable picnic on the crater of a volcano. They know the volcano could erupt any moment, but they keep saying how terribly dangerous it is, and arguing, and only when the earth shakes underneath them and lava shoots up do they realize that the situation is really serious. And that it's too late to do anything to save themselves.

Having knocked several glasses over, Mrs. Lawrence had attracted the attention of everyone present. Some of the teachers jumped up because their juice or water was dripping over their clothes. Mrs. Cook, with great presence of mind, picked up the vase of daffodils and got it to safety, and all the students sitting near us started whispering.

Mrs. Lawrence was around forty, and with her finely drawn features, dark hair, and long, graceful neck, she reminded me of that French movie star with the long bangs—Sophie Someone. She liked to wear pale blouses, Chanel suits, and high-heeled shoes in which she could move amazingly fast. Her hair was pinned up in a style that was elegant but still looked casual, and she could glare at you quite sternly if you hadn't done your French homework. In general, she looked the very image of the ideal French teacher, and we'd always felt as if Mrs. Cook hadn't appointed her in the normal way but had hired her straight from a movie set.

But that image had taken a bad knock now. Totally unfazed by the chaos around her, she stood on the teachers' table surrounded by the used dishes and overturned glasses and flung out her arms in a dramatic gesture.

At first I thought she might be going to make some kind of *Dead Poets Society* speech, quoting Walt Whitman, which would have been odd enough, anyway, since English poetry wasn't her subject, but unfortunately I was wrong.

"As you may know, because anyone could have read it in the blog of some little tart calling herself Secrecy, Giles Vanhagen here and I have been having an affair for the last two school years," she announced in the clear voice that usually made her students tremble, and not only the younger ones. Mr. Vanhagen, who had just been trying to mop up the contents of the spilled glasses with a napkin, froze rigid, and all the color drained out of his face.

You could have heard a pin drop in the cafeteria.

"An affair," repeated Mrs. Lawrence, turning the corners of her mouth down scornfully. "I hate that word. It makes everything so shabby, so petty and despicable, when it seemed to me so pure, wonderful, and sweet. I was so in love, so happy, and so sure that we had been made for each other."

Thinking about it later, it struck me as remarkable that in a room full of adolescents, who aren't famous for the delicacy of their feelings, no one giggled, or laughed, or brought out a cell phone to record this astonishing moment. I saw nothing but shocked faces. And no one moved. You could bet that a teacher at that venerable institution, the Frognal Academy for Boys and Girls, had never before climbed up on a table. If people ever did go out of their minds here, you could be sure they did it in a very correct and proper way, behind closed doors.

"I believed him when he swore he was going to leave his wife," Mrs. Lawrence went on, pointing a shaky finger at Mr. Vanhagen, who was obviously wondering whether the better course of action would be to hide under the table or sprint for the exit.

"But I should have known better!" Mrs. Lawrence turned on her heel, knocking another glass over. "Girls, are you listening? You must never trust men. All they want is to steal your heart and then tread it underfoot!" She looked around the cafeteria. "Would you like me to prove it?" she cried. "Would you like me to show you what he did to my heart?"

That was undoubtedly a rhetorical question not expecting any answer, although a fervent *no* or a projectile accurately aimed at her head might have prevented the catastrophe that now took place. But we were all too stunned to do anything.

Slowly, very slowly, Mrs. Lawrence unbuttoned her Chanel jacket and let it slide down over her shoulders to fall into Mr. Daniels's plate of salad. Then she undid the buttons of her blouse one by one.

"Look at this," she cried as she did so. "I'll show you where he tore the heart out of my breast."

I realized that I was holding my breath. We were all holding our breath. Two more buttons, and we'd see what color bra Mrs. Lawrence was wearing.

Mrs. Cook was the only one who summoned up the strength to move. She cautiously put the vase of daffodils down on the floor and reached out her hand. "Christabel, my dear! Do please come down from that table."

Mrs. Lawrence stared at the headmistress, irritated. "But my heart," she murmured. "I must show them my heart."

"Yes, I know," said Mrs. Cook, and her voice trembled a little. "Come along, let's go to my office."

"Where . . . ?" Mrs. Lawrence lowered her hand and looked down at herself. The heel of her left shoe was parked in Mr. Vanhagen's soup bowl, and when she took it out, pea soup dripped off it. "What happened? How did I . . . ? Why . . . ?" Her expression was one of pure horror now, and she began swaying slightly. Like someone awoken from deep sleep and not sure where they are.

"It's all right, Christabel," Mrs. Cook reassured her. "You

just have to get off this table. Andrew, could you give her a hand?" she asked Mr. Daniels.

"Who . . . where . . . ?" Mrs. Lawrence looked around the room in panic, her eyes disorientated as they wandered over our faces.

A thought shot through my head—she looked just like my sister, Mia, when she had been sleepwalking, and understanding rose in me, along with a bit of stomach acid. Mrs. Lawrence hadn't just lost her mind; there was method in her madness. And it had been staged especially for us. Someone had manipulated Mrs. Lawrence like a puppet, in order to show us something.

To show us he was far superior to us—and more than a little way ahead in the game as well.

"This is a dream, isn't it?" Mrs. Lawrence managed to say. "This *must* be a dream."

"Unfortunately not," whispered a girl behind me, and I was sure that all of us in the place felt as sorry for the stammering, swaying woman as I did.

All of us but one.

While Mr. Daniels and Mr. Vanhagen, who was still white as a sheet, helped Mrs. Lawrence down from the table, and Mrs. Cook put her arm around her and led her out of the cafeteria, I slowly turned my head and looked at Arthur. He seemed to have been waiting for that because, for once, he held my gaze with his clear blue eyes. Held it until Henry and Grayson were staring at him too. Without a shadow of doubt, all three of us had come to the same conclusion.

Arthur smiled. Not even triumphantly, but with a horrible kind of deep self-satisfaction.

While all the students around recovered from their shocked

rigidity and began streaming out of the room, Arthur gave us a little bow.

"And that was only for a start, you guys," he whispered as he passed us in the crush a split second later. "Try to improve on it if you can."

HENRY WAS THE first to pull himself together. "Well, so much for the reformed version of Arthur."

"Shit" was all that Grayson said, burying his face in his hands.

"How did he do that?" I asked, and the horror in my voice made me even more scared than I was already. "How could he manipulate Mrs. Lawrence in a dream, so that she'd climb on the table at lunchtime and set about wrecking her own life like that?" I was staring at the chaos around the teachers' table.

Henry shrugged his shoulders. "A particularly nasty kind of hypnosis, I guess. He only needed some personal thing of hers, and then he just had to find her door."

"Easy as pie," agreed Grayson ironically.

"But why poor Mrs. Lawrence? What . . ." I stopped for a moment because Emily's brother, Sam, was just pushing past our table on his way out of the cafeteria. Since all the fuss about Mr. Snuggles, the topiary peacock, he would mutter quietly, "You ought to be ashamed of yourself," whenever he passed me, and recently he'd taken to saying the same thing to Grayson, but today he seemed too upset to think of that. I waited until he was out of earshot, and then I asked again, "Why Mrs. Lawrence? What has she ever done to Arthur?"

"Nothing, as far as I know." Grayson was as baffled as I was. "Arthur gave up French two years ago."

"I don't suppose it was anything personal," said Henry. Unlike Grayson, he didn't seem upset, but strangely animated. "He probably picked on Mrs. Lawrence just by chance, to show what he could do. To show *us* what he could do." He looked at his watch. "Come on, Grayson, we have to be in class discussing futurist cubism in Russian avant-garde art with Mrs. Zabrinski."

Sighing heavily, Grayson reached for his jacket. "Hell, I still have goose bumps all over. I'd never have expected to feel so scared of Arthur. But right now it seems to me like all the other villains in the world are still in kindergarten by comparison."

"Look at it in a positive light." Henry gave Grayson an encouraging slap on the shoulder. "At least we know now why he's been keeping so quiet these last few weeks. He's worked out how to dominate the world."

Although that last bit was obviously meant as a joke, neither Grayson nor I could laugh at it.

"If Arthur can manipulate people in their sleep so that they'll do what he wants in real life, then world domination isn't such a far-fetched idea," I murmured. "And we can't even warn anyone—or we'd end up in a psychiatric hospital faster than you can say *dream doors*."

"Yes, well." Henry gave a wry grin. "It's just a shame we're the only ones who can stop him."

"Although we don't have any idea how," I added quietly.

"But . . . but we must do something." For a few seconds, Grayson looked utterly determined. "Let's all three of us meet at our place after practice tonight. We need to make a plan." As he put his jacket on, however, something seemed to occur to him, and the determination vanished from his expression again and gave way to sheer desperation. "That bastard! He really has picked one hell of a time. How are we supposed to save the world *and* pass our final exams at the same time?"

Henry laughed briefly. "At least he has the same problem himself. I don't think that Arthur is about to fail his exams for the sake of world domination."

I just hoped he was right about that. Although of course you don't necessarily need A levels if you plan to dominate the world.

In the two classes after lunch, no one was talking about anything but Mrs. Lawrence's nervous breakdown and her near striptease act. Apparently Mrs. Cook had driven her straight to a hospital, and she probably wouldn't be out again in a hurry. Mr. Vanhagen wasn't teaching that afternoon either. Maybe he'd also had a nervous breakdown, as my friend Persephone suspected. Or maybe he'd gone home to his wife and was looking for a new job. You didn't know whom to feel sorrier for.

By the time I set off for home with my little sister, Mia, the story had spread to the lower school students. Of course Mia wanted to know the details. "Is it true that she was wallowing in pea soup and left a slimy trail all over the school building?" she asked as soon as we'd left the schoolyard.

I was about to answer her, when someone put an arm around me from behind. Automatically, I put both hands up.

"Leave out the kung fu, please. It's only me!" Henry strolled along beside us. He still seemed to be in an inappropriately good mood, but I could just have been misinterpreting it. "Hi, Mia!" he said. "Nice hairdo."

"Lottie calls it the Empress's Nest." Mia put her hand to the braids pinned up on top of her head. "Liv and I call it the Empress's Compost Heap."

"Very useful if you don't know where to hide your boiled egg from breakfast," said Henry, taking his arm off my shoulder and reaching for my hand instead. "Okay if I come part of the way with you? Why aren't you on the bus, come to think of it?"

"Because it's such a lovely sunny day." Mia was staring at our entwined hands and frowning. Before she could ask anything embarrassing (like "Are you two an item again or not? And if not, why are you holding hands?"), I added hastily, "And because there's always a boy from Mia's class on the bus who calls her Princess Silver Hair. His name is Gil Walker, and he writes her love letters. In his own rhyming poetry."

"How ghastly." Henry laughed, and I forced myself not to look at the crinkles at the corners of his mouth and think of what it felt like to kiss them.

"You're dead right." Luckily, Mia let that distract her. "At last, someone who doesn't think it's sweet and touching. Lottie, Mom, and Liv have been trying to persuade me to think up delicate things to say, so as not to hurt his feelings."

"So she told him, with the utmost delicacy, that he'd damn well better find some other princess to worship," I explained.

"Adding that otherwise I'd stick his poems where the sun never shines." Snorting, Mia kicked a pebble along the sidewalk. "Unfortunately that didn't put him off a bit. It just inspired him to write another poem."

She was right. Even I had to admit that it's no fun riding on a bus with someone behind you trying, at the top of his voice, to find rhymes for *eyes of heavenly blue* and *teeth with a glittering brace*.

"Mia and I have been thinking of fighting back with a poem of our own, called 'Walker the Stalker,' " I said.

The crinkles at the corners of Henry's mouth were still there. "Ah, yes, that's love!" he said with a theatrical sigh. "Makes one do peculiar things. By the way, Mia, do you still remember South Africa and a certain Rasmus?"

All of a sudden the joke was over.

"Rasmus?" repeated Mia.

Oh my God. Please don't. I had stopped dead in alarm. That was the trouble with lies—they always caught up with you sometime. Now Henry would not only realize that I'd made up my ex-boyfriend, he'd also find out that Rasmus was a dog. And then the pity in his eyes would be only too appropriate.

"Rasmus? You mean the Wakefields' Rasmus?" asked Mia.

I was still standing there as if rooted to the spot on the sidewalk, trying to tell her telepathically to keep her mouth shut. Unfortunately the telepathy didn't work.

Mia and Henry just looked at me, mildly intrigued.

"Er . . . hmm, yes, the Wakefields' Rasmus. Rasmus Wakefield," I said, pointing frantically at someone's front garden. "Oh, look at those beautiful daffodils!"

My pathetic attempt to change the subject failed dismally.

Without waiting for me, Mia and Henry turned around and went on. I stared helplessly after them.

"What was this Rasmus like?" I heard Henry ask.

"Why do you want to know?" Mia asked suspiciously back.

"Oh, no special reason. Did you like him?"

At last I managed to get moving again.

"Rasmus? Yes, sure," said Mia. "He was really cute. Maybe rather pushy. Kind of possessive. The Wakefields had spoiled him rotten."

Oh no! Please no! She'd be talking about his blue tongue next.

"Pushy and possessive, was he?" Henry looked briefly back at me and raised one eyebrow.

"Wait for me!" I got between them.

"Liv always called him a *little slobberer*, didn't you, Livvy? Ouch."

Unfortunately my elbow hit her in the ribs just a second too late. I linked arms with Mia and Henry, uttering a small, artificial laugh. "No, I didn't. Does anyone have a spare mint?"

It was useless. Mia was enjoying her memories, and as for Henry . . . well, as so often, it was difficult to make out the expression on his face.

"Yes, you did, Livvy. You had all sorts of silly pet names for him, don't you remember? Buttercup was terribly jealous. She bit his leg when you'd been tickling his tummy. . . ."

Oh, for heaven's sake! "Can't we please talk about something else?" I said, maybe a tad too vigorously. "Mia, don't you want to know about Mrs. Lawrence? Henry and I saw the whole thing live."

This time it worked. I finally had Mia's attention, and for now her mind wasn't on the subject of my ex-boyfriend, a.k.a. ex-dog. Although I was afraid that Henry would go back to it at the first possible opportunity.

Mia listened, fascinated, to the tale of Mrs. Lawrence climbing up on the table and delivering her speech. And nearly showing us the very place where Mr. Vanhagen had torn out her heart. Henry and I told the story by turns, and Mia sighed sympathetically.

"How terrible to think that unrequited love can send you out of your mind," she said after we'd described Mrs. Cook leading the totally shattered Mrs. Lawrence out of the cafeteria. "A nervous breakdown in front of so many people—I should think you'd never get over it."

"It wasn't a nervous breakdown," said Henry. "Unrequited love didn't send her crazy, and she wasn't under the influence of drugs either. She was in the same kind of state as you when you were sleepwalking and tried to jump out the window."

I looked at him in alarm. I hoped to goodness that he wasn't about to reveal the truth about Arthur and the dreams. We'd been disagreeing about that for weeks. "Don't you have to turn off here?" I asked rather brusquely.

Henry thought that we ought to let Mia in on the secret, if only so that she could protect herself. Grayson and I were against it. She was only thirteen, and she'd stopped sleepwalking. By now Mia's subconscious mind had taken plenty of precautions (her dream door was as safe as Fort Knox), and Arthur had new aims in view. Knowing that he had invaded her dreams and made her do things while she was sleepwalking, things that almost cost her her life, would worry and confuse Mia unnecessarily.

"What do you mean?" Mia was staring at Henry.

As for Henry himself, he looked at me and sighed when he registered my stony expression. "You'll have to ask your sister. Yes, I do have to turn off here. Nice to talk to you both, though." He dropped a kiss on my cheek. "See you tonight."

"Does he really think Mrs. Lawrence was walking in her sleep?" asked Mia as I watched Henry walk away. As usual, his hair was standing out in all directions. I used to think he styled it every morning in front of a mirror, using all his fingers and both thumbs, until it looked as wild and casual as that, but now I knew that he had no less than fourteen cowlicks on his head doing all the work for him. I'd found every one of them myself, and stroked them, and . . .

"It's terrible to see what love does to people," said Mia.

"Yes, poor Mrs. Lawrence," I hastily agreed.

"I'm not talking about Mrs. Lawrence." Mia jumped up on top of a low wall and made her way along the flat top. "What's up with you and Henry? Are you together again, or aren't you?"

"Kind of. One way or another," I muttered, relieved that we had indeed changed the subject. "I mean, we haven't explicitly discussed it. There are still a few things I have to clear up. And then I stupidly went and . . . er . . ."

Mia sighed and jumped down on the sidewalk again. "Then you went and what?"

"Went and invented an ex-boyfriend that I'd slept with."

Mia was staring at me, horrified. "Why?"

"So that Henry won't think he's the first." Put like that, it sounded even worse than I'd thought.

"Why?" asked Mia again.

"Because . . . because . . ." I groaned. "I don't really know myself. It just sort of happened. As if it wasn't me saying it, but a nasty-minded ventriloquist's dummy yakking away. And now Henry thinks I had a boyfriend in South Africa. And had sex with him."

"I really don't want to keep asking *why*, but I can't help it."

"It . . . well, he always seemed so sympathetic . . . and then there was that . . . oh, you don't understand."

"You bet I don't. Please, dear God, don't let me ever fall in love and do silly things without knowing why I do them myself." Mia linked arms with me. "Oh well, at least it's not boring being around you and Henry. I can't wait to see how you're going to get out of that fix."

Me neither. "One more thing. If Henry asks about Rasmus again, don't say he kept panting in a funny way, or . . ."

Mia stopped and began grinning all over her face. "Oh, I get it now. That's why Henry took such a burning interest in the Wakefields' pudgy dog." She was giggling unstoppably. "You said your ex-boyfriend was called Rasmus."

"It was the first name I thought of." I was beginning to see the funny side of it myself.

"Oh God, Livvy, only you could do a thing like that!" gasped Mia. "Rasmus Wakefield. Good thing I didn't say he stopped to lift a leg at every streetlamp."

"Or stank in rainy weather."

"Or howled when you played the guitar."

"Or once got stuck in the cat flap."

When our front gate came in sight, we were still falling over laughing, and we almost collided with an unshaven young guy who was carrying two moving boxes, a floor lamp, and a saxophone along the sidewalk.

"Are you moving in here?" asked Mia, pointing to the house next door.

The guy nodded, which wasn't so easy, because two books were jammed between the top box and his chin, and they now started sliding out of place. "Oh, good." Mia smiled at him, pleased. "The people who've been living there are dead boring. The woman's been sweeping the front path every day and swearing at the blackbirds."

"My mother has a blackbird phobia." The guy sighed, and the books slipped out from under his chin.

"Oops," said Mia.

I caught the books before they could hit the ground. One was a heavy tome entitled *Criminal Law*, the other was a much-worn paperback copy of John Irving's *The Hotel New Hampshire*. Obviously a law student with good taste in literature.

"Hello, the return of the prodigal son." Florence got off her bike beside us. As usual, she looked simply stunning, not in the least worse for wear after a long day at school. Her brown ringlets were tied back in a ponytail, with one gleaming strand of hair loose and falling decoratively over her face. If you considered her enchanting smile, bright eyes, and cute little dimples, you'd never have believed she would ever do or say anything unkind. But impressions were misleading. Florence had been in a particularly bad mood recently. "I heard about your girlfriend throwing you out of her apartment," she told the unshaven guy. "Your mum thinks she's the most horrible person that ever lived. You too?"

"The second-most horrible, right after Poison Ivy." The guy smiled too, showing nice teeth. He didn't even notice me holding his books out to him. "Hi, Flo. You've grown."

Florence put the loose ringlet back behind her ear. "Time doesn't stand still, Matt. I'll be starting at university this fall. You'd better watch out that I don't finish studying law ahead of you. I heard you failed a couple of exams. Your mum thinks it was unrequited love of the girlfriend."

"Ex-girlfriend." Anyone else would probably have been writhing with embarrassment, but Matt didn't seem to feel the least bit awkward. He looked like someone who was at ease with himself even with a floor lamp under his arm, and even though he was moving back in with his mother.

"You're better off without her, Matt." Florence patted his arm, overdoing the sympathy a bit and making the standard lamp wobble. "She's telling terrible lies about you. Saying you split up because you had something going with her best friend. And her best friend's sister. And that you'd rather hang out in clubs than study for your degree. And didn't pay your share of the rent for four months because of what you owed on some ridiculously expensive vintage car with a hood about four times as long as its trunk, something like—no, *exactly* like that one." She pointed to the red car parked beside the sidewalk. It really did have rather a long hood. "What a shocking liar she is."

"It's not a vintage car; it's a Morgan Plus 8, made in 2012," Matt explained with satisfaction. "The father of a friend of mine was selling it at such a ridiculously low price that only an idiot wouldn't have wanted to buy. The downside is that I'll have to live with my parents for a few months and cook my own food every day. But I'll survive. With such nice neighbors." He winked at Florence. "I bet Mum has kept the love letters you wrote me. Maybe we should reread them together."

Now Florence was having trouble keeping the pitying smile on her face. "I was twelve at the time," she said, pushing her bike on. Her ponytail was bobbing up and down angrily.

Matt grinned at her retreating view. "Seems like only yesterday to me," he said while Florence and her bicycle disappeared down the path to our house. Then he turned to Mia and me. "And who are you two?"

A couple of girls who had been listening, openmouthed.

"Florence's future stepsisters," said Mia helpfully. "I'm Mia, and this is Liv. She used to have braces on her teeth too."

"Nice to meet you, Mia and Liv. I'm Matt. The character who'll be sweeping the path here and chasing blackbirds away for the next few months."

"That's good to know." I put *Criminal Law* back on the top box, and Matt wedged it down with his chin and set off up the path to the house next door.

"Thanks. Be seeing you again soon, I'm sure," he said over his shoulder.

It was amazing to see how long he could juggle the boxes and the floor lamp, not to mention the saxophone, which was already at a dangerous angle.

Something else seemed to occur to Mia. "Did your mother really keep Florence's love letters?" she called after him. "And if so, would you sell them to me?"

Matt laughed. "Why not? I could use every penny I can get."

"Don't look so reproachful," said Mia as we finally started up the path to the Spencers' house. "I only want them in case of emergencies."

"For your career as a blackmailer?"

"Better a blackmailer than a thief. I was watching when you stole his book. What for?"

"Oops." I took Matt's paperback out of my blazer pocket, pretending that I was surprised to find it there. "Oh yes. *The Hotel New Hampshire*. I just wanted to read it again." That was a lie—we had a copy of our own on the bookshelves, even signed by the author with a personal dedication to Mom. In fact, it had come to me spontaneously that it might be useful to have a personal item belonging to Matt around the place. You never knew when such things might come in handy. And what could be more personal than what was obviously a favorite book, since it had been read several times already?

TITTLE-TATTLE BLOG

**The Frognal Academy Tittle-Tattle Blog,
with all the latest gossip, the best rumors, and
the hottest scandals from our school.**

ABOUT ME:
My name is Secrecy—I'm right here among
you, and I know *all* your secrets.

3 March

J'ai tremblé

tu as tremblé

il/elle a tremblé

nous avons tremblé

vous avez tremblé

ils/elles ont tremblé

And didn't we all just tremble in Mrs. Lawrence's lessons
when she had us conjugating French verbs! Woe to anyone
who turned up late. In the first year, I thought her stern
L'exactitude est la politesse des rois meant "Exactly like a
politician," or something like that, and I connected it with
being late and wearing the school uniform. (It really means

"Punctuality is the politeness of kings"; I add that just for those who opted to learn Spanish rather than French and who complain that my blog is too difficult for them.)

Anyway, that's all over now. Maybe no student will ever be trembling in Mrs. Lawrence's French lessons again. The last thing she taught us was never to get involved with a married man. Very useful. Could be even more useful than conjugating irregular verbs. Although I'm sure none of us can imagine ever getting involved with someone like Mr. Vanhagen—even if he wasn't married. Well, would we?

One way or another, what happened in the cafeteria today is terrible, so terrible that I wouldn't run a picture of it even if I had one. I owe Mrs. Lawrence that, although she did call me an anonymous slut. Well, the anonymous slut will tell you something now, Mrs. Lawrence: You were much too good for Mr. Vanhagen, anyway. And you'll be okay. It's said that psychopharmaceutical drugs work wonders these days. Who knows? One day you may be back teaching at Frognal Academy. Or you might meet the love of your life in the hospital and be happy somewhere else. I think you deserve it. *Chaque chose en son temps.* (Go and look that up, those of you who don't do French. I'm not your interpreter, I'm only the anonymous school slut.)

Speaking of school sluts: In view of today's drama in the school cafeteria, all other news pales, of course. So here are only the main headlines: At this very moment Jasper Grant is on the ferry from Calais to Dover. He was really supposed to be staying in that French dump until the end of the school year, but his father had to go pick him up today. Because he's been expelled from the school there for breaking the rules, and his host family wanted to be rid of him as soon as possible. For now we can only guess what he did that was so bad, but the great thing is that tomorrow we can ask him ourselves.

I for one am glad—I've really missed Jasper.

See you soon!

Love from Secrecy

"JUNE? YOU DON'T mean June this year, do you?" Mrs. Spencer Senior, a.k.a. Grayson and Florence's grandmother, a.k.a. the Beast in Ocher, a.k.a. the woman who on principle left her Bentley occupying two parking spots, a.k.a. just the Boker for short, stared at Mom, horrified. "But that simply can't be done."

"Oh, there's another three and a half months before the wedding." Mom was sitting at the kitchen table beside a mountain of essays that she had to mark, but before the Boker arrived, she had put her feet up and was basking in the afternoon sun. She laughed happily. "We can take it easy."

"We?" Florence wrinkled her nose. "You can leave me out of that *we*." Although she officially thought Lottie's presence in the household unnecessary, she had taken to hanging around the kitchen every afternoon, wolfing down the cookies that Lottie baked. Today there were tiny apple and cinnamon muffins that tasted as delicious as they smelled. When Florence bit into one, an expression of bliss involuntarily came over her face for a moment. But when she noticed that Lottie and I were watching, she said quickly, and as crossly as possible, "Anyway, Grayson and I can't help you with the planning. We have more than enough to do with our A levels. And then there's the end-of-exams ball in June. Maybe you really should think of putting it off until the fall. Or next spring."

"Yes, or 2046, so that your grandmother could celebrate her eightieth birthday at the same time." Mia picked up three muffins and looked thoughtfully at them for a moment, as if wondering whether they would all fit into her mouth at once. They did.

"Don't worry, there's nothing to plan." Mom gave us all a relaxed smile. "We'll just spontaneously improvise. Those are always the best parties."

"But . . ." The Boker looked as if she had to gasp for air. "But this is a wedding, not a child's birthday party. It takes more than a few balloons. The guest list alone . . . I mean, normal people have already made their summer plans by this time of year."

"Yes, let's hope that includes Great-Aunt Gertrude," muttered Mia.

"Oh, that doesn't matter. Anyone who has time to come can come, and never mind the people who can't," said Mom. "It's not going to be a big occasion, just a nice, uncomplicated little party. . . ."

"But I hope Lottie can wear her party dirndl." Mia grinned.

"And I'll bake a wedding cake, anyway." Lottie was beaming. "A three-tier wedding cake."

"That would be terrific," said Mom enthusiastically.

The Boker groaned. "All possible venues will have been booked for June already, of course—in the end, you'll be having the party in the garden here." She gave a little laugh showing she meant that sarcastically, but Mom didn't notice.

"Yes, that's a good idea," she said appreciatively.

"It would be a disaster," said the Boker.

"Not if we make sure that Grandma, Great-Aunt Gertrude, and Great-Aunt Virginia don't appear as the Supremes," I said, and the Boker went pale. It didn't seem to have occurred to her that we had a family of our own.

"Oh, how I look forward to meeting even more of you." Florence rolled her eyes. She might be Grayson's twin sister, but when it came to being good company, she took entirely after her grandmother.

Who had a vein beginning to throb on her forehead. "A little garden party! That's probably all very well if you're marrying a nobody without family or obligations." She began pacing busily up and down the kitchen. "Unlike you, however, my son can't simply ignore the traditions and principles that he owes to his social standing. You obviously haven't the faintest idea of all that."

"And there's smoke coming out of your ears," Mom said cheerfully.

"Nonsense," said the Boker, but Mom was right: little white puffs were unmistakably coming out of the Boker's ears, accompanied by sounds like a steam locomotive. That was when I realized that I was only dreaming all this, although the actual conversation had taken place, in just the same words, in the kitchen this afternoon. Except that the Boker's ears hadn't been smoking, and there hadn't been a green door in the wall beside the fridge. I noticed the door only now.

The Dream-Boker had followed my eyes. "I never did think much of arts and crafts, far too fussy," she said. "And that kitschy lizard doorknob really is utterly tasteless . . . oh, my word!"

The doorknob had moved. Her fine black and red scales shone in the light, while the lizard stretched, uncoiled her tail, and opened her eyes.

"You're not at all kitschy," I said, charmed by her beauty as I always was. When I first saw my dream door, the lizard had been made of brass and was much smaller than she was today. Apart from a friendly wink now and then, she had never moved, but these days she scuttled up and down the door and condescended to act as a door handle only when I really wanted to go out. Her eyes were bright turquoise and—unlike the eyes of her twin on the other side of the door—always looked friendly. I was still looking for a name that would do her justice: mystical, musical, and kind of pleasantly familiar. After all, she was a creation of my sub-conscious mind and thus a part of myself. Just like her sharp-toothed, hissing sister on the other side of the door.

"Far too brightly colored," said the Boker. "And totally unrealistic. The proportions in front and behind are all wrong."

I waved a hand to dismiss the Boker from my dream. It was bad enough having her drop in on us so often at home in real life, noticeably picking days when Ernest was away on business and Mom had an afternoon when she wasn't giving a lecture. Mia and I thought it was sheer bloody-mindedness, but Mom and Lottie, who persisted in believing in the good in people, thought the poor old lady just wanted to take part in family life and make herself useful.

Sure. And the Earth was flat.

I cautiously ran my fingertip over the lizard's smooth

scales. To my delight, she began purring like our cat, Spot. Unrealistic but kind of nice.

"Call her Liz," suggested Mia. She, Lottie, and Mom had turned up beside me to admire the lizard. Florence had obviously disappeared with the Boker. "I think she looks like a Lizzie."

"No, too . . . too prosaic," said Lottie. "Maybe Salamandria. Or Nyx, like the goddess of night."

"Barcelona would suit her." When Mom looked at our inquiring expressions, she added, "You know, like Gaudí's famous lizard that . . . Oh, forget it, you two philistines."

As so often in a dream, I found it a bit creepy when my subconscious mind dug up information from the depths of my brain that I thought I'd never heard. I'd type "Gaudí" and "Barcelona" into a search engine tomorrow. And hopefully I would find more than just lizards.

Someone was knocking at the door.

The lizard obligingly rolled up like a good little doorknob, while her twin on the other side of the door put her head through the mailbox slit and hissed, "It's Henry."

"That's what I call an innovative spyhole," said Mom.

"You could call her Mata Hari," said Lottie.

I bent down. "What did Grayson's room smell of this evening?" I asked through the mailbox slit.

"The bottle of cologne that Grayson dropped on the rug, which is probably going to smell like his grandfather forever now," replied Henry on the other side of the door. "I bet he dreams of him tonight."

I opened the door. Henry had propped one hand against the frame and was grinning at me.

"Hi, cheese girl. May I come in?"

"I don't know," I said, acting flirtatious. "It's the middle of the night. My mother would never allow it."

"Nonsense," said Mom behind me.

Henry put his head around the door. "Ah, a nice, comfy family dream. And it smells delicious too . . . freshly baked cookies, and cinnamon . . . incredible, all those good smells in your dreams these days."

It was even more incredible that he could smell what I was dreaming about. That was so crazy that I avoided thinking about it for long. Because whenever I did that, I felt afraid—afraid that in the long run there might not be any logical, scientifically verifiable explanation of this whole dream thing. Which in turn would mean that . . .

"Hello, who's this?" said Henry, interrupting my train of thought.

A rather fat chow had suddenly appeared under the kitchen table and was looking at us with his head to one side. Rasmus, as large as life.

"He always looks like that when he's begging for a treat," said Mia, giggling. "What's little Ras—"

"Ouch!" Henry was rubbing his arm. I had pushed him into the corridor, slipped out after him myself, and slammed the door behind us both—all before Mia could finish what she was saying. I could move faster in a dream than Superman if I had to.

"That little scamp. Let's check up on the dream corridors around here," I said, linking arms with Henry. "For instance, we could go and see whether Grayson is right, and it's really impossible to get past his dream door anymore."

"But it was so comfortable in there." Henry looked regretfully at my door. "While out here there could presumably be invisible spies and psychopaths up to all sorts of things."

Right, or demons. You could never be absolutely sure. The corridor with its different colored doors and soft lighting could have looked cheerful and peaceful, but it didn't. There was something sinister about its silence, and I couldn't make out where the light came from anyway—there were no windows and no ceiling lights, in fact not even a ceiling that the lights could have hung from. A little way above the walls there was a vague kind of void that could be compared only with the pale-gray sky that hung over London on many days. There seemed to be no end to all the branching corridors; they just lost themselves somewhere in the shadows. All the same, I liked this place, and the idea that there was another human mind dreaming behind each door, so that everyone in the world was linked by this labyrinth. It was a magical place, mysterious and dangerous—a mixture that, to me, was simply irresistible.

I moved a little closer to Henry and took a deep breath. "We can have as many comfortable dreams as we like for the rest of our lives. Once we've saved the world from Arthur."

Henry moved away from me, only to put both arms around me this time. "That's why I love you so much, Liv Silver," he murmured into my ear. "Because you're always ready for an adventure."

It was just the same with him. Without another word, we both turned into jaguars and padded forward side by side. I always felt a little safer here in nonhuman shape, and by now I could control being a jaguar so well that it didn't take much concentration to keep the transformation going. Unlike difficult shapes such as flying insects, immovable objects, and, that most difficult transformation of all, a breath of air, I could maintain a jaguar for hours on end. Sometimes when I woke in the morning after an intensive night dreaming in jaguar shape, I had taken on the role so well that I had to suppress an urge to lick my paws, and once I had even growled like a jaguar at Florence because she was standing between me and the coffee machine in the kitchen.

And speaking of Florence, the elegant reed-green door that was next to Grayson's tonight was certainly hers. Unless the initials F.C.E.S., in silver lettering on the wood, meant something other than Florence Cecilia Elizabeth Spencer, but that was rather unlikely.

We hadn't yet found out what the rules for the arrangement of the doors were, and why they changed places now and then. But it was certain that the doors of people close to you in some way, whether positive or negative, were never too far from your own. You could tell who owned many of the doors just from the look of them—for instance, Grayson's door was a perfect copy of the front door of our house, and Mom's door even had her name on it: MATTHEWS'S MOONSHINE ANTIQUARIAN BOOKS—OPEN FROM MIDNIGHT TO DAWN. Other doors weren't so easy to identify, but by now I was sure that the plain door painted an elegant gray next to Mom's Moonshine Antiquarian bookshop belonged to Ernest. Wherever Mom's door went, the gray door was always beside it. And the door painted bright red, with a showy golden door knocker, was a perfect match for Persephone's character, particularly as it kept getting closer to mine when we'd been spending time together during the day.

Not that I'd ever felt I needed to look behind one of those

doors, but it kind of reassured me to know which door was whose. If you spent as much time as Henry and I did in this corridor, you got to know all the doors in the corridors near it pretty well—even if they changed places or altered their appearance. I'd spent half the day wondering how the hell Arthur had managed to find Mrs. Lawrence's dream door. There were a great many doors here that might have suited her, but no real clue on any of them, like—oh, how would I know? Maybe like a picture of the Eiffel Tower carved on it, or a doormat saying BIENVENUE. Or at least a doorknob shaped like the stopper of a bottle of Chanel perfume. But Arthur had probably set about it pragmatically. Having laid hands on some personal possession of Mrs. Lawrence's, he'd only have had to try all the likely doors until he found one that would open. It would have taken him some time, but that just showed how doggedly he kept pursuing his unpleasant plans. And if Mrs. Lawrence hadn't built any insuperable obstacles into her door, it would have been easy for Arthur to get into the room behind it. And do whatever he had done there.

I felt the fur on the back of my neck stand up at the thought of it. And for another reason too: by this time, Henry and I had turned off our own corridor and were now in the one where we were likely to find both Arthur's and Anabel's doors.

Just in case Arthur was watching us somehow or other, we always used to stroll along this corridor in a particularly calm and confident way. We didn't want him to think we were afraid of him. So I cast only a brief glance—a glance as scornful as my jaguar face could manage—at the words *Carpe Noctem* hammered into the smooth metal surface of his door, and then I turned my head away and went on scanning the surroundings. There—that plain silver doorbell on the door opposite was new. And even as I stared inquiringly at it, it melted and flowed like a silvery shining stream down the wall to the floor, where it formed again, grew taller, and finally turned into a girl with long, wavy hair and a striking similarity to Botticelli's Venus. Except for being much, much more beautiful, and wearing jeans and a T-shirt instead of standing naked in a scallop shell. Anabel Scott, probably the best-looking psychopath in history.

"Why, if it isn't the kitty-cat patrol." Anabel had an attractive smile, which had failed to impress me ever since she tried cutting my throat.

I wasn't so sure about Henry. He had changed back to his own shape and was smiling just as attractively back at her. "Nice to see you, Anabel. Is that your door, right next to your ex-boyfriend's? Interesting. Or are you hanging around as a doorbell to spy on him?"

"You'd like to know where my door is, wouldn't you? So that *you* can spy on *me*." Anabel gave a little laugh and then added, with a sigh, "Although spying isn't so easy since everyone has found out how to be invisible. . . . I never ought to have taught Arthur so much."

She had a good point. *One* brilliant psychopath around the place would have been quite enough. And there was no denying it: Anabel was brilliant. Somehow or other, she had managed to lure her psychiatrist into these corridors, and while he had been living out his megalomaniac fantasies here, like a child given the run of a toy shop, believing he had everything under control, Anabel had found a way of locking him inside his own dream—after he had signed her discharge papers, by the way. Now Dr. Anderson, or Senator Tod, as he had called himself in the dream corridors, was lying in a care home somewhere in Surrey being fed through a tube—and was fast asleep. The doctors could find no conclusive diagnosis for his condition. Anabel had assured us that he was feeling fine because he was dreaming a life for himself and couldn't tell it apart from real life. All the same, and although Senator Tod hadn't been exactly a nice character, I felt sorry for him when I thought about all that. I had no idea how Anabel had managed to lock the man into his dream, but maybe he could be woken if his door was opened from the outside. But we'd have to find the door first, and unfortunately only Anabel knew where it was. She was right: invisibility made spying very difficult.

I growled softly.

"I'm afraid that now Arthur can do things even you haven't mastered," said Henry. He didn't mention the fact that we did actually know where Anabel's door was. Once, it had indeed been right opposite Arthur's, but since Anabel's breakdown last fall, her showy double door with gold fittings in the Gothic style had disappeared without a trace. Which meant that it had changed its appearance entirely, because Anabel herself was haunting the corridors as busily as ever. We'd been looking for it for ages, sometimes in corridors quite a long way from ours, but Henry had tracked it down only a week ago, thanks to his detective instincts and some under-handed shadowing tactics, as he claimed. But later he admitted that it had been pure chance—and luck—because he had been exploring the corridors invisibly when a bright-pink door with a Hello Kitty picture on it opened and Anabel cautiously stepped out into the corridor. When you were disguised as a breath of air or something as insubstantial as that, it was difficult to the point of impossibility to move objects or do something as simple as pressing down a door handle, and it reassured me to know that Anabel obviously had the same difficulties. A second later, she had made herself invisible again, but that brief moment had been enough for Henry. He had waited for her to come back, so as to make quite sure that it wasn't the door of someone else whom Anabel had been visiting in a dream. Of course we'd seen the Hello Kitty door hundreds of times before; it was far and away the most tasteless in the corridors, and we'd never have expected to find Anabel behind it. You had to admit that her camouflage was perfect, in line with the principle that people who draw attention to themselves aren't likely suspects. How she had done it was a mystery to me; I was pretty sure that you didn't have any influence on the appearance of your own door. It seemed to suit its owner's frame of mind just like that. However, maybe Anabel had developed a special trick—it wouldn't be the first time she'd proved capable of doing something when we hadn't the faintest idea of it. Now, for example, she even seemed to be capable of reading Henry's thoughts.

"You mean that scene with Mrs. Lawrence. I read about her nervous breakdown in Secrecy's blog." Anabel glanced up and down the corridor again. "Arthur's been visiting her in her dreams these last few nights, so I knew at once he must have something to do with it. I did wonder what he wanted with her, of all people, after he gave up French."

"We think he picked her by chance, as a kind of guinea pig. He wanted to try out a new method of hypnotizing people in their dreams so that they'll do what he wants in the daytime."

Anabel nibbled her lower lip. "But why would he want Mrs. Lawrence to climb on a table in the school cafeteria and tell all about herself and Mr. Vanhagen?"

It was a good question. I looked at Henry with my jaguar head to one side.

He shrugged his shoulders. "Well, just like that. To show that he can ruin people's lives." There was a short pause in which he looked around. "Because he can."

"Yes. Yes, maybe," murmured Anabel, and her eyes were slightly glazed. "That would be just like Arthur. Or, anyway, the person that Arthur has turned into."

I found it hard to imagine that Arthur had ever had moral scruples and something like a conscience, but Henry and Grayson also kept assuring me that their former best friend had once been a really nice guy. Before he fell hopelessly in love with Anabel and then realized that he had been exploited, manipulated, and misused for her purposes. However, I kept my sympathy well within bounds. Where would we be if everyone who suffered a bitter disappointment automatically mutated into a criminal? I felt sorrier for Anabel. After all, she hadn't been born a crazy psychopath. Her early childhood with her mother in a sect that worshipped demons and went in for weird rituals had made her the monster who tried cutting my throat. And now that monster had created another monster—a nastier and more dangerous one than Anabel herself.

We knew it was risky, and neither of us was happy with the idea, but if we were to be a match for Arthur, we needed Anabel as an ally. Even worse than facing him without her help was the idea that she might get back together with him in the end. We had to prevent that, at all costs.

Henry cleared his throat. "No one knows what Arthur has in mind, but with the abilities he's developed, I guess every opportunity is open to him. He must be doing something like what you did to Senator Tod to get him to sign your discharge from the hospital. You must tell us how you did it, Anabel."

"So that you two can interfere as well?" Anabel gave Henry a thoughtful smile. "I can well imagine that you'd try everything, Henry Harper. No, thanks! It's quite enough to think that Arthur could spoil my plans."

"And what plans would those be?" asked Henry with a deep sigh.

"You've known that long enough." The light suddenly changed. It was as if a shadow were falling over the invisible sources of light in the corridors. Anabel made a sweeping gesture with her hand. "You both know who we have to thank for all this, and what we still owe him."

The air around us was noticeably chillier. I was very glad I was still a jaguar. That way, I could stare hard at Anabel without her noticing how uncomfortable I felt.

"Isn't all that about the demon over and done with?" asked Henry gently. "I thought you'd realized in the hospital that it was only part of . . . part of your sickness."

"Yes," said Anabel. "Or so they tried to convince me. And I may be crazy, but I'm certainly not stupid. I do take it into consideration that . . . that the Lord of Shadows and Darkness may have existed only in my sick imagination. But suppose that isn't so? Wouldn't you, too, rather be safe than sorry?"

No, we wouldn't. Heaven knows we had plenty of other problems as things were.

"Are you still taking your medication?" asked Henry, frowning.

"Always so splendidly direct." Anabel was smiling again. "As it happens, I've stopped taking it. Just to see what happens. Or if anything happens. So we can wait and see." Suddenly she seemed to be in a hurry. She threw her hair back over her shoulders. "Well, nice to see you, as always." She walked away without waiting for us to say anything, and after she had taken three steps, her outlines blurred and became more and more translucent, until a few feet farther on she had disappeared entirely. She had taken the cold temperature with her.

"DID HE REALLY say Perpetua?" I asked automatically, for what was probably the hundredth time that day. "I mean, you can easily mishear something. And you know what Jasper's like. He always calls me Liz."

"It's different for you." Persephone's lower lip began trembling ominously again, and I hastily propelled her on ahead of me down the school corridor, making for the main exit.

Since all that Jasper had said to Persephone this morning was a brief, throwaway *Hi, Perpetua*, her world had turned upside down. She had always admired Jasper, but only while he was away in France had she fallen desperately in love with him, don't ask me why. Meanwhile, Jasper had obviously entirely forgotten that Persephone even existed, at least if you interpreted that *Hi, Perpetua* less charitably and more realistically. Which of course I didn't, because Persephone was crushed anyway, so the last thing she needed right now was realism. In today's break periods, she had made her way through two family packs of tissues (and we had discovered that her mascara probably wasn't waterproof), and it hadn't done any good for me to invent a disorder called face-and-first-name legasthenia and suggest that Jasper suffered from it. I was running out of helpful ideas.

At least school was over for this week; it was Friday, the sun was shining, and it was the start of the weekend. I'd been longing for the peace of my own room for hours, so as to get away from Persephone's wailing and think a few things over clearly. With a bit of luck, I could even allow myself a relaxing afternoon siesta before kung fu practice—I had a lot of sleep to catch up on, and maybe clear thoughts would come of their own accord if I wasn't so tired.

It was now two nights since Henry and I had met Anabel in our dream, and we had walked up and down the corridors without much of a plan, keeping an eye on the doors of the people we loved and looking out for Arthur or Anabel, always hoping to find some new clue. But in vain. Absolute silence had reigned, a silence that I found suspicious, but Henry thought it was reassuring. So reassuring that last night he had even begun talking about Rasmus in the middle of the corridor. Apparently he had found a Rasmus Wakefield on Facebook and wanted to know if he was "my" Rasmus Wakefield. At least I could deny that with a clear conscience and tell him that "my" Rasmus wasn't a fan of social media. So then Henry had asked what his hobbies had been.

"He liked playing ball games," I said. And to avoid having to say any more about my invented South African ex-boyfriend who was really a dog, I began kissing Henry, ignoring any potential observers. It was a distraction maneuver that always worked. But this time—if only after a while in which I for one forgot everything else: Rasmus, invisible spies, danger-ous demons—it just made Henry ask what Rasmus was like at kissing.

It was enough to drive me crazy. I'd never get rid of the wretched guy I had invented.

"If I didn't know better, I'd say you were a tiny bit jealous," I said, instead of saying, "Wet kisses with a lot of licking."

Henry nodded. "Very likely" was all he said, stroking my cheeks and throat with his fingertips. "I'm just interested to know who taught you to kiss so well."

Hmm. Not Rasmus, anyway.

"Who says he taught me kissing and not vice versa?" I murmured. "Could be I'm a natural talent." But, anyway, I was a bad, bad liar. I wouldn't be able to keep this up for much longer: sooner or later I'd have to tell Henry the truth. I just didn't know how to do it without sinking into the ground in my embarrassment.

"But that wasn't all," Persephone was wailing again. "Jasper didn't even really look at—"

"What's going on over there?" I said in a loud voice, point-ing to the main exit, where a crowd had gathered. Sometimes diverting another person's attention was the only thing to do.

And it worked. Persephone wrinkled her nose, smoothed out her plaintive expression, and hurried inquisitively over to the circle of students, eager for a sensation, listening to a con-versation that was obviously going on in the middle of the crowd. I followed her, rather more slowly. But when I saw who was at the center of the circle, I stood on tiptoe, just like Persephone, to get a better view.

Although he haunted my mind almost all the time, I hadn't seen Arthur again in daytime since Mrs. Lawrence's nervous breakdown. Even in the school cafeteria, we never seemed to come across each other, and I couldn't say that I was missing the sight of him. But I kept catching myself expecting someone else to stand up and do something crazy or outrageous. Henry and Grayson said they felt the same during basketball practice. And the fact that so far nothing like that had happened didn't set our minds at rest. Far from it—it just heightened the suspense. Who was going to be Arthur's next victim? And what would he do to that victim?

I was beginning to sound paranoid—for instance, I asked Mia as casually as possible, every evening, whether she had lost anything (having checked up on my own things), and only when she assured me that nothing of hers had gone missing could I go to bed with an easy mind. I thought a lot about when an object became personal. Did a pencil you had just bought count? Or did you have to chew the end of it to give it that personal touch? And how long did the effect last? After a while, wouldn't it count as the possession of whoever had taken it, and then it wouldn't work anymore for the previous owner? Last time, it had been a glove that let Arthur invade Mia's dreams, and I knew I'd sooner die than go through that again. So I didn't mind knowing that in the end Mia was bound to think my constant questions were odd. I'd really have liked to tell *everyone* to take extra good care of their personal possessions, especially when Arthur was around. But of course that wouldn't do. And presumably he'd acquired what he needed ages ago by now. I imagined him collecting his loot in his room, labeling every item conscientiously with its owner's name, and wondering, every evening, whose dreams to haunt that night. To keep from being taken by surprise in his own sleep, of course he had stopped using the secret hiding place for his key that had allowed Grayson to break in and retrieve Mia's glove in January. And as Grayson had found out, the secret way to Arthur's house, a route that the boys had known and used since childhood, had recently been blocked off by a new fence, so there was no way of getting at Arthur in his sleep, or the stuff that he had stolen. All kinds of influential, famous figures went in and out of his parents' house, musicians, politicians, industrialists—it was scary to think of all the people Arthur might be spying on after stealing something of theirs.

At the moment, however, he wasn't dealing with influential friends of his parents, he was confronting the number-one hate object at Frognal Academy, who went by the name of Theodore E. Ellis.

Theo Ellis wasn't, as you might think, unpopular because he was a puny, scheming show-off, or a fat, nasty bully, or unpleasant company in some other way—no, the trouble was that he was outstandingly good at basketball, a huge talent, always scoring points, someone who'd do any team credit. He was also good-natured, smart, and attractive. The problem was that Theo Ellis wasn't a student at Frognal Academy but at Roslyn High. In other words, he played for the wrong team, which was a good enough reason to hate him like poison.

Theo would surely never have ventured into enemy territory of his own free will, but it was his bad luck to be studying Ancient Greek as an exam subject, and since not many students were learning that language, Frognal Academy and Roslyn High School shared the course. And the lessons were here in our school.

When Theo came for Ancient Greek classes on Fridays,

the booing that met him in the corridors and the rest of the school building was not by any means the worst of it. If rumor was correct, the Ancient Greek teacher, Mrs. Ritzel, always gave a test and extra homework when there was an important game against his team coming up. Mrs. Ritzel was a great fan of the Frognal Flames.

And over the last few weeks, the situation had deteriorated, if possible, even more. Because Theo's team looked likely to win the school championship, while the Flames had slumped to number four in the rankings. And since, as everyone knows, fans are even worse about losing than their teams, there was even a "We Hate Theo Ellis" forum on the Internet, where people made up rude rhymes about Theo.

He must feel sorry he hadn't opted for Spanish instead, but I kind of admired him for walking so casually along our corridors every Friday, ignoring the concentrated hostility of all present with stoic calm.

Like today.

At least, if he was feeling at all uncomfortable, he didn't let it show. With his legs apart and his arms crossed, he was standing in front of Arthur, looking like nothing so much as a massive oak wardrobe. Arthur, over six feet tall and very fit, looked feeble by comparison. That didn't keep him from calling Theo names. Not such primitive names as the Frognal Flames fans shouted, but names in Arthur's own line, which were even nastier.

"Not that your A levels are suffering," he was saying in a soft voice. "After all, your mother expects at least one of your family to amount to something. But I heard that your brother is on probation."

Murmurs of approval from the onlookers. I saw Emily's

shining brown hair among the other heads and was surprised. She'd taken no interest in basketball when she was going out with Grayson. All the same, she was listening to the conversation as if spellbound. Her brother, Spotty Sam, who was always telling me to be ashamed of myself, was standing beside her, filming it all on his cell phone.

"What interesting things you do hear, little Goldilocks," said Theo, and Persephone, who was clinging to my arm, took a deep, audible breath. "I expect you pick them up at the hairdresser's when they're putting the curlers in your pretty hair."

Arthur favored him with a tolerant glance. "It must be awful, being under such pressure, and the only member of your family who can read and write, at that. Can't be nice imagining yourself ending up as a house cleaner, like your father." He sniffed ostentatiously, looking at Theo. "Well, good cleaners are always in demand."

A few of the crowd giggled, and some idiot from the lower school murmured, "Theo, Theoderant, doesn't use deodorant."

Theo sighed, sounding bored. "Of course I always knew what a snob you are, little Goldilocks, but you used to be better than that. Before your team made you captain. Why, as a matter of fact, did they do it?"

Aha! That hit home. I was beginning to like Theo a lot.

Arthur kept his superior smile going, but I wasn't the only one who could see him losing his cool. Theo had found a sore point. No one was giggling now; they were all waiting to hear what Arthur had to say in reply. Because no one but us knew the reason for the obvious bad feeling between him and his former best friends Grayson, Jasper, and Henry, which dated from last fall.

While Arthur was still at a loss for words, Theo shouldered his schoolbag. "Well, we can't all be popular, Goldilocks. Don't take it so hard; you have rich parents to make up for it. I must be going," he added, making his way through the crowd of students. "I'm off to practice with my team. Who, incidentally, voted unanimously to make me their captain last week."

Strolling along at his ease, he disappeared through the double glass doorway, and I couldn't suppress a small smile of glee. Because everyone present, not just me, could see only too well that Theo Ellis had won that little exchange. And Goldilocks hadn't.

"I think Theo Ellis is definitely sexy," I said to the girl next to Persephone and me.

"Me too," admitted the girl. "But I hate him, all the same."

The gawping onlookers were dispersing, muttering angrily, and I was about to urge Persephone to move on as well, when Arthur's eyes fell on me. Although it was the briefest of glances, it was so cold that I spontaneously tried to turn into a jaguar.

"That stupid Theo is just jealous. Arthur's hair looks great," said Persephone, dreamily, staring at Arthur as he turned away. "Do you have any idea how difficult it is to style natural curls so that they'll look masculine and cool?"

I ran my hand over the place where the fur at the back of a jaguar's neck would be standing on end, and looked at Persephone, shaking my head. She was a hopeless case.

"Let's go, or we'll miss the bus," I said, pushing her toward the door. Unfortunately that meant passing Emily. As usual, Emily ignored me but greeted Persephone effusively, probably hoping that would make me feel ignored twice over. And in the normal way, Persephone would indeed have felt flattered, but then Emily made a grave tactical error.

"Do you have hay fever, you poor thing?" she asked sympathetically. "Your face is so swollen. Like me to write down the name of the stuff that helped my brother, Sam, so much?"

"No, thanks." Persephone sniffed and threw back her hair. "Does my face really look swollen?" she asked me as we went on.

"Oh, it's not too bad." Anyway, not too bad considering all the tears she'd shed since that morning. I was afraid Persephone might start on about Jasper again, but her thoughts were still with Arthur.

"I feel sorry for Arthur," she said when we had reached the bus stop. "Without his friends, he's kind of . . . oh, I don't know. Henry, Grayson, Jasper, and Arthur were like the Four Musketeers. It's funny that they don't get along anymore." She gave me an inquiring glance. "I still think it's something to do with Anabel. He must have done something last fall, and she can't forgive him for it. And I think you know what it was, but you just don't want to tell me."

She was dead right there. "Persephone, the closest of friends grow apart when they develop in different directions," I said, realizing that I sounded like Lottie in one of her instructive moods. "As Theo Ellis pointed out just now: Arthur is a terrible snob. And who wants to be friends with a snob?"

Persephone looked as if she were having difficulty not saying, "I do!"

"Hmm," she said instead, not sounding very convinced.

"You and I are totally different, but we're best friends all the same."

"Yes, you're right," I said, and I couldn't help laughing. At first I'd thought Persephone was a horrible, superficial girl, a real pain in the neck, and in fact, she probably was. I'd never have expected to get so fond of her, but now there'd certainly be something missing from my life without her.

As the bus stopped and its doors opened with a hiss, I put an arm around Persephone and hugged her. "Mind you take good care of your things, won't you?" I told her. "Especially little things like key rings, jewelry, hair scrunchies, gloves . . ."

"You keep saying that lately. As if I were totally scatter-brained." Persephone pushed an underclassman aside and forged a way up to the top deck of the bus for us. "Or even worse, as if you were my granny, warning me of thieves all over the place. She even puts out her garbage cans at the last moment in case someone makes off with them before the truck comes to take the garbage away." She dropped into an empty seat and began crying again. Don't ask me why, but obviously the garbage cans had somehow reminded her of Jasper again.

"Perpetua!" she sobbed. "He might as well have called me Aphrodite!"

"Well, at least he got the initial of your name right," I said, sighing. Yes, it was a fact, there'd be something missing from my life without Persephone. All the same, I was glad when she got off the bus at her stop and I knew I wouldn't have any-one weeping all over me for the rest of the day.

But unfortunately I'd rejoiced too soon. Because instead of relaxing in heavenly peace and quiet, as I intended, Mom summoned Mia and me to the kitchen for a crisis meeting. No hope of relaxation after that. All I really wanted was to crawl into bed with Mr. Twinkle, my favorite teddy bear from early childhood, and cry into his soft, brown, nice-smelling teddy-bear fur. But stupidly I didn't have him anymore, because I was way too old for cuddly toys and I'd already thrown dear old Mr. Twinkle away in Utrecht. I could always cry into a pillow, but it wasn't the same. I wanted Mr. Twinkle back. I wanted to be the right age for cuddly toys again. Four, or thereabouts.

Of course Grayson wasn't to know that when he burst into my room, without knocking, a few hours later. He hadn't come home after school, and he'd not been there for supper either. If I hadn't been distracted by recent events, I'd have been worried, because Grayson never skipped a meal.

He looked excited, and he hadn't even stopped to take off his jacket. I pushed my damp pillow aside and stared at him in confusion. Or more precisely, I stared at what he was holding out to me. Was that by any chance . . . ?

Yes. It was. Grayson really was holding a black sock out to me, looking as pleased and proud as if it had been a red rose.

"There," he said. "I've ticked off number one on my to-do list. Take good care of it."

"Of a *sock*?" It wasn't like Grayson to burst in just like that. He seemed strangely full of himself. And what did the sock mean? Was this another British custom that I didn't understand? Or had Buttercup run off with the other sock, and now he wanted compensation? I looked more closely. "Yuck! Is that . . ."

"Yes, of course. Fresh from the man's own foot," said Grayson. He somehow reminded me of Buttercup when she retrieved an enormous branch instead of a little stick, and wanted to be praised for it. "Otherwise it wouldn't be a personal possession. Here, you look after it."

I was still skeptical. "It smells cheesy."

"Liv, this is no ordinary sock!" I was so slow on the uptake that Grayson shook his head. "It belongs to Senator Tod, a.k.a. Dr. Otto Anderson, a.k.a. Anabel's psychiatrist. Armed with this, we can open his dream door. You remember— phase one."

Oh, yes! Phase one! This afternoon's events had driven it right out of my mind.

The three-phase plan was Grayson's own idea. He had explained it right after the humiliation of Mrs. Lawrence in the cafeteria—a plan to rid the world of Arthur. Unfortunately, in spite of its impressive name, the whole thing wasn't really worked out yet. To be honest, it wasn't even a proper plan, just a kind of statement of intent. Phase one was clear enough: take as many precautions as possible, check up on everything, and collect information, materials, facts, and ideas. But when you reached phase two, it was more vague. All the statement said was *work out a concrete plan to keep Arthur from doing whatever he's planning to do*. Grayson hadn't actually read phase three aloud to us (presumably because it would send us into fits of laughter), but we could make a guess at the gist of it: *finish Arthur off according to plan*.

And so we would too. Always supposing he hadn't finished us off first. And if we knew how.

"Hey, have you been crying?" Grayson gave up offering me the sock, dropped on the chair at my desk, and looked at me reproachfully. "To be honest, I'd expected a little more gratitude. And appreciation," he said, folding his arms. "Not everyone would go all the way to Surrey just for a sock."

He was right there. Getting hold of some personal possession of Senator Tod's was definitely part of our plan, but we hadn't really known how to go about it. However, Henry and I had found out what hospital he was in. That had been easy: a few clicks on the Internet and two phone calls, and we had the information we wanted. There weren't very many nursing homes in and around Reigate that took in long-term coma patients, and luckily for us, they didn't seem to take data protection all that seriously.

"But wasn't getting into the hospital difficult?" I asked.

Grayson rolled his eyes. "No problem at all. I was going to say I was his nephew, but no one even asked me." He looked almost disappointed; presumably he'd thought up another three-phase plan for breaking into hospitals with hostile action in mind. "Poor guy," he said. "Just lying there asleep. Sleeping twenty-four hours a day, for over a month now. Did you know they can run feeding tubes directly through the abdominal wall instead of down the esophagus? It's called percutaneous endoscopic gastrostomy. They recommend it for long-term patients. Obviously they don't hold out much hope that he'll ever wake up again." He rubbed his nose, clearly affected by his discoveries. "I don't know the man at all, but even if he wasn't a good character and Anabel had her reasons, I don't think anyone deserves a fate like that, do you?"

No, I didn't. Not even Arthur. Even though Henry thought that Anabel's method might be the only way of putting Arthur out of action if we weren't actually going to murder him.

"We have to help him." Grayson looked at Senator Tod's

sock with a melancholy expression. "One of the nurses told me his mother comes in every day to get him dressed, just in case he wakes up. Poor woman—I bet she'll wonder where the second sock of that pair is."

I bit my lower lip. Grayson was right; we must at least try to help Senator Tod. If only for his mother's sake. I almost began crying again. "Weren't there any other personal possessions lying around?" I asked quickly, blinking the tears away. "Maybe something not quite so revolting?"

Grayson looked guilty. There had probably been all kinds of personal things there, but he couldn't bring himself to steal one of them. "Don't be so ungrateful, Liv. That sock is ideal. You can simply wear it every night, and then you'll be ready if we find the door. Or if Anabel shows it to us of her own accord. Anyway, what can *you* tick off your to-do list today?"

Hmm, well. I didn't want to admit that I hadn't drawn up a to-do list at all and had not, therefore, been able to contribute to the three-phase plan to save the world from Arthur. My day had been horrible enough as it was, and it occurred to me that Grayson didn't know anything about that yet.

"Forget the to-do lists," I said, sighing deeply and moving to the edge of my bed. "Something bad has happened." And I wanted my dear old teddy Mr. Twinkle back!

"Has Granny finally made Dad agree to get a wedding planner in?" asked Grayson sympathetically. "Is that why you were crying?"

Oh heavens, we had to think of the wedding planner too! Apparently the Boker had engaged the best in the business, and if she had her way, he would make Mom's informal little party into a gigantic social event. But that wasn't what our crisis meeting this afternoon had been about. I shook my head.

"Lottie told us today that she's going to leave us after the wedding," I said, and I nearly did begin to cry again.

"Really?" Grayson seemed genuinely concerned. "I thought there wasn't any question of that anymore."

"So did I," I said. But that wasn't really true. Deep down inside, I'd known this day would come sometime. Mia and I were far too old to need an au pair, and had been for a long time, and now that Mom couldn't be said to be bringing us up on her own and we had a real home, our Mary Poppins would have to take off for somewhere else. It wasn't that we didn't understand. We simply couldn't imagine life without Lottie. She was the best thing that had ever happened to us. I wasn't so sure whether that applied the other way around. After her au pair year almost thirteen years ago, she'd originally been going to train as a teacher in Munich, and she would be teaching in elementary schools if she hadn't been traveling the world with us instead. She'd probably have married and had children of her own by now. As things were, she was thirty-two years old, and she didn't even have training to do anything.

"But what is she going to . . . er, I mean what will she . . . ?" Grayson obviously didn't know how to put his question tactfully, but I understood him all the same.

"One of her cousins has offered her a job in his hotel in Oberstdorf," I said. "Beginning on the first of July."

Grayson looked really shocked. "In Germany? But what about Uncle Charles? I thought he and Lottie were really serious about each other."

I shrugged my shoulders. "No, I'm afraid nothing is going to come of that. Your uncle is so . . . so undecided. And I think Lottie's feelings have cooled off a bit too. She doesn't stammer anymore when Charles is in the room."

"We'll have to do something," said Grayson firmly. "If Lottie and Charles are a couple, she'll have to stay in London. That would be the best thing for Charles as well."

"Put it on your to-do list," I said. I meant to sound sarcastic so that he wouldn't notice how touched I was. And I could have hugged him for worrying about Lottie—and maybe also worrying a bit about Mia and me.

"At least that's one thing I can do." Grayson grinned at me. "You wait and see, I'm not just brilliant at stealing socks—I'm good at pairing people off as well."

I grinned back and suddenly felt much more confident. Okay, so we had no plan, but we all had one another. Which was more than could be said for Arthur.

The only question was, how long did we have left to arm ourselves to thwart whatever he was going to do? Which brought my thoughts back to personal possessions. Did things that the owner had thrown away count? And how long would an ordinary black sock, for instance, keep a personal note about it?

Grayson couldn't answer that question.

"For a while at least, I guess," I said, thinking out loud. "T-shirts that you've thrown out and I wear as pajama tops work fine, anyway."

Grayson took a deep breath. "First, I haven't thrown those T-shirts out; you simply found them in the basket of clean laundry. . . ."

"Yes, but only when you hadn't worn them for weeks."

"And second, I want you to stop trying to get into my dreams."

"It's only for test purposes." I ignored his frown. "You know—phase one, security checks and so on. I'm only seeing whether the door would open if I wanted to get in. Which of course I don't. Although I could."

"Leave that right out," said Grayson categorically.

"I'm afraid I can't." I realized that in spite of the Lottie disaster a big grin was spreading over my face, and there wasn't a single thing I could do about it. "You'll have to improve your security precautions, Grayson. I bet it would be easy as pie for Arthur to answer Frightful Freddy's question. I mean, if I could do it . . ."

Grayson laughed incredulously. "Oh, come on, you're making this up, Liv. Since when have you been a whiz at mental arithmetic?"

"It really wasn't difficult." Well, actually, it had taken me three nights even to notice the silly arithmetic puzzle and then get my calculator to work it out. "If you multiply the root of sixty-three thousand and one by a hundred and eighty-six, what is the result?" I said, trying to imitate Freddy's squeaky voice. "And then if you subtract from that the product of one thousand three hundred and fifty plus six, take away from the result the root of sixty-three thousand and one, and look at it the other way around, what do you get?"

"If you can recite it off by heart, you must really have heard it many times," said Grayson sarcastically, still pretty sure of himself.

"Thirty-eight thousand three hundred and seventeen," I said.

"Good arithmetic but wrong answer," said Grayson, both relieved and gleeful. "Math isn't everything, you know."

"Yes, I do know. But if you look at thirty-eight thousand

three hundred and seventeen the other way around, you get—*Liebe*—which means love, in German." I was the one who probably now looked like Buttercup when she wanted appreciation. But I was also proud of grasping all the laborious arithmetic quickly enough to see that looking at the result the other way around only meant reading the number on the display upside down, a trick that every schoolchild knew. That made the 7 a letter *L*, the 1 a letter *I*, the 3 a letter *E*, and so on. "I'd call that a very romantic password."

In fact, I hadn't checked whether it really worked, because when I was standing outside Grayson's dream door and Freddy was looking expectantly at me, it had suddenly seemed stupid to mention the password itself—too dangerous in this corridor, where you never knew if you were really alone. Even if I just whispered it into Freddy's ear, someone could be eavesdropping, someone who might be invisible but still might not have thought of simply turning the calculator upside down. And Grayson had played fair with me by putting it in German—*Liebe*.

"Oh, hell," said Grayson quietly, from which I concluded that *love* really was the right answer. "Then I'll have to think up something else for tonight." At that, his frown went away, and he smiled. "Even though I bet Arthur isn't as clever as you."

"Fair enough. But he makes up for it by having a nastier mind." I thought of the showdown with Theo Ellis inside the school entrance, but just as I was about to tell Grayson about that, I thought of something and stood up to search my bag. "Here, this is for you, from Henry. He wants you to wear it tonight."

Grayson stared at what I was offering him, as baffled as I

had been by the sock just now. "A pair of glasses with only one lens? Why? Who does it belong to?"

"He didn't say, but if I were going to make a guess . . ." I held up the lilac scarf that Henry had provided for my own use and smelled it. "I'd say to a woman born before 1950, who likes eating cabbage and douses herself in lavender perfume. I hope tying it around my leg will do. I'm not wearing it around my neck, anyway."

Grayson grumpily turned the glasses over in his fingers and stood up. "Oh, wonderful. No refreshing good night's sleep again." Yawning, he made for the door. "But I'll tell you one thing: I'm not going to bed on an empty stomach. Do you think there's anything left over from supper?"

I nodded. "In the fridge. And Lottie hid your share of the meatballs on the terrace, to keep it safe from Mia. They're in the green dish on the windowsill."

Grayson's expression cleared at once. "I just love Lottie. How I'm ever going to live without her and her meatballs I can't imagine." He smiled at me once again before closing the door behind him. "See you soon, then. In that damn corridor."

"HERE WE ARE." Henry put his hand on a clunky bronze door-knob. "In you go."

Grayson looked skeptically at the door in question. "Can one of you please explain why we have to invade some stranger's dream room, at a distance of what feels like miles away from our own doors, just to talk?" he asked, looking back along the corridor. "Aside from the fact that I'm sure I for one won't find my way back on my own, Ar . . . er, an invisible person could have followed us here as well as anywhere else."

"Correct," said Henry. "But anyone who doesn't know whose door this is can't steal one of its owner's possessions and therefore won't get through the doorway." He gave the door a friendly pat. "We're sure to be undisturbed here. And we'll always have somewhere to take refuge if . . . if we happen to need it."

Grayson still didn't look convinced, and I myself did not really think Henry's argument entirely conclusive. "Hang on a moment. How about Amy's door? I didn't have any personal possession of hers," I said. Amy was Henry's four-year-old sister, and it was in one of her sugar-sweet sky-blue dreams of balloons and soap bubbles that Henry had first said he loved me. He couldn't have chosen a more romantic setting. Well, maybe the rainbow-colored ponies had been rather over the top.

"You could get into Amy's dream room only because I opened the door for you and took you in with me," Henry explained with a touch of impatience in his voice. "And because you had a personal possession of mine with you. Come on."

I still didn't quite like it. "Ar . . . *someone* invisible could simply smuggle himself in with us. The way I followed you into B's dream not so long ago as a breath of air. Don't you remember?"

Henry sighed. Maybe with impatience, maybe because he didn't want to be reminded of that episode. "In this case, for one thing, *someone* would need a personal possession of mine, and, for another, would have to break through all the energy fields that I set up behind us on the way here." He pointed to a wall of flickering air that he had brought into being just now with a casual wave of his hand, about sixty feet away from us. "They'll last only as long as we can see them, but that's enough to deter anyone following us."

"Energy fields keeping invisible people out," muttered Grayson. "That sounds so silly that, if this was a movie, I'd walk out of the cinema."

You bet. "A movie about people who are so powerful in their dreams that they can even make themselves invisible but are supposed to be kept away by energy fields dreamed up by other people," I added. "Doesn't sound likely to win any

Oscars." Never mind the fact that it would be dead difficult to get invisible actors performing in such a movie.

"Well, I've seen worse movies. Come along, you two." Henry had opened the door, held it open, and pushed us through the doorway one after the other. "And no need to beware of the mastiff. It won't hurt you."

When I heard that, I felt like going back, but Henry was quick to close the door behind us and lean back against it. I looked around. Luckily there was no sign of a mastiff. We were in a living room crammed with furniture and bric-a-brac. Stylistically, it was a perfect match for the scarf that Henry had given me (I had tied it around my waist like a belt before going to bed). The patterns of the flowered upholstery of the sofas and chairs, and the flowered shades of the floor lamps, competed with embroidered cushions, colorful Persian rugs, and traditional Victorian wallpaper. Framed prints of oil paintings showing ballerinas in blue and pink tutus hung on the walls, and pots full of magenta Alpine violets in flower stood on every spare space: the windowsills, the piano, and the dark, heavy cupboards and chests of drawers. There was a parrot in a huge gilded cage near the piano, scratching its chest feathers and looking at us with interest.

"What a nightmare place to come," said Grayson, astonished.

"Nightmare yourself, scum!" screeched the parrot.

"Corky, that's no way for a well-brought-up bird to talk!" The speaker was an old lady sitting beside the fireplace in a flowered armchair, knitting something very brightly colored. Small and thin, with hair tinted pale lilac and a flowered dress, she merged so perfectly with the optical effect of the armchair that I hadn't noticed her before. She pushed her glasses down to the end of her nose so as to look at us over the top of them. "But the blanket isn't finished yet," she said.

"Never mind, Mrs. Honeycutt," said Henry gently. "Don't let us disturb you, just go on with your knitting."

"You aren't disturbing me." The old lady's knitting needles clicked. "I don't like people putting pressure on me, that's all. It will take as long as it takes."

"Quite right too." Henry slowly pushed Grayson and me past Mrs. Honeycutt's chair and the parrot to a group of chairs standing around a little circular table. "We'll just sit here for a little while, and you'll forget we're even in the room. Go on knitting, and you'll feel relaxed and happy." There was something in his voice that suggested hypnosis as shown in some ancient film, but it seemed to work.

"I always feel relaxed and happy when I'm knitting," said Mrs. Honeycutt, more to herself than to Henry. "That's the wonderful thing about it. I always say, if everyone in the world knitted, it would be a better place."

"Sit down," Henry told us. He turned one of the chairs around, sat astride it, and looked at us, satisfied.

"Where's the mastiff?" I whispered.

"Mrs. Honeycutt doesn't always dream of it. Usually she has perfectly harmless dreams of herself sitting in her living room, knitting." The crinkles at the corners of Henry's mouth deepened. "Which is exactly what she does in waking life."

"How awful," whispered Grayson, and I wasn't sure whether he meant our surroundings, or the fact that Mrs. Honeycutt's dreams were a boring copy of what she did every day.

"You can talk aloud; she's hard of hearing in her dreams as well as real life." Henry pushed a pot of Alpine violets aside and propped his elbows on the table. "She lives on the other side of the road from us, and she feeds our cat when we go away. In return, we water her flowers when she goes to see her brother in Bath. It took me ages to find her door, but the more often I . . . er, visit her, the closer her door moves to mine, and so to yours too." He let his eyes wander around the room and then smiled at us. "The perfect headquarters, don't you think?"

Grayson gave him a dark look. "Yes, it's such a great feeling, stalking a poor old lady. I don't see how that's going to help us solve our problems. Or what use it is spending night after night in these corridors, anyway." He sighed. "I'm going to be dead tired again tomorrow morning."

"I know you hate all this," said Henry, in the same gently hypnotic tone of voice that he'd used to Mrs. Honeycutt. "But you've seen what happens if you simply keep away. Arthur and Anabel have had months to perfect their abilities every night. So we must practice all the harder, try experiments to keep up with them—"

"You mean you must, not all of us," Grayson interrupted in such a loud voice that we looked at him in alarm. "Oh, come along, you know I'm right. It's not just Arthur and Anabel who have perfected their abilities, so have you two. And to be honest, I'll never learn the things you can do."

"Never ever," screeched the parrot, and I was afraid it might be right. Grayson didn't have a great deal of imagination— and you needed imagination here more than anything.

For a second Henry looked as if he were thinking of something else. "It's all a matter of training," he said, and at that very moment he disappeared without a trace. Just like that, without advance warning, without leaving a breath of air behind or making the slightest sound.

"At least a little plop like a soap bubble bursting would be nice," I murmured.

"Very funny." Grayson put out his hand to the air above Henry's chair. "Yes, okay, Henry, a great demonstration. That's exactly what I meant. I'll never learn how to do that. And now you can stop it and reappear."

"Grayson, I'm afraid he hasn't made himself invisible; he simply woke up." I looked over at Mrs. Honeycutt, sitting with her back to us and knitting peacefully away. There was something homely about the click of the knitting needles. "We could wait a little while, in case Henry manages to go back to sleep quickly. But he's probably been woken, and then it takes longer." I knew about this already. On weekends, Henry's mother used to go out, leaving him to look after his brother and sister. Those were usually restless nights; little Amy, in particular, was often sick and got thirsty or lost her cuddly toy. Or sometimes Henry was woken by his brother, Milo, who thought he had heard someone breaking in or simply had a bad dream. And if Amy, Milo, or the family cat didn't keep Henry on the go, it would be his mother coming home drunk and waking everyone with the sound of her high heels tapping on the floor like gunshots. Too bad if she stumbled over the toys in the hallway. She would begin shouting, and she often burst into tears. Henry hadn't told me that, but those sounds and voices in real life sometimes mingled with his dreams and I could hear them myself, before he woke up and disappeared.

"Let's go." Grayson rose to his feet quickly. "Because if

you stop dreaming too, Liv, I'll have to find my way back alone, and I'll get hopelessly lost."

"Lost, cost," screeched the parrot, and then, in an alarmingly human and very deep voice, it added, "Permafrost."

"Oh, great, you're giving me goose bumps, you stupid bird," said Grayson. "Liv, are you coming?"

Presumably there wasn't any real point in waiting around here for Henry. I reached for the hand that Grayson was impatiently holding out to me, and let him haul me up. "The first thing you have to learn, Grayson, is how to wake if you don't like the dream or it gets too dangerous. That's much more important than any shape-changing tricks."

The grandfather clock against the opposite wall struck twelve. That was the time in Mrs. Honeycutt's dream, but in reality it must be well after two in the morning. I knew I hadn't fallen asleep until long after midnight, because Mia had climbed into bed with me and we had tried to comfort each other, saying it would be best for Lottie to begin a new life. Without us.

Even as the clock struck, echoing through the room, a door in the wallpaper beside the clock opened with a slight creak, and a pale, skinny middle-aged man came through it. He was wearing nickel-framed glasses, and he had a round, doughy face and a deep part in his hair on one side of his head. Although he wasn't exactly a terrifying sight—if only because of the plump flowered cushion wedged under his arm—Mrs. Honeycutt dropped her knitting. Grayson had jumped in alarm as well, letting go of me and sweeping a pot of Alpine violets to the floor. Neither the newcomer nor Mrs. Honeycutt seemed to take any notice.

"Alfred!" gasped Mrs. Honeycutt.

"Yes, it's me." Alfred laughed. It wasn't a nice laugh, not the sort you'd expect from a harmless little man with nickel-framed glasses and a flowered cushion, more like what a serial killer might come up with. His voice was the same. "So you triple-locked and checked everything, did you, Becky? But you forgot this secret door."

"Oh heavens, I get *this* kind of dream myself," whispered Grayson.

Alfred wasn't distracted. Without more ado, he raised the cushion and advanced on Mrs. Honeycutt.

"Please don't." It sounded as if Mrs. Honeycutt were short of breath already; her voice was hardly more than a whisper. "Please don't, Alfred." She was sitting with her back to me, so I couldn't see her face but I had a very good view of Alfred's. There was a wicked gleam in his eyes.

"Begging won't help you, Miss Know-It-All." He came even closer to her. "You are about to take your last breath. Oh, how I shall enjoy the twitching of your limbs beneath my hands . . ."

Grayson cleared his throat. "I don't want to disturb you, but wouldn't you rather leave committing murder to a time when there aren't any witnesses in the room? Hello? Hello, cushion murderer! Can you hear me?" He snapped his fingers wildly in the air.

Alfred frowned but stayed where he was. Mrs. Honeycutt turned and said, "Oh!" as if seeing us for the first time.

I gave her a friendly smile.

"What are these kids doing here?" asked Alfred.

"We were just going," I said, making my way past all the chairs to the door. "Come on, Grayson!"

"You can't be serious!" Grayson looked at me indignantly. "I'm not leaving this poor old lady alone with a murderer."

"It's a dream, Grayson! Mrs. Honeycutt won't even remember it first thing in the morning."

"Never mind that," said Grayson. "It's not right."

I sighed. "Okay. Then here's a wonderful opportunity for you to get some practice." I leaned back against the door and crossed my arms. "There you go. The murderer is all yours."

Rather undecidedly, Grayson raised his arm and pointed to Alfred. "Go away," he said. "Or . . . or I'll call the police."

I rolled my eyes.

And Alfred had no intention of going away. Far from it. With Grayson's outstretched forefinger pointing at him, he began growing and getting more muscular. The large, well-manicured hands with which he was clutching the flowered cushion turned into strong paws that you could easily imagine smothering someone, even without a cushion. One-handed, if necessary.

"Okay," growled Alfred, who didn't look at all like the Alfred I'd seen at first, and he threw the cushion away. "Your turn first, then, boy!"

"Oh, that's really . . . ," said Grayson, taking a step back, which almost landed him on Mrs. Honeycutt's lap.

"That's what happens if you let your fears take control," I pointed out, offstage.

"You might lend a hand, Liv." Grayson was standing protectively in front of Mrs. Honeycutt, trying not to sound panic-stricken. "You can do kung fu. Did you hear that, Alfred? My friend over there can do kung fu."

Alfred wasn't in the least impressed. He took no notice of me at all, but reached his enormous, clawlike hands out to

Grayson, who snatched up a brass candlestick from the table and brandished it threateningly.

"I warn you," he said. "Not a step closer, or I'll hit you with this!"

I groaned. "Do stop acting as if all this was real, Grayson. You can deal with Alfred easily, no trouble at all. You can—oh, think of something yourself—you can be Spider-Man and immobilize him with cobwebs in a flash. Or beam him up to the moon with an intergalactic ray of energy. Or you can turn him into a guinea pig or a strawberry lollipop. You can blow him up like a balloon and let him burst, or—"

"Yes, I get the idea," said Grayson, angrily interrupting me without taking his eyes off Alfred, who still seemed to be growing larger. "Easier said than done, that's all."

Mrs. Honeycutt tugged at his sleeve. "Do you mind, young man?" She picked her knitting up from the floor, stood up herself, and pushed Grayson and the candlestick aside. Then, faster than you'd believe possible, she had thrust both knitting needles into Alfred's chest. Breathing heavily, he staggered back against the door in the wall.

"Take that, you monster," cried Mrs. Honeycutt. "And this!" As she picked up a lamp with a marble base in order to bring it down on Alfred's side part with a yell of triumph, I took my chance to take hold of the totally baffled Grayson's arm and get him over to the door.

"You see, Mrs. Honeycutt understands the principle too," I said, slightly breathlessly, once we were out in the corridor and I had closed the door behind us. "Only, unlike you she put it into practice perfectly." An inappropriate giggle escaped me. "Who'd have thought it?"

Grayson just stared unhappily at the candlestick that he

was still holding. "I'm a hopeless case! I didn't just turn a feeble would-be murderer into a dangerous strangler, I made a killer out of a harmless old lady." He was going to try opening the door again, but I barred his way.

"We're not going back in there! Or do you want to help Mrs. Honeycutt get rid of the corpse?"

"I was only going to put the candlestick back," he said meekly.

He really was a hopeless case, but I didn't want to discourage him even more. I made the candlestick disappear with a snap of my fingers and took his arm.

"All you need is a bit of practice," I said as optimistically as I could. "And a little more self-confidence."

And a sense of achievement. He badly needed that.

THE WAY BACK took us a good deal longer than the way to Mrs. Honeycutt's room had earlier. That was because while we were there, the weird door that could have belonged to Sleeping Beauty's castle, and was one of the things that helped me to work out where I was, had obviously changed place. Unfortunately that dawned on me only when we had taken two wrong turns.

Instead of cursing me, Grayson just nodded wearily when I told him we still had quite a long way to go.

"It's a comfort to know that you're not infallible," he said. "Although I know it ought to worry me, of course." He looked briefly behind him for about the thousandth time. "It's so quiet here."

"Quiet is good," I assured him, just as Henry was always telling me. We really did seem to be alone, if I could trust my gut feeling. True, I had briefly glimpsed a shadow out of the corner of my eye, but when I looked more closely, it had gone. But then I made an unexpected discovery, and for once it wasn't gruesome but a really nice surprise.

I stopped so suddenly that Grayson collided with me.

"Matt's door!" I pointed enthusiastically to my new find, which was painted a shiny bright red. "We'd never have found it if we hadn't lost our way."

"Who's Matt?" asked Grayson, intrigued.

"Matt next door. I don't know his surname. The son of the woman who's scared of blackbirds. He's moved in with his parents again—didn't Florence tell you? And this door has to be his."

"What makes you so sure?" Grayson looked at me, shaking his head. "And why are you so pleased about it?"

I pointed to the words in black ink in the middle of the space above the mailbox slot. "*Keep passing the open windows.* That's the motto of the Berry family in *The Hotel New Hampshire*, which is Matt's favorite book. And if you want more proof, the red paint is exactly the same color as his Morgan's Plus Minus something or other."

"Morgan Plus 8," Grayson automatically corrected me, before adding, "Don't say you're an admirer."

"Oh, I don't know the first thing about cars." As we walked on, I watched the doors carefully so as not to miss our turn. Yes, unless I was much mistaken, we ought to turn left beside that opaque glass door.

"I didn't mean the car," said Grayson. "Why are you interested in the whereabouts of Matt's dream door?"

I left that question unanswered. "We go along here and turn left again just ahead. Then we ought to be in the right corridor."

"Liv?" Grayson was giving me an intent, sideways look. "What are you planning to do with Matt?"

"Nothing." Nothing concrete, anyway. I just had a few

half-formed ideas that I didn't want to tell anyone about. Least of all Grayson. "I was pleased to see his door, that's all." And now I was very sorry I'd pointed it out to Grayson.

He was still looking hard at me. "I've no idea what it is that makes all the girls so keen on that guy. Florence was in love with him for years. It didn't do her any good, because Matt never saw her as anything but the little girl next door."

"Yes, that's the trouble with boys," I said, incensed. "If you're inexperienced, they dismiss you as a little girl and just look at you pityingly. But if they hear that you've had a boyfriend before them, then, er . . ."

"Then, er, what?" asked Grayson.

"Then they want you to act that way. I mean, like someone experienced. Only—well, maybe you can look it up somewhere—how to act like an experienced person, that is— but it doesn't feel genuine all the same." I was talking myself into a temper, and without noticing it, I was walking faster. Grayson lengthened his stride and never took his eyes off me. "And that's the problem," I said. It suddenly came bursting out. "If you have to act like someone experienced, then the only way is actually to *have* experiences first! And then it gets really complicated. Like flying a plane. Right, so suppose I said I could pilot a plane, and it was a lie, but I only said it because people don't really want to pride themselves on flying planes, but they can do without those pitying smiles they get just because they're not pilots. Only, suppose that now I have to fly a Boeing 747, and of course I haven't the faintest idea how to do it. How would I? Do you see the problem? I can't go on just acting as if I knew anything about flying, or I'll never get the plane off the runway. So what do I need? Exactly! Experience! Flying lessons of some sort. And here the flight simulator comes into it. And—" I abruptly stopped talking. Oops. Now I'd gone and told Grayson all about it. But he hadn't been able to follow me, anyway. The look in his eyes was no longer penetrating but plain confused. Very confused.

Thank heavens.

"Poor Florence," I quickly added. "And stupid old pilots."

"Absolutely. What a conceited crowd they are," said Grayson, and he smiled for the first time that night. I had no idea what he thought was so funny, but to be on the safe side, I didn't ask. In silence, we passed heavy oak double doors and turned into the corridor where our own doors were. Even for Grayson, this was familiar territory. Judging by his sigh of relief, he'd probably thought I would never find the right way back.

But at almost the same time, he gave a start of surprise, and I almost yelped in alarm myself. Someone was standing there ahead of us, right in front of Grayson's door. I quickly drew Grayson back into the shadow of a navy-blue door that I always thought might belong to our headmistress, Mrs. Cook. It was the same color as our school uniform, and the Frognal Academy coat of arms stood proudly in the middle of it. There were plant tubs to the right and left of the door, with fine specimens of box trees trimmed into pyramids growing in them, and we quickly got into cover behind those tubs. (Although why Mrs. Cook's door should be so close to ours was another question. Personally, I didn't feel really close to her—and I hoped the reverse was also true.)

Grayson had turned pale. Because the person ahead of us, obviously trying at this very moment to get into his room, was none other than Emily.

"I don't understand," he whispered.

"I'm so sorry," I whispered back, and I meant it.

"If you multiply the root of sixty-three thousand and one by a hundred and eighty-six, what is the result?" we heard Frightful Freddy saying in his squeaky voice. "And then if you subtract from that the product of one thousand three hundred and fifty plus six, take away from the result the root of sixty-three thousand and one, and look at it the other way around, what do you get?"

"I thought you were going to change it." I gave Grayson a reproachful nudge in the ribs.

"Haven't had time yet," he whispered.

"Seventy-one thousand three hundred and eighty-three," announced Emily solemnly, putting a strand of her gleaming brown hair back behind her ear.

"Wrong password," Freddy politely told her.

"Oh, no it isn't!" Emily's eyes flashed at him. "The answer to the sum is thirty-eight thousand three hundred and seventeen, and if you look at the figures the other way around, you get seventy-one thousand three hundred and eighty-three. So now let me in, you stupid vulture."

"Wrong password," repeated Freddy, who was not a vulture but half lion, half eagle, and who, in spite of being overweight and having a squeaky voice, made a very majestic impression.

Emily stamped her foot. "I've done the sum ten times, and I'm right." She furiously rattled the door handle. "I haven't spent five nights making sure I knew that silly question and answer by heart, just to have you turn me away again. Seventy-one thousand three hundred and eighty-three! What else can the other way around mean? Minus thirty-eight thousand three hundred and seventeen?"

"Oh, that's enough." Grayson straightened up and came out of cover. Emily didn't see him until he was almost beside her, because she was still busy shouting at poor Freddy. Unfortunately I couldn't see Grayson's expression, but Emily's couldn't have been more horrified. Her eyes were wide open, and her jaw had dropped. And as she slowly closed her mouth, her face flushed dark red. It was worth Grayson giving himself away just to see that highly unusual sight.

"Hi, Emily," he said casually. "Arithmetic problems? What a good girl you are, with nothing but school on your mind even at night!"

Emily laughed nervously. "I'm just dreaming all this."

"Hmm," said Grayson, agreeing. "In principle, yes."

"You're not really here," said Emily. Her voice was higher than usual, almost a bit hysterical. "I'm just dreaming that you're talking to me."

"Exactly right. You'd look pretty silly if I'd caught you intruding on my privacy in real life." Grayson leaned back against the wall beside his door and dug his hands into the pockets of his jeans. "My God, Emily, I could hit you, I really could."

Emily stared at him. "The real Grayson would never do that," she said. Her face was gradually returning to its normal color.

"And you're so sure of it because you've been analyzing my dreams?" inquired Grayson scornfully.

"As if anyone wouldn't have done the same in my place," said Emily. "I mean . . . I sensed that you were moving further and further away from me, and then those strange dreams began . . . and when you simply called it all off, I . . . oh, what am I talking about? None of this is real. Anyway, you're not making me feel guilty, Grayson."

"Obviously not." Grayson looked at her, shaking his head.

"All's fair in love and war." Emily came closer to him. Then, to his (and my) great surprise, she closed her eyes and raised her chin. "Kiss me!"

For a split second, I was afraid that Grayson would go along with her, but instead he said quietly, "It's not that kind of dream, Emily. And you don't know anything at all about love."

Emily wasn't giving up so easily. She opened her eyes again and wound her arms around Grayson's neck. "This is *my* dream. And I want you to kiss me. Now."

"And I want you to go away," said Grayson, pushing her back. "Now." Emily slid several feet back, as if the floor had suddenly turned into a smooth, icy surface.

She stared at him in horror. "What are you doing?"

"I told you it wasn't that kind of dream." Grayson had raised his hand. Emily went on sliding down the corridor as if invisible threads were pulling her. "Your door is somewhere back there, right? The one with a horseshoe and an ugly knocker like a horse's head on it?"

Emily didn't reply; she had enough to do keeping her balance as she slid on, going faster all the time. She slid away past me, beginning to whimper in fright. When Grayson finally lowered his hand, she sobbed, cast him one last, bewildered glance, and turned on her heel. She ran around the next corner as if the Furies were after her, and then I heard a door latch and something made of metal—a horseshoe?—fall to the floor with a clink.

"Sweet dreams," said Grayson.

I could have hugged him as I came out of cover from behind Mrs. Cook's box tree. I wasn't even sure if I ought to let him see how proud of him I felt. So all I said was, "Not bad."

"Not bad? Not bad?" Grayson held his hands in front of my nose. "Listen, it was sensational! I pushed her halfway down the corridor by pure energy. Crazy! I think I get the principle now." He grinned at me. "Unfortunately it doesn't work for me unless I'm really, really furious."

"You were great!" I glanced over at Henry's door. A pity he hadn't seen it. "There are only two things I'm sorry about: first, that I didn't have anything with me to film Emily's stupid face. And second, that she thinks she was only dreaming it all."

"Or she could have been just pretending to be stupid," said Grayson.

I shook my head. "She wasn't pretending; she really doesn't have any idea. Arthur may have shown her the way to this corridor, but he didn't give her any user instructions. He probably didn't even turn up himself but just let her loose here for fun. Released into the wild, if you see what I mean."

"Well, all that about kissing wasn't really in character," Grayson conceded. "She's usually rather . . . unforthcoming that way."

I could well believe it. "We get to know someone's real personality in dreams. Now the only question is, do we confront Emily with the truth, or do we simply ignore her when she crosses our path here and let her think she's only dreaming it all?"

"Oh heavens." Grayson suddenly looked very tired. "Could

we discuss that tomorrow? I feel I've done more than enough for one night."

"Yes, we really ought to get some sleep." I took one last glance at the black door with its three keyholes. "It doesn't look as if Henry is coming back. See you tomorrow morning when we're racing each other to the coffee machine."

Grayson bent down to whisper his password in Freddy's ear and opened his door. "Good night," he said. Then he turned back and smiled at me. "Oh—and, Liv, whatever you may think, I'm just about sure you could fly a Boeing 747. Even without flying lessons. All you need is a little more self-confidence."

TITTLE-TATTLE BLOG

The Frognal Academy Tittle-Tattle Blog, with
all the latest gossip, the best rumors, and the
hottest scandals from our school.

ABOUT ME:
My name is Secrecy—I'm right here among
you, and I know *all* your secrets.

7 March

Oh wow! I decide to sleep late, just this once, and
something like THIS goes and happens. It's not fair. You
know how I wear myself out, bringing you all the latest
scandals and stories hot off the press. I go to every darn
party, even if I wasn't invited. I hang around half the night
on Instagram and other social media so as not to miss a
thing. At two in the morning, I'm still reading your e-mails
and comments hoping to find something interesting. (Yes,
your comments too, Hazel. Here's a little tip. If you want to
stay anonymous, you have to log out of Facebook first. . . .)
So at least in the near future, please be kind enough to wait
until after ten in the morning, on the weekend anyway,
before you do anything crazy.

And don't be like Theo Ellis, who broke into a jeweler's shop
on West End Lane at seven this morning and was arrested
while he was emptying the display cases.

Yes, you read that correctly: Theo Ellis, that model of admirable behavior, good-looking, ambitious, hard-working, talented, fair, friendly, broke the security glass of the shop with a sledgehammer at dawn. I still can't believe it, but you can even find it in the police reports in the press— "the eighteen-year-old, who has no previous police record, was tested for drugs and alcohol with negative results." That's Theo Ellis. "Those responsible for security will explain why the fireproof metal grille had not, as usual, been lowered after the shop closed yesterday." And I must say, that's not all that needs explaining.

Why did Theo do it, for instance? And why didn't he stop when the alarm went off after the first noisy hammer blows rang out, and local residents not only told the police but even came out of their houses to watch Theo at work? Someone even filmed it on a cell phone (look for "Crazed Boy with Sledgehammer" on YouTube). And all the witnesses confirm that Theo didn't let anything disturb him. It took him quite a long time to break the security glass, and when he was finally able to climb into the shop, the sirens of the police cars were already close. But instead of running for it, Theo began carefully clearing out the glass cases and putting the jewelry in his jacket pockets. When the police arrested him, he did not resist; on the contrary, apparently he smiled at the officers and asked whether they were interested in wedding rings, platinum or white gold, and diamonds, because he could offer them some particularly fine specimens.

Do you think that sounds like someone who tested negative for drugs and alcohol? I guess they ought to run the tests again. I just can't imagine Theo waking up this morning stone-cold sober and thinking, "Hey, why don't I pick up a sledgehammer and ransack a jeweler's shop?" Let's hope he's allowed to do his A levels from prison.

See you soon (but not until after ten tomorrow morning, please)!

Love from your still stunned Secrecy

PS—I've just heard that the first T-shirts printed with *Theo Ellis, I'd like you to give me a ring!* are being made already. Tasteless, you guys, tasteless! (But I'm ordering one all the same, size S.)

7

TOO LATE.

Someone else was just taking the last pint of blueberries off the shelf. And that someone was a girl whose long golden-blond hair seemed to me decidedly familiar. I stopped so suddenly that Mia rammed the supermarket cart into my heels.

"Hey!" she protested, and the girl with the blueberries turned around.

Sure enough, it was Anabel. Unlike me, she didn't seem particularly surprised to meet me here. She smiled, while I felt goose bumps coming up all over me, and my heart began racing.

"Oh, hell," said Mia. But she didn't mean Anabel; she meant the fact that the last blueberries had been snapped up from under our noses.

I was unable to say a word at first; I could only stare at Anabel. For some reason, I hadn't expected to come across her anywhere but in a dream, where I felt comparatively strong and secure. Yet I ought to have realized I might meet her near home sometime. After all, we lived in the same part of town and knew many of the same people. If I'd anticipated this, I could be smiling as normally as Anabel instead of having to fight off the irrational, icy-cold wave of fear that was washing over me.

Although maybe my fear wasn't as irrational as all that. Last time I had met Anabel in real life, she had tried to hit me over the head with an iron torch holder, so that I'd needed four stitches. And that was almost the least dangerous thing to have happened that evening.

As I was trying to get my heart rate under control, Anabel calmly put the blueberries in her cart and looked me up and down. "Very chic outfit, Liv Silver," she said, and the little hairs all over me stood on end at the sound of her sugar-sweet voice. "The romantic country-girl look. Earth under the fingernails and all." Her eyes moved to Mia. "And how cute, the partner look as well."

I was slightly sorry now that we'd been in such a hurry to get away from home. And the rubber boots were the most stylish thing about us. Anabel was right: we had dirty fingernails, and if I looked like Mia, then I had some earth in my hair and on my glasses as well. But we'd had to seize our chance to get out of the garden when it came up.

There was a Saturday morning of disillusionment behind us, and the reason for that was montbretias. Members of the Iridaceae plant family.

Mia and I had always wanted a garden, so when we came to live with the Spencers, we had been keen to do some gardening, not least so as to wear the pretty, flowered rubber boots that Lottie had ordered for us all on the Internet.

Our enthusiasm for gardening had suffered a teeny little bit in January, when we had wanted to teach the Boker a lesson because she was so consistently nasty to Mom and us, and had attacked her beloved Mr. Snuggles—a box tree clipped in the shape of a peacock and apparently famous all over Britain. We'd meant to prune him to look like some other creature, but it all went terribly wrong. Maybe we ought to have realized back then that our thumbs weren't as green as we thought. (There was now a memorial plaque on the spot where the topiary peacock used to stand.)

But we hadn't given up our romantic idea of gardening. You didn't have to begin with topiary, which is dead difficult. Even Ernest said so, and he was a keen gardener himself. There was so much to be done in a garden, and never enough helping hands, he said. So this morning he had solemnly invited us into the garden and given us two brand-new spades, bought specially for us: lady's spades with hand-forged blades and handles made of ash wood. Almost as pretty as our rubber boots. We had set to work with a will.

Unfortunately we couldn't have foreseen that our future stepfather—usually the most patient and tolerant person I knew—would mutate into a pedantic spoilsport in his precious garden. He must have inherited that side of his character from the Boker, although, as we had to admit, without her sheer nastiness. On the contrary, he was particularly happy when he was in the garden, but it seemed that we couldn't do right. So our original enthusiasm drained away with every passing minute as he told us what we were doing wrong (in a friendly, polite, English sort of way). The edges of the lawn must be chopped off exactly half an inch farther forward, leaves were swept up from east to west and not all over the place, and orange montbretias must not on any account grow near pink phlox. The montbretias didn't seem to know that; they'd seeded themselves in corners where their color would be all wrong. Ernest called them horticultural terrorists and told us to dig them up and destroy them whenever we found them. But then he realized that we couldn't tell the wicked montbretias from the obviously desirable irises. Well, how could we, when neither was in flower, but they both had very similar leaves, which looked to us identical? By now I was hating the montbretia terrorists I'd never known about before. It wasn't just malicious; it was downright sly the way they'd made sure we dug up the innocent iris plants instead.

"Do you have a tissue? I think he's going to cry," whispered Mia as Ernest inspected the plants we'd pulled up and talked soothingly to them. Apparently they were precious rare varieties with names like Bonnie Babe and Mallow Dramatic.

"Is it very bad?" I asked hesitantly.

"No, no, don't worry," said Ernest, obviously trying hard not to sound too upset. "These things happen. And I'm sure I can save a few rhizomes. . . ." He turned back to the plants and started murmuring to them again. "With luck, you'll grow again, won't you?"

"Doesn't he remind you of Great-Aunt Virginia and her room of glass animals made by craftsmen glassblowers?" whispered Mia.

"Yes, it's terrible." I looked longingly at Grayson, who was freeing the paved surfaces from lichen with a pressure washer. Even if he was staring rather grimly ahead of him (he was probably thinking of Emily), his work looked like fun, and by now I'd happily have changed places with him. Sighing,

I leaned on the ergonomically shaped handle of my spade and watched a brimstone butterfly fluttering past. It was probably out too early in the season for butterflies, but it seemed to be having fun too. The weather was so fine that you could even take off your jacket in the sun. Florence was sitting on the upholstered window seat of her room one floor higher up, with the window wide open, reading her chemistry book. At least, pretending to read it—from where she was, she had a perfect view into the garden next door, where Matt was just giving the lawn its first cut of the year.

Buttercup, who was frightened of the pressure washer, had stayed in the kitchen with Lottie. Ever since Lottie had announced that she was going back to Germany in the summer, Butter wouldn't let her out of her sight and followed her everywhere. Don't try telling me that dogs don't understand human language. The rest of us were acting as if we'd never heard the announcement, because we didn't know how to talk about it without bursting into tears. It was a small consolation that Papa had just been moved from Zürich to Stuttgart, which wasn't far from Oberstdorf, so at least we'd be able to visit Lottie on our vacation.

Lottie had originally been going to help in the garden too. But today, of all days, she had started making some bread dough that took a lot of watching. I felt sure she was glad to have escaped the gardening now. Mom, marking essays at the kitchen table, had been clever enough to claim all along that she for one didn't have a green thumb. As if she'd guessed.

Now she opened the terrace door.

"Is something wrong?" she shouted above the noise of the lawn mower and the pressure washer.

"We've killed an iris," Mia told her. "And Ernest is look-ing to see if he can bring it back to life."

Horrified, Mom clutched her breast. It was a little while before she realized that Iris was not the name of next door's cat. "Oh well," she said, looking cautiously at Ernest. "Maybe you ought to stop work for today. It's such lovely weather, you could sit out in a deck chair with a book. . . ."

"Only a non-gardener could say a thing like that." Ernest put one arm around Mia's shoulders and the other around mine, and smiled bravely at Mom. "The girls can't help hav-ing grown up without a garden. With proper teaching and a little concentration, they'll soon grasp the basics. I must just keep a closer eye on them next time." He obviously felt full of missionary fervor to make up for our lack of gardening know-how. "We were having such fun that a deck chair is no alternative, right, girls?"

"Yes, I last had that much fun when I was helping Great-Aunt Virginia dust her glass animals," said Mia under her breath. "Or maybe the other day, when my hair band fell into the drain and I had to clear out all the yucky hairs and so on—wow, what fun. Not to be compared with gardening, of course."

Luckily Mom and Ernest didn't hear that because they were too busy staring lovingly into each other's eyes.

"You're a wonderful, wonderful man," said Mom, drop-ping a kiss on his bald patch. "And so British when it comes to your garden. But I think the girls could make themselves use-ful somewhere else. Where they can't do as much damage." She winked at us. "And I need them to go shopping. Lottie wants to make a blueberry tart for our breakfast meeting when we plan the wedding tomorrow, and she'll need blueberries for that. And mascarpone."

So of course we had instantly exchanged our spades for the shopping basket, and we'd gone off all muddy and relieved before Ernest stopped smiling lovingly at Mom and realized that it didn't really take two people to buy a pint of blueberries and some mascarpone.

And we couldn't have guessed that twenty minutes later, standing in front of the fruit display, we'd meet Anabel.

In fact, on closer inspection, I saw that Anabel herself wasn't perfectly styled. No doubt about it, in real life she was as pretty as in dreams, although so thin that her jeans were hanging loose around her legs. Her hair, always flowing over her shoulders in spectacularly shining waves in the dream corridor, almost looked a little dull in the artificial light of the supermarket. There were dark shadows under her unusual turquoise eyes, and while her fingernails were clean, unlike ours, she had obviously been biting them.

But her voice was absolutely the same. "So you're Liv's little sister," she said, looking at Mia with her head on one side. All the alarm bells instantly started going off in my mind. "You're exactly as I imagined you."

"Oh," said Mia. Secrecy had written a good deal about Anabel in her blog last year, and because of the photos, Mia presumably knew exactly who this girl was. But she had no idea of my personal experiences with Anabel: conjuring up demons in general and cutting people's throats in particular. If she'd known, she probably wouldn't be giving her such a friendly smile.

"I love your door," Anabel went on. "There's something so optimistic about that forget-me-not blue. Self-confident, playful, and profound all at once, don't you agree, Liv? Isn't it surprising how much the doors can tell us about their owners?"

I wasn't sure whether the mention of Mia's dream door was meant as a veiled threat (along the lines of *We know where you live*) or whether she was only beating about the bush a bit to find out if, and to what extent, Mia knew about the dreams.

"Mia, this is Anabel Scott," I said quickly. "Arthur's ex-girlfriend—remember how Secrecy wrote about her last fall, when she had to go into hospital with a psychotic disorder?" *That's why she says all this confused stuff about doors and their owners. Unfortunately she's stopped taking her pills. And if you knew that she poisoned her own dog, you wouldn't be looking at her so trustfully.*

Anabel sighed.

"Blue is my absolutely favorite color," said Mia, whose unprejudiced smile hadn't changed a bit. "And blueberries are my favorite fruit." She was gazing sadly at the punnet in Anabel's cart, and for a moment she managed to look much younger and cuter than thirteen. "What a shame those were the last. Lottie will be terribly cross." She swallowed with difficulty. "It's going to be ages before she gets another chance to bake us a blueberry tart."

Anabel sighed again. "Well, I can just as easily use frozen raspberries," she said, giving Mia the blueberries.

"Oh, that's so kind!" Mia was beaming radiantly. "Thank you very, very much. You really are amazingly nice."

Yes, so long as there wasn't a dagger lying around.

"You're welcome." Anabel turned to me again. "Are we seeing each other this evening?"

"You're going to Jasper's welcome-home party?" I asked, taken aback.

The corners of Anabel's mouth turned up in amusement. "I was thinking about it. There's something I ought to show you."

Yes, several things. Like Senator Tod's door, for instance. And how she'd managed to lock him into his own dream. But apparently Anabel was thinking of something else. As she pushed her shopping cart on, she bent her head and whispered into my ear, in passing, "*He's* back!"

And when she said that, my wretched goose bumps were back as well.

Anabel gurgled happily. "See you sometime, Mia," she said over her shoulder, in dulcet tones. "It was nice meeting you."

"Same here," said Mia in equally dulcet tones. "And thank you so, so much for letting us have the blueberries!" She waited until Anabel had disappeared toward the frozen foods section, then grinned at me and said, "Totally nuts, poor thing! I'm surprised they let her out of hospital, aren't you? But I expect she's harmless."

Unfortunately not. Compared to Anabel, the orange terrorist montbretias were the purest of angels.

8

THE VICTORIAN ROW house where Jasper's parents lived was so small and cozy that even with just the thirty guests officially invited to the party, there wouldn't have been much space. But when Grayson, Henry, and I turned up at quarter past nine, there were at least twice as many people there, and we could hardly get through the door, the front hall was so full. We had to get past Emily leaning decoratively over the banisters on the stairs, wearing a short, tight skirt not right for her at all. She had obviously been waiting for Grayson. Lost in thought, she was playing with her necklace and acting as if she didn't see us. Well, we could play the same game.

Except for Grayson.

We'd almost made our way to the kitchen when he turned back. "I know I ought to ignore her," he said. "But she's still wearing the necklace I gave her, even though she . . . oh, this is just too much. I must talk to her. Now."

"Have fun." Henry playfully punched Grayson's upper arm.

"Call me if you need someone who can do kung fu," I said.

"Don't worry, I can deal with this on my own," said Grayson grimly.

I'd have liked to go right back with him, so as to miss none of it, but Henry led me on. All the guests we passed were talking about Theo Ellis. His amateurish burglary of the jeweler's shop in West Hampstead was the talk of the town. I had looked at the video posted on the Internet myself that afternoon. Theo's confused behavior reminded me in every way of Mrs. Lawrence in the cafeteria on Tuesday. I was convinced that Arthur was behind it. He just couldn't accept the little victory that Theo had scored in the school entrance hall. It was alarming to think that he'd needed only a single night to put his plan of revenge into practice. He was good at it. Diabolically good.

It was really annoying to have to put my mind to him again, instead of just being a perfectly normal girl at a perfectly normal party for a couple of hours.

"Terrific atmosphere, right? The beer ran out at eight thirty," Jasper shouted on seeing us. We had found him in the kitchen, wedged in with half the basketball team and busy opening wine bottles. He favored us with exuberant hugs.

France hadn't changed him in the least, outwardly anyway. He still looked just like a live version of Barbie's boyfriend Shaving Fun Ken, with his thick fair hair, bright-blue eyes, and three days' growth of stubble, plus the beaming, always slightly dopey smile that regularly made not just Persephone but other girls, too, feel weak at the knees. I'll admit that I had missed him a bit. Although so far Jasper had drawn the short straw where relationships were concerned, and was much nicer and less macho than everyone thought (including Jasper himself). He carefully polished up his image as a ladies' man and a breaker of hearts, and it seemed to work splendidly, at least with the younger girls. They all thought he had done something totally scandalous at the school in France, so it had had to throw him out and send him home sooner than planned. Rumors ranged from an affair with the school's married English teacher to getting the headmaster's daughter pregnant.

"None of it's true," he cheerfully explained to me as he took the cork out of a bottle of wine that he had brought up from his father's cellar, along with several others, to make up for the shortage of beer. "I'm sorry to say!"

Henry wiped dust off the labels with his fingertips, in the same cautious way that he sometimes used caressing me. As if I were something especially precious and fragile. Even watching him gave me butterflies in my stomach.

"Are you sure your father doesn't mind if we drink this?" Henry asked.

"Of course he doesn't mind," said Jasper with total conviction, "or he'd have locked the cellar. They've locked the gun cabinet and the bedroom. After my brother's last party, Mum insisted on new mattresses. That was quite a party!" He sighed. "Whereas the French . . . I can tell you, they're nothing like as free and easy and amusing as you might think from their movies."

"Not even the girls?" I inquired.

"Particularly not the girls," said Jasper.

Well, that was good news for Persephone.

Jasper pulled the cork out of the neck of the bottle and, with a flourish, poured wine into a glass. I'd been looking around for soft drinks, but like the beer, they all seemed to have gone already. And judging by the used plates standing on the work surfaces in the kitchen here, there had even been something to eat. Now there was nothing left but a single cube of cheese and a small sprig of parsley.

Jasper waved his glass in the air. "Want to know the truth?"

You bet I did.

The truth was that Jasper had almost died of homesickness with his host family and had begged his parents, in tears, to let him come home early. Instead of wild parties and easygoing French sophistication, there had been nothing at all going on in that little French town. He didn't even think much of the French food.

"Totally overrated," said Jasper, taking a large gulp of red wine, and then he made a disgusted face. "Yuck! The French can't even make decent wine. Well, never mind that, if it works."

Henry had taken the bottle from him and was studying the label. "You do realize this is the 1972 vintage, don't you? Tipping it down your throat like beer strikes me as positively criminal." He placed himself protectively between the wine and the thirsty boys from the basketball team.

"Oh, come on!" said Jasper. "We're going to empty them all. Shut your eyes, and down the hatch! I want to celebrate being back with my friends at last. You've no idea how lonely I felt in that French dump!"

He offered me a glass, but I shook my head.

"In the end, I was so bored that I even read a book. Me! I read it from beginning to end and then began again at the beginning. When my mother heard that, she knew I was in a bad way."

"You poor thing. It sounds terrible," I said. Henry had

given up defending the bottles from the other guests, and red wine was gurgling into glasses on all sides. Henry took one for himself.

Jasper's forehead was wrinkled in an untypically philosophical frown. "Yes, it was ghastly. All the same, I gained by the experience. I've kind of matured. Now I know what really matters in life."

"Everyone knows that," said Persephone. Even as I was trying to work out how she had managed to materialize out of nowhere beside us (quite apart from the fact that she hadn't even been invited to the party), she reached over and poured some wine into a water glass for herself. The wineglasses had run out by now. "The only really important thing in life is love."

Jasper looked at her in some confusion, but he wasn't going to have his train of thought interrupted. "Really? I was going to say friends! But it comes to the same thing in the end. Friends are the same as love." Jasper's philosophical frown had given way to his beaming Shaving Fun Ken smile again. "Did you come with your sister, Penelope?"

Persephone raised the glass to her lips, and when she put it down again, it was half-empty. "No," she said. "With my boyfriend. Gabriel."

"Oh, I just sent Gabriel off with Dave to organize a few more drinks." Jasper looked around in search of them.

"I know," said Persephone, and she actually managed to empty the glass completely in a single long draft. "Gabriel's tremendously good at kissing, you know."

But Jasper didn't hear that; he had just spotted Grayson trying to squeeze into the kitchen and lunged at him to give him a hug. Unfortunately they both disappeared toward the living room. A pity. I'd have liked to ask Grayson how his conversation with Emily had gone. But first I had to look after Persephone, who was helping herself to more wine, even though she couldn't usually tolerate alcohol at all. Still, she looked okay, apart from the little dark-red mustache that the wine had left on her upper lip—not a trace left of reddened eyes and swollen eyelids.

"Didn't you say Gabriel's tongue feels like a slug?" I whispered to her. Henry was busy with his smartphone.

"Yes, I did." Persephone smiled happily. "But Jasper doesn't have to know that. I want him to feel jealous, not sorry for me."

I was about to say, "That's silly," but unfortunately her abstruse line of reasoning struck me as familiar. Yes, I was the last person who could shake her head in disapproval. Unlike Rasmus, Gabriel really existed.

"Do you like this dress? Pandora bought it today. She's going to murder me when she sees me wearing it." Persephone giggled. "But she's babysitting for our neighbors, so she isn't likely to turn up here before midnight."

"Oh. No. Shit," said Henry, still staring at his cell phone.

"What's the matter?" I looked at him in concern. Hopefully it wasn't something wrong with his family again. Last night, when he had disappeared from Mrs. Honeycutt's dream so suddenly, his mother, trying to make an omelet, had burned her hand and arm badly enough to scream with pain. That had woken Henry, and he had insisted on taking her to the emergency room at the nearest hospital to get the burns treated. He hadn't given me all the details, but I was assuming that someone who burns herself so clumsily making an omelet at 3:00 a.m. couldn't have been stone-cold sober at the time. No wonder Henry was always on the alert for something to go wrong at home.

But it wasn't his family this time. "The 1972 Château Margaux they're tipping down their throats here is traded on the Internet at over four hundred pounds a bottle."

"I could tell from the flavor." Persephone swirled the wine around in her glass and smacked her lips like a real wine expert. "A really good vintage. Velvety and with an elegant aftertaste . . ."

Henry grinned. "Not forgetting the slight blackberry note," he said.

"Exactly," agreed Persephone.

"Jasper's father will kill him." I was quickly counting the bottles that had already been opened. "Two thousand pounds down the drain, just like that. Put back by people who'd rather be drinking beer."

At the word *beer*, the boy beside me immediately perked up. "Hey, are there more supplies?" he asked, and put his half-empty wineglass down on the platter with the solitary cube of cheese. "Because this stuff tastes like horse piss."

Henry jammed the last two unopened bottles under his arm. "I'd better get these to safety."

"Wait a moment, I'll come with you." Persephone picked up the corkscrew and followed Henry through the crowd. Only now did I notice that the zipper of her dress was only half done up, and the two sides of the dress were open from the waist upward at the back, flapping about as she walked. I quickly chased after her. But it was some time before I could get from the kitchen to the living room, and when I finally made it, I couldn't see Persephone and Henry anywhere.

It wasn't too crowded in here, but the stereo system was

turned up so loud that the windowpanes were shaking. A few people were dancing, including Jasper with a bottle of wine in one hand and his half-empty glass in the other—dangerously close to one of the cream-colored sofas. I could only hope the sofa hadn't been as expensive as the wine. I was beginning to feel really sorry for Jasper's parents.

Grayson was leaning back against the bookshelves and gave me an exhausted smile as I passed him.

"What did Emily say?" I shouted.

Grayson mimed that he couldn't hear what I was saying. I shouted my question again, and Grayson yelled back something that sounded like, "Shot that muddy feckless mac."

"What?"

"Sort out Sunday brainless quack!"

"Really?" I asked incredulously. Why in heaven's name would I do that? What sort of quack, a bird or a doctor?

But Grayson nodded angrily. "The hell with it," he seemed to be saying if I read his lips. He jerked his chin at the other side of the room, where Emily was standing beside the music system jiggling her foot in time. A very unusual thing for Emily to do. She wasn't usually the foot-jiggling sort.

"Threw a bit of shellfish logistics!" shouted Grayson above the noise.

I realized that acoustically we weren't going to get anywhere if we carried on like that. So I just danced past Jasper and the others and over to the stereo system, ignored the foot-jiggling Emily as well as I could, and turned the sound down a bit. When no one objected, I turned it down some more. That was much better. The music was still rather loud, but at least the windowpanes had stopped clinking and my ears weren't giving me so much trouble. I could even make out what Emily was saying when she leaned over and said, "Don't be so stuffy, Liv! This is a party. People don't want to talk; they want to dance."

Very odd to hear that from someone whose middle name might have been Spoilsport. Was she trying to make out that by getting into that daringly short miniskirt she had mutated from teacher's pet to party girl? If so, she ought to have taken that sour smile off her face.

I saw that she was no longer wearing the necklace that she'd been toying with so coquettishly earlier, and all at once I worked out what Grayson had been saying to me. It was really *Got that bloody necklace back*. Aha!

"What did you say?" I shouted. "The music's so loud I'm afraid I can't hear you. Did you really throw a fit of selfish hysterics?"

"Silly cow," said Emily, back to normal again.

"Thanks very much. Same to you!" As I moved away from her, I smiled as brightly as possible.

Over by the bookshelves, I finally found Henry and Persephone as well as Grayson, and Jasper stopped dancing for a moment to hug his two friends again and tell them once more how glad he was to see them. In order to do so, he stood his glass of red wine on the white piano. Well, at least his father would have a memento of his good wine in the form of red circles left on the white paint.

For a split second, it looked as if, in his high spirits, Jasper was going to hug Persephone as well. She had quickly moved within hugging distance, but at that moment, precisely when a new song, the Rolling Stones' "Sympathy for the Devil" began, Arthur came into the room and attracted everyone's attention. He had three six-packs under his arm and looked like an angel in a cool ad for beer. Presumably that was why everyone was so pleased to see him.

Everyone except Grayson, Henry, and me, of course. We instinctively drew closer together, and as Henry reached for my hand, he said reproachfully, "Don't say you went and invited him, Jasper!"

Jasper spread his arms wide. "Hey, guys, what do I keep trying to tell you? About friendship, and what I found out about it in France? Friends matter more than anything! I think you've all been at cross-purposes too long."

"Did you lose your memory in France as well? Have you forgotten what Arthur did?" Grayson was watching grimly as Arthur, like Santa Claus in person, handed out beer cans left and right, coming closer all the time. Mick Jagger was singing, *Pleased to meet you. Hope you guess my name. But what's puzzling you is the nature of my game.*

"Oh, come on, make an effort," said Jasper. "Forget all that silly, childish stuff about demons and dreams, and grow up! Arthur has been friends with us since we started school. Okay, so he's made mistakes, but first, who hasn't, and second, most of what happened last fall was due to Anabel's mischief-making. . . ."

"Really?" exclaimed Persephone, her eyes wide as she followed this exchange. "I knew she had something to do with it. Only, with what, exactly?" She was beginning to mumble. I took a moment to pull up the zipper of her dress, although unfortunately that meant letting go of Henry's hand. Persephone thanked me with a little hiccup.

"It does no one any good to keep harping on about it," stated Jasper, ignoring both Henry's look of annoyance and the way Grayson was rolling his eyes. "You just have to break the habit and begin again. Real friendship lasts forever. And we're the best friends who ever were, back then and now as well. Isn't that so, Arthur?"

"He's right. You were the Four Mosquitoes." Persephone was mumbling like anything now that she joined in again. "And you may not be the nicest mosquito, but you're the best-looking, Arthur. Because of your hair. And that amazing skin. Like porcelain."

"Thanks, Persephone." Arthur was right in front of us now. He had handed out all the beer cans and was smiling almost shyly. "Hi, everyone."

No one returned Arthur's smile except Jasper. We just stared at Arthur in silence: Persephone wide-eyed with curiosity, the rest of us with as much cold indifference as we could summon up. The last thing we wanted was for Arthur to think we were afraid of him.

Although unfortunately we were—or at least, I was. I thought of poor Theo Ellis again, and how Arthur had punished him for daring to stand up to him.

Just call me Lucifer, 'cause I'm in need of some restraint, sang Mick Jagger, and Henry raised one eyebrow and said, "Your signature tune, Arthur?"

Jasper gave him a reproachful nudge, went over to Arthur, and ostentatiously put an arm around his shoulders. "Good to see you back, man. Grayson and Henry are glad too; they just don't like to show it. But deep down inside, they know that a friendship like ours can get over a few differences of opinion. Come on, everyone, do make up your quarrel."

"Give them a bit of time," said Arthur indulgently. "Sometimes you don't realize how much you need your old friends until things get serious. Which might be before the rest of you think." He leaned forward slightly, and the shy smile he'd assumed had given way to his usual self-confident expression. "All I'll say is *Saros Cycle*."

We stuck with our tactic of indifferent glances and didn't reply. I for one couldn't think of anything to say except "Er?" or "What?" I'd never heard of any Saros Cycle. And my attention was diverted because now of all times Persephone was moving away from us. I watched as she left the living room in a hurry. Had the alcohol made her feel sick? Or had her sister turned up sooner than expected, and Persephone needed to hide herself and the dress from her?

Arthur interpreted our silence correctly. "Oh, didn't Anabel let you guys into the secret of her"—here he drew quote marks in the air with both hands—"'mysterious death threats'? Didn't she mention that you probably won't survive the coming eclipse of the sun?"

No, she hadn't. But she might well do so yet.

"She's been back in touch with him again for some time," Arthur went on, while familiar goose bumps stood up all over my arms. "Back in touch with her demon, I mean. The Lord of Darkness. Or maybe it was the demon who got in touch with her." He gave a little laugh. "And the demon isn't very well disposed to us, if Anabel is to be believed."

"But he must really have taken you to his heart," said Grayson, sounding pretty cool about it, as I felt for Henry's hand, because I had remembered that there really was to be an eclipse of the sun in two weeks' time. We were going to observe it from the schoolyard, wearing protective glasses and using measuring instruments that we were putting together out of cardboard in physics class.

Arthur smiled faintly. "Seriously—it might be more

sensible to remember the old days and stick together again. The situation could come to a head sooner than we'd like."

"What do you . . . ," Henry began, but he then fell silent and held his breath. He wasn't the only one. Everyone stopped talking at once, and people who were dancing froze in the most unlikely positions. If the music hadn't still been booming out, there would have been a deathly hush. And it was all because Persephone was back again, standing in the doorway.

My friend Persephone, the girl whose only interests were good-looking boys, fashion, and makeup, who could spend hours talking about lipstick colors and the choice between "dark raspberry" and "pearly mauve." The thing she was holding as she stood there was so out of place that I had to stare for at least five seconds before I realized my eyes were not deceiving me. Persephone really was standing in the doorway with a gun in her hand. A very large and very genuine-looking gun.

And Persephone looked as if she knew just how to handle it, too, as she slowly raised it and pointed the barrel at us. The sheer terror that had frozen everyone else in the room came over me as well, with a few seconds' delay.

What scared me most wasn't the gun itself, but the weird, dreamy, glazed look in Persephone's eyes. Mrs. Lawrence had looked exactly like that.

Arthur laughed quietly. "Sooner than we'd like," he repeated.

EMILY TURNED THE music off. That made her the only one who stirred. The rest of us were still incapable of any movement. We simply stared at Persephone.

And she stared back.

Without the music, it was perfectly quiet in the room. All we could hear were scraps of words and laughter from the kitchen, where they obviously didn't yet know what was going on in here.

Not so long ago, we'd been told in school what to do if someone ran amok. It could be reduced to a simple formula: *run away, hide, wait.* We were simply waiting. Maybe waiting for the whole thing to turn out to be a bad joke.

I'd lost all sense of time, but presumably it was only seconds since Persephone came back. However, it already felt like eternity. Henry's hand lay cold as ice in mine.

Finally Jasper managed to break the silence. "Is that . . . one of my father's shotguns?" His voice was faltering.

"Yes," said Persephone, as if it were the most natural thing in the world. "Your father keeps the key to the gun cabinet under an old flowerpot in the laundry room. Second shelf from the top."

Old flowerpot. Laundry room. My brain was clinging to separate words, but I couldn't make the connection between them.

What was going on here?

Grayson took a step forward, which made Persephone move the gun a little way. Somewhere behind me a girl stifled a scream, and Grayson stopped moving.

"Better put that thing down, Penelope." Jasper gave a nervous smile. "I know it's not loaded, but all the same . . ."

"Persephone," she corrected him. Her voice expressed no emotion at all. "My name is Persephone. And you reload a repeating rifle by pulling back the bolt of the barrel so that spent cartridges are ejected. If the magazine is empty, you open the bolt of the barrel, let new cartridges slide into the cartridge chamber, and turn the locking lever to one side. It's really simple." She took a couple of steps into the room and raised the gun with both arms. "Then the gun is ready to use. Breathe calmly."

She was clearly doing that better than the rest of us, who were either holding our breath or gasping with horror. And the barrel was pointing our way.

Or to be precise, my way.

"The stock has to be properly held against your shoulder. Relax your hand, forearm, and upper arm, at the same time keeping your wrist firmly braced. Take off the safety catch, aim carefully, with your forefinger outstretched," Persephone went on. She sounded as if she was quoting straight from the

Proceedings of the Fiftieth Anniversary Jubilee of the Duck-Shooting Association. Except that I wasn't a duck. And I didn't like the idea of shooting anything.

"Persephone!" I couldn't get out anything but a hoarse whisper. And I couldn't think of anything else to say either, not at the moment. I knew I must do something, but it all felt like one of those nightmares when you can move only in slow motion because the ground beneath your feet and even the air feel like sticky syrup. I was thinking so slowly that my brain seemed to be stuck in the syrup as well. Or alternatively, everything was happening far, far faster than my brain could take it in.

Persephone wasn't paying attention to me anyway; she was too busy aiming at my heart. Judging by the expression on his face, Grayson, who was closest to her, seemed to be desperately working out how much time it would take him to reach her. But however fast he moved, a bullet would be faster.

"Place your fingertip on the trigger. Now begin slowly crooking your finger," said Persephone. I was sure now that this was all happening in some weird kind of slow motion. I mean, how long could it take someone to crook her finger?

There can't have been much color left in my face. Anyway, it felt as if most of my blood had gone down into my legs.

"Persephone! Stop it!" cried Henry beside me. He had let go of my hand, and now he moved so that his whole body was in front of me. "Bloody hell, stop that stupid stuff!" I admired his ability to move and speak. I couldn't even bat an eyelash, let alone do anything sensible.

But it was no use. Persephone didn't even seem aware of us. She just went on with what she was doing.

"Keep your finger steady," I heard her saying. "Go on

breathing calmly, and don't blink or you can easily miss the target."

This was clearly the moment for me to scream, but I couldn't even manage to open my mouth. Any moment the shot would be fired and hit Henry. . . .

Arthur (whose presence I'd entirely forgotten for the moment) cleared his throat. Then he said, quietly but firmly, "Persephone Prudence Porter-Peregrin! Put the gun on the floor at once."

I still couldn't see Persephone because Henry had planted himself in front of me like a rock, but I could tell, from the reaction of the others, that Arthur's words were taking effect.

Everyone started breathing again. The air was no longer like syrup. I could move properly.

Then an uproar broke out. All the party guests began talking and laughing hysterically at the same time. One girl burst into tears, and it seemed as if the flight reflex had been activated only now in many of the guests. They ran through the terrace door and out into the garden.

But what about Persephone? Oh my God, Persephone! I pushed Henry aside and hurried to her as fast as my knees, which felt soft as butter, would carry me. She had collapsed on the floor with the gun and was kneeling on the floorboards, her eyes wide open.

"What . . . ? Why . . . ?" she stammered, just like Mrs. Lawrence. "The process of taking aim must not take more than five seconds," she went on, "or your eyes will begin to water . . . why is everyone looking at us?"

I knelt down beside her and put an arm around her shoulders.

"Everything's all right," I said, hating myself for not

thinking of anything better. What's more, nothing was all right. Not even a bit. I glanced at Arthur, who was surrounded by people clapping him on the back. The hero of the hour who had persuaded Persephone to put down the gun.

"What are we doing on the floor?" asked Persephone. "Have you lost a contact lens again?" Then she saw the gun and flinched. "What's that? Is it loaded?"

"Yes, I'm afraid so." Henry picked it up carefully and handed it to Jasper, who put the safety catch back on. His hands were visibly shaking.

"That was close!" he said, looking down incredulously at Persephone. "Good heavens, girl, what put a crazy idea like that in your head? And how did you know where my father hides the key to the gun cabinet?"

"I don't," faltered Persephone. "Take it away. I hate guns."

"You really ought to put the thing somewhere safe right away, Jas," said Henry, indicating the gun. "Take the cartridges out first. And listen . . ." He let his eyes wander around the room, where small groups had gathered and were whispering excitedly in low voices. "We ought to be able to tell the police a convincing story if someone happened to call them just now. For instance, we could say Persephone was drunk and playing a practical joke, but of course the gun wasn't loaded."

Jasper nodded in agreement with Henry. I could tell how grateful he was that someone had taken control.

"You're right," he said to everything Henry suggested, and then he left the room quickly, with the gun under his arm like a badly behaved tiger cub.

"What have I done? I don't remember. . . ." Persephone put both hands to her burning red cheeks. "I must have blacked out. Did I really drink all that much? And how come . . . what was I doing with that gun? I don't understand." She began crying.

"You know alcohol has a bad effect on you," I said.

"That's right." Persephone sniffed. "Even in makeup remover."

"We'll get you home. Wait and see, tomorrow morning you'll be . . ." I hesitated. What would she be tomorrow morning? Perfectly all right again? Probably not. And we certainly wouldn't be laughing at this incident. Ever.

"Tomorrow is another day," I said at last. It sounded lame and didn't really console Persephone. She just cried even harder.

"Is your middle name really Prudence?" I asked. Anything to change the subject. And for a few seconds, it worked.

"What?" She looked at me indignantly. "Prudence? Who's called Prudence? I don't have a middle name. A double-barreled surname is quite enough." She let Henry help her up and blew her nose on the tissue I gave her. But then, unfortunately, she began crying again.

"What did I do? Everyone's looking at me as if I was some kind of monster."

"No, they aren't," I said quickly. "If anything, they're feeling sorry for you." Okay, so that was a lie, considering the way most of them had put their heads together and were enjoying the sensational details, but luckily Persephone was too exhausted to notice. Over by the bookshelves, Arthur was accepting congratulations for saving the day, while Grayson, who still hadn't moved from the spot, stared at him furiously.

"He must have been controlling her somehow. Maybe by what he said." I drew Henry a little way away from Persephone.

"A word or phrase to set it off?" Henry nodded. "Yes, that shot through . . . er, crossed my mind too." He frowned. "Persephone went off to get the gun when he was talking about Anabel, right?"

Exactly right. "And she stopped aiming it at us when he called her by her middle name. The one she doesn't have. So Prudence was probably the word programmed to make her stop."

"And the word to start her off could have been Saros Cy—" Henry began, but I hastily interrupted him.

"Better not say it aloud."

Although Persephone was crying into my tissue too much to hear us.

"I suppose we should be grateful to him for stopping her just in time," I murmured with my eyes on Arthur.

"I knew it," growled Henry.

The whispering around us was gradually turning back into the normal noise of a party. It was crazy, but with every minute that passed, the mood seemed to be more and more ordinary, as if nothing at all had happened just now. Or as if everyone had secretly agreed on the story that we had really thought up for the police. And maybe that was better, for Persephone too—no one would believe the truth, anyway.

Someone—Emily?—had even turned the music on again. Although not so loud as before, so that we could clearly hear Arthur's cheerful laughter. He seemed to be in a very good humor. And so were all the others around him.

Except for Grayson, of course. He had clenched both hands into fists, and he looked as if he might burst with rage any moment. Like a bull who's been staring at a red rag for too long.

"You'd better get him out of here fast," I murmured to Henry. "Before he breaks Arthur's nose again."

"Let him go ahead and do it," said Henry.

"No! Arthur would only turn it to his own advantage. Please look after Grayson, will you?" I tried to smile, but even I noticed that I wasn't succeeding very well. "I'll take Persephone home. Then we can meet later at Mrs. Honey . . . at our old friend's place, okay?" I took Persephone's arm. "And—Henry?" I had to stop again and turn toward him.

"Hmm?" Was I imagining it, or was Henry's smile a little shaky?

"Thanks for getting in front of me," I said. "That was very . . . very chivalrous of you. Also very reckless."

"Yes, well." Now Henry was smiling properly, with all the crinkles at the corners of his mouth. "I simply couldn't help it. We're powerless against our instincts."

10

"THE TREE WANTS peace, but the wind will not stop blowing." Why my Californian kung fu teacher Mr. Wu's saying came into my mind just now I had no idea. After all, there wasn't a breath of wind blowing just after midnight in this attractive London suburb.

And I wasn't a tree.

But I still wanted peace. Instead, another few problems turned up to be solved every day. I couldn't see them as mere challenges anymore; there were simply too many of them—and too few solutions, if any. There seemed to be no prospect of any improvement. And obviously there was no way of stopping Arthur, who was like a tsunami. We couldn't do anything to stop him; we couldn't even get our friends to safety on higher ground.

I had taken Persephone home and made sure she reached her room without her parents getting a glimpse of her tear-stained face. Luckily they had both gone to bed early, and they were sleeping soundly.

"At least I got drunk for the first and last time ever on 1972 Château Thingy worth four hundred pounds," muttered Persephone as I helped her to take her makeup off, get into her pajamas, and hang the dress back in Pandora's wardrobe. "Isn't it funny that I remember all about the wine, but nothing about what happened later?"

Yes, it was. But how was I to explain the whole thing, without leaving her unable to trust herself to go to sleep ever again?

After all, sleep was vitally important, and the whole situation was so complex that it would have been hopelessly overwhelming even for someone stone-cold sober.

Fortunately Persephone was too exhausted to ask any more questions. So I had simply let her fall into bed, puzzled as she still was, and I hoped she would sleep like a log. Waking tomorrow morning was going to be bad enough. I knew all about that: just after you awoke, there was that weird little moment when you felt normal, warm and safe under the soft duvet. But if you then realized—as you usually did right away—that what seemed to you like a ridiculous dream had really happened, you just wanted to die.

I had covered Persephone up, had gone downstairs quietly in the dark, and cautiously latched the front door behind me, greatly relieved not to have met one of her family in pajamas at the last moment, taking me for a burglar.

As I was passing the bus stop not far from Persephone's house, a bus was just arriving, but I thought I'd rather go home on foot, hoping that my head would clear in the cool night air. Although a church clock was striking midnight somewhere or other, I wasn't frightened. I'd lived in much more dangerous places, and Hampstead was calm and peaceful by night and day alike. The full moon gave extra atmospheric light. Furthermore, in the unlikely case that a criminal might be lying in wait in one of the neat front gardens, I could do kung fu. Not that kung fu had been any use to me tonight when Persephone made her dramatic appearance.

During the ten minutes it took me to get home, I gave every stone I could find a vicious kick, but as I turned into our road, I was still furious. And not just with Arthur, the cause of the trouble, but with myself as well. Because I hadn't done anything to stop it, I'd just stood around helplessly in the background. And because I'd known all this week that something bad was going to happen, yet all the same I hadn't managed to prevent it.

The magnolias were coming into flower outside our house. I could see their pale petals a long way off, and I stopped kicking stones and quickened my pace. Maybe Grayson was home already and could tell me whether the police had turned up, and, if so, whether they believed the story we had planned to tell them.

Coming closer, I saw that there was still a light on in Lottie's room on the top floor, and I wondered whether to slip upstairs and let her comfort me a bit. Like in the past when I'd had a bad dream and got in under her quilt with her. There'd always been a faint smell of cinnamon and vanilla, and Lottie had stroked my hair soothingly and assured me there was nothing to be afraid of. It was like magic: if Lottie told me everything was all right, then it was—life was as simple as that in those days. Then she used to sing me German lullabies in her soft alto voice. The moon rose behind the trees in those lullabies, stars like little sheep grazed the sky, and shone their friendly light in at every window. Worries had gone to sleep, and God had watched over everything, including our sick neighbors.

I hadn't heard those lullabies for ages. And if Lottie was going to Germany in July, I'd probably never hear them again. I blinked a few tears away. Why couldn't everything simply stay the way it was? Why did life have to get more and more complicated the older you grew? A life without Lottie in it seemed to me very bleak.

I'd never been able to keep secrets from her, at least not for long; she'd always noticed when something was on my mind. And she still did, but there were secrets that I couldn't tell anyone, not even Lottie. And worries that wouldn't go away even in the light of the kindly moon. To be honest, I wasn't even sure whether God was really watching over us all.

Presumably that was why I no longer had the right to climb into Lottie's bed and let her comfort me.

Because I'd been staring up at the light in her window for too long, I almost missed seeing that someone was leaning against the wall that divided our drive from the garden next door.

When he emerged from the shadows, his hair shone like gold in the moonlight. It was Arthur.

"Oh, it's only you," he said, disappointed. He was obviously waiting here for Grayson, which in turn meant that Grayson wasn't home yet.

I had stopped, automatically raising my fists. Now I let them sink again. In the last few hours, too much had happened for my adrenaline level to rise any further.

"Haven't you ruined enough lives for one day?" I asked. I realized that I wasn't even feeling furious anymore.

"I'd have thought I saved yours," he replied.

"Interesting way of looking at it." I tried to see the expression on his face, but it was too dark for such details. Although it didn't look as if Grayson had beaten him up—no black eye or split lip. What a pity.

"I'd never have let Persephone shoot Henry," said Arthur, so quietly and seriously that it took me a couple of seconds to understand what, fundamentally, he had just admitted. But even that didn't stir up my anger again. I suddenly noticed how terribly tired I was. And sad. It had been a long, long day.

"You mean that if Henry hadn't moved in front of me, I'd be dead now and Persephone would be a murderess?"

Arthur's teeth flashed white in the moonlight for a split second. "I wanted to make something clear to you and the others, that's all."

"You wanted to make it clear that you're rotten right through, and you have no scruples at all?" I snorted contemptuously. "Sorry, but we already knew that. It's just surprising to see how much further you can go."

"Oh, Liv, you're only a little girl still. A little girl who naïvely divides the world into good and bad." He sighed. "You don't understand what an incredibly powerful tool we have within our reach." Now he was speaking fast and urgently, almost as if he feared I wouldn't let him finish what he was saying. "To you, all this is just a game. You don't want to see that in reality we have the key to changing the world, making it a better place, in fact making it what we want."

"You want to improve the world, is that it?" I meant to sound sarcastic, but it came out almost despairingly. Because Arthur obviously really believed what he was saying. I took a deep breath. "All I see so far is how good you are at hurting people. Mrs. Lawrence and Persephone never did anything to harm you. And Theo Ellis was only answering back when you insulted him. Why are you being so horrible?" That final question had simply burst out of me, and as soon as I'd asked it I wished it unsaid. Because it sounded so childish. Like Little Red Riding Hood and the Big Bad Wolf. *Why do you have such big teeth, Grandmother?*

Arthur promptly laughed quietly. "Oh, why am I here arguing with you? I just wanted to shake up Grayson and Henry a bit. So they'd realize that we can't go on fighting each other. If we remember our friendship, then we can do anything and everything together."

"Surely you don't think that, after all you've done, they will ever be able to trust you again?"

"Yes, indeed I do," said Arthur. "You've no idea how deep our friendship goes. We've known each other since we were small. And we've gone through a great deal together. That makes a bond between us."

He sounded almost like Jasper earlier in the evening. Or then again, maybe Jasper's sentimental comments on the subject of "friends for life" had come straight from Arthur. In fact, that struck me as quite likely.

"I could never hurt my friends," Arthur went on, and there was such deep feeling in his voice that I almost laughed out loud. But then it occurred to me that, so far, he had in fact never attacked Grayson and Henry directly. He'd turned his beady eye on others—for instance, me and my sister.

"I don't think you've understood the principle of friendship," I said. "If you hurt people that Grayson and Henry love, then you're hurting them as well."

Another bright-white flash of Arthur's teeth. This time his laughter sounded scornful. "Speaking of yourself, are you, little Livvy? It must be great to feel that two boys love you at once. You think you're really important, right? But until six months ago, Grayson and Henry didn't even know you existed. And believe me, they'd have forgotten you again just as quickly. Want to bet on it?" He held his hand out to me.

I felt like spitting on it. All of a sudden, my anger had come back, and I welcomed it like an old friend I'd been missing badly. It was so much better to be furious than sad. I was wide awake again. "I'd really love to go along with that," I said, sounding as cool as possible. "Not that I'd get anything out of it, because if I win the bet, the stupid thing is that I won't know."

"It's all the same to me," replied Arthur. "In fact, I just have to prove it to myself. Yes, so I spared you today, but I'm beginning to regret it."

And now I was *really* angry. Okay, so he had "spared" me, but all the same, Persephone was going to be exposed to the mockery of the whole school for weeks. Not to mention poor Theo Ellis. No one would believe that he himself didn't know why he had broken into that jeweler's shop, and of course he'd doubt his own reason. At best, he'd end up in a psychiatric hospital. He might never recover from the experience.

"Seriously, what would keep me from clearing you out of the way?" asked Arthur. "By means of anyone I like, in any way I like. What's more, at any time and any place . . ."

That did it!

"And what's going to keep me from breaking your jaw again? Right here and now?" I snapped back, taking a step toward him. To my satisfaction, Arthur retreated. As for what

I was going to do next—to be honest, I didn't know. And unfortunately I was not going to find out, because at that moment a red sports car raced up and stopped, tires squealing, at the edge of the sidewalk beside us.

Matt's style of driving was all his own, and he didn't waste time parking neatly either. His car was always at a slight angle from the side of the road, and it was a miracle that so far no one had at least knocked his side mirror askew.

Unfortunately it hadn't hit Arthur, who seized his opportunity, turned around, and made off. I supposed he felt it was too dangerous to hang around waiting for Grayson here.

Matt saw me only when he got out of the car, and although I couldn't be quite certain in the dark, I felt pretty sure that he was grinning.

"Oops!" The smell of beer and a tangy eau de toilette wafted toward me. "Hope I didn't disturb you and the boyfriend."

"Not at all," I said.

"But I obviously scared the poor guy off. Don't you want to go after him?"

"I don't think I'll bother. But if you want to do me a favor, you could run him down in your car. That would solve at least a few of my problems."

Matt laughed. "That bad?"

Yes, that bad.

Arthur didn't turn to look back. And he was not walking particularly fast, but from his manner, treading rather more firmly than usual, I thought I deduced that he was furious too. Well, that was something, anyway. Even if it probably meant that he would now spend the whole night making sadistic plans to do away with me. What use was it for me to protect my own dream door like Buckingham Palace if Arthur could set someone on me anytime he liked? Someone who didn't even know what he was doing when he pushed me under a bus or whatever fate Arthur intended for me? I'd probably be looking behind me for the rest of my life.

"How old are you, Liv? That's your name, isn't it?" Matt was looking at me curiously. I could see *that*, even in the dark.

"Yes, that's my name. And I'm seventeen," I replied.

"Oh. Much too young for me. What a shame," said Matt regretfully.

"Yes, probably. Although I'm not sure whether I'll get to be much older." I smiled at him. "I think I'll go in now and write my will. Good night, Matt."

"Good night, Liv. Stay away from open windows."

I most certainly would. That, at least, was something I could do.

11

"WELCOME TO OUR little practical course in flying for beginners, Miss Silver!" The captain of the aircraft placed my hand on a lever in the middle of a control panel between us. It was covered with countless switches and small lights blinking on and off. "There's no time to lose, am I right? I believe you have to fly a Boeing 747 tomorrow?"

"Maybe not tomorrow, but in the near future," I said, embarrassed.

"Well, let's start, then. This is the throttle lever, and you work the landing flaps with this switch. To start the plane—"

"Just a moment," I interrupted him, going rather red in the face. "You do know all that about flying was only a metaphor, don't you? What I really have to learn is, er . . . something else."

"Oh, that's perfectly clear," said Matt. Because it was his face under the pilot's cap. "But flying and sex are practically the same thing. It's all about the equilibrium between delay, thrust, the gravitational pull, and air resistance—that's the whole secret. And of course you mustn't be afraid."

He pushed a green button, and a flight attendant appeared.

"Anything I can do for you, Captain?"

"Yes." Matt smiled at her. "You can keep the copilot away from me for the next half hour, and we'd like some coffee to keep us awake, a piece of cake for later—and oh, yes, could you kindly lend Liv your bra? The one she's wearing is a total turnoff."

I looked down at myself in horror. Only now did I see that I was sitting there in my underwear, and certainly not the nicest I had. In fact, they weren't even my own. The panties went right up to my waist, and, like the bra, were made of some kind of fabric the color of pork sausage. Mom sometimes wore a bandage on her hand for carpal tunnel syndrome, and it was that sort of thing. This was exactly the kind of underwear I could imagine my great-aunt Gertrude wearing.

"Yes, it's hideous," the flight attendant agreed rather pityingly. "Mine comes from Victoria's Secret. You'll like it." She willingly slipped out of her uniform, which was blue and yellow, its colors clashing with the green cockpit door in the background. The bra that she now revealed was made of plain black lace.

"Stop!" I cried.

Both Matt and the flight attendant looked at me in annoyance.

And it really was annoying too. Me in Aunt Gertrude's undies, with Matt and a flight attendant doing a striptease in the cockpit of a plane—it just didn't make sense.

My glance went back to the green door behind the flight attendant. It wasn't only the color that didn't fit the picture as a whole. You didn't get ornate wooden doors like that in airplanes, and you certainly didn't get door handles in the shape of lizards screwing up their eyes to squint at you.

"A dream!" I said in relief. "A stupid, feeble-minded dream."

"If you don't like it here, you're free to go," replied Matt, sounding offended. "I'm sure we can have fun without you. At least I don't have to teach Patricia here anything now."

Patricia giggled flirtatiously.

"Fine. Have a good flight." I made her disappear with a wave of my hand, and Matt and the entire cockpit after her. To compensate, I imagined a sunny meadow and breathed deeply. As always when I began a lucid dream, I had no idea how late it was. After meeting Arthur, I had fallen asleep surprisingly quickly, so I didn't know when (or even if) Grayson had come home, but sometimes my body indulged in more deep sleep than normal, as if it knew it wouldn't be able to recover from the stress of waking life in the REM phase later. That was the exception rather than the rule, but it could happen that I didn't begin to dream until the early hours of the morning, and there wasn't much time left before I woke when I finally spotted my door.

Barcelona, as I had now christened the lizard on the inside of the door, purred when I stroked her scaly head. She was an enchanting creature, so beautiful that when she kept still you might have thought she was a delicate piece of jewelry made from onyx and garnets. Her still anonymous sister on the outside of the door put her scary double tongue out at me when I passed her in the corridor. With her sharp, vampire teeth and the adhesive pads of her feet, which allowed her to scurry up and down the door like lightning, she was every bit as frightening as I wanted her to be.

"But it's okay for you to be nice to me," I said, closing the door behind me. At that moment I realized that I was still wearing the nightmarish sausage-colored armored under-clothes.

The lizard hissed gleefully as I conjured myself up a prettier outfit and, still feeling embarrassed, looked up and down the corridor, staring particularly hard at the gleaming black door of Henry's dream room opposite.

But all was quiet. With a bit of luck, no one had seen me in those old-lady undies. I hoped that Grayson and Henry were waiting for me in Mrs. Honeycutt's dream.

Frightful Freddy nodded majestically as I said hi to him in passing. I stopped for a second outside Lottie's door. Today there was a slate hanging under the notice saying LOTTIE'S LOVE BAKERY—DELIVERIES PLEASE USE THE BACK DOOR, and the message in white chalk on the slate said CLOSED TODAY BECAUSE OF UNREQUITED LOVE. Oh, poor Lottie. Obviously she was still upset about Charles, even if she claimed they were just good friends and that was a good thing because he really wasn't her type. Who did she think she was fooling? That stupid, balding dentist who couldn't make up his mind had broken her heart with all his dithering. Maybe it was his fault that she was going to leave London. I sympathetically stroked the pretzel-shaped handle on her door. There must be something I could do to make Lottie feel better.

Farther away down the corridor, I heard something that sounded like the quiet squeal of a door. I immediately ducked down and turned into a jaguar. Of course, taking the shape of a breath of air would have been a more sensible alternative because a breath of air is invisible, but I could do that trick only when I was completely relaxed and, at the same time, concentrating. And the corridors were far from relaxing at this moment. Even the most harmless sound, like the squeal of a hinge that needed oiling, was enough to make my heart race. Anabel's "*He's* back" was still echoing in my mind.

I looked over my shoulders, first the left shoulder, then the right, but there was no one in sight. As I wasn't sure where the sound had come from, I prowled a few doors farther on, keeping close to the wall, and peered around the corner and down the next corridor.

The figure was standing right in front of the next door.

If I'd put out a paw, I could have touched it. Unconsciously, I'd been so sure of meeting Arthur saying that he could make me disappear any time he liked, or Anabel saying, "It's only just begun," that my first reaction was to sit down on my jaguar hindquarters in relief.

It was only Emily.

She was standing outside her own door, in flowered pajamas, and seemed to be wondering what to do next. She was biting her lower lip in such confusion that I almost felt sorry for her. What was she doing there? Pinching her own arm, maybe? Now I really *did* feel sorry for her.

"It hurts, but I won't have any bruises in the morning, so I'm only dreaming," she murmured. "And if I'm only dreaming, then none of this is real. But then why does it hurt?"

Oh my word. She clearly needed someone to explain a few basic principles to her—even if it was only that she ought to lock her door at night and never go out into the corridor again. But when I turned the corner, she looked anything but pleased to see me; in fact, she opened her eyes very wide and stared as if I were a dangerous beast of prey. Which in fact—oops!—I was. If I wanted to gain her confidence, I'd have done better to turn into a horse than a jaguar. On the other hand, the mere sight of me made her do exactly what I'd wanted to persuade her was a good idea. She reached behind her and pressed down the handle of her door.

"I hate this place," she said fervently, stepping backward into her room and slamming the door. I heard her shooting several bolts in place on the inside. If I hadn't been a jaguar, I'd have had to laugh.

Feeling much more cheerful, I trotted on. Jaguars may not be able to laugh, but at least they can smile. I was already looking forward to telling Grayson and Henry about this encounter.

When I turned left, just past a striking opaque glass door that I'd already noticed as a landmark on the way to Mrs. Honeycutt's room, the light suddenly changed. It was like a cloud suddenly covering the sun on a fine day. At the same time, the atmosphere felt colder.

Not a good sign.

I ought not to have made that comparison with the sun, because it immediately reminded me of what Arthur had said about Anabel, the demon, and the eclipse of the sun that we weren't going to see.

My heart beat faster, and the fur stood up on the back of my neck.

There wasn't far to go now, but at this moment I felt it would be wiser simply to turn around and get to safety behind my own dream door. That would take longer, but I would be on familiar ground, with other doors that I could open if I needed to be safe.

I turned around.

That wasn't a good idea either.

Because the doors behind me were in deep shadow. I could hardly make them out. The air seemed to be full of tension, as if a storm were brewing and about to break. And now the shadows seemed to be getting denser, flowing into each other to form an impenetrable pitch-black wall, cutting off my way of retreat.

I felt sick to my stomach and dizzy at the same time, while the temperature around me seemed to drop to freezing point within seconds.

I stared at those shadows, as if hypnotized. I didn't know why that black wall of darkness scared me so much; all I knew was that I must not on any account come into contact with the shadows.

At last I managed to move and ran in the opposite direction. My claws dug into the ground with every step, and I was lashing my tail behind me. The cold seemed to get even worse, and I couldn't shake off a feeling that the darkness was following me, was right behind me, but I was too scared to look around. Scraps of thoughts shot through my mind, as if reason was fighting panic inside my head.

There are no such things as demons. Someone—Arthur or Anabel—is putting on a big show. None of it is real.

It was no good. My panic grew with every step I took and with every split second that passed without a sight of Mrs. Honeycutt's door. Even the doors nearby seemed to be changing shape and turning against me. Scornful laughter rang in my ears in one place, sharp teeth flashed in another, out of the corner of my eye I thought I spotted grotesque faces looming from the shadows, only I was running much too fast to see them properly.

Maybe, whispered the sensible voice inside me, *maybe these are just your own fears taking shape. A nightmare surfacing from your subconscious mind and getting worse and worse the more scared you are.*

Something seemed to brush against my furry back, but I wouldn't have looked behind me now for anything. Where the hell was that door?

I went faster and faster, I was almost flying. Now the walls of the corridor in front of me also seemed black as night, and I could scarcely make out the doors. It was as if the darkness wanted to surround me on all sides and then swallow me up.

There, just ahead! Mrs. Honeycutt's door! With a great leap I sprang at it, got my claws around the door handle, and opened the door as I flew in. I landed on the other side of it with all four paws on the floor and flung my entire weight against the door from the inside.

Done it! Not very elegant, but I was safe at last. I gave a triumphant hiss.

Only then did I see that Mrs. Honeycutt was staring at me from her flowered armchair and had dropped her knitting in her fright. The parrot had opened its beak and looked as if it might fall off its perch any moment now. Closer to the back of the room, Grayson was staring at me, equally horrified. He and Henry were sitting at the little, circular tea table that I'd noticed last time.

Henry was the only one to smile at me. I turned back into human form as fast as possible. Henry stood up and bent down to pick up Mrs. Honeycutt's knitting.

She put one hand to her throat. "There . . . there was a . . . a leopard in here!" she stammered.

"To be precise, a jaguar, but a very nice one, Mrs. Honeycutt," said Henry in the same soothing, hypnotic tone of voice that I remembered from our last visit. "And look, there's only a girl here now. A very nice girl too—you needn't be afraid of her. Everything is all right. You'd better just forget that we're here at all and go on knitting that beautiful blanket."

"It's a stole," Mrs. Honeycutt corrected him, "but you're right, it's beautiful. Thank you." With a sigh, she began sorting out her needles. "Thank goodness nothing's tangled up. You have to concentrate very hard on this leaf pattern."

"We won't disturb you," said Henry, grinning at me. "You're doing wonderfully. There's a lot of skill in your leaf pattern. . . ."

I tiptoed past the birdcage, over to Grayson, and dropped into a chair at the table. The parrot seemed to have recovered from its fright, because it croaked, "If you've escaped all other harms, we welcome you with open arms."

"It's weird the way everything here looks just the same as last time," I whispered. "How can she dream her knitting pattern, and the flowers, and the rest of the stuff exactly as it was before?"

Grayson just gave me a dark look.

"Simple," said Henry. "This is what Mrs. Honeycutt's living room looks like in real life. In all the years she's been sitting here knitting, every ghastly detail must be imprinted on her mind." He gave me a kiss before sitting down again himself. "Thank goodness you're here at last. We've been waiting for ages, right, Grayson?"

"Is that why he looks so cross?" I asked.

"No, he looks so cross because a jaguar just raced through that door, hissing, and scared him silly," said Grayson, injured.

"Oh, that." I stretched out my legs and was glad to see

that they weren't shaking anymore. Or only a very little bit. "Then you should be glad you weren't out in that corridor." I cast an eloquent glance at the door. "I'm not going back through it tonight, anyway."

"Oh God." Grayson lowered his head to the tabletop. "Don't say Arthur's waiting out there."

Was he? I didn't really have any idea what had just happened in the corridor. In retrospect, I only half understood it. It had simply been . . . very, very dark. Maybe I ought to have held up a light.

On the other hand, it had felt truly dangerous, and I'm all in favor of trusting one's instincts. "Listening to the inner tiger," as Mr. Wu put it.

"I don't know," I said truthfully. "It was either Arthur or crazy Anabel. Or alternatively the demon that wants to see us dead by the time of the solar eclipse." I meant it to sound like a joke, but somehow I didn't have my voice properly under control.

Grayson promptly groaned.

"Or else it was a monster conjured up by my own subconscious," I quickly added. "Anyway, everything was horribly dark and weird and . . . and I think it followed me."

"Followed you here? What exactly did it look like? Is it still out there?" Henry was about to stand up again.

I clung to his arm. "That door stays closed, okay?"

"Okay." One corner of Henry's mouth was raised, as if he were laughing at me, but then he thought better of it. Looking at me, he seemed to realize that I meant what I said seriously.

"Then how do we get back into our own dreams?" asked Grayson desperately. "I've been afraid all this time that the two of you would wake up and leave me here on my own, and the flowered-cushion murderer would come back. . . ." He stopped. Obviously he realized what a fuss he was making.

On any other night, I'd have wound him up a bit, but today I understood just how he felt. The scene Persephone had made at the party, Arthur's death threats, and the thing out in the corridor—more than enough for a single night.

"When did you get home?" I asked Grayson.

"Henry and I helped Jasper to clear his family's place up a bit, and we tried getting him to see that Persephone freaking out, and Theo Ellis, and Mrs. Lawrence were all Arthur's doing. But he didn't want to believe us."

"How's Persephone?" asked Henry. "Oh, silly question. Forget it."

"Arthur was waiting outside the door at home for Grayson to come back, but he met me instead. We had a delightful conversation. . . ." I fiddled with the Alpine violets on the table in front of me. "He said if I died, in six months' time you two would have forgotten that I ever existed. And he said he'd like to prove it."

Neither Henry nor Grayson said a word. Then Grayson sat up straight and told us, "Forget everything I said about Arthur before, both of you. I couldn't care less whether or not he spends the rest of his life in a coma, dribbling—we have to stop him, never mind how."

"Yes, but we need Anabel for that." Henry joined me in pulling petals off the Alpine violets, touching my fingertips as if by chance in the process. "And she's, well, concentrating on her demon at the moment. At least Arthur wasn't telling lies about that. Anabel herself has told me that '*he*' is back again. And that our names are written in blood, which will flow at the time of the eclipse of the sun . . . and other crazy stuff like that. It's a pity she decided to stop taking her medication."

"Maybe Arthur's blood will flow first," I murmured hopefully. That might even make me a fan of Anabel. Or of her demon, depending on who was responsible.

Grayson hit the table so hard with his fist that the flowerpots clinked, and Mrs. Honeycutt instinctively raised her curly lilac-tinted head. "We're going about this the wrong way. If Anabel is the only one who can help us to stop Arthur, then we must talk to her."

"I've tried," said Henry, adding quietly, with a sideways glance at Mrs. Honeycutt, "More than once. But I'm afraid it's impossible to have a reasonable conversation with Anabel. She talks about blood and death in Latin, in a sinister, echoing voice, and black feathers float down through the air. What's more, she keeps turning invisible."

"We can't have a reasonable conversation *here* either," said Grayson vigorously.

Too vigorously for Mrs. Honeycutt. She turned and looked at us. "Now my knitting's all tangled up," she complained. "And what are you doing with my *Cyclamen persicum?* You're not pulling the leaves and petals off, are you?" She narrowed her eyes. "You're that tall Harper boy. Weren't you going to clean out my roof gutter?"

"Did it ages ago, Mrs. Honeycutt." Henry lapsed into his hypnotic whisper again. "Everything's fine. Just carry on knitting. You have to finish that lovely blanket."

"Stole!" Mrs. Honeycutt turned around, grumbling. "You'd do better to knit than play cards yourselves."

We exchanged surprised glances. The fact that we were

sitting around a table didn't mean we were playing cards. But that made no difference to Mrs. Honeycutt.

"It leads to no good; you can see that from Alfred's example," she went on. "My sister, poor soul, always stood up for him. She even knitted him pullovers. And how did he thank her? He gambled their money away, that's what he did. And wept crocodile tears when he found her dead in bed. Asthma, indeed! I know what he did, but no one would believe me." Her grumbling was drowned out by the click of her knitting needles, and we breathed sighs of relief.

"I mean, it's no use talking to Anabel in a dream," whispered Grayson. "We must do it where there are no demons and no chance of turning invisible. In real life! Where I don't feel a total idiot. Where common sense always wins out in the end."

"With Anabel?" I said doubtfully. "Even the psychiatrist got nowhere with her." Although he himself had been rather crazy.

"I can do it!" Grayson very nearly thumped the table again, but he stopped himself at the last minute. "I know Anabel from before she went . . . before she got sick. She was well-above-average intelligence, someone who could think very logically. And she still is. Do you see what I mean?" He cast a skeptical glance at us. "That stuff about the demon as an explanation for all this is perfectly logical. In itself, I mean."

"Absolutely logical," I agreed. "If demons existed."

"Exactly," said Grayson, pleased to find that someone understood him. "So we don't need to convince Anabel that she's nuts, only that her demon doesn't exist."

Hmm, easier said than done. And of course it assumed that the nonexistence of demons was a fact.

"It's worth a try," said Henry, shrugging.

"I'm no use to anyone here in these corridors, anyway." Grayson folded his arms.

"I've told you hundreds of times . . . ," Henry began, and Grayson interrupted him. "Yes, I know, you've told me that it's all a matter of practice. But I'm afraid Arthur will have finished us all off long before I've had enough of that."

Something rustled, and he looked at the door in alarm. "Did you two hear that as well?"

"It was only Mrs. Honeycutt scratching her head with a knitting needle." Henry laughed.

"You're only saying that. I'm not going out of here on any account." Grayson straightened his back and stretched. "Oh, shit, how can anyone be asleep and so tired at the same time?"

That had always seemed strange to me as well. In reality, we were all lying in our beds fast asleep, although some of us must look rather odd. Me, for instance, with a flowered scarf around my waist, assorted hair clips on my head, two arm-bands on my wrist, and a tattered notebook under my pajama shirt. The trendy look for a woman of the world haunting dream corridors by night. (But I had passed on Senator Tod's sock to Henry—I couldn't bring myself to wear it.)

"You can wake up anytime you like," Henry told Grayson. "You just have to want to."

"The trick is to imagine all the details of coming awake. As intensely as you can." It had taken me some time to learn the trick myself. It was simplest in your own dream, but much harder, I thought, in the corridor or in other people's dreams. And most difficult of all was waking when you were under stress. "Close your eyes, and when you open them again, you'll find yourself in your bed. In your room. Try to imagine yourself lying there, imagine what the quilt feels like, how the moonlight is falling in through the window, or—"

"It doesn't work!" Grayson had closed his eyes and opened them again at once. "I'm just afraid that you two will disappear the moment I'm not looking."

"Would we do a thing like that?" Henry grinned. "Come on, try again. And then we'll meet at twelve noon tomorrow to study."

"Oh, hell." Grayson rubbed the back of his hand over his forehead. "I'd entirely forgotten the chemistry test on Monday."

"We'll be okay," said Henry kindly. "We'll concentrate on aromatic hydrocarbons. . . . I have a kind of feeling they may come up in the test."

Grayson looked at him suspiciously. "You haven't been . . . ?"

"No," said Henry. "There are dreams that even I would rather avoid, and Mr. Fourley's are definitely among them. Now, wake up! Before we do."

Reluctantly, Grayson closed his eyes. "So what else do I do?"

"You're lying in your bed. You feel the pillow under your head," I prompted him. "Keep your eyes closed. You're lying in bed with the quilt over you. . . . Imagine it in detail. When we were talking about Emily and the necklace at Jasper's party, you said something about shellfish logistics. I've thought it over this way and that, but I can't make it out. Selfish hysterics, or what?"

"No idea," murmured Grayson.

"If that was to do with Emily, probably something about a hypocritical tart," suggested Henry, winking at me.

"Yes, right, hypocritical so-and-so. The hell with eternity. Not with me," said Grayson crossly. "I got that damn necklace back."

I knew it.

Mrs. Honeycutt's grandfather clock began striking.

"Keep your eyes closed, and breathe deeply in and out, Grayson," I told him, but then I was gasping for air myself, because without advance warning, a door in the wallpaper that hadn't been there before opened, stupidly not on the same wall as before. And even more annoyingly: flabby, little Alfred didn't come through the door slowly this time; he leaped into the room with a hoarse cry and the cushion under his arm, moving like a jack-in-the-box, at the very moment when Grayson opened his eyes in alarm.

And then . . . then Grayson disappeared.

12

"IT WORKED THIS time," said Henry, pleased.

Yes, it obviously did.

"Alfred," gasped Mrs. Honeycutt.

"Becky!" Alfred swung the cushion in the air. "Your last hour has come!"

"We'd better wake up too," I told Henry. "Before he smothers Mrs. Honeycutt and the dream collapses."

"Definitely not." He took my hand. "I'm so glad to be alone with you at last. Have you noticed that, with all these problems, we never have any time to ourselves?"

"Well, we're not exactly alone with each other here either. . . ."

"Please," begged Mrs. Honeycutt. "Don't hurt me, Alfred. You have what you wanted after all."

Alfred laughed his hoarse, serial-murderer's laugh. "Becky, Becky! What's to prevent me from cashing in your life insurance too?"

Exasperated, Henry rolled his eyes. "Excuse me, please," he said, going over to Alfred. As he didn't let go of my hand,

I had to follow him. "Mrs. Honeycutt doesn't have time for you now, little fatso." And as he spoke, I saw Alfred shrinking until he was no larger than my little finger, a tiny, little doll with an even tinier flowered cushion under his arm. He was opening and closing his mouth, but you couldn't hear a word he said.

"Wow," I said, impressed.

"Where is he? Where did Alfred go?" whispered Mrs. Honeycutt. "He came to smother me. The way he killed my sister. In her sleep, on the sly."

"Alfred will come back another time. At a more suitable moment." Henry bent down, picked tiny Alfred up between his forefinger and thumb, and put him down on the windowsill, under a glass dome that already had a tiny little pot containing an Alpine violet cutting underneath it. He did all that without letting go of my hand. "He can act the part of garden gnome here for a while. And you can finish knitting your beautiful stole in peace. Everything is fine. There's nothing to be afraid of."

Mrs. Honeycutt looked at the shrunken figure of Alfred with his head on one side, under the glass dome (at that size, he looked positively cute, and so did the cushion). "They never believed me," she said sadly. "Because he looked so harmless. And he shed such heartrending tears at Muriel's funeral."

"Go on knitting, Mrs. Honeycutt," whispered Henry as he made the open door in the wallpaper vanish by snapping his fingers at it. "That will give you something else to think about."

"Knitting till the break of day drives all pain and grief away," squawked the parrot.

Mrs. Honeycutt nodded and picked up her knitting again. "Muriel and I loved to knit, even when we were children." As her needles began clicking, she smiled. "Muriel used to knit things to suit everything and everyone. She described it as beautification. Our guinea pigs, rolls of toilet paper, telephones, doorknobs, Alfred—even he wasn't safe from her. Once—she was already thirty-five too—once she knitted her vacuum cleaner a pullover."

"Wonderful," whispered Henry as he cautiously moved back to the tea table, with me still in tow. "Simply wonderful, Mrs. Honeycutt. Keep thinking of your lovely stole and how beautiful it will look when it's finished."

"Not bad," I whispered.

"Thanks. Where were we?" Henry pulled me into his arms and kissed me on the mouth. Long enough to make me weak at the knees, but not for me to forget that Mrs. Honeycutt was there. She cleared her throat disapprovingly when I propped myself on the tea table, trying to keep my balance, and almost dragged the tablecloth and an Alpine violet off it.

"It . . . I think it was about us not having anywhere private to go," I said a little breathlessly, as I quickly got all the stuff on the table back into its proper position.

"Yes, it was." Henry was keeping his eyes on me. He put out one hand and smoothed a strand of hair back from my face. His touch was very gentle, but it immediately sent an electric shock right through me. "We're not alone together nearly often enough. But I have some good news."

"Mhm," I said in as neutral a tone as possible. I didn't mind the lack of time for just the two of us so much until I'd disposed of Rasmus. On the other hand—in view of the way Henry kissed me (and he was doing it again)—I'd better deal with that problem as soon as possible. Because this felt just too good. I couldn't help it; I wound my arms around Henry's neck and drew him closer to me. It was great to be so near him, and for a moment I couldn't have cared less about all the imaginary ex-boyfriends in the world. I concentrated exclusively on Henry's soft lips and his hands. One of them was on my back, holding me firmly and securely, as if he never wanted to let go of me again; he had the other on the back of my neck, and his fingertips were very gently stroking the sensitive skin there. That alone would have been enough to deprive me of any ability to think straight. And then his kiss again . . . I sighed.

Lovely dream. Lovely, lovely dream.

It was some time before Henry reluctantly let go of me. There was a light in his eyes. And presumably in mine too, or at least that's how I felt. A bit like having a high temperature.

"Back to my news." Henry's voice sounded hoarse, and his hair was even untidier than usual, which I supposed was my doing. He took a step back, as if he deliberately wanted to put a little distance between us. "Listen. My mother is flying to Ibiza to stay with friends over the spring vacation, taking Amy and Milo. She doesn't want me there so that she can drink white wine beside the pool every evening without a guilty conscience." His voice was matter-of-fact, and as so often, he had raised one corner of his mouth derisively, but there was something else in his eyes, something that almost broke my heart. "Which means I have the house all to myself for two wonderful weeks. No one will be wanting me to read *The Gruffalo* aloud for the hundred thousandth time, no one will be burning herself on an omelet pan or throwing a tantrum because one of his Legos has gone missing, no one will want to have all the math he's supposed to have learned in the last month explained in five minutes flat, and no one will come running in and throw up on the rug." He laughed. "Well, except maybe the cat. Why are you frowning like that?"

Because these glimpses of Henry's family life were rather like a cold shower to me. The proverbial cold shower. Never mind how amusing he made it sound, it always brought a lump to my throat. But because I knew he hated sympathy like poison, I tried to assume a less skeptical expression.

"Aren't you glad?" He looked genuinely disappointed.

"Glad you won't by lying on the beach for vacation?" Of course I knew that alcoholism is a sickness, but all the same, and without even having met her, I felt a deep dislike for Henry's mother.

"Glad we can finally have a place where it's guaranteed no one will disturb us," said Henry.

Oh my word. Only now did I see what he was getting at. "When actually is the vacation?" I asked in a slight panic.

"It starts on March the twenty-eighth."

As soon as that? Only three weeks to go, at the most. Three weeks in which I must either learn to fly, or come out with the truth. Preferably the latter, here and now at that. You had to approach it as something like pulling off a Band-Aid. Don't stop to think too much, just do it.

"Henry . . . ," I began. My mouth was suddenly very dry. I began pacing up and down, although I ran the risk of startling Mrs. Honeycutt. But I couldn't help it. When I was so close to Henry, I was simply unable to think clearly—as if my brain wanted to switch to autopilot and register only Henry's nice smell, and the way his chest muscles felt under his T-shirt, and how . . .

Stop it! This was getting us nowhere. I had to pull myself together and summon up all my courage.

"Henry, about—"

"I know," Henry quickly interrupted me, suddenly looking embarrassed. "And you're right. It's strange that you've never been to my place, and now you'd be coming only because the house is empty, and we'll have a place where we can sleep together undisturbed. I thought that, to keep it from feeling weird, I'd ask you to visit next Sunday." He took a deep breath. "To meet my family officially. And for them to meet you."

I could only stare at him, taken aback. He suddenly seemed even more nervous than me, standing there with his hands in his jeans pockets and a guilty look in his eyes as he gazed at me.

"It's a fact, I've done all I could to keep them and you apart, and I was rather—well, I know I upset you. That business of B and my father, and the way I acted later . . ." He took a step toward me. "But now we're together again, I don't want to make the same mistake a second time."

Another step.

He put out his hands. "You see, Liv . . ."

Now he was close to me, looking at me with as much concentration as if I were a puzzle that he had to solve, and I noticed something inside me skip a beat. Probably my heart. "You see, Liv, whatever happens I don't want to lose you again."

Tears were prickling my nose, and I let my head sink quickly against his chest. I couldn't have him see them glittering in my eyes.

All the same, he seemed to sense how I was feeling. "Hey,"

he whispered in my ear, laughing quietly, "if anyone can cope with a family like mine, it's you."

"Sure, I have nerves of steel," I replied, grateful for the chance to get back in control of myself. Although my voice still sounded rather shaky. "Don't worry." I could trust myself to look straight at him again; I'd smiled away my tears. "Your family isn't as peculiar as you make out. I mean, I know Amy and Milo already."

"Yes, so you do," said Henry ironically, and his eyes narrowed slightly. "That was the day when you also met my father and his girlfriend face-to-face and heard the way they shouted at my little brother. What a delightful afternoon."

I gave him a quick kiss. I could cope with sarcasm myself—that, at least, was familiar ground. "Exactly," I said. "And on the same occasion I made off with that pretty snuff box." The one that later helped me to get into Henry's father's dreams and convince him to change his reckless plans. I was still a little proud of that. "Did you give it back to him?"

Henry shook his head. "I'm keeping it. In case of bad times." His gray eyes looked intently at me. "Are you ever going to tell me how on earth you did it, Liv?"

I shook my own head. "I'm keeping *that* to myself—in case of bad times," I retorted. "If we ever run out of things to talk about, I can tell you that story."

"Hmm. One way or another, talking is overestimated, anyway." Henry grinned, put both hands on my waist, drew me close, and began kissing me again, and this time I forgot that we were really dreaming, I forgot that Mrs. Honeycutt could see us, I forgot practically everything.

There was only Henry and me and . . . that damn parrot.

"Go find a room," it screeched somewhere close to us.

We couldn't help laughing.

"A good thing we cleared that up." Henry sat down on one of the chairs, pulling me down on his lap. "Right, then, tea at our house next Sunday at three." I leaned against his shoulder. "And about . . . about the vacation, we have a bit of time yet to discuss some things."

"Hmm." I stared at the attractive curve of his lips and thought what it would feel like to trace it with my forefinger. "Like what, for instance?" I absentmindedly asked.

"For instance, like what we do about contraception."

I sat up abruptly and had a coughing fit. "What?"

"Well, we ought to think about it first, don't you agree?" Unfortunately Henry wasn't a bit embarrassed.

"Er, yes . . . ," I stammered. Damn it, what had I just been thinking about telling the truth before it was too late? Maybe I ought to have another shot.

"What did you and Rasmus do about it?" asked Henry.

I felt myself blushing and faked another fit of coughing until I felt I had the blush under control. Luckily that happened much faster in a dream than in real life.

"Livvy? Do you feel awkward talking about it?"

You bet I did. "No, you're right. We ought to think about these things. And Rasmus and I . . . er . . ." Rasmus and I only went for walks together. Because he was a dog. *Say it. Just tell him, Liv. And then you'll be awake and biting your pillows.*

"Condoms," I managed to say.

Henry nodded slowly. "Yes, that's the most sensible thing. For a start, anyway." Was I just imagining it, or had his face gone a little red too? "Well, three weeks is still a ways off. . . ." He sighed. (And at that moment the way he looked really did have a fatal resemblance to Rasmus. Rasmus when he wanted a dog treat.) "An eternity, in fact."

An eternity . . . for him, maybe. On the other hand, he was right: a lot could happen in that time. Who knew whether we'd even be in the land of the living then? After all, Arthur and Anabel's demon had both clearly announced their murderous intentions.

"When was that eclipse of the sun?" I asked. But Henry couldn't answer—he had disappeared.

And without his lap there, I fell against the edge of the chair, and the parrot laughed gleefully.

TITTLE-TATTLE BLOG

The Frognal Academy Tittle-Tattle Blog,
with all the latest gossip, the best rumors, and
the hottest scandals from our school.

ABOUT ME:
My name is Secrecy—I'm right here among
you, and I know *all* your secrets.

8 March

Do you remember those weeks last winter when NOTHING
AT ALL happened? You know—that boring time when
there were so few scandals to be revealed that I almost felt
like inventing some myself. Journalists call a phase with as
little news as that the silly season, and you may remember
that I used to write a lot about totally uninteresting people
or revive stories that had already and probably rightly been
forgotten. Well, what can I say, except that right now I don't
have any space to spare for boring people even in the PS.
Because you out there are doing the craziest things every
day! Thanks, you're the greatest. (Although maybe we ought
to have the drinking-water supply in Hampstead officially
investigated, because there's something not quite right
going on here. . . .)

So here's a quick rundown on Jasper's welcome-home party
yesterday, for those who weren't present:

7:00 p.m., an hour before the official beginning of the party . . . The party begins.

8:00 p.m.: The beer runs out.

8:15 p.m.: Emily Clark is wearing such a short skirt and such a tight top that Jasper flirts with her by mistake. Until he looks at her face (presumably also by mistake) and recognizes her.

9:00 p.m.: The fresh supplies of beer also run out. Guests begin looting the contents of Jasper's father's wine cellar.

9:21 p.m.: Persephone Porter-Peregrin turns up in a dress that her sister bought in Harvey Nichols that afternoon. As the photo shows, she obviously forgot to zip it up the back. Doesn't matter, it's a really sexy dress, Pandora. It's a shame you'll never wear it without someone pointing at you and saying, "Oh, look, the dress that girl was wearing when she ran amok."

Between 9:30 and 9:45 p.m.: The toilets are always occupied, so Ben Ryan pees secretly in the umbrella stand in the cloakroom. Without taking the umbrellas out first. Little does he know that he's being watched by someone standing behind the coats who has turned into a pillar of salt.

At about the same time: Persephone drinks until her alcohol level rises from zero to well above the limit, and disappears down to the cellar.

9:57 p.m.: Persephone appears back in the living room with

Jasper's father's shotgun and tries to shoot her best friend, Liv Silver, who always makes out she's a nerdy four-eyes but manages to hook the cutest boys all the same. Unfortunately Persephone doesn't explain why. But she seems to be in earnest. Arthur Hamilton saves Liv's life by persuading Persephone to put the gun down. It turns out that it wasn't loaded, but too late for Maisie Brown, who has already wet herself in terror. (And yes, Maisie, I know I've read eleven e-mails in which you say you sat in some lemonade, that was all, and there are witnesses, only it's a fact that all those witnesses, without exception, say that the lemonade smelled of pee).

10:00 p.m.: The party is in full swing now; but without Liv and Persephone, who have gone off somewhere. (And without Maisie, who has gone home because of the lemonade on her dress.) Rather mean of Liv, if you ask me, not to thank Arthur for his courage in saving her—no one could have known that the gun wasn't loaded.

11:30 p.m.: Someone kicks over the umbrella stand in the cloakroom, and now the whole hall smells like Maisie's lemonade. Jasper decides to end the party. It was terrific all the same, Jasper. We're so glad to have you back!

And we'll see each other again. Just carry on in the same way. But do go carefully with the local drinking water.

With love from your totally exhausted friend

Secrecy

13

THE WEDDING PLANNER was called Pascal de Gobineau, and he was an extremely well-groomed, very good-looking man with dark hair. The floppy bit combed to the side fell over his forehead so often as he talked that, after a while, I felt sure his elegant gesture as he pushed it away from his face was simply part of his general styling, like his French accent and his charming smile.

That smile was in complete contrast to the sourly puckered lips with which the Boker had greeted me when I turned up in the dining room, at ten on the dot. Which hadn't been so easy, because until five to ten Florence had been mercilessly hogging the bathroom, so when she finally emerged, perfumed, with her hair done, and her makeup on, I had exactly five minutes to shower, get dressed, comb my hair, and run downstairs. I hadn't managed to apply any makeup, or I could have been in *The Guinness Book of Records*.

All the others were already sitting at the table, so I had to make do with the last available chair—right opposite the Boker, and next to Florence, who in spite of her perfect styling and the gigantic mug of coffee in front of her, looked tired and wore an expression that would have suited someone having a colonoscopy.

I could think of better ways to spend my Sunday morning than at the dreary discussion of the wedding as decreed by the Boker. "Then no one can claim later that they never had a chance to put forward their own ideas," she had said, insisting on the presence of all members of the family, including Charles, who looked even balder than usual to me today, compared to the wedding planner with his floppy hair. He didn't look wide awake either.

Mom and Ernest had tried to sell us the whole thing as a relaxed family breakfast when we would just happen to discuss the wedding casually, but Ernest's choice of vocabulary had already shown that there would be nothing relaxed or casual about it. When he was on edge, he always lapsed into a curiously stiff kind of legal language full of difficult phrases—and he was on edge nearly all the time when the Boker was around. "Our intention is solely to configure a few ideas," he had said. "And maybe on the same occasion we shall succeed in consolidating aversions that one or another of us may harbor for important occasions in general, or weddings in particular."

If that didn't mean that he was scared out of his wits, then I didn't know how else to interpret it.

"The only aversion that *we* harbor is to pink organza dresses," Mia assured him. (When she was five, she had been forced to carry the bride's train at a wedding, and ever since then she had suffered from a pink organza phobia. So had the bride.)

We hadn't told Ernest that we also harbored an aversion

to bridegrooms' mothers who assumed, without asking, that they could order us around and commandeer our time. The last thing we wanted was to spoil his and Mom's fun in looking forward to their wedding, although we were a bit scared by the Boker, the size of the celebration as she envisaged it, and the expense of it all. And we were sure it also scared Mom, but today she didn't once mention her preference for small, informal garden parties. On the contrary, she immediately agreed with Pascal that there was no better place for a wedding party than a classic English country house hotel. That made Pascal very happy, because just by chance one of the finest such country house hotels, usually booked for years in advance, happened to be available on the planned wedding date of the last weekend in June. Which was as much of a miracle as the fact that Pascal himself had been available at such short notice, as the Boker never tired of emphasizing. Because Pascal, too, was booked for years in advance, and many famous couples had him to thank for unforgettable festivities. The couple who had changed their minds at short notice, thus leaving the booking open for Ernest and Mom, were also famous, but unfortunately Pascal wouldn't tell us who they were.

"All I say is that it is better for many people if they notice that they are not right for each other before the wedding" was the only comment he would make before turning to his "famous, or infamous, de Gobineau wedding checklist." I don't know whether that checklist really was famous, or even infamous, but if so, it was probably for its enormous length. In spite of his charming smile and his accent, Pascal's voice droned monotonously on, and he had obviously decided to tell us about absolutely everything that was in the folder on the table in front of him, from the two thousand ways of folding linen serviettes worldwide, to the effect of floral decorations featuring globe-headed alliums in square glass vases, to the best height for pedestal tables. With the best will in the world, it wasn't possible to show any genuine interest in the difference of quality between brands of lined envelopes, so I did what I do in boring classes: I allowed an interested expression to come over my face, and let my thoughts wander. That way you couldn't exactly catch up on the sleep you'd missed, but you reached a state of deep relaxation, which was better than nothing. And it didn't annoy anyone.

Now and then a few words got through to me, like *embossed printing*, *floribunda roses*, *seating plan*, and *almond mousse filling*, but I could easily fit those into my vague thoughts while dozing.

For instance, there must have been almond mousse filling instead of brains in my head last night, after Henry had left me alone in Mrs. Honeycutt's dream, and instead of waking up myself, I had decided to venture out into the corridor again. Because however frightened I'd been of the darkness that swallowed everything before, there was something now that frightened me even more: our spring vacation.

Usually Mia and I always went to stay with our father on school vacations, but this time we were staying at home for once, because Papa was away on business so often and until he finally moved from Zürich to Stuttgart he was living in hotels. (Although he was going to come to London for a few days in May, allegedly to see us, but no doubt also to get a look at the man Mom was going to marry.)

The corridor had been peaceful; there was nothing to hear but my own footsteps—so whoever had let the darkness loose might perhaps be awake by now. Or else there was no such person, and it was only my own fears and gloomy thoughts that had come to life. My thoughts were no longer gloomy, just very complicated, but they were leading me deliberately into a certain corridor. I let my eyes wander over the doors, and there it was, just as I'd expected: Matt's red door.

It must be early morning, I had worked out. My sleep would probably be interrupted any moment now, because I had a very reliable alarm clock known as Little Sister. Mia never slept in for long on weekends, and ever since I could remember, she had come scrambling into bed with me on Sunday mornings. Staring at Matt's door, I persuaded myself that the time for me to wake would come very soon.

Of course I had known only too clearly that my idea wasn't a good one—but then again, I couldn't think up anything better. Spring vacation began in less than three weeks' time, and Matt . . . well, Matt would have to be my flight simulator.

I had glanced briefly down the corridor. Still no one in sight, no sense of anyone about. I was alone and could still turn back. But I didn't. I had taken a deep breath, turned the door handle to the right, and opened Matt's door. . . .

"Love isn't what we expect to get, but what we are prepared to give," said Pascal all of a sudden. Hopefully, I raised my head. Had I missed anything important? Had he by any chance finished?

No, it didn't look like it. The file was still more than half full of papers.

I cast a searching look around the table. The Boker, Mom, and Lottie seemed to be the only ones following Pascal's remarks with genuine interest. Everyone else appeared to be paying as little attention as I was. Florence was secretly fiddling with her iPhone under the table, Ernest was holding

Mom's hand and had a vague smile on his face, but his eyes were looking into space. Mia was building castles of scones on her plate, and Grayson was making up for the sheer boredom of it all by eating. He had already consumed vast quantities of scrambled egg on toast and about half of Lottie's blueberry tart. When I smiled at him, he didn't smile back but just glanced up at the ceiling.

Charles had half closed his eyes, and his chin was sinking lower and lower, but whenever his head was nearly touching his plate, he looked at Lottie and sat up straight again.

And Lottie looked particularly pretty today in her close-fitting ivy-green cardigan. It really suited her brown hair, which she had tied together loosely at the back of her neck. Maybe I was only imagining things, but it seemed to me that Pascal smiled at her especially often.

"I've been working for years with the same gardener on the little baskets of blooms for the flower children to scatter. She provides organically grown and freshly picked flower heads on the wedding morning, in perfectly matched shades of color." There was something hypnotic about his voice. Maybe that was why no one interrupted him, for instance to ask what all this was going to cost. Organically grown flower heads—I ask you! Good old rice did the same job. And who was going to scatter the flowers, anyway? But I didn't intend to ask a single question. That would just drag it all out unnecessarily.

I felt as if I'd been sitting at that table for days, but it was only eleven in the morning.

Was Persephone awake yet? And had Secrecy already exposed what she'd done at the party in her blog? I bet she had. I was going to call Persephone as soon as I was through with this wedding stuff, hoping she could manage without me that long. By now she'd certainly be wishing she could turn the clock back and cancel last night.

And speaking of canceling things: my mind wandered back to Matt's red dream door. Maybe I'd have withdrawn in time, if it hadn't been so easy to get in. Most people unconsciously protect their doors with an obstacle of some kind, but with a few, you can simply walk in during their dreams. Matt was one of those.

When I crossed the doorstep, I found myself in the foyer of an obviously enormous modern building with a huge amount of glass and gigantic steel constructions. To right and left, people were streaming past me toward broad escalators, and they all looked very busy. I was greatly relieved to be in a comparatively normal dream; you never knew what people would be dreaming, and especially in the small hours of the morning, the dreams often turned rather crazy, at least mine did. It took me a few seconds to locate Matt himself. That was because, like most of the other people here, he was wearing a dark-blue suit, so he didn't stand out from the crowd. He was standing in front of the electronic security gates leading to the elevators, talking to a woman sitting behind the reception desk. They were flirting, as I could see at once from the way Matt was leaning against the desk and smiling. The woman tossed her hair back provocatively, and when I came closer, I saw that the jacket of her business suit was unbuttoned rather a long way down, and she was leaning well forward on purpose for Matt to look inside her neckline. Which he was doing very thoroughly.

Okay, so it was that sort of dream. At least that meant the general atmosphere was right for what I had in mind. Much better than if Matt had been having a nightmare in which he was pursued through an empty multistory parking lot by a serial killer or chased through the jungle by cannibals. Or than if he'd been dreaming he was still a little boy, going for a walk in the park with his granny. No, this was perfect.

Now I only had to get rid of the woman at the reception desk. And of my own inhibitions too.

That bit was better than I'd hoped. I simply imagined that I was a secret agent who had been told to seduce Matt. It was like an improvised theatrical show but much better, because in the morning none of the other actors would know anything about it.

Secret Agent Silver generated herself an outfit as much like what the woman behind the desk was wearing as possible, a figure-fitting, dark-blue skirt suit and blue pumps, with heels so high that in real life, I could never have taken more than a couple of steps in them without stumbling. I let my hair flow over my shoulders, like hers, and I even gave myself lipstick the same color, somewhere between pink and dark red. Persephone would certainly have known its name at once. Then I put on my glasses (because so far Matt had only ever seen me in glasses, and might not recognize me without them), and I stalked toward the reception desk like a model on the catwalk, holding a stack of folders out in front of me with both arms. I dropped the folders right beside Matt and let out a little cry of alarm when one of them landed on his foot.

"Oh, excuse me, I'm so sorry!" I said breathlessly, and as Matt bent down to help me pick the folders up (how nice that he had such good manners even in a dream), I quickly made the woman at the desk twenty years older and gave her yellowish teeth and a wart under her left eye, but the wart looked so disgusting that I removed it again.

"Thank you so much," I murmured, beaming at Matt through my glasses. "That's really so kind of you."

"You're welcome," said Matt. Then he did a double take. "Liv? Is that you?"

"Yes." I blinked at him as if surprised. "Oh God. Hi, Matt. I didn't recognize you in that suit. What are you doing here?"

Matt straightened up and put the folders on the desk. After a glance of annoyance on seeing that the object of his flirtatious attentions had aged so suddenly, he turned back to me and said, "I work here. My office is on the thirty-second floor."

Aha. So in the dream corridors he obviously wasn't an unsuccessful law student who had moved back in with his parents.

"Mr. Davenport will soon be a partner in Strong and Jameson," the woman behind the desk explained. "The youngest partner in the history of this legal practice."

Ho-ho-ho. In his dreams—literally.

"Oh wow!" I tried to inject genuine admiration into my voice. "The view from up there must be staggering—I'm working as an intern in the admin department," I added, hoping to heaven that there was indeed such a department in this outfit, "and I've never been higher up than the twelfth floor."

"Really?" Matt gave me a slightly pitying smile. "You can go right to the top in the elevator anytime. That's what the tourists do."

Damn it. "Well, er, yes. I will as soon as I get time." I gave Matt a trusting smile. "This is only my third day here. I'm afraid my boss, Mr. . . . . er, Smith, is terribly strict."

"Oh dear," said Matt. The sympathy dodge seemed to be working, so I decided to lay it on even thicker.

"I think he's upset because I don't like it when he calls me 'sweet little thing.'" I pushed the hair back from my face. "Although I'm taller than he is. I mean, the man is about two hundred years older than me, and he has bad breath too."

"That's disgusting." Matt indignantly shook his head. "In fact, it obviously comes under the heading of sexual harassment. Even aside from the fact that you're still underage. A child!"

Damn it again. *Child* wasn't what I wanted. I must correct him about that. "I'm eighteen," I said untruthfully. If Matt had promoted himself from law student to partner in a legal practice, I could easily add a year to my age; his dream logic wouldn't have any difficulty in coping with that. "But I don't want to be groped by a slimy character like that. . . . It's not how I imagine my first time." I held my breath for a moment, afraid I might have been going too fast. On the other hand, we were in a dream, and every second counted. Seeing that Matt didn't look particularly shocked but interested instead, I quickly went on. "Yes, I know. I realize it's not right myself—but it's not easy to find someone who . . ." Here I fell silent. Not on purpose, but because at this point Secret Agent Silver's talent for improvisation simply let her down. Like in real life.

"Oh, I can't imagine that." Matt looked me up and down. "I mean, you're a very pretty girl."

Very pretty. In boy language, didn't that mean exactly the opposite of *stunningly beautiful*? I obviously wasn't his type. All the same, I gave him a warm smile. "Thank you. But the men I meet don't like . . . er . . . girls without any experience. Well, apart from Mr. Smith. But on principle he isn't choosy."

Matt said nothing.

Oh God. It wasn't working. Maybe I ought to change the scenario a bit. Stage an earthquake. Or an attack by aliens. That always brought people closer to each other in movies.

Or maybe I should simply give up.

I looked around surreptitiously for Matt's dream door. It was standing in the foyer, looking lost and totally out of place, but no one else seemed to notice it.

"I . . . I must go," I murmured. Secret Agent Silver had failed. "To give Mr. Smith my notice. I can't stand it here another day. Good to see you."

The foyer blurred before my eyes, and then the sun was dazzling me instead. A city lay spread out far below me, and at first I thought I was flying. Then I realized that I was looking down at London from the window of a very tall skyscraper. Ravines of buildings, rooftops, towers, the dome of St. Paul's Cathedral, the glittering ribbon of the Thames with its bridges. Someone put a hand on my shoulder from behind.

"Impressive, isn't it?" said Matt's voice, close to my ear, and the back of his hand was caressing my throat.

"Yes." I swallowed. It really was impressive to see how quickly Matt had changed his dream backdrop and how nimbly his subconscious mind had simply skipped any unnecessary preliminaries. I was half-relieved to find that I was obviously his type after all. But only half. When he put both hands around my waist, turned me to face him, and held me close, I felt distinctly queasy.

"The couch over there not only has the best view in

London, it's also very comfortable," he murmured in my ear. "And I promise that you will never forget your first time."

He began kissing my throat, from the collarbone upward, and I immediately felt even queasier. Although what he was doing was really exactly what I'd wanted. A training session in the flight simulator. No one would ever know. All the same . . .

"No kissing!" the words involuntarily escaped me.

Matt slackened his grip. "What? No kissing? Hello? And maybe no undressing and no touching?"

"Does that work?" I asked hopefully.

Matt rolled his eyes. "No, it doesn't work. What's the matter with you? I thought you were dead keen on it."

Yes, what was the matter with me? I'd reached this point, and now I was about to spoil everything again. Surely I hadn't gone to all that trouble for nothing?

"Sorry," I said remorsefully.

"That's all right." Matt let his hand slip under my jacket. "No kissing, then."

I had to summon up all my willpower not to push him away. I was Agent Silver on a secret mission, and this was only a dream. Only. A. Dream. If I closed my eyes, maybe I could simply think of it as Henry's hand. But it didn't feel like Henry's hand. It felt like a stranger's hand. A hand that had absolutely no business on my bare skin.

And a hand that now suddenly froze when it reached the hook of my bra. "What on earth is *that*?"

Oh no, not again. My subconscious mind had fitted me out in Great-Aunt Gertrude's armored flesh-colored underwear. I'd lost control of this.

"Hey, that's mine," said Matt, but this time in Mia's voice.

There was a tweaking sensation in my hair—and then I was awake.

Even though Mia had pulled out at least ten hairs to get back the frog-shaped hair clasp I'd stolen from her, at that moment I had thought how lucky I was to have a reliable Sunday alarm clock called Little Sister.

And it was also Mia who now brought me back from the depths of my embarrassing memories to the breakfast table and made sure that Pascal was interrupted in the middle of his monotonous lecture. She had stacked seven scones on top of one another, but when she added an eighth, the entire structure collapsed, knocking over a glass.

"Oops," she said, to which the Boker responded with an acid, "You mean *sorry*, child."

"Sorry, child," Mia repeated.

Pascal smiled, just as we might have expected. "I was about to move on to the next point on my checklist anyway," he said.

"That would be point three thousand and forty-four," murmured Grayson.

I was about to drift back into my state of half sleep, but against all expectations, things suddenly turned exciting. The guest list was under discussion. It turned out that the Boker had already done some work in advance and had written down, on her deckle-edged notepaper, the names of the eighty-four people whom Ernest must at all costs invite, and another ninety-eight names of those who really ought also to be invited, but could be dispensed with if absolutely necessary.

She had also started a list for Mom's guests "at a rough reckoning." Mom stared at it in consternation.

"Brother of the bride with companion," she read out loud. "I don't have any brothers. Or sisters."

"All the better," said the Boker, delighted. "I hoped I'd put the figure too high rather than too low."

Mia leaned curiously over to Mom. "Oh, great, you can invite your best friend and your second-best friend. Who's your best friend, and who comes second best? Papa?"

The Boker gave a start. Presumably "ex-husband of the bride" hadn't made it to the deckle-edged paper.

"Oh goodness, I don't rank them in any order. I love all my friends the same. But that doesn't mean they have to come to my wedding." Mom cast Ernest a quick sideways glance. She really did have friends all over the world, and quite a number of them were men. "Particularly as they all live so far away."

"Yes, that's what I thought." The Boker smiled, extremely pleased with herself. "Someone from Ernest's second list, the reserves, can be invited instead of every guest of yours who doesn't want to make the long journey from the States or wherever else."

"Everything depends on good planning," Pascal agreed.

"Can I see those lists, please?" asked Ernest.

"Of course." The Boker passed several sheets of deckle-edged paper over his empty scrambled-egg plate, and Ernest studied them, frowning.

"Who's Eleanor?" he asked.

"Eleanor?" The Boker looked at him as if he had gone out of his mind. "Why, my cousin Lucy's daughter, of course, the one who married Lord Borwick. You used to play with her as a child."

"Yes, very likely, but I never saw her again after that," said Ernest.

"As I have always deeply regretted," replied the Boker. "It is extremely useful for a man in your position to be in contact with members of the House of Lords."

Ernest skimmed the lists again, then put them down and took off his reading glasses. "Mother, these are all names of people I don't know from Adam."

"That's the list of reserve names. And of course you know them. Or at least you ought to know them." The Boker compressed her lips. "But if you don't want my help, then by all means draw up a guest list of your own by tomorrow evening, complete with full names and addresses. Pascal has to order the printing of the invitations by the weekend at the latest, isn't that so, Pascal?"

Pascal nodded. "I work with a very exclusive little printing press in Highgate. They also do very fine stamps for embossment work." He looked at his file. "Well, I think we're *almost* finished for today. . . ."

Grayson groaned. "I really don't want to be uncivil, but exactly why do we have to sit through all this?"

"Because it's a family matter, Grayson," said Florence, although he hadn't been asking her. "And because I want to be sure that no one puts Liv, Mia, and me in the same silly dresses."

"Don't you worry! I'd sooner die," said Mia.

Grayson looked at Florence in annoyance. "Surely we have better things to do than bother about dresses and silly stuff like easy-iron tablecloths? Such as studying our chemistry, for instance."

"You think I'm enjoying this?" Florence venomously retorted. The Boker cleared her throat, but Florence ignored her and glanced at the clock on the mantelpiece. "As far as I'm concerned, you're welcome to push off, Grayson. Emily is coming at quarter to twelve to do some studying with me, and we don't want her seeing you."

"Why not? Am I supposed to go into hiding whenever Emily comes to visit you?" asked Grayson indignantly.

"Yes," said Florence. "If you were a more thoughtful person, you'd spare her a meeting until she's recovered from you dumping her." She sniffed. "Although, if you were a more thoughtful person, you'd never have started something with my best friend in the first place."

"Now you're finally going crazy! Emily can damn well stay at home if she doesn't want to meet me."

The Boker cleared her throat again. This time it sounded like a sick horse. "If you could *kindly* keep your private conversations until later! Pascal's time is valuable."

"So is mine," said Grayson. He was unusually quarrelsome today.

"We're nearly through," said Pascal amiably, before the atmosphere could finally become impossible. A vein was already standing out on the Boker's forehead, and Charles looked as if he wanted to jump up and walk away. Mom and Ernest were holding hands tightly. "There's only the question of who supports the bride and groom to be considered."

"Oh, that's easy," said Mom, relieved, and she smiled at Ernest. "Charles is going to be Ernest's best man, and of course Lottie will be my maid of honor."

Charles nodded loyally, and Lottie beamed.

"Oh, how exciting!" she said happily.

"Yes, indeed," murmured the Boker. I was waiting for the insult that was bound to follow, but it never did, because someone rang the front doorbell and the next disaster got going.

"I'LL ANSWER IT!" cried Grayson and Florence in unison, leaping up at the same time. Buttercup, who until now had been sleeping peacefully on the sofa, looked up in alarm.

Grayson and Florence stared into each other's eyes across the table.

"That's Emily," snapped Florence. "And no way are you going to let her in, or she'll be upset and angry all day."

"So what? Can't I even answer the door in my own house these days?" Grayson snapped back. The rest of us looked alternately at one and then the other, like when you're watching a tennis match.

"It could be Henry. We're studying for chemistry ourselves."

And zoom, all heads turned back to Florence. "Yes, that's just typical! Studying at the last minute, just so long as you don't miss any parties."

"Mad because you missed something at Jasper's the other night?"

The doorbell rang for a second time, and Buttercup

couldn't stand it anymore. She jumped off the sofa and barked at us. Grayson and Florence took no notice of her; they just shouted even louder to be heard above the noise.

"Hardly likely. Maybe your immature basketball friends getting drunk is exciting—personally, I think my A-level results are more important, if you can imagine such a thing!"

"For heaven's sake, how old are the two of you—five?" asked Ernest.

The doorbell rang for the third time, and the Boker said, to no one in particular, "I feel so ashamed!" Buttercup was still barking. She hated quarrels.

"I'll answer it." Mia stood up. Relieved, Buttercup wagged her tail and followed her out into the hall. "If it's Emily, I'll whistle so that Grayson can hide behind the sofa," Mia called back over her shoulder.

"What a delightfully lively family! Too, too wonderful!" Smiling, Pascal closed his folder. "Separately we are words; together we're a poem," he said. I supposed he meant to tell us he'd finished.

"Amen," whispered Lottie, much moved. Everyone else, including Mom and Ernest, stretched inconspicuously as if they had been on a long rail journey. The Boker massaged her temples.

"All clear!" By now Mia had opened the door. "It's only the guy from next door, the one that Florence used to be in love with," she called, and my heart missed a beat, "And he has—shit!"

"He has shit?" repeated Mom.

Spot, our ginger cat, came racing into the living room, closely followed by Mia, Buttercup—and Matt.

Shit.

Spot leaped over the sofa and landed on the piano, where he crouched beside the bust of Beethoven and stared at us crossly, his face all fluffed out.

"What's that in his mouth?" asked Florence, while I sat back in my chair and tried to look as small and inconspicuous as possible so that Matt, standing at the end of the table, wouldn't notice me.

"A blackbird." He blew a black feather off the sleeve of his sweater. "Sorry, but he dragged it into our conservatory and let it go flying about there. My mother almost fell down in a faint. Luckily your cat caught the bird again, but in the process, he knocked over two containers planted with some kind of exotic greenery, so I picked him up and—"

"And brought him here, so now he can let the bird fly about in our dining room? Thanks very much," said Florence. She cautiously approached the piano. "Poor little Spottikins! Did nasty Matt hurt you?"

"More like the other way around. Spot scratched poor little Mattikins quite badly," claimed Matt. "Not to mention what he did to poor little birdikins. And about the plant containers . . . I've been told to ask if your insurance will cover them. Seems they were rather valuable."

"Then maybe your family ought to keep their conservatory door closed," snapped Florence.

"Good Lord, you're in a temper." Matt inspected her, shaking his head. "And you used to be so cute."

Florence's eyes flashed angrily. "Huh! Since then I've found out that being cute doesn't get you anywhere in this world."

"But common civility does." Ernest had risen to his feet. "Mr. Gobineau," he said to Pascal, "I think we'd better show you the way out before things get even more chaotic in this—what did you call it?—delightfully lively family."

Pascal was still smiling. I was beginning to get the creeps.

"I must be going too." The Boker quickly stood up and reached for her beige cardigan. "I can feel a migraine coming on, and bad-mannered domestic pets and children only put an unnecessary strain on my nerves." For once, her withering glance was not for Mia and me, but for her real grandchildren.

"Would you like a slice of the tart to take home?" asked Lottie, but the Boker had already disappeared into the hall without another word. Mom, Pascal, and Ernest followed her.

"We'll talk about this later. You see to the cat," Ernest told us, while Pascal waved good-bye—still smiling. For the first time, I thought maybe he didn't smile like that all the time because he wanted to; he could be suffering from facial paralysis of some kind. Was that the secret of his success?

"Oh, what a nice man," said Lottie with a deep sigh. "So positive! Probably because he's busy all day setting the scene for love and happy endings."

"All that posturing and grinning is only a dodge to rustle up more business." Suddenly Charles looked wide awake. "To give people the feeling that they can buy love and happy endings."

"Only an unromantic person who doesn't believe in love could say a thing like that," said Lottie, tucking a strand of hair back behind her ear and looking at him challengingly. "Someone who doesn't know what passion is."

"Just because I don't tie bows around everything doesn't mean I'm unromantic," said Charles, annoyed. "Or that I don't know what passion is."

"Really?" Lottie shrugged her shoulders. "Excuse me, that's only my personal impression."

I looked incredulously from one to the other of them. Here we went again. There seemed to be something in the air today, turning everyone into quarrelsome kindergarten kids. All we needed was someone saying "Yah, boo!" after every remark.

"And you think that everything presented to you with a smile is romantic," retorted Charles. "Speaking of smiles, I for one wouldn't smile as superciliously as that guy if I had a nasty inflammation of the gums."

"He wasn't being supercilious, only charming. And he doesn't have an inflammation of the gums," said Lottie.

"Yes, he does, around the canine tooth top left! Only, you couldn't see it because you were sitting on his right." Even Charles himself seemed to notice that he sounded childish. "Can I have some of that tart before the bird gets away again and leaves droppings on it?" he asked in a more conciliating tone.

"I don't think it can still fly," said Matt. So far his glance had fallen on me only briefly, and I had calmed down a bit. Not many people could remember their dreams once they were awake, and if they did, it wasn't for long. But even in the unlikely case that Matt did remember, it was still *his* dream, and he hadn't the faintest suspicion that I had smuggled myself into it and manipulated the whole thing a little. If anyone had to be embarrassed about the dream, it was Matt. So why did I still feel I wanted to crawl under the table and hide until he had gone away again?

Spot growled at us quietly.

"That poor cat is totally traumatized," said Florence, casting Matt a furious glance. "I hope *you* are insured against *that*."

"Stop taking your bad temper out on Matt, Florence. If anyone around here is traumatized, it's the blackbird." Grayson picked up Spot and carried him out to the terrace. The idea that the bird might really leave droppings on what was left of the tart had probably made him step in. Not a stupid idea, because it turned out that the blackbird was alive and well and perfectly capable of flying. Spot must be sorry that he had opened his mouth, but with Grayson gently shaking him, he couldn't help it. He grumpily watched the blackbird as it flew straight into Matt's parents' garden (stupid creature), but then, without further protest, he let Grayson carry him back indoors, where he curled up on the sofa with an injured expression and didn't favor us with another glance. Buttercup showed solidarity by lying down beside him and looking at us reproachfully.

"At least that makes two who aren't quarreling," said Mia cheerfully.

"Anyone for blueberry tart?" asked Lottie.

"I wouldn't say no," replied someone in Henry's voice, and I spun around at once. Henry was standing in the open doorway of the dining room, and there was Emily behind him, peering over his shoulder. They had both obviously come in while Mom and Ernest were saying good-bye to the Boker and Pascal—as they were still doing, to judge by the voices coming from the hall.

"I'd like a piece of the blueberry tart as well," said Matt.

The dining room was beginning to look to me like a theater with too many actors suddenly on stage all at once, performing a play that made no sense.

Mia was whistling. And many of the others had peculiar lines to say. Mia was brilliant at prompting, in a tone of voice that could be heard only onstage. "Grayson, hide!" she whispered. "Emily is here!"

"I'd rather have a piece of blueberry tart, if it's all the same to you," muttered Grayson, sitting down at the table again.

Florence didn't know who to attack first. "You've already eaten half the tart on your own," she told him indignantly, and correctly, at that. "You're not getting another slice until everyone else has had one, if there's any left. Emily, would you like some blueberry tart?"

Emily strolled into the room in Henry's wake and looked at the almost-empty breakfast table. It didn't look to me like she didn't want to meet Grayson, in fact on the contrary. Right, so she wasn't as scantily clad as at yesterday's party, but her jeans were very tight and her T-shirt neckline was cut extremely low. She had put on makeup too.

"No, thanks," she said. "Looks like too many calories and saturated fats."

"I wonder how I knew she was going to say just that?" murmured Henry, dropping into the chair beside me where Florence had been sitting before, and giving me a light kiss on the cheek. Meanwhile, Matt took the chair that the Boker had just vacated.

And I felt, well, rather hemmed in.

Lottie handed both of them a plate of blueberry tart, pointedly ignoring Charles.

"Come on, let's go somewhere there isn't so much testosterone in the air! We'll use my room." Florence led Emily offstage—sorry, I mean out of the dining room. Emily still seemed to be looking for something appropriate to say, but nothing occurred to her. Instead, she swayed her bum in her close-fitting jeans. It was a terrible theatrical show. Charles for one hadn't been able to follow the course of events for several minutes and was just looking crestfallen.

"Would you girls like some blueberry tart yourselves?" Lottie asked Mia and me.

I'd have loved some, but with Matt and Henry at the same table, I felt rather choked. "Maybe later," I said. First I had to phone Persephone, whose nerves must be worn to a shred by now. And I had to know what Secrecy had written in her blog. "Could you lend me your iPad, Lottie?"

"It's in the kitchen," said Lottie, whereupon Mia ran off at once to grab it herself.

"This is the most delicious tart I ever ate," said Henry, and Matt nodded, with his mouth full. Charles went on looking crestfallen.

High time for me to make my own exit. I had to get the iPad out of Mia's hands.

When I pushed back my chair and stood up, Matt swallowed his mouthful and said, all of a sudden, "I had a dream about you last night, Liv!"

Oh no.

Both Henry and Grayson raised their heads and looked at me too. I quickly let my hair flop forward so as to hide as much of my face as possible, because it was sure to be going scarlet. At least, it felt very hot.

"I hope it was a nice dream," I said as casually as I could. I had my voice at least under control.

"Well . . . well, kind of nice." Matt grinned. "Rather crazy, but yes . . . nice. We were in the Leadenhall Building together."

"Should I know it?" And could I simply walk out, or would that *really* make me look suspicious? Henry was still looking at me attentively, although I couldn't see the expression in his eyes because my hair was hiding my view like a curtain.

"The Leadenhall Building is a skyscraper in the City," he said, and then turned to Matt. "Tell us more about that dream. It interests me a great deal."

"Me too." Grayson gave me one of his penetrating glances.

"Oh, well." For a split second Matt looked embarrassed, which was long enough to tell me that he remembered the details of the dream very well indeed. "It was all confused stuff, the kind you get in dreams. . . ." He cleared his throat. "I . . . there were these escalators. And I, er, I was playing the saxophone as I rode up on one. Liv came past me at high speed carrying some heavy folders." He was getting increasingly fluent; obviously he enjoyed inventing all this nonsense. I just wished he hadn't turned his eyes up in such a striking way. "And then there was this circus clown juggling coffee cups and cookies on the escalator ahead of us and giving everyone his business card. He wanted to give one to Liv too, but she didn't have a hand free, and she was ranting and raving because she couldn't get past him. He simply put the business card in her mouth, and that shut her up. I don't remember any more. Oh, I do, the clown's name was Mr. Smith. Yes, that's what it said on his business card." Laughing, Matt forked up a piece of blueberry tart. I could see how proud of himself he was. "Funny, don't you think? I'd like to know what an interpreter of dreams would make of it."

"Hmm. I'm not an interpreter of dreams," said Henry regretfully. "But I'm a fairly good amateur psychologist, and as such, I'd say you've just made up the dream out of your head." While the smile temporarily disappeared from Matt's face, Henry turned to me again. "What do you think, Liv?"

"I've had crazier dreams than that," said Matt, sounding slightly hurt, but Henry and I took no notice. We were much too busy staring at each other.

"Me?" Instead of feeling I'd been caught out, I was rather angry. With Henry and his claim to be an amateur psychologist, and also with Grayson, who was watching from the other side of the table like one of the Spanish Inquisition at a witch trial. "I think you're showing a hell of a lot of interest in the dreams of perfect strangers," I said aggressively. My God, there really must be something in the air today.

"Only when you come into them," replied Henry.

I swept the curtain of hair away from my eyes and looked straight at him. With a little luck, the color of my face would be back to normal. "Oh yes? Or only when it's about the dreams of good-looking characters?"

"Good-looking characters who play the saxophone." Henry was smiling, but there was a glint of suspicion in his eyes. I could see that clearly.

"Oh, thanks," said Matt, back to his old confident self again. "Although I play better in dreams than real life. Unless I'm having the dream where I'm on the stage at Carnegie Hall, and I can't play a single note. . . . But that's the best of dreams: there's no one to see you making a fool of yourself."

"Exactly." Grayson had exchanged his inquisitorial look for a remorseful one and rubbed his forehead. "Dreams are very private, and they're no one else's business."

"That's a nice way of closing the subject," I said. I gave

Henry a quick kiss on the forehead and smiled at the other two. "Well, I'll leave you to your studying, then." And this time I didn't hesitate; I left the stage without a backward look at the other actors.

All I regretted was the blueberry tart.

15

"NO LEOPARD TODAY?" Anabel was leaning back against the blue door that I still thought belonged to Mrs. Cook, the headmistress. When I glanced at it a moment ago, Miss Possessed-by-a-Demon (if she didn't take her medication) had not been there. That's to say, she had been there, all right, but she hadn't made herself visible until I was almost past her. Presumably she wanted to enjoy seeing me jump in alarm, which of course I did.

"Jaguar," I automatically corrected her.

Anabel shrugged her shoulders. "It comes to the same thing. Are you meeting Henry? He went past here a little while ago."

"That's nice to know." I didn't want to, but I couldn't help staring at her. In the twilit corridor, her turquoise eyes were trying to outshine her golden hair, and her complexion was like a work of art. It was as if she had a hidden spotlight fitted to show her—and only her—in soft focus in gentle evening sunshine. Anabel really was astonishingly beautiful, like a painting that you can't see enough of, and it was hard work making myself remember that she didn't look so supernaturally perfect in real life. All the same, I instinctively wondered whether Henry hadn't stared at her just as fascinated, if he had really come this way recently. When Anabel went on, I felt irrational jealousy rising inside me. Jealousy and a certain amount of anger.

"I hear you met his mother this afternoon." She smiled gently at me.

I gritted my teeth. Did her information come from Henry? And if so, why had he told her, of all people?

"Amazing!" Anabel's delicate nostrils were quivering. "How long was it before he took you home with him? Only six months?"

I tried to make her shut up by frowning, but it didn't work. She simply went on probing for sore spots. "Do you at least know why he always tried to keep you away from his family? Or was it just a kind of proof that he trusted you, so that you'd finally sleep with him?"

How on earth did she do it? She was saying exactly what that suspicious little voice inside me whispered, the one that I thought was the voice of my inferiority complex. The inferiority complex that had landed me with Rasmus—and indirectly with Matt. I had steered particularly clear of his dream door tonight. Although Henry hadn't said another word about Matt, I'd put my flight-simulator plan on ice for now.

Not very clever of you, Liv, the inner voice whispered. *Because it's soon going to be spring vacation, and you're still an inexperienced virgin with no idea of anything, so people feel sorry for you!*

Anabel was smiling as if she heard every word the voice

said. But I didn't want to listen to either her or my inferiority complex. They were both poison to me.

"Jaguars and leopards are not the same at all," I replied firmly. "Jaguars have a broader forehead and wide jaws, and their coat patterns are different. The jaguar has larger rosettes, and leopards have no light spots inside their rosettes, and in addition jaguars like to swim, whereas—"

Anabel folded her arms and gave me a pitying smile. "I understand that you don't want to talk about your relationship problems," she interrupted me. "Although maybe I could give you a tip or two. I know Henry really well. Even the way he kisses."

Oh, I hated her.

She laughed. "Don't worry, that was long before your time. Henry and I have a lot in common. For instance, dark family secrets, and a childhood that . . . that has left us scarred. That kind of thing brings people together. We both have mothers that we can't necessarily feel proud of." Her glance seemed briefly to turn in on herself, and I promptly felt a surge of pity. Poor Anabel—it must have been dreadful, growing up in that sect. "Although my mother was kind enough to hang herself with the belt of her bathrobe after she'd ruined my childhood," she went on, "so at least I never had to introduce my friends to her."

Immediately a small horror movie unreeled before my mind's eye, featuring an older version of Anabel sharpening a ritual dagger. Poor Ana . . . stop that! I had to force myself to remember who this was, the most manipulative person in the world, well known for her subtle insinuations. And comparing Henry's childhood with her own was only another trick to make me feel sorry for her. Stupidly, it had worked.

But the comparison was very misleading. Henry's mother certainly wasn't going to win any prizes for Mother of the Year, but compared to Anabel's, she was harmless. At least, our meeting this afternoon had gone off perfectly smoothly— in fact, it had been positively boring. I was still wondering why I had been imagining all kinds of ghastly scenarios this whole week. Maybe because Henry had issued such a solemn, official invitation to afternoon tea and had even baked a cake with his little sister's help. And because he had been even more nervous than me.

But it hadn't been a solemn, official occasion at all.

I hadn't been sitting at the table for long before I realized that Henry's mother had no particular interest in me. It was as simple as that. I hadn't been exposed to keen glances or embarrassing questions, as I'd secretly feared, nor had she lapsed into babbling, risen from her chair, and pointed an accusing finger at me claiming that I was going to take her eldest child away from her. And although I looked out for cliché signs of addiction to alcohol and prescription drugs, like wide pores, bloated features, and a drinker's nose, I couldn't see any. Henry's mother was tall, very well groomed, and had one of those pretty faces that you think you've seen hundreds of times before. Strange that she should have had three such distinctive children. She seemed perfectly normal except that she never really looked you in the eyes. Her gaze passed fleetingly over everything, as if she didn't want to look closely, not even at the display on her cell phone, which kept lighting up and distracting her attention. She contributed almost nothing to the conversation, although she smiled in a friendly way, and she was taking only half an hour to sit having tea with us, saying she had an engagement after that.

She shook hands with me when she left, and dropped kisses on her children's foreheads. When she said she might be home late, and they weren't to keep supper waiting, they all nodded as if they were used to that. Maybe she ate almost nothing on purpose to keep her model's figure. At least, she hadn't eaten any of the cake that Amy and Henry had "baked," but that could have been because half of it consisted of M&M's, and that's not everyone's idea of the perfect cake.

I was astonished to find how quickly and easily the afternoon had passed. Henry, too, seemed relieved when he escorted me to the door. We'd really meant to have a little time on our own in his room, but that didn't work out. First, Henry's little brother, Milo, spent half an hour asking me questions about kung fu (which I can heartily recommend as a hobby if you want to impress your boyfriend's little brothers), and then Amy dragged all her thirty-four favorite stuffed animals into Henry's room so that I could say hi to them all by name and shake paws with them.

But even without romantic moments alone, and despite my fears, it had been a really nice afternoon, not at all embarrassing, and I was positively exhilarated when I left, after Amy had solemnly invited me to her birthday party in August.

At the door, Henry had difficulty in kissing me good-bye because he was carrying Amy and Amy was carrying Molly the donkey and Herby the crocodile. But he managed, and Amy chuckled with delight and wanted a good-bye kiss as well.

"Even the cat didn't misbehave," said Henry with a funny little smile. "Odd, don't you think? And a bit weird."

"Oh, I'm sure it will turn out as expected next time," I consoled him. "When you've been lulled into a false sense of security."

There was a gleam in Henry's eyes, but before he could reply, Amy wanted me to kiss her toys good-bye too. It seemed the crocodile couldn't get enough of it, and I finally had to slap his long muzzle.

"Put your tongue in, Herby!" I said sternly. "That's not the way to kiss when we've only just met."

Amy fell about laughing, and Henry's eyes gleamed a little more.

"Well, there's one toy misbehaving at least," I said.

"See you later at Mrs. Hon . . . at headquarters," said Henry, "and maybe we'll find a little peace and quiet there for . . . er, misbehaving."

Yes, a bit of peace and quiet would definitely be welcome.

That is, if I ever arrived at Mrs. Honeycutt's door. I wasn't even out of my own corridor yet, and unfortunately Anabel looked as if she had a good deal more to get off her chest.

"I don't entirely understand why you two don't simply fix to meet in your own dreams," she said.

"Well, I'm sure you'd like to know," I replied, trying to match her own supercilious smile. Although I didn't quite understand it myself. Of course I realized that no one could follow us into Mrs. Honeycutt's dreams when they didn't know her door, and so couldn't get hold of any personal item to let them in. But our own doorways were well protected, and furthermore they were much closer. That would mean far less danger of meeting Anabel and Arthur and that encroaching darkness.

But then again, the unconscious mind was more powerful in your own dreams than anywhere else, so I was glad that our headquarters were not behind *my* door, where presumably a chow called Rasmus might appear every ten minutes.

Anabel tilted her head on one side and looked at me curiously. "But that's probably too . . . intimate for you and Henry, right? It would be typical of him not to let anyone get a real insight into his mind. The question is, does that secretly bother you, or do you find it sexy?"

Both, to be honest. But that was no business whatever of Anabel's. I wondered whether to have another shot at telling her the difference between a leopard and a jaguar, but then I decided to go for the direct approach instead. "Look, is there anything in particular you want, or are you simply spraying venom around the place at random?" I asked, as if I were very busy, glancing at the watch I'd conjured up on my wrist at that very moment for purely dramatic reasons. "I'm in a hurry."

Anabel smiled again. "Yes, you are, aren't you? It's terrible the way time passes so quickly."

Sad to say, that was right. It was particularly terrible the way time passed so quickly when you didn't want it to. And vice versa. The last week had raced past me, whereas to Persephone it must have seemed like the longest week of her life. But she was bearing up better than I'd feared, thanks basically to Secrecy and her nasty remarks about the lemonade stain on Maisie Brown's dress.

"However bad what I did was, and however hard everyone was staring at me and making silly comments—wetting yourself is a hundred times more embarrassing than anything else," Persephone kept saying. I refrained from pointing out that, even if Secrecy's story was true, Maisie had wet herself only because she was scared stiff of Persephone. I was glad my friend was putting up such a good fight, and I genuinely admired the self-possessed way she strolled down the school corridors, although I knew she'd rather have kept out of sight at home until grass had grown over the entire incident. Persephone had guts—you had to give her that. When she wrinkled up her nose and tossed her hair back, many of the students probably decided against saying the unpleasant things that had been on the tip of their tongues, ready to let fly. And she could cope with being on Emily's silly brother Sam's list of people he thought should be "ashamed of themselves."

"It's tough, but so long as they don't print T-shirts with my name I'll survive," she assured me.

Speaking of names, one positive side effect of the whole thing was that, at long last, Jasper knew Persephone's. All week he called her Persephone, if not in a particularly friendly tone, but in the circumstances she could understand that. Especially since Jasper was much nicer to her than her sister, Pandora. Pandora had taken it badly when Persephone borrowed her new dress, and wasn't speaking to her.

At home, on the other hand, the atmosphere was rather better. Florence and Grayson had buried the hatchet, the Boker was busy with a golf tournament in aid of a charity and was leaving us alone, and Lottie—well, Lottie was baking for all she was worth.

On Monday she baked fluffy madeleines as light as air; on Tuesday she experimented with seven different flavors of macaroons, each more delicious than the last; on Wednesday we were devouring the best lemon tarts that any human being has ever eaten. Not until Thursday, when crisp butter croissants and strawberry jam were on the menu, did it strike me that these delicacies were all typically French. And when, on Friday, Lottie put tiny little cakes on the table, saying, "*Voilà, mes enfants! Cannelés bordelais. Bon appétit,*" we could no longer help noticing that Pascal, the wedding planner, had done more than just inspire her. She obviously thought his fixed smile as charming as his accent and not at all sinister. As bridesmaid-to-be, and empowered by Mom to make all the decisions, she had phoned him several times, and next week she had a date at the florist's. She wouldn't admit that her phase of French baking had anything to do with Pascal. But the notice saying CLOSED BECAUSE OF UNREQUITED LOVE was no longer on her dream door, and instead there was a message saying DON'T EXPECT MIRACLES—LIVE FOR THE DAY, as Grayson and I both noticed. Much too late, he remembered his boastful promise to pair his uncle off with Lottie.

"What's wrong between you and Charles?" he had asked her yesterday when she was busy kneading the dough for French baguettes, and humming "La Marseillaise" to herself. "I thought you liked each other."

"We do," replied Lottie. "I think Charles is a very good dentist."

Hmm. Even Grayson had to admit that things didn't look good for Charles. *I think he's a good dentist* came high on the list of the most disillusioned, unromantic remarks ever made, almost on a par with *Let's stay friends*.

But Grayson wasn't defeated yet. "It's not as bad as all that about the wedding planner," he said. "Competition is good for business. Some people don't realize what they want until they can't have it anymore."

I guessed he was referring to Emily. Twice that week, I'd seen her standing outside Grayson's dream door, shouting at poor Frightful Freddy and calling him *silly goose* and *pompous chicken* when he wouldn't let her in.

Watching that had been the secret highlight of my week.

Otherwise, I'd spent most of my time suspiciously checking out anyone who came near me. Almost any of them could, without knowing it, have been programmed by Arthur to murder me, by pushing me down the flight of steps outside school or hitting me with a medicine ball—I kept thinking of new methods of murder every minute. Very likely Arthur was observing me from a distance, tremendously amused to see how often I looked around or jumped nervously.

"How pale you are," said Anabel now, in passing.

Well, not all of us needed to conjure up such a flattering sunset light in soft focus. But I didn't feel like quarreling with her. If I had to talk to her, I could at least try appealing to the reason that, according to Grayson, was still slumbering somewhere under her insanity.

"I know," I admitted. "I'm not feeling too well. I'm afraid. Of what Arthur will think up next. And a little afraid of you too."

For some reason, that seemed to flatter Anabel, like the soft-focus effect. "Afraid of me—or *him*?" she asked.

A cool breath of air fell on my arms, and it turned a little darker. I suppressed a sigh. Here we went again. I just wanted to get into Mrs. Honeycutt's dream. Preferably before going down all these damn endless corridors first. Was that too much to ask?

"Are you afraid of me or *him*?" Anabel repeated. "The Lord of Shadows and Darkness. You swore to be true to him, and then you broke your oath."

Well, in view of the fact that the Lord of Shadows and Darkness had picked me as a blood sacrifice from the first, I didn't consider breaking my oath such a terrible thing to do, even apart from the fact that in a way I'd been cheating when

I swore it in the first place. But it probably wouldn't be a great idea to tell Anabel what I was thinking.

"Both of you," I said instead. *Because you're one and the same person, you crazy girl. When will you finally grasp that? There. Are. No. Demons. And it doesn't scare me a bit that this corridor is getting darker, and there are shadows lurking in the corners. . . .*

Hell. It did scare me. I concentrated entirely on Anabel's face, which was still shining. "What was that about the eclipse of the sun? Didn't you say we might not live to see it?"

Anabel shook her head. "I didn't say that myself. I only passed on what the Dark Lord told me: faithless blood will flow when the sun moves into the shadow of the moon, the one hundred and twentieth year on the Saros Cycle governing eclipses."

Or maybe you're just having your period? I quickly shook my head. Whenever Anabel spoke in such a sententious tone of voice, I was inclined to get really silly ideas.

But they were going away again. Even the warm radiance of Anabel's face was beginning to fade now. She leaned slightly forward. "It could equally well be my blood—after all, I have disappointed the Feathered Commander of the Night more than all the rest of you put together."

Correct. She hadn't succeeded in cutting my throat, although she had certainly done her best to. I could bear witness to that.

"Feathered?" This was new. "Does that mean you've seen him?" I asked, rubbing my arms. It had turned even colder by a couple of degrees.

Anabel shook her head again. It could well be fear reflected in her eyes, but whether mine or her own I had no idea. "I only saw his shadow on the wall. And he had wings. Huge black pinions on which he can soar through dreams and the night. And through time and space."

As she spoke, something dark came floating down between us. It was a shining black feather, and it landed on my outstretched hand. I looked up. More feathers were falling on us, spinning through the twilight and falling on the floor as soundlessly as snowflakes.

Looks like the Lord of Shadows and Darkness is molting. The more sinister all this felt, the sillier my thoughts were. And the more Anabel's eyes shone. More and more feathers came drifting down from the nonexistent ceiling. Anabel had stretched out her arms as if she were enjoying a warm summer shower of rain. I had a sinking feeling that nothing was going to come of my plan to meet Henry in Mrs. Honeycutt's room today. It would probably be more sensible to awaken before things became even more sinister. On the other hand, I must take this chance to get as much out of Anabel as possible. That damn solar eclipse was due on Friday.

I cleared my throat. "And . . . did he give you any orders?"

Anabel cast me a scornful glance. "You still don't believe he exists, do you? You think I'm mentally ill, hearing voices and seeing hallucinations, right?"

Yes, absolutely right. "At least it's a possibility that we should consider," I said, trying to sound casual and unimpressed, and not breathe in any of the feathers that were falling faster and more densely all the time. "It's only since you stopped taking the medicine that you've been seeing and hearing the de . . . the Winged Prince of Darkness again."

"You sound exactly like Grayson," replied Anabel. By

now the feathers covered large areas of the floor, and many of them had landed on Anabel and me too. Anabel's arms were still outstretched, so she looked as if she were sprouting wings. "Did you know that he came to visit me at home today? Kind of sweet. He thinks if he can only prove to me that there's no demon, I'd show you all where Dr. Anderson's dream door is and tell you how I took him out of circulation." She gave me a fleeting smile. "The only problem is that he *can't* prove it. Do you really think I excluded the possibility that it might all be just the product of my sick imagination from the first? I may be crazy, but I'm not stupid. If I didn't have incontrovertible evidence of his existence, you and I wouldn't be talking like this. . . ."

I wanted to ask her what kind of evidence, but a feather drifted into my mouth, and I had to retch until I'd spat it out again. After that I kept my lips pressed together. The feathers were now falling so thickly that I could hardly see through them, and I could only guess where Anabel was. Another few minutes and we'd be entirely covered with feathers; my ankles were already buried in a soft black sea of them. This was the right moment to end the nightmare.

"I sense his power!" I couldn't work out how Anabel could talk without breathing feathers in. I felt I was being slowly smothered, although I kept my mouth firmly closed. But it wasn't possible to breathe properly even through my nose; there were feathers everywhere. I had to close my eyes as well. There was nothing to be seen, anyway, apart from swirling darkness.

High time to awaken. But it wasn't so easy to concentrate on that if you couldn't breathe normally.

"And if you listen to yourself, deep down inside, Liv, you will feel it too," I heard Anabel saying in her soft, melodious voice. "You know in your heart that he exists."

I knew in my heart one thing above all others: this was only a dream, and I was lying in my bed at home in Hampstead. . . .

This time it worked. I sat up, gasping. Damn Anabel! I breathed in and out deeply, trying to slow my racing pulse, and then I looked at the illuminated numbers on my alarm clock. Three thirty. Henry was probably waiting for me in Mrs. Honeycutt's dream, but I couldn't be sure of dropping off to sleep again at once. I still felt as if I had feathers on my body. And the one that had landed in my mouth . . .

I quickly got out of bed and went over to open the window. Damp, cold night air streamed into the room. The fine spring weather seemed to be over for now; it was pouring with rain outside. Ernest would be glad; the garden badly needed rain.

Back in bed, my heart was still beating faster than usual. It was no good—Henry would have to wait until I had calmed down. I switched my bedside light on, propped myself up on the pillows, and looked at the pile of books on my bedside table, including Matt's copy of *The Hotel New Hampshire*. It was lying under a volume of Emily Dickinson's poems, and they seemed to me just the right medicine. After a few pages, I might feel tired enough to get back to sleep.

When I opened the book at random and began to read, something dropped out of my hair, floated down, and lay on the pages.

It was a shining black feather.

TITTLE-TATTLE BLOG

The Frognal Academy Tittle-Tattle Blog,
with all the latest gossip, the best rumors, and
the hottest scandals from our school.

ABOUT ME:
My name is Secrecy—I'm right here among
you, and I know *all* your secrets.

16 March

You have to give Mrs. Cook one thing; she never makes the
same mistake twice. For instance, like engaging attractive
women teachers who will embark on affairs with their
colleagues and end up climbing on tables to do a striptease
act. There was no chance at all of Mrs. Fatsourakis, the
substitute teacher who is taking over French classes from
Mrs. Lawrence (officially for the rest of the school year,
unofficially forever), doing that kind of thing, as anyone who
has seen her rolling around school will agree. If she ever
climbed on a table, that would be the end of the table. And
for heaven's sake, what kind of name is that? Okay, so the
lady is of Turkish and Greek origin, but surely people who
call their bouncing baby Fatima when her surname is
Fatsourakis can't have thought of the consequences? I guess
that FatFat can't have been a very happy child. It's about
101 percent likely that she was teased mercilessly by the
other kids, and so is the probability that FatFat has hated
children to this day. You don't need to be a psychologist to

suspect that she became a teacher only to avenge herself on kids. Thanks a bundle, Mrs. Cook. That's just the kind of teacher we need these days.

See you soon!

Love from Secrecy

PS—That entry has been online for only twenty minutes, and there are already twenty-four comments telling me how primitive and nasty fatso-bashing is, and what an incredibly nice teacher Mrs. Fatsourakis is, after she even brought muffins she'd baked herself to her first class. Speaking personally, I'd sooner be mean than fat. Well, thank goodness I gave up French!

16

"THE NEXT SUCH total eclipse of the sun can be seen in Central Europe in the year 2081," said our physics teacher, Mr. Osborne. "If you lead a healthy life, you may even get to see it yourselves, but I'm unlikely to live to be a hundred and twenty, so today is a very special day for me."

He had pushed his table over to the door of the physics lab, and we had to file past him as we went out so that he could check whether we all had our eclipse-viewing glasses and our parents' permission to leave the building during the eclipse. These precautions seemed doubly ridiculous in view of the cloudy sky—we couldn't even guess where the sun might be. Although the lab had huge windows, we'd had to switch on the light as if it were a gloomy November morning.

"Poor thing," Persephone whispered to me as we stood in line. "The last solar eclipse of his life, and then the weather turns out miserable. At least it isn't raining. How do I look?"

"Fine," I said without glancing at her. Just now, Mr. Osborne had proudly revealed that we had the honor of using the limited space on the school roof for our observations, along with the physics classes of the two years just above us. Which meant that we'd also join Henry, Grayson, and Jasper up there.

And Arthur.

Unlike Persephone, I was not overjoyed at this prospect, if anything the opposite. The idea of standing on a high roof near Arthur, who boasted that he could dispose of me any-time he liked, was uncomfortable enough even without a solar eclipse. *Faithless blood will flow when the sun moves into the shadow of the moon. . . .*

"Really?" Persephone was still thinking about her appear-ance. "Have I overdone the blush? Somehow that brush always picks up too much powder."

"No, you look great." I glanced at the sky outside again. That monotonous pale-gray cloud cover obstinately hiding the sun reminded me only too well of the absence of any ceil-ing in the dream corridor. And not just that: I saw a large black-bird perching in one of the three trees in the schoolyard. I swallowed. It hadn't been there just now, had it? It seemed to be staring at me, boding no good. And the tree was a copper beech, with leaves the color of blood. Surely it couldn't be just coincidence.

Persephone gave me a small shove to make me walk on. "The blush is *nude velvet*. It looks orange in the jar, but when you put it on, it suits your own skin tone. Absolutely natural. I'll show it to you later. I think you look rather pale."

"Yes, I know." And at that moment I felt quite sure that

there wasn't going to be any "later." Something terrible would happen up on that roof. The schoolyard would soak up my blood, and black feathers would rain down from the sky. . . .

I was grateful to Persephone for pushing me again and interrupting my train of thought. What was the matter with me? A crow sitting in a tree, and I felt like throwing a fit!

Okay, so that feather had been weird. But not weird enough to make me believe in demons and their prophecies. There were any number of logical ways to explain a black feather getting into my hair. Henry and Grayson had said so when I told them about it. After all, a keen blackbird hunter lived in our house and also liked to sleep on my bed—and blackbirds, surprise, surprise, have black feathers. One of them could easily have been caught in my hair.

Even if it was a strange coincidence, it would take more than a silly feather to convince me that demons existed.

"Your turn!" Persephone dug me in the ribs and pointed to Mr. Osborne, who was looking at us expectantly. We handed him our letters of permission and showed him our glasses.

Mr. Osborne nodded, satisfied. "And the camera obscura?"

Persephone held out the thing we'd made from a shoe box and some wax paper. To keep it from looking too plain and simple by comparison with the structures, some of them very complex, made by the other teams, and because we got so bored in physics class, Persephone and I had beautified it with a great many strips of decorative sticky tape. We'd taken a lot of trouble, and now it paid off.

"B plus," said Mr. Osborne, making a note of the grade in his little red book and smiling at us. "See you up on the roof. Next, please."

Persephone could hardly believe it. When we were out of earshot, she hugged me. "B plus! For a shoe box covered with sticky tape, like in elementary school. I think this is our lucky day."

Chance would be a fine thing. But her good humor was kind of catching. On the way up to the roof, my gloomy thoughts seemed to me rather silly. It was like this: if you were looking for bad omens, you really did see them everywhere and you immediately suspected every innocent crow that crossed your path.

There was plenty of traffic going the other way because of the classes who were going to watch the eclipse from the schoolyard. Mia waved cheerfully to me from the middle of the crowd. The general mood was happy, almost relaxed. Presumably because a solar eclipse, even under a cloudy sky, was more fun than learning math or French.

However, it's the exception that proves the rule. Sam Clark, standing near the door to the rooftop, looked miserable as sin. Especially when he caught sight of Persephone and me.

"Should be ashamed of yourself. Should be ashamed of yourself," he said emphatically, casting us a scornful glance.

"Or you could put the whole thing into the plural," I told him. "Then it would do for both of us at once. Just say *You should be ashamed of yourselves*. Much more effective, and a little less ridiculous."

"Exactly," said Persephone. "But maybe saying everything twice is your idea of fun, is it, Spotty Sam, is it, Spotty Sam?"

Sam frowned. "And what do my skin problems have to do

with you two and your moral depravity?" He liked to talk in a rather pretentious way, just like his sister. Or the Boker.

"Nothing at all, nothing at all," replied Persephone cheerfully. "Your spots aren't our business any more than our moral depravity is yours."

She made me go on.

"Huh. Sounds like someone doesn't understand the difference between the common good and the rights of the individual," nagged Sam, behind us. "You two really *ought* to be ashamed of yourselves."

Well, at least he'd grasped the idea of the plural now.

"What's his idea? Does he think his spots don't offend the common good? I disagree." Persephone tossed her hair back. "How do I look?"

"Morally depraved but still stunning," I said.

When we reached the rooftop, the sky was as gray as ever, still gloomy and overcast. I had never been up here before, and I looked suspiciously at the metal railings dividing the flat part of the roof from the sloping surface. They looked stable. But unfortunately they were no higher than a normal balustrade.

I automatically took a couple of steps toward the middle of the roof, where I thought it would be safer. Particularly as Grayson and Henry were there too. And so, a little farther away, was Arthur. Persephone strolled off without me to the east side of the roof, where Jasper was sitting on the railings dangling his legs. Mrs. Cook sternly told him off.

"Heavens, doesn't he know that this is the day when faithless blood will flow?" I murmured, forgetting for a split second that Jasper had broken with "demons and dreams and all that childish stuff." It was to be hoped that the demon had also broken with Jasper.

Henry smiled, pleased to see me. "I'm glad you're up here too. We ought to share an epoch-making experience like this with the people we love. So that then we can tell our grandchildren there was absolutely nothing to be seen during this solar eclipse."

Grayson was looking at his iPhone. "They have a spectacular view everywhere else. All of them beside themselves and tweeting cool pictures. While here we don't even notice that it's begun."

"Yes, we do. I think it's darker already," I said, and I wasn't lying.

"Everyone put your glasses on, please!" Mrs. Cook told us, and Mr. Osborne added, "Those who want to watch through the camera obscura, please put your black cloth over your head and shoulders. Keep a record of the eclipse in your exercise books."

"Yes, if you wouldn't mind telling us where the sun is supposed to be," Grayson grumbled, but he put on his protective glasses.

"Are we really supposed to stand up here for two hours staring at a gray sky?"

I gave a start of alarm because that muted question was Arthur's. And because he was standing right behind me.

He laughed quietly. "Why so jumpy, Liv? Did Anabel's crazy talk maybe scare you? Do you think the demon will punish you today for being a bad girl?"

"No, I think he'll set to work in alphabetical order and sort you out first," I said, gratefully aware of Henry moving closer to me and putting his arm around me. But Arthur wasn't to be deterred. As if naturally, he joined us and winked conspiratorially at us over the rim of his protective glasses.

"Faithless blood will flow when the sun moves into the shadow of the moon," he whispered. "Spooky stuff. But seriously, guys, you don't believe that nonsense, do you?" He looked around with exaggerated caution. "I for one don't see either Anabel or her demon, so I'm assuming we're safe here. Although of course a demon like that can fly." He laughed, pleased with himself. "And can possess human beings. Don't you think Emily, over there, looks possessed by the demon?"

"Strictly speaking, it isn't really a demon, but a kind of deity," Grayson began, but he fell silent when Henry gave him a warning glance. He was right: it might not be a great idea to let Arthur know about Grayson's latest discoveries.

Grayson had gone back to phase one of his three-phase plan, in the firm conviction that knowledge is power and the basis of every sensible plan. His attempt to reason with Anabel herself hadn't exactly been crowned by success (she had made the same cryptic threats as she did in the dream corridor, minus the hocus-pocus with the feathers and the stage effects with lighting and temperature), but she had been willing to talk about her childhood and among other things had told him the name of the sect with which it had all begun, when Anabel was still a baby.

The members of the sect called themselves "Wayfarers on the True Shadow Path" and had been a small group of about twenty-five who dedicated themselves to worshipping the deity of an ancient, long-forgotten religion. Grayson had found some disturbing websites about it on the Internet, because on New Year's Eve 1999, the Wayfarers on the True

Shadow Path had hit the headlines on account of what looked like a tragic mass suicide at the turn of the millennium. The remains of the leader of the sect and sixteen of its members, including three children, had been found in a barn burnt right down to its foundations.

Anabel had been three years old at the time. Why, and how long, her mother had been a Wayfarer, and what position she had held in the outfit we didn't know. Nor did we know how she and her daughter had escaped the mass suicide. Grayson thought that Anabel herself didn't know much about it, because she had never been able to discuss the subject with her mother. Once Anabel's father had won custody of her, he naturally enough kept her away from her mother, who herself didn't make any attempt to stay in touch. She had been diagnosed with schizophrenic psychosis and committed to various hospitals; she killed herself in the last of them a few years later. The notebook that had been burnt in the Hamiltons' family vault in Highgate Cemetery last year had been in the box of her personal possessions that Anabel had inherited, and it had contained assorted handwritten formulas and instructions for performing rituals intended to revive the demon—sorry, the dark deity. Anabel hadn't touched the box of souvenirs for years, but when she finally did and opened the notebook, something had happened to her. At least, that was how Grayson told the story. She had suddenly decided that she was intended to reawaken the deity—better known to us as the Lord of Shadows and Darkness—and take up the inheritance of the Wayfarers on the True Shadow Path herself. We knew the rest of the story— after all, we had been part of it.

"A deity? You mean an actual god?" Arthur looked attentively at Grayson. "Well, well, you *have* been busy investigating Anabel's fantasies. Interesting. I wonder what you expect to get out of it?"

Grayson didn't reply. The facts he had discovered and put together were sad, and they had shaken him, but he had doggedly stuck to the idea of proving to Anabel that her demon didn't exist.

"Maybe you hope Anabel will tell you a few of her tricks so that you can use them against me," Arthur went on, getting quite close to the bull's-eye. We did need Anabel on our side, as an ally, if we were to be a match for Arthur. He shrugged his shoulders. "A clever idea. She hates me. If she wasn't so busy with her schizoid delusions, she probably *would* help you—look at it that way, and maybe I ought to be glad to have a raving lunatic as my ex-girlfriend. On the other hand, I'm not as easy a victim as Senator Tod." He paused for a moment, to make sure that he still had our full attention. Then he said, "Okay, so Anabel is good—but I'm better."

In other words, even with Anabel we wouldn't stand a chance against him.

"Oh, shut your trap," said Grayson, loud enough to make the teachers turn and look at us. Mrs. Cook, the headmistress, came closer to see what was going on.

"Yes, and then get lost," said Henry, taking his arm off my shoulders and adjusting his protective glasses just before Mrs. Cook reached us.

We all raised our heads and stared at the gray sky, trying to appear fascinated.

"You're looking the wrong way," said Mrs. Cook in passing. "The east is over there."

Arthur waited until she was out of earshot and then said,

"To think of us all standing up here on the roof, forced to pretend we're watching something interesting. It's about as likely that the sky will suddenly clear as that Anabel's demon will turn up to shed our blood."

"Suppose he's been here all along?" said Henry, looking keenly at Arthur over the cardboard rim of his protective glasses.

Arthur raised his eyebrows. "What do you mean?"

"You said it yourself: Anabel could be dangerous to you if she wasn't so busy with her demon," said Henry. "So you'd have more interest than anyone in convincing her of his existence."

Arthur laughed incredulously, earning himself a disapproving glance from Mrs. Cook. Then, lowering his voice, he asked, "Are you joking?"

I'd have asked that question myself, if he hadn't. I stared at Henry in confusion. Grayson seemed to feel the same. At least, he was frowning heavily.

Henry shrugged. "It really isn't such an absurd idea, Arthur. As long as Anabel was in the hospital and concentrating on her own problems, she wasn't any threat to you. But it's different now. You saw what she did to Senator Tod, and maybe you were afraid she still had scores to settle with you. So you had to give her something else to think about in a hurry." Had Henry only just come to these conclusions, or had he reached them some time ago? If so, why hadn't he told us? But the longer I thought about it, the less weird his ideas seemed to me.

"As soon as Anabel stopped taking her pills, you took to haunting the corridor yourself," he went on quietly. "You know Anabel pretty well, so presumably it was easy for you.

You projected winged shapes on the walls, made a shower of feathers fall, and whispered exactly what she expected to hear: the demon is still around and needs her services . . . and voilà—Anabel has her hands full, and no spare time to thwart you one way or another."

"You're crazy yourself." For a moment Arthur looked honestly annoyed. Then he pushed an angelic golden curl back from his forehead and said, "Here I am showing my cards at last, and you still insinuate that I'm deceiving you. Honestly, guys, I'm the one who wears the T-shirt with *The Bad Guy* printed on it in large letters, and I stand by what I've done. Or may yet do," he added with a little laugh. "But please don't make me responsible for my deranged ex-girlfriend's wild fantasies about demons into the bargain."

His voice sounded as if he genuinely meant it. Difficult to know whether he was being honest for once, or simply a good actor . . .

Persephone appeared. "What are you all doing here?" she asked. We were probably an odd sight, standing there staring at each other in silence through our silly cardboard glasses.

"Waiting," I said.

"For something to happen at last," added Arthur.

Persephone sighed. "I guess you'll have a long wait. I hate living in London! Seems like they're having supercool eclipse parties all over the rest of Europe. Here, your turn!" She held our camera obscura under my nose. "This thing is terrific— you see nothing at all! I wonder when Mr. Osborne will finally realize that the last solar eclipse of his life was a total flop. But I do think it's a little darker now, don't you?"

"At this very moment we would be seeing maximum coverage of the sun, with only a crescent still visible at its lower rim," announced Mr. Osborne promptly from under the black cloth that he had put over his head and his observation device. He still sounded hopeful. It was slowly getting rather cold up here as well.

"May I take a look?" Arthur was about to take our shoe box out of Persephone's hands, but he flinched. Cursing quietly, he looked at his thumb.

"You've cut yourself," said Persephone in surprise. She was right: blood was coming from a cut on Arthur's thumb. "And I thought we'd covered any sharp edges with sticky tape. I'm terribly sorry. Do you want a tissue?"

"That's all right." Arthur was staring at the wound in surprise. Henry, Grayson, and I also watched, fascinated, as a drop of blood collected on the cut in the skin, flowed down to his thumbnail, and dripped to the roof below our feet.

"Blood will flow," I murmured, and I didn't know whether to shiver or laugh.

Arthur for one burst out laughing. "You have to hand it to Anabel's demon," he said. "Turns up on the dot. But to be honest, for the sake of drama there should have been more in it. Doesn't it strike you as a little like this solar eclipse? Talked up in advance, and then it turns out to be a disappointment." Still laughing, he walked away, and we simultaneously heaved a sigh of relief.

Persephone sighed too, but not with relief. She was looking through the camera obscura at Jasper, who was talking to a girl from his own class.

"I think I left my exercise book over there by mistake," said Persephone. "I'll be right back, and then you must tell me what Arthur meant by Anabel's demon."

"Er, yes." I wondered whether to credit Anabel spontaneously with a new dog called Demon. But maybe Persephone would have forgotten her question by the time she came back.

As soon as she had gone away, Grayson leaned forward. "Do you really think Arthur is behind the revival of Anabel's demon, Henry?"

Henry shrugged his shoulders again. "Could be," he replied. "I mean, there are only three possibilities. First, Arthur leads Anabel to believe in a demon to keep her under his control, without her knowledge. Second, even without any help from Arthur, Anabel is still suffering from delusions. And third . . . well, the third is unlikely."

"The third possibility is that the demon really does exist." It burst out of me—well, someone had to say it. "It's odd that Arthur cuts himself today of all days, don't you think? Just in time for the complete solar eclipse. And then . . . the dreams, the black feathers, and . . ." I turned aside and pointed down. Yes, it was still there. Or it was there again. "See that crow? It's been perching in that copper beech all day, staring at me."

"It's an acacia, really," said Grayson, and Henry looked at me, shaking his head.

"What's the matter with you, cheese girl? You were always the one who could laugh at demons."

"Yes, I know." I watched, feeling slightly ashamed, as the crow flew away. It was stupid to go worrying about a demon that very probably didn't exist, when we had plenty to worry about with Arthur. Because Arthur existed, for sure, and it was only a question of time before he struck again. I hadn't forgotten his threats of murder, and I expected I ought to be glad that he'd resisted the temptation to make someone throw me over the roof railing.

He let slip that he had at least thought of it later in the day, when we had been told to leave the roof and go back to classes and I met him in the hallway.

"Did you know that if you fall twenty-five meters through the air, you can reach a speed of eighty kilometers per hour?" Arthur was obviously enjoying the way I jumped at the sound of his voice—for the second time today. I had noticed, too late, that he was only a few steps away from his own locker. My thoughts had been elsewhere, in fact with Theo Ellis, who had passed me in the hall only a minute earlier.

Like everyone else, I'd only been able to stare at him. But it was real: Theo Ellis! Of course it was Friday, so he had his Ancient Greek class, but no one had expected to see Theo here again, me least of all. I'd thought he was either in prison or in a psychiatric hospital, and to see him striding through school as upright and self-confident as ever made me feel happy and hopeful. Theo Ellis didn't just look like a wardrobe made of solid oak; he obviously had a mental constitution to match. And a good attorney.

Unfortunately my brief hopeful mood went away at the sight of Arthur. I was on my own, so for a moment I considered coming back later, but I didn't want to let Arthur feel triumphant because he had put me to flight simply by being there.

So I tried a scornful glance in Sam's manner and wondered whether to add a *You should be ashamed of yourself*.

"Eighty kilometers an hour! Imagine what it would look like when you hit the ground!" Arthur went on with relish.

"Yes, anyone can easily imagine it if that's their idea of fun," I said, repelled.

"I only mean—well, in terms of generating blood, anyway, it would have produced more than this silly cut." Laughing, Arthur held his wounded thumb out to me. I hated the way he was always in such an outrageously good mood. "But sad to say, I didn't know that your physics class would be up on the roof with ours, or I might have planned something nice," he said, laughing even more. I wondered whether to hit him, which might not be the cleverest option, but would certainly make me feel better.

"But right now I have more important things on my mind, and I'd really miss the cute way you always jump at the sight of me." While Arthur tapped the numerical code into his own locker, he winked at me. "A solar eclipse is so exciting, don't you think? I'm sure Anabel—sorry, her demon—will soon come up with a substitute date for bloodshed. Demons have such a wide choice. Full moon, new moon, witches' Sabbaths, the solstice, lunar eclipses . . ." He pulled his locker open and reached into it. Something brown shot out of the locker—something that looked like a snake's flat head.

Arthur screamed.

I held my breath and stared, incredulously. A snake had dug its fangs into Arthur's hand. It withdrew its head again just as quickly as it had shot out.

Arthur slammed the locker door. "Did you . . . did you see that?" he gasped. The draft had swirled up a small black feather that now sank slowly to the floor.

"Yes," I said, feeling breathless myself. "It looked like a snake. And a feather."

Arthur's scream had attracted more students, who crowded around us curiously, so I couldn't see the feather any longer.

"It *was* a snake," said Arthur, more to himself than me. It was almost as if he had to explain it to himself, because otherwise he wouldn't believe it. He was clutching his hand, and I tried feverishly to remember what I'd learned about first aid for snakebites.

"There's a damn snake in my locker!" I heard a touch of hysteria in Arthur's voice now. "And it bit me."

Snake! The whispered word went around, was passed on down the corridor louder and louder, and set off a little panic. Some people began screeching and stamping their feet. I couldn't see the feather anywhere in all the confusion. I'd probably only imagined it, anyway.

"Calm down," I said. "The snake is shut up in Arthur's locker. It can't hurt you. And we don't know if it's really dangerous. Maybe it's . . ." I fell silent, because at that moment Arthur staggered and then slowly slid down the smooth locker door to the floor.

"I think it would be a good idea for someone to ring for an ambulance," he said quietly but with surprising composure. "And get someone from the zoo to come and identify the snake. I might need an antidote."

Oh God, yes. The hand with the snakebite was swelling more and more.

"You have to suck the venom out," someone called, but I shook my head. From my time in India, I knew that sucking venom out after a snakebite was an urban myth and did more harm than good to the healing process. And Arthur himself didn't look as if he were going to try. Maybe he was too weak already. But while all around us people were frantically getting out their cell phones, or running for help, he managed to smile at me all the same. "Looks like the demon has demanded his victim after all."

Yes, it looked very much like that.

17

When I got home, the Boker's Bentley was parked in the drive, and I thought of disappearing straight into my room. My need for excitement had been more than satisfied for today. But first, a delicious aroma was wafting out of the kitchen, and second, the coffee machine was in there. If I wanted to survive the rest of the day, I needed caffeine. So I took a deep breath and walked into the kitchen. To my relief, the Boker was conspicuous by her absence. Instead, Florence and Mia were sitting at the kitchen table, Buttercup was on the chair between them, and they were all three staring at the baking sheet that Lottie was just taking out of the oven, with their tongues hanging out. Well, only Buttercup's tongue was really hanging out, but the other two looked at least as hungry.

And there was also someone else in the kitchen: Charles, leaning back against the fridge. "You're home at just the right moment, Liv," he said. "Lottie has been baking scones."

"Not scones—they're French brioches," Florence corrected him.

"*Oui, ma chérie*," trilled Lottie cheerfully, and Charles murmured, "Just think."

I went over inconspicuously to the coffee machine, put a cup under it, and pressed the double espresso button.

"Where's the Bo . . . er, Ernest's mother?" I asked as the beans were being ground. "Her car's outside the front door."

"She's in there. With Mom." Mia pointed to the dining room. "The wedding invitations have to go out today."

"And then there'll be no going back," said Charles in a sepulchral voice.

My coffee had finished brewing, and I pressed the same button again. "So you are here because . . . ?" I asked, not very politely. Since Lottie had put that notice on her door, saying it was closed on account of unrequited love, my sympathy for Charles was well within bounds.

He blushed slightly. "Oh, I . . . I just wanted to borrow Ernest's fretsaw, and besides that . . ." He took a deep breath and looked at Lottie, who was just arranging her brioches on a plate, humming cheerfully. "And besides that, I wanted to ask Lottie whether she's doing anything tomorrow evening."

Lottie went on humming to herself for a few seconds. Then she noticed that he was staring expectantly at her, and said, "Oh, was that the question? No, I'm not doing anything tomorrow evening. Why do you ask?"

"Because—because I have a spare concert ticket, and I spontaneously thought you might like to go to the concert with me," said Charles.

"Spontaneously?" repeated Lottie. "You spontaneously had a spare ticket?"

Charles nodded.

"Meaning that the ticket was originally intended for someone else?" asked Lottie, putting the plate of brioches down on the table. "Someone who maybe spontaneously couldn't go?"

Charles looked alarmed, but he couldn't think up a reply.

Lottie energetically wiped her hands on a tea cloth. "No, sorry, it's a fact that I didn't have any plans for tomorrow evening, but spontaneously I feel like doing something other than being used as a stopgap. Where's my cell phone? Oh, I think I left it upstairs. Just a moment . . ."

"But . . . but it's not like that," said Charles. "I've had the tickets for some time, but . . ."

By now Lottie had left the kitchen.

"But I . . . somehow forgot to ask her," concluded Charles sheepishly.

Florence turned her eyes to the ceiling. "You somehow forgot? Aren't you old enough to know what you want, Uncle Charles?"

"Well, yes." Embarrassed, Charles rubbed his knuckles. "I just wish everything wasn't always so complicated."

"Hmm," said Florence. "Then you'd better forget about women and concentrate entirely on golf and your dental practice."

"Exactly," Mia agreed. "He can put all his sadism into that without having to break anyone's heart."

"I haven't broken anyone's heart," Charles began, but he fell silent when all three of us rolled our eyes.

"Not intentionally, anyway. I'm just a bit slow on the uptake sometimes," he said remorsefully.

"Very slow on the uptake is more like it," said Mia.

"Irresolute, cowardly, no finer feelings at all," added Florence.

"Woof," agreed Buttercup. If she could have rolled her own eyes, I bet she would have joined us there too.

I was beginning to feel sorry for Charles. "If I were you, I'd go after Lottie right away and talk to her before she makes a date with that Pascal," I suggested.

Charles looked doubtful. "But suppose she'd sooner spend her time with that grinning Frenchman? I'm not the fighting sort, you know."

"Good heavens!" Florence was looking daggers at him. "Then it's high time you tried to be. If you don't fight for Lottie, she'll be off and away, and you'll regret it for the rest of your life."

I stared at her, astonished. Well, well! Florence, of all people, who hadn't even wanted Lottie in the house at first, standing up for her now? Could be that my stepsister had a heart.

At least her words took effect. Charles straightened his back. "I don't really have anything to lose, do I?" At the door, he turned back once more. "If it works, I'll show you my gratitude, girls."

"And if it doesn't, we'll change our dentist," said Mia when the door had closed.

Florence helped herself to a brioche and moved Buttercup, who was wagging her tail hungrily, off the chair. "I'm so glad I'm not a man. They're all so silly."

"My own opinion exactly." Mia opened Lottie's iPad, but after a brief glance, she closed it again.

"Nothing new on the Tittle-Tattle blog?" I asked, and Mia shook her head. "Do you think Arthur's still alive?"

"If he wasn't, we'd have heard by now," said Florence. "That kind of news spreads like wildfire." She rubbed her arms. "I still can't believe it—a venomous snake in the school lockers. I just hope the police are searching all the lockers thoroughly, or I'm never going to open mine again."

Yes, I felt the same. In fact, it had been one of my first thoughts as I crouched beside Arthur waiting for help: had the de . . . had someone left snakes in our lockers as well? If so, I was really glad Arthur had held me up making that speech of his and had opened his locker before I opened mine.

Maybe that was why I'd stayed with him until the doctor arrived. All the time—it was only a few minutes, really—I was expecting Arthur to say something else, something dramatic like "Tell Henry and Grayson I always loved them," or even "Liv, I swear that if I survive this I'll be a better person!" But he just sat there perfectly still, clutching his hand, with his head against the wall. He was obviously in great pain. I could imagine what that felt like; I had once been stung by a scorpion in India.

"Anyway, we know now that Arthur isn't Secrecy," said Mia. "Unless he wrote up his blog from intensive care." She opened the iPad again. "Have you noticed how inconsistent Secrecy is these days? Today, for instance, she seems to have been watching the eclipse of the sun both from the roof and from the schoolyard. See that? The photo of the sky dated 10:05 in the caption was taken from the yard. You can see part of its fence at the edge."

"Where?" Florence leaned over the display. "But that could be all kinds of other things."

"No, it's the fence, I'm sure. I magnified it a lot." Mia was wearing her best Sherlock Holmes expression. "Later, in the account of the eclipse, at about the time Arthur was bitten, there's this picture of Mr. Osborne's behind sticking out when he had the black cloth over himself and his camera obscura. *Watch your ass*, says the caption."

"Someone else could have taken it and sent it to Secrecy," I said, and Florence nodded vigorously.

"Yes, but the whole account reads as if it's by someone who was on the roof—and what's more, whoever wrote it seems to know physics pretty well, which brings us to the next inconsistency." Mia ran her finger down the screen. "Here, on February 20, Secrecy posted a piece calling physics a subject for mentally disturbed nerds who like to show off. And she says she's glad she gave it up. That was what she said about French, too, last Monday. But apparently it was her favorite subject back in January."

"Maybe she was just trying to create confusion," said Florence. "Seems to work, too, from the way you talk."

Mia shook her head. "No, if anyone is confused, it's Secrecy. Analysis of the different style and content of parts of the blog shows that quite clearly."

"Analyzing the posts in the blog stylistically? Who on earth would do a thing like that?" said Florence scornfully.

"I would," said Mia. "A good detective has to follow every trail—and most of them are left by Secrecy herself in her blog. Until a little less than a year ago, it was all consistent in style and content, but recently Private Detective Silver has found clear differences. Secrecy is always malicious, but sometimes her style is witty and elegant, sometimes more ponderous and stilted; sometime she likes French, sometimes she doesn't; sometimes she's still studying physics and makes herself out the guardian of our morals, and so on and so forth."

"Sounds kind of schizophrenic," said Florence.

"That hits the spot, I'd say," replied Mia, looking Florence in the eyes.

Florence shook her head. "I mean you and your detective act, Private Detective Silver." She pushed her chair back and stood up. "Not even the IT specialist brought in by the headmistress has managed to find out who's writing that blog and is, therefore, Secrecy. So don't waste your time." Florence grabbed another brioche and left the kitchen.

Mia watched her walk away. "Did you get the feeling she's mad about something? I did."

"Yes, a bit. When did you analyze all that, clever little sister?" I asked curiously. I had a feeling that she was keeping something important from me.

Mia grinned. "You know, there are great advantages to steering clear of boys. It gives you much more time for other things."

"So who do you think Secrecy is? Is Florence still on your list of suspects?"

Mia made a great business of closing the iPad and looked at me intently over the rim of her glasses. "Let's say the list has narrowed down quite a bit now," she said, lowering her voice. "Given the present state of my investigations, I can say no more just yet, but you will be the first to know when the time comes."

I couldn't help laughing. Judging by the expression on her face, she was longing to tell me all about it, and I knew that if I really pressed her I could get some information. I was about to say, "Oh, come on, we don't have secrets from each other." But then I realized that wasn't true. In fact, I had any number of secrets from Mia, dark secrets, and my laughter faded when I thought of her reaction if she knew that Arthur had been spying on her in her dreams so that he could pass information about me on to Secrecy.

"Do be careful, Mia," I said. "Secrecy knows all kinds of tricks—she's an unscrupulous snake, and directly or indirectly she has methods that . . . well, that maybe you can't even dream of."

"Don't worry." Mia spoke in her normal voice again. "I'm always reckoning with the impossible, whenever and wherever it turns up. Secrecy may be cunning and malicious, but at least Private Detective Silver is brighter than she is. So far I've solved all my cases." She seemed to listen for a moment. "Hey, don't you think it's rather quiet here? Maybe we should check that Mom is still alive, in case the Boker tried clocking her with the guest list." She picked up a brioche, divided it accurately into two, and gave one half to Buttercup, who was sitting patiently beside her, panting. "Do you think Lottie and Charles have made up?" she asked with her own mouth full.

"You tell me, Private Detective Silver." I finally took a gulp of my coffee. What with all the excitement, I'd forgotten to drink it, and now it was cold. Never mind, the caffeine was still in working order.

18

"A WHAT?" ANABEL'S eyes were open wide. We had met her, as so often, in the corridor, where she had obviously been waiting for us, this time in the shape of a letter box on Mrs. Cook's door.

"A Malayan pit viper," repeated Grayson, who had come out of his door at almost the same moment as me. He had jumped even more nervously than I did when the mailbox began talking.

"Very venomous," he said. "So the police will probably investigate it as a case of attempted murder."

Really? Or was Grayson just making it up to make Anabel drop her guard?

"Arthur was lucky that they knew what to do at the hospital," he went on. "In Thailand, a great many people die from the bite of this snake every year." He shook himself. "You don't ever want to Google images of *snakebite*."

"So he's going to survive, is he?" asked Anabel, who of course was no longer a letter box. She was twirling a strand of golden hair in her fingers.

Grayson nodded. "Yes," he said, and an *unfortunately* almost escaped me. Horrified, I gasped for air. So it had come to this: I'd rather have seen Arthur dead than able to go on where he had left off.

Anabel's expression was one of neither regret nor delight. "But how did the snake get into Arthur's locker?" she asked, and for the first time since I'd known her, she seemed a bit slow to catch on. Grayson and I exchanged a brief glance.

"Yes, that's the question," I said slowly. "Whoever put it there must have known the numerical combination to the locker, because the lock hadn't been broken open."

"Yes, but . . . I mean, where would anyone get a poisonous snake like that from? Can you just buy one in a shop?" asked Anabel.

Grayson shook his head. "No. Normally anyone keeping poisonous snakes would have to show a certificate saying he was fit to be in charge of them, and what's more, no one seems to be missing a snake, not the zoo or in any other collection of reptiles in and around London."

"That's odd." Anabel was biting her lower lip. "Because . . ." She fell silent and briefly looked around.

"Because you're the only one who knows the combination to Arthur's locker?" I completed her sentence. "That's what Arthur says, anyway,"

"What?" Anabel looked confused. "Yes, I do know the combination, unless he's altered it. But what's that to do with . . . oh, I see what you mean!"

Thank goodness. It had taken her long enough.

"*Was* it you?" asked Grayson straight out.

"No, of course not," replied Anabel. "My goodness, I have

a snake phobia, I could never bring myself to touch one! I wouldn't know how. Honestly, to think you'd believe that!" She shook her head vigorously.

"Well," said Grayson slowly. "You might not do it of your own free will, but if the de . . ." He cleared his throat. "If someone ordered you to do it, someone that you, er . . ." Grayson had lost the thread. He didn't notice a change in the light or the black feather floating down from the ceiling.

Oh no, not again! I didn't know whether to feel annoyed or frightened. Unfortunately my body decided on fear: at the sight of the feather, I got goose bumps all over, and my heart began beating faster.

"It wasn't me," repeated Anabel. "Not even in *his* service."

The light dimmed even more.

"Maybe . . ." Grayson hesitated. "Maybe you just don't know it anymore."

"What don't I know anymore?" asked Anabel, irritated. "You mean I don't know I stole a venomous snake from somewhere or other and took it for a walk in my old school to attack my ex-boyfriend?" She snorted briefly and tossed back her long hair. This was the Anabel we knew. "I don't think I'd have forgotten a thing like that."

"But wouldn't it be in line with the symptoms of your sickness?"

"I don't have brainstorms!" Anabel angrily interrupted Grayson. Then she went on, a little less furiously, "Don't you two understand? If I'd done it in *his* service, I wouldn't deny it. Why should I?"

More feathers were drifting down, and Anabel caught one on the palm of her hand. The sight seemed to both soothe and please her, because now she was smiling. "The Winged

Commander has incalculable power—when will you finally grasp that? If he wants to send a snake to punish Arthur, he doesn't need anyone else to help him." She put back her head and raised her hands, and her voice grew louder and more solemn. "For he is lord and master of the creatures of the night, snakes grow upon his head . . ."

"That was Medusa," murmured Grayson, but I urged him to walk away. I'd been in this damned corridor with Anabel in her psychotic mood once too often, and the way she was now working herself up, in her sermon about the demon, suggested that the situation might well escalate. Which presumably meant that it would then rain snakes instead of feathers.

Grayson, too, seemed to have noticed that this was not the best moment for a sensible conversation. He willingly followed me around the next corner, where we started trotting along, as if by mutual agreement.

"If he has shown Arthur mercy, there may also be hope for you two unbelievers," Anabel called after us. "You can still repent."

"Or just run faster," gasped Grayson.

I glanced back over my shoulder. Anabel had stayed put around the corner. To make sure, I raised a finger. No telltale breath of air following us, no stray letter box in sight. It wasn't raining snakes or feathers either.

All the same, it couldn't hurt to take Grayson's advice, so we were rather breathless when we opened Mrs. Honeycutt's door.

"Come in unless you're Death," screeched the parrot.

Mrs. Honeycutt was sitting in her armchair as usual. When the door latched shut behind us, she let her knitting sink to her lap and looked at us curiously.

"It's only us. Not Death," Grayson hastily assured her.

"I'm not afraid of death," said Mrs. Honeycutt, and Henry, leaning against our table at the back of the room, involuntarily made a face. "Only of dying. What's that door?"

"Don't let it bother you, Mrs. Honeycutt," said Henry gently, as he signed to us to come over. "You have to finish that cardigan, and the pattern will call for all your attention. You do it so well."

Mrs. Honeycutt picked up her knitting again and went on with it as we stole past her on tiptoe, not that there was any need for that.

"I can see you," she said with a mischievous smile. "I can do a waffle pattern without looking at my work, you know. But now I must watch carefully as I shape the armhole."

"Exactly," murmured Henry. And turning to us, he said, "That was a close shave. Let me guess: something nasty has been chasing you along the corridors again?"

I dropped onto one of the chairs. "Anabel, feathers, darkness—the usual, that's all."

"Anabel says she wasn't to blame for the snake; it was the demon's doing. Hey, that wasn't here last time, was it?" Grayson pointed to the flowered china dish full of candies standing in the middle of the table.

"No, it's new," said Henry, sighing. "Mrs. Honeycutt's subconscious mind must have laid it specially for us."

"How nice." Much moved, I cast Mrs. Honeycutt a friendly glance. Her curly lilac-tinted head was bent over her knitting again. We each took a candy—mine was lemon-flavored, Henry's was a peppermint. Grayson complained that his didn't taste of anything, and then told Henry what Anabel had said.

"Suppose she really didn't have anything to do with it?" I finally asked, changing the flavor of my candy to orange for the sake of variety. "Could be that someone else really did hide the snake. Someone who wanted to teach Arthur a lesson."

Like the demon himself, for instance? According to Anabel, he had snakes conveniently growing on his head. Although she had just mentioned that for the first time ever, as if it were Arthur's snake that had given her the idea.

Henry seemed to guess my thoughts. "The demon doesn't exist, Liv," he said mildly, "and you know that yourself when you listen to your healthy human reason."

"But while the demon exists in Anabel's mind, he's almost as dangerous." Grayson took another candy and unwrapped it. It didn't seem to bother him too much that he couldn't taste anything. "I for one wouldn't want to be bitten by a snake, or punished in some other nasty way. Which is what makes it more important than ever to convince Anabel that the demon isn't real."

"And me too, if you don't mind," I said. "My healthy human reason is having a few problems right now with snakes and feathers."

"Okay, nothing easier." Grayson leaned forward and propped his elbows on the table. "I've found out more about that sect."

Henry and I exchanged a quick glance. "Ah, yes, the three-phase plan," said Henry rather slowly. "Are we still at phase one?"

But Grayson wasn't misled by the note of mockery in his voice. "Listen, and you'll be surprised," he said. "The Wayfarers on the True Shadow Path were founded by an unemployed roofer from Liverpool called Timothy Donnelly.

He was the son of an Irish steelworker and a schoolteacher, and for the first twenty-five years of his life, he apparently seemed perfectly normal. Until he'd just been fired from two jobs in quick succession, and he began getting messages from some kind of limbo, where a demonic deity had chosen him to create a new earthly paradise and lead humanity back to the True Path." He took his elbows off the table, leaned back, and grinned at me. "How does that sound to your healthy human reason?"

"It sounds like the poor old roofer had a screw loose himself," I admitted. "Or else didn't fancy doing an honest day's work anymore and thought he'd try something else."

"Exactly," said Grayson, pleased. "If you ask me, the probability of a demonic deity choosing an unemployed roofer from Liverpool to lead people back to the True Path is somewhere in the region of zero. The guy was either nuts or a fraud—or both."

"Still, he did manage to convince a few people of his idea." Henry had begun building the candies into a pyramid. "He made those people his disciples, and in the end, they died with him in that barn, for whatever reason. . . ."

"Oh, you mean that terrible thing in Surrey?" said Mrs. Honeycutt, surprisingly joining in the conversation. "I remember it well. The newspapers were full of it at the time. Those poor little children. Their own mothers and fathers, misguided souls that they were, poured kerosene over them and . . ." Mrs. Honeycutt put her knitting down. "Dreadful. And apparently no one noticed anything in advance. But that's always the way."

Grayson nodded. "Because they were living in a remote

old mill somewhere in the country, cut off from the outside world."

"A terrible place. I still remember the pictures." Mrs. Honeycutt shuddered. "The walls had diabolical symbols all over them, painted in human blood; that's what the *Daily Mirror* said."

"Must have made it a difficult building to sell," murmured Henry.

My mind was on Anabel again. And the human blood. "But just because back then the demon . . . ," I hesitantly began.

Grayson jumped up. "Damn it, Livvy, once and for all: demons do not exist! More particularly this one! Don't you both remember what a fuss Anabel always made about that dusty old book where she'd found all those rituals and incantations? The book that was supposed to have been passed on from generation to generation of her family?"

I nodded, remembering the notebook with the bloodred seals that had gone up in flames in the mausoleum in Highgate Cemetery, to the accompaniment of Anabel's dreadful screams. It hadn't looked nearly as old as I'd expected, but Arthur had explained that it was a copy of the original. I did know that I hadn't been able to suppress my disappointment when I saw the scribbled handwriting in ballpoint pen.

"Of course I remember," Henry said too. "Anabel, and later Arthur, always kept it locked up as far as they could. There were those gruesome fingerprints in blood among the incantations, and the last pages were sealed, although I'd really have liked to know what they said. . . ."

"Yes, exactly," said Grayson, "but if that book was really

so special, how come anyone can go to the Internet and read all about those strictly secret rites for opening a door to our dimension for the Lord of Darkness and Shadows, etcetera, etcetera?"

"*What?*"

Grayson nodded, pleased with himself. "I knew you'd be interested. Our secret spells come from a serialized novel posted online by some guy calling himself BloodySword66, in a fantasy fan fiction forum."

I stared at him. Henry stared at him. Even Mrs. Honeycutt stared for a moment, before turning back to the cardigan that she was knitting.

"Are you sure they're the same secret rites?" asked Henry at last. "Or just something like them?"

"If so, would I be here?" Grayson was looking very full of himself. "Five have broken the seal, five have sworn the oath, and five will open the gate. A circle of blood, wild, innocent, upright," he declaimed. "Allow the Keeper of the Shadows access, *sed omnes una manet nox.*"

I gawped at him. "You still remember all that stuff by heart?"

"Yes, here we go again," said Grayson. "I fed all the silly ideas and set phrases about the demon that I could remember into a search engine, including the Latin tags that Anabel was always quoting from her book. The trick was not to look for them individually but all at the same time." He paused for a moment for effect, and in the silence, only the click of Mrs. Honeycutt's needles could be heard. "And," he went on with a triumphant expression, "seek and you shall find, as the saying goes. *Nights of the Bloody Shadows*, a serial story in eleven chapters."

"Wow," said Henry, impressed.

I couldn't have put it better myself.

Grayson grinned. "Surprised, are you? And hey, next time you two make fun of my three-phase plan and show off because you can turn yourself into—oh, how would I know what? Let's say a pair of skates gliding along these stupid corridors in perfect harmony. Well, just remember that a proper piece of research can get you a good deal further."

I was irresistibly reminded of Mia. The two of them could set up a detective agency together some day. But of course he was right.

"Skates!" Henry was chuckling.

"But what does that have to do with this fan fiction forum you were talking about?" I asked. "Could Anabel have posted the text on it? Or Arthur?"

Grayson sat down again. "If they were able to write and use a computer at the age of two, yes," he said. "But no, *Nights of the Bloody Shadows* was published by that forum in 1999."

"1999? Did the Internet even exist then?" I murmured, and Henry was frowning as if working out a complicated mathematical problem in his head.

But Grayson was already going on. "You do realize what that means?" He looked at us solemnly. "I have no idea how or why, but BloodySword66 wrote the novel that we know from Anabel's notebook, so to speak."

Slowly, Henry nodded. In waking life, his pyramid of candies would have collapsed long ago, but here it had reached a considerable height. "So now the only question is, which came first—the notebook or BloodySword66's literary efforts? And what does it all have to do with the sect?"

"And do they belong together?" I said. "That's another

question. Did all that demonic garbage really come out of a story thought up by some would-be writer for a fan fiction forum?"

"That's what I'm hoping," said Grayson with his eyes shining. "It's a shockingly bad story, incidentally. I don't think I ever saw so many adjectives all at once. And its basic plot is nothing new either. An ancient, demonic deity with all those names we already know comes back to life in a London museum specializing in the art of the ancient world, after being brought here from what was once Babylon or some such place in an old amphora, along with other things found in archaeological excavations."

"How original," said Henry.

"And the rest is more of the same." Grayson leaned back, grinning. "A nerdy young archaeologist, not particularly successful with women but good at heart, is chosen by the deity to help it take physical form again by means of assorted incantatory spells and rituals, all described in detail. Because at first this deity is only a voice, and it consists of dark smoke, wind, and shadows. And an iron will that it can impose on anyone."

"And—let me guess—it wants human sacrifice in the shape of a virgin," I said, and Grayson nodded. "Exactly, and the virgin picked for that part is the younger, mousy sister of the silly cow who has already turned down our young archaeologist's advances in no uncertain terms. The chosen victim is actually much nicer than her sister, but the archaeologist realizes that only later."

"Sounds quite exciting," I had to admit.

"But I'm afraid it isn't. Also it's terribly confused, too

many characters with too many names. More deities appear, including a talking scarab beetle that later takes possession of the nice sister, there are endless dialogues, sword fights for no special reason, and boring descriptions of everyday life. After chapter eleven, the story breaks off. The people in the forum weren't all that enthusiastic about it themselves. By the end, it was getting more brickbats than praise, and I'm afraid BloodySword66 lost the plot, or else he simply got tired of it."

"Or he went off and founded a sect," I suggested. "Or it was all entirely different, and—"

"Whatever happened then, I'm going to find out," Grayson interrupted me, sounding very self-confident. "Unfortunately that fan fiction forum closed down several years ago, and it didn't include any contact information. But I've already tracked one of the administrators down to another forum— these fantasy enthusiasts give themselves the same names everywhere—and I've gotten in touch with him. Maybe he can help me to find out who was hiding behind the name BloodySword66. Then I could go into the case thoroughly and finally prove to Anabel that her delusions are based on nothing but a poor work of fiction."

Yes. It was possible. And a great idea. But all the same . . .

"Are there feathers in this poor work of fiction? I mean, does the demon have wings?" I asked. "And how about dreams? Are dreams another part of the story?"

Grayson didn't reply. Instead, he looked up at the ceiling. "Did you hear that? Sounds like a ventilator. The ventilator in my room."

We stared up ourselves. There was only a light with a

brightly patterned shade hanging over us. And there was no sound but our own voices.

"But that's . . . ," said Grayson, and then he had suddenly disappeared.

"No one knows how long he will live until his last hour strikes," screeched the parrot.

TITTLE-TATTLE BLOG

**The Frognal Academy Tittle-Tattle Blog,
with all the latest gossip, the best rumors, and
the hottest scandals from our school.**

ABOUT ME:
My name is Secrecy—I'm right here among
you, and I know *all* your secrets.

21 March

Hey, are you all afraid of opening your lockers tomorrow?
Are you wondering what's going to happen next at our
school? Have you maybe already signed the petition put
forward by Mrs. Pritchard? The petition calls for several
specially trained security officers to be engaged at the
Frognal Academy.

Well, if the police and Mrs. Cook are to be believed, all that
about the snake was a one-off incident. In their opinion, it's
an adolescent trick, a joke that went wrong, but of course,
all the same, it has to be investigated.

You bet it does! Is it usual for students to put exotic
venomous snakes in other students' lockers, just because
they're bored and their hormones are playing up again?
I mean, it really gives you ideas, when of course those
annoying venomous snakes are easily available all over
the place.

Anyway, Mrs. Pritchard doesn't see it the same way as the headmistress and the police. Her petition demands, before school is reopened to the students, a thorough inspection of all cupboards and lockers by a pest exterminator specializing in snakes.

Sounds like a good idea! It could be that the snake is a common British locker viper, rearing its young among sports bags and shredded textbooks, and sooner or later biting everyone who's given up French, or has been eating too many carbohydrates for lunch again. You can't be too careful. And who knows, while the inspectors are at work they may find a few tarantulas, scorpions, and Siberian tigers lurking in the lockers, left over from other amusing student pranks, or simply never cleared away by the cleaners. Mrs. Pritchard has been complaining of their bad habits for some time. Seems like the dirt in the cloakrooms has ruined her daughter's cashmere coat.

But now, seriously, and for anyone who's interested: It was a Malayan pit viper that bit Arthur, and no one knows how it came to be in his locker rather than anyone else's. What's certain is that he was incredibly lucky, because the bite of that snake is often fatal. Arthur is still being treated in the hospital, where he had to be given adrenaline and an antidote to the poison, and he's still not well.

So I just hope the police catch whoever thought it would be an amusing prank to play. And as soon as possible, before that person tries anything like it again. Because somehow we don't share the same sense of humor.

See you soon!

Love from Secrecy

PS—And no, guys, it wasn't Theo Ellis trying to keep Arthur from taking the helm for the Frognal Flames again in the last match of the season! That is really the silliest conspiracy theory I've ever heard. Because first, Theo has plenty of other problems on his plate already (being prosecuted for breaking and entering, theft, damage to property, and disturbance of the peace isn't to be taken lightly, even if Theo is allowed to attend school until the trial), and second, the Flames, unlike the Roslyn Raptors, have no chance now of winning the championship or getting a place among the top three teams, anyway. If you ask me, even the theory that the snake got into the locker by itself because it knew the combination is more credible than the theory of Theo's revenge. ☺

19

˙NO ONE KNOWS how long he will live until his last hour strikes," screeched the parrot again, while we were still staring at the empty chair from which Grayson had just that moment disappeared.

I had instinctively reached for Henry's hand.

"Death stops for no one, young or old," agreed Mrs. Honeycutt. "Only think of my poor sister. Snatched away in the prime of life, maliciously suffocated by her own husband . . ."

I had goose bumps now. "Please say that Grayson simply woke up," I whispered to Henry.

He reassuringly pressed my hand. "That's right. He simply woke up," he assured me. "It's a pity. I was going to show the two of you something else. Something that I found out some time ago . . . a very interesting discovery."

Another one? Had everyone but me been doing nonstop research? I almost felt guilty because I'd been so lazy in that respect.

Henry smiled, as if he was reading my thoughts. "I found

it out entirely by chance, when I was showing off again, gliding down corridors in the form of a skate."

I couldn't help laughing with him, but only briefly, because Mrs. Honeycutt lowered her knitting, turned, and looked at us thoughtfully. "I used to be afraid of death myself. But I think now there's nothing to be afraid of. You just swim over into the next world. . . ."

Even as she was speaking, the colors in the room changed, the bright hues of the patterned furniture and wallpaper paled, a cool, peaceful light streamed into the room. The ceiling seemed to lift and turn into glass, the room grew larger, and the flowers, the parrot's cage, and all the ornaments hovered in the air and became translucent. I clung to Henry as the chairs were gently washed away from under us. Mrs. Honeycutt floated past us in hers, waving cheerfully. No doubt about it: her room was gradually but unmistakably turning into an aquarium. The furniture disappeared, the walls retreated, and with a touch of panic I saw that the door to the corridor was moving farther and farther away. I was going to say something to Henry, but only bubbles came out of my mouth. The room was full not of air, but of water bathed in light.

Now I was really scared.

"It's dying itself that I fear," I heard Mrs. Honeycutt's kindly voice saying. Unlike me, she could obviously talk, but neither she nor her armchair was in sight any longer. Instead, wonderful shimmering fish swam past us, looking as transparent as if someone had drawn them in silver ink straight on the water. "No, I am not afraid of death, only of that moment when I must say good-bye to my body," Mrs. Honeycutt went on. "The moment when I draw my last breath."

For me, that moment seemed to have come. I was in urgent need of a diving suit—or gills. . . . Help!

Glancing at Henry, I saw panic in his face, which didn't improve things. Henry was never afraid of anything.

He pointed to the door in the still retreating wall. I couldn't nod, but I let go of his hand and swam toward it as fast as I could. I was still short of air, although I knew perfectly well that this was a dream, and in a dream, you could breathe underwater even without anything to help you. Except that I couldn't seem to manage it.

Also, this was no ordinary water; it seemed to me like cool, liquid light, neither too cold nor too warm, in fact not even wet when I felt it properly.

"And then you simply let go and drift away into the next world." Mrs. Honeycutt's voice seemed to come from very far away now, and it sounded so happy that all of a sudden I calmed down.

Opening my mouth, I let the water simply flow into my lungs. It didn't hurt at all. The water made me weightless, and like the fish, I had a silvery sheen, becoming part of the liquid light that was carrying me on wherever I wanted, into another world where there was nothing bad.

Henry's face appeared beside mine. He grabbed my arm, my head hit something hard, and the next moment I landed with a bump on my behind, gasping.

"Damn it!" exclaimed Henry. We were on the other side of the door in the corridor, and we hadn't brought a single drop of water from Mrs. Honeycutt's dream with us. A strange sensation of regret came over me as Henry closed the door firmly behind us. It had been so peaceful in there. Whereas out here . . .

Henry gave me his hand to help me up. "Are you all right?" His face was even paler than usual. "It looked as if . . . as if you were going to dissolve."

"Yes, that's what it felt like too." I was still busy getting my breath back and was surprised to find that I didn't even have to cough. "Maybe dying isn't so bad after all. Maybe you really do just swim over into another world where everything is peaceful and bright and good."

Henry took me by the shoulders. "Don't say it so wistfully, Liv. You frighten me." He drew me close. "I need you so much," he murmured into my hair.

I suddenly had a large lump in my throat, so I couldn't answer. If I'd said something, it wouldn't have been very original anyway, just an ordinary *I need you too*. So I wound my arms around his neck and kissed him. That was a kind of answer in itself, and maybe not a bad one.

At least, Henry sighed quietly and held me even closer. Briefly, a hesitant little voice inside me spoke up, trying to remind me of the coming spring vacation, but I made it shut up. Henry kissed much too well for me to torment myself with such thoughts. Although the vacation really was very close, and furthermore . . .

"Mrs. Honeycutt didn't really die, did she?"

"No, don't worry. She just sometimes dreams of dying," murmured Henry, ensuring in his own way that I stopped thinking of that. He really ought to patent his way of stroking the nape of someone's neck, I thought. And he seemed to know exactly what he was doing, because he smiled with satisfaction, as he interrupted our kiss to look over his shoulder.

Which—unfortunately—brought me back to reality.

"Weren't you going to show me something else?" I asked when he had turned to me again.

"Was I?" Henry was looking intently at my mouth, and I was about to put my arms around his neck again, but then he himself seemed to work out that here and now wasn't the right time and place for it.

With a regretful sigh, he took his hand away from the back of my neck and turned me around in his arms until I had my back to him. "See that door over there?"

I nodded as I leaned back against him. In his embrace, I felt as safe as I had felt in the water just now.

I looked at Henry's discovery. It was a wooden door painted a cheerful yellow and obviously led to a shop called "Little Sister's Yarn Barn," as an oval shop sign above the door frame told me.

"Has that always been here?" I'd never noticed it before, but until now I'd always been in rather a hurry when I went this way. I admired the amusing door handle with its brightly colored knitted cover. The two flowerpots full of sunflowers to right and left of the door also had bright, striped knitted covers over them. There was a glass pane in the door, with wording in curved letters: ALL YOU KNIT IS LOVE. And under that: COME IN AND FIND THE WOOL OF YOUR DREAMS.

"That shop could easily belong to Mrs. Honeycutt."

"Exactly." Henry let go of me, took a few steps in both directions up and down the corridor, and came back to me after installing two of his mysteriously sparkling energy fields. "I just want to make sure that Arthur isn't getting bored in his hospital bed and roaming around somewhere here," he explained. Then he pointed to the door of the wool shop again. "See those initials on the doormat? I'm just about sure that M.H. stands for Muriel Honeycutt, Mrs. Honeycutt's sister. In her dream, she obviously kept her maiden name."

I touched the knitted cover of the door handle. Yes, it was a perfect fit. "Mrs. Honeycutt said that Muriel was always knitting covers for everything, even her bicycle." I hesitated. "But if she's dead, what's behind this door? Or . . ." I looked hopefully at Henry. "Or did she maybe die only in Mrs. Honeycutt's nightmares?"

But Henry shook his head. "No, Muriel is really dead. Died in 1977; I checked up on it. In *real life*," he added with a little laugh. Then he turned serious again. "She died in her sleep. Apparently it was due to her asthma, but to this day Mrs. Honeycutt suspects her brother-in-law, Alfred, of hastening the process. He, too, died, not long after Muriel—not a nice death; he had cirrhosis of the liver."

I thought of our meetings with Alfred and his flowered cushion, and the fear in Mrs. Honeycutt's eyes, and I nodded grimly. I thought cirrhosis of the liver was just what the man deserved.

"How terrible that Mrs. Honeycutt still has nightmares about him." Sadly, I stroked the painted wooden door. "The sisters must have been really fond of each other, if their doors are still so close, after all these years. Even the name Muriel gave her shop: Little Sister's Yarn Barn. That's sweet, don't you think?" Of course it made me think of Mia, and before I got so sad that I started crying, I quickly turned back to face Henry. "But it's strange that dead people keep their dream doors." I let my eyes wander down the corridor. "I wonder how many of the doors here belong to the dead?"

"None of them," said Henry firmly. "That's the point. When people die, their doors disappear along with them."

I looked at him doubtfully. "How do you know for certain?"

"Do you remember hearing of Tom Holland?" asked Henry.

"The boy who died in a car crash?"

"Yes." When I came to the Frognal Academy, Tom Holland's death was already several months in the past, and I knew only what I'd read about it in Secrecy's blog. Tom had been Anabel's boyfriend before Arthur, and for a while I had suspected that the car accident hadn't been chance but was directly or indirectly the demon's doing.

"Tom Holland had an unusual door—the kind you get in an old-fashioned elevator, with an ornate wrought-iron grating that you push aside, and one of those semicircular display panels over it telling you what floor the elevator is at. Arthur and I visited him once or twice." Henry cleared his throat. "Arthur probably visited him more often. Only for . . . well, reasons of information."

The idea of Arthur and Henry once walking along the corridors together was something I could hardly imagine today. But it wasn't all that long ago. At the time, moreover, Arthur hadn't let his real nature show; his sadistic tendencies and crazy notions of conquering the world came to light only later.

"I see," I said. "For reasons of information. Of course. The same way as I'm always wandering around your ex-girlfriends' dreams."

Henry grinned. "Speaking of that, have you found Rasmus's door anywhere here?"

Oh no! I wasn't letting myself in for this. Not today.

"You were telling me about Tom Holland and his door," I reminded Henry.

He sighed. "Yes, so I was. Tom's door disappeared on the night when he died. We never saw it again. The same thing happened to our old janitor's door when he died last August. When people die, their doors don't exist anymore."

"That's logical enough," I said. "The dead don't dream. Then why is Muriel's door still there, if she died all those years ago?"

"I've been thinking about that for a long time." Henry rubbed the bridge of his nose. "I can find only one explanation, and it's rather crazy."

"Don't worry, I'll visit you in the nuthouse and hold hands in between the electric shocks," I reassured him.

The corners of Henry's mouth twitched. "Let's assume that Mrs. Honeycutt is right, and poor Muriel didn't die a natural death but really was smothered by Alfred with a cushion in her sleep . . ."

He paused for effect, as Grayson had done a little while ago, but this time I guessed what he'd worked out.

"Just as she was dreaming," I finished his sentence for him.

"Exactly," said Henry. "And so the dream simply . . ." He raised his shoulders. "I don't know how to put it."

"The dream stopped. Like a clock. Or an old gramophone record." I thoughtfully bit my lower lip. "Could be that's what always happens if someone dies in the middle of a dream." I thought again. "Or if someone's murdered in their sleep."

"One way or another," said Henry, "the fact is that Muriel is dead, but her door is still there."

"The only question is, what's behind it?" I was getting goose bumps again.

"That's exactly what I want to find out today." Henry put his hand out to the door handle.

I looked at him in alarm. Okay, so now he really *had* gone crazy. "But you can't just walk into a dead person's dream! That would be like . . ." I swallowed. "And anyway, you'd need something personal of hers."

"What do you think I've been doing these last few days?" The corners of Henry's mouth twisted, but his smile wasn't quite as confident as usual. "Mrs. Honeycutt gave me the necklace Muriel got for her christening. That ought to be personal enough."

"She *gave* it to you?" I asked incredulously.

"Well, she didn't directly give it," admitted Henry, pushing the handle down. "But she won't miss it, let's put it that way." He obviously didn't want to go into detail.

I clutched his arm. "For heaven's sake, Henry! You can't do this. Please! We can't simply walk in."

"Only me for a start. You must stay here. Someone ought to know where I am, in the unlikely case that . . ." Henry looked seriously at me. "Listen, Liv. I've thought this right through. We absolutely have to know what's behind that door. It could open up entirely new opportunities for us."

"Or it could kill you," I whispered, while Henry, ignoring me, let the door swing open. I imagined I heard a rushing sound; there was nothing to be seen. My hand was still clutching Henry's sleeve. "It could . . . it could be the gateway to the world beyond the grave."

"Very dramatic today, aren't we, Miss Silver?" said Henry mockingly, but he did hesitate for a moment. Then he took a deep breath. Gently but firmly, he took my hand off his arm. "I'm going in. See you in school, and I'll tell you about the special offers in Muriel's wool shop, okay?"

Without waiting for an answer, he opened the door entirely

and walked in. The hand that I put out to hold him back met empty air.

Talk about pigheaded!

But no way was I going to let him stay in there on his own. Before the door could close again, I closed my eyes, held my breath, and took a great stride into the unknown after Henry.

For a moment nothing happened, and then I heard his sigh of resignation.

"You can open your eyes again, Liv," he said as the door latched behind us. "We're still alive. At least, I think so."

I did as he said. "Oh, we're at the seaside!" A great expanse of calm water lay before us, with a sunset sky veined with pink light above it. It was certainly beautiful. "But suppose it isn't really the sea?" I asked with a slightly hysterical note in my voice. "It could easily be the next world. Eternity Beach, like where they made that movie with Deborah Kerr."

"More likely Clevedon Beach, my angel," said Henry, pointing to his right, where a large, old-fashioned pier on stilts went out into the sea. He looked his usual easygoing self, but if you listened carefully, there was clearly something like relief in his voice. "I think we're in Somerset." He turned to me with a wry smile. "It was very sweet of you to want to follow me into the next world, Liv, but you do realize now we have no one out there who knows where we are, don't you?"

Yes, that might have been a little shortsighted of me. Never mind. I couldn't have borne to stand outside without knowing whether Henry would ever come back. That made me look around for the dream door into the corridor. There it was—in the quay wall right behind us. I breathed a sigh of relief myself.

Henry put an arm around my shoulders and gazed out at the sea. "Looks like Muriel was having a really lovely dream, when Alfred arrived with his cushion."

I was about to say, "That's a comforting thought," but at that moment I heard the noise. A shrill scream, excited voices, a dog barking, and it all got louder and louder, as if someone had turned on a radio right beside us. And then Henry, the sunset sky, and the sea had disappeared, and I was staring into darkness.

Only the noise was still there.

It took me a second to realize that I had woken up, and that it was Buttercup barking like crazy in the hallway.

"What on earth is going on?" I heard Mom ask sleepily. "Hush, Butter! Oh, for heaven's sake!"

I threw off my duvet, jumped up, and flung open the door of my room. The first thing I saw was Florence, standing in the doorway to Grayson's room as if turned to stone, with a hand to her mouth. The second thing I saw was feathers. Black feathers, lots and lots of them.

For a moment I felt weak at the knees, but I managed to stagger past Florence and Mom and into Grayson's room. Oh God—I remembered how Grayson had just vanished, and the parrot had repeated . . .

"What's this supposed to be—some kind of midnight meeting?" Grayson snapped at us, annoyed. He was standing in the middle of the room, obviously busy picking up the feathers that had fallen all over the furniture, the rug, and Grayson himself, and stuffing them into his wastepaper basket. I was so relieved to see him alive that I almost burst into tears.

"For heaven's sake!" Ernest, wearing a pair of checked pajamas, put his head around the door. "Where did all that black stuff come from?"

Buttercup was still jumping around in the feathers, very excited, but at least she had stopped barking. She was sneezing instead.

"Such a shock!" said Florence with her hand still in front of her mouth. "Feathers everywhere . . ."

"That's no reason to scream the house down and rouse everyone." Grayson was looking at her impatiently. As if to make his point for him, Mia now came out of her room and blinked in confusion at the sight of the chaos.

"There are hundreds of them." Mom picked up a feather from the floor, and I felt like snatching it from her hand and shouting, "Don't touch! They're dangerous!"

"Yes, hundreds," Grayson groaned. "When I woke, my door was open, and the ventilator was turned up to maximum. These feathers were flying all over the place. I'd have picked them up to spare the rest of you the sight, only Florence had to scream like a lost soul. You'd have thought she was auditioning for a horror movie."

As Florence indignantly gasped for air, Grayson cast me a brief glance and raised his eyebrows inquiringly. I helplessly shrugged my shoulders. I still didn't trust myself to stay on my feet, so I was leaning back against his wardrobe.

"Well, what would you have done in my place if you just wanted to go to the toilet, and you found feathers flying out of your brother's room?" Florence defended herself. "In the middle of the night! Have you been killing crows in here, or what?"

Being a practical person, Mom had picked up Grayson's duvet and was shaking it. "Well, they didn't come out of this, anyway," she said.

Yes, that would have been too easy. But anyway, what duvet is stuffed with black feathers?

Ernest scratched his head. "Okay, how did these get into your room, Grayson? Is this meant to be some kind of a joke?" For I don't know what reason, he was looking at Mia. "Or a silly prank?"

Mia snorted indignantly in her turn. "I'd never think up something as silly as this. My jokes are funny."

"Yes, I expect Mr. Snuggles is still laughing his head off," murmured Florence.

"I'm sorry, Mia," said Ernest. "It's just that I'm rather baffled."

He wasn't the only one.

Gritting his teeth, Grayson cast me another glance. I'd have liked to help him out, but for once I couldn't think up a good lie on the spur of the moment to use as an explanation. We couldn't even try the truth because, well, we ourselves had no idea what was going on.

Of course, Grayson could have said, "Could be that the feathers come from the wings of a demon in limbo who wants to give me a warning," but that was not the kind of explanation to satisfy his father.

I didn't like it either.

Grayson avoided answering by heaving a deep sigh. "Why don't you all go back to sleep?" he asked, exhausted. "I'll tidy up in here by myself."

Ernest shook his head. "We'll do it together tomorrow," he said. "And we will also find out where these feathers came from." He took Mom's hand. "Grayson, you'd better sleep in the guest room." He yawned. "Good night, everyone."

Florence also disappeared into her room, grumbling. Only Mia stayed put for a few seconds, looking hard at us. I was already preparing to fend off her questions, but much to my surprise, she turned without another word and stalked off to her room, taking Buttercup with her.

Grayson waited until her door had closed and then looked at me. "You do know you have a book strapped to your waist, don't you? *The Hotel New Hampshire*. Interesting."

Damn. I'd forgotten all about it in the chaos. "Yes, it's a good book. You should read it sometime," I said. "As soon as we've thought how you can explain all this . . ." And I pointed to the feathers lying around.

Grayson sighed again. "For now I'd be happy enough to understand it myself."

I opened my mouth to say something, but he didn't want to hear me. "No, don't say it, Liv! Someone or other must . . . oh, I don't know either! But there'll be a logical explanation. An explanation without any demons in it."

"Of course," I said, bending down to help him pick up the feathers. "Because demons don't exist."

20

THE DAY AFTER the demon's feathery shower, as I thought of it, was wonderfully uneventful. Unlike me, Grayson had managed to drop off to sleep again after we'd cleared up the feathers, and in the morning, when we met by the coffee machine in the kitchen, he seemed as if he'd not only had a fair amount of sleep, he was also in a very good mood.

Even after two espressos, I was close to falling asleep again on my feet. And sad to say I couldn't find any reason at all to feel good. There had been rather too many feathers, snakes, and unsolved riddles over the last few days. When Grayson put some of the feathers in a transparent plastic freezer bag, which he then stuffed into his jacket pocket, I promptly got goose bumps again.

"Why don't you throw those in the garbage?" I asked. "And why are you so disgustingly cheerful? Do you know something that I don't know?"

"Not yet! But every scrap of evidence brings us a little closer to the truth," replied Grayson, rustling the freezer bag in his pocket in a meaningful way. And whistling merrily (the *Sherlock Holmes* theme, but out of tune), he left the house.

I didn't get to see him again until early evening, when he stopped at home to pick up his gear for basketball practice, and he was in so much of a hurry that he had time only to whisper to me, "You'll be amazed by what I've found out," with an extremely mysterious smile.

I very much hoped it was something about the snake, because out of all those unexplained phenomena it struck me as the most sinister. Right, so Arthur was still in the hospital, but according to well-informed sources (i.e., Secrecy), he was to be discharged today.

In spite of Mrs. Cook's reassurance that there were no snakes at all in the school building, I'd seen countless other students hesitating to open their lockers. Emily even had her pepper spray at the ready.

When she saw me, she made a face. "I don't know which I like less, a venomous snake in the lockers or a four-eyes gawping stupidly at me." She pointed the pepper spray in my direction. "Want some of this?"

"Okay, if you want a broken hand yourself," I retorted.

"Oh yes, you can do karate." She rolled her eyes. "Don't worry, I'm not in the habit of resolving conflicts by violence. My IQ is too high for that."

"Kung fu, not karate," I corrected her. "And what conflicts? We don't have any conflict, apart from not liking each other. By the way, you look tired. Have you been having nightmares lately?" That was the right thing to say, although the rings around my eyes were dark today, as the espresso that hadn't been enough to get me properly awake. But instead of rubbing it in, Emily briefly gulped.

"Valerian tea is supposed to be good for that," I quickly added. "And so is just accepting things as they are."

Now Emily was looking as if she'd love to make an exception and settle her conflicts by violence after all. "I'm just so sorry for Florence, having to live under the same roof as you," she hissed, slamming her locker shut and hurrying away. A pity—I'd been about to ask whether she liked solving arithmetic problems in her dreams.

In spite of my exhaustion, I got through the school day well enough, presumably because of Arthur's absence. I didn't have to fear all the time that he might pick some random person to turn into a zombie and push me downstairs.

But there was no chance of relaxing after school, because as I turned into our road, Matt raced past me in his sports car, laughing and waving, which reminded me that demons, feathers, and snakes weren't the only problems facing me. Recently I'd been very remiss about the Rasmus business, just letting it slide, but in the bright light of day, and seeing Matt's rear lights, I couldn't put it out of my mind as easily as last night in the corridor. Probably because Henry wasn't here to distract me with his kisses.

The spring vacation would begin in only four days, and it turned my stomach to think how disappointed Henry would be by the lie I'd told. No one likes being lied to, particularly not if his own girlfriend is telling the lie. And how was I to explain why I hadn't simply told him the truth, when I didn't understand that myself?

Yes, possibly Henry had felt a bit superior when he'd thought I was a virgin, and yes, maybe that was why his expression had really sometimes been pitying and amused. But I hated to think how he was going to feel when he found out that I was a pathetic person with an inferiority complex and thought it necessary to invent an ex-boyfriend.

Obviously Mia was right to say love makes you stupid. Or at least, it makes you do silly things. And the worst of it was that, clearly, it didn't get any better with advancing age. Mom and Lottie were prime examples. Well, Mom had made great progress since falling for Ernest, but the ridiculously grand wedding certainly came into the category of things you do just for love, even though you hate the prospect. Did she see how this event staged by the Boker and Pascal, in charge of the infamous guest list, was going to turn out? Because if not, nothing could be guaranteed. Mom was well known for her spontaneous changes of plan, and in my ghastliest fantasies, I saw Ernest waiting at the altar with its floral decorations in a church crammed full, while Mom, in her wedding dress, made us race through the Heathrow departure lounge so that we could catch the next plane to Sydney, or Addis Ababa, or somewhere else we hadn't lived yet.

And Lottie—Lottie wasn't her usual self at all. Yes, she had finally gone to that concert with Charles, but his U-turn didn't seem to have impressed her much. Far from it. On Sunday morning, she and Pascal had visited Suffolk to see the country house hotel where the wedding reception was to be held, and because Mom and Ernest had chickened out of that (saying they had perfect faith in Lottie's judgment), it had been as if they were on a date. At least, Pascal had kissed Lottie's hand when he arrived and then escorted her to his showy Mercedes convertible, gallantly holding the passenger door open for her.

Charles, who was going to pay Lottie a surprise visit on Sunday evening (with a bunch of flowers too), knew nothing about either the kiss or the car door being held open, but all the same he was wild with jealousy when he realized who Lottie was out with. While he waited for her (which was a long time, because apparently Pascal's wedding checklist also included an inspection of the hotel grounds in the romantic evening light), I felt a little sorry for him. Mom gave him a glass of red wine, but that didn't make things much better. First he sounded off about the French, claiming they were nothing near as charming as their reputation but were well known for their unscrupulous dealings with women, and adding that they needn't pride themselves on their thick hair because that was genetically determined and scientifically shown to go hand-in-hand with diminishing masculine vigor as they grew older. Then he began worrying, said the French were also notorious for their dangerous, showy driving, and wondered whether we ought not to call Lottie on her cell phone and make sure she hadn't been in an accident. In the end, he went so far as to claim that all Frenchmen were potential murderers of women, and it had been very careless of us to let Lottie drive off with a total stranger. Finally, he just shook his head sadly and murmured things like *Of course an ordinary British dentist can't compete with a French accent and a diploma in canoodling*, and *Life has a nasty surprise in store if you come to the party too late.*

All the same, he seemed to have taken Florence's advice about Lottie to heart, because when she finally came home, safe and sound, and obviously in a good mood, he surprised us all by smiling casually and saying she looked wonderful, as in fact she did, with her rosy cheeks and bright eyes. And he asked if she'd like to go to a movie premiere with him on Wednesday, mentioning that the famous supporting actor in it had him, Charles, to thank for his brilliant new smile. Lottie accepted the invitation with a nonchalant smile of her own.

Mia and I were amazed. This was a new Lottie, one we'd never met before, and our new Lottie seemed to be enjoying herself in her unaccustomed role as a vamp with a man for every finger, or in her case a man for each hand. Her only problem was that she had nothing to wear for a movie premiere.

"This is how men like it," she explained that afternoon, when we and Florence, who had turned up in the kitchen on the dot, as usual, at that time of day, were sitting at the table, and spreading warm scones with clotted cream. "If you show them how much you like them, it puts them off hopelessly. You should never serve up your heart to them on a silver platter."

"Exactly," Florence agreed. "It's a terrible cliché, but men always need a sporting challenge. If you make it too easy for them, they immediately lose interest."

"Do you mean that if I write Gil Walker the Stalker a love poem, he'll leave me alone?" asked Mia.

"No, not him," I said. "And don't let Florence and Lottie talk you into anything; they're just kind of temporarily—er, disillusioned. Men aren't so bad."

"Not all of them, anyway," Lottie agreed at once. For a moment she was the old Lottie again. Florence only snorted. "You can go on indulging in your taste for romanticism, Mia."

The idea of Mia and a taste for romanticism was so funny that we all burst out laughing, and Mia nearly swallowed her mouthful of scone the wrong way.

When she could speak again, she said, "Charles or Pascal, I don't mind which you finally decide on, Lottie. The main thing is for you to stay with us in London."

But Lottie turned serious. "One way or another I must go

back to Germany, darling," she said. "It's time I stood on my own two feet, independent of your family—and independent of any man."

"But you can do that here too," wailed Mia. "You don't have to move away."

Lottie sighed. "I have a job waiting in Oberstdorf, and I can keep going with that for now. I don't expect I'll stay there forever, but for the time being, I'll try to get a footing there." She passed the jam to Mia, who was looking at her with her lower lip sadly thrust out. "It's very pretty there. Mountains, cows, lakes—you girls will like it if you come to see me. And it's not about to happen yet. I'm still here," she added. "I'm going to make the best of every day!"

"That's the right attitude," said Florence, and Lottie beamed at her.

"Yes, times are changing, and we have to change with them," she said enthusiastically.

Florence looked at Lottie with her head to one side. "My green dress would probably fit you, if you'd like to borrow it for this movie premiere . . . ?"

Mia and I exchanged a glance. Times were certainly changing if Florence and Lottie were friends and swapping clothes. It really made me wonder what might happen next.

But I was just too tired to think much about that. And instead of waiting for Grayson, as I'd originally meant to do, I decided to go to bed early that evening. It was only because by now I worked to a strict routine that I managed to strap, tie, and clip assorted items to myself, including *The Hotel New Hampshire*, before my eyes closed. My last conscious thought was that it would surely be a long time before Anabel and

Henry went to sleep. Maybe I could make it to Matt's dream door by then, just to see what happened.

As so often, however, when my body needed to catch up with its sleep, I fell first into a long phase of deep sleep, and when I finally began dreaming, I noticed at once that something was wrong.

My green dream door with the lizard was nowhere to be seen. Instead, the structure of an old-fashioned pier on a sandy beach, going out into the sea, rose on my right, and behind me there was a quay wall with rocks enclosing a bay beside it. Farther away I saw trees and houses. The view was very familiar: it was exactly the small stretch of beach in the evening sunlight that Henry and I had found last night. We had been standing right here looking out to sea when the noise in the corridor at home had awakened me.

Without a doubt, this was dead Muriel Honeycutt's dream, and I had no idea why I had landed in it.

I had often woken in someone else's dream, but the next time I went to sleep, I had always found myself in my own dreams. Until today. It was disturbing enough to have landed in a stranger's dream, and to make it worse the dream of a stranger who was dead, but the worst thing of all was still to come: there was no way out of it.

Whether I liked it or not, I had to acknowledge that fact an hour later, when I dropped on the sand, exhausted.

The door to the corridor through which Henry and I had reached the seaside had disappeared without a trace. Yesterday, it had been set in the quay wall, but there was no sign of it now, however desperately I searched.

I had tried everything I could think of. I had set out in

every direction, and at different speeds, only to find myself back exactly where I had started from after several feet. I had turned into a seagull, I had swum out to sea, I had thrown stones, I had shouted for help. But none of that had changed anything. The waves were still breaking lazily on the sand, and there was no sound apart from the gentle splash of water and the cries of the seagulls, always flying the same way back and forth. And the sun hadn't sunk an inch lower in the sky. Time seemed to have frozen, and the door was gone.

Slowly but surely, the conviction seeped into my mind that I was really caught. Caught in the dream of a woman who had died nearly forty years ago.

The only way out that occurred to me was to stop dreaming.

And luckily there was no problem in waking. When I sat up in my bed, my first feeling was relief. By now I had imagined what it would be like to be stuck forever in Muriel's dream. Never anything but sand underfoot, no company except a few seagulls—no one could bear that in the long run.

I got up and went to the bathroom. On the way back, I checked that all was quiet in the house. Everyone but Spot the cat was sleeping peacefully, and after I had let him out of the front door, I lay down in bed again, reassured, and went to sleep almost at once.

Only to find myself back on Muriel's beach again.

This time I didn't even try looking for the door. I let myself drop on the sand, clasped my hands around my knees, and did my best to keep calm. This eternal sunset scene no longer struck me as peaceful and atmospheric but threatening in an oppressive way. I'd never have thought that I'd miss the corridor with all its dangers so much.

Why hadn't I woken Grayson just now, when I put my head around his door to make sure he was all right? I couldn't bring myself to do so, that was why, because he was lying in bed so peacefully, with one hand between his cheek and the pillow. But now I regretted it. I ought to have told someone that I was stuck here. The best thing would simply be to wake up again. . . .

"Ah, there you are!" said someone right behind me.

I was so startled to hear a voice in the silence all of a sudden that I hit my chin on my knee. But it was only Henry, looking down at me with a broad smile.

"Sorry I didn't get here until now," he said, holding out his hand to help me up. I'd seldom felt happier to see him, with his clever gray eyes, the crinkles at the corners of his mouth, and his hair looking as untidy as if he'd strolled here through a tornado. All the same, I gave myself only a couple of seconds to give him a delighted smile, and then I turned around.

Thank heavens! Muriel's yellow door was shining in the quay wall as if it had never been away, and I felt a heavy weight lift from my heart. So it still existed. And at last I could get out of here.

Couldn't I?

"I was rather late working it out that you'd be shut in here as well," said Henry.

"What do you mean, *as well*?" I brushed the sand off my jeans. Now that Henry was here—and even more important, the door—I felt relaxed enough to make sure, quickly, that the jeans were a perfect fit.

"Well, I landed here myself after I fell asleep." Henry looked really pleased with that. He seemed to be in high spirits. "Like you, I woke up yesterday while I was still looking around Muriel's dream. I didn't imagine I could land back here again tonight. You should have seen my face! Luckily I'd thought ahead and had put the christening necklace around my wrist so that I could walk through the door and out of the dream." He was looking at me thoughtfully. "But you obviously couldn't."

I shook my head. "In my version of the dream, there wasn't even a door there at all. And absolutely no way of getting out—believe me, I tried everything. The only thing that worked was waking again. But then, after I went to sleep for the second time, I was back here."

Henry seemed even more pleased to hear that. "Do you know what that means?" he asked.

"It means I'll have to spend every night on the beach now, does it?" I retorted.

"No, don't worry," he reassured me. "Once you're out of here, everything will be back to normal. I tried it just now."

"But you have the christening necklace," I said, shaking the door nervously. "I'd rather try it for myself."

Henry reached past me, pressed the handle down, and opened the door. "There you go!" He pointed to the corridor outside.

"Thanks." I heaved a deep sigh of relief once I was out in the corridor and Henry was closing the yellow door after us. "If you ask me, sunsets are really overrated."

21

"IT'TH HIGH TIME we tried getting Anabel on board with uth," said Grayson with his mouth so full that I could hardly make out what he was saying.

I moved Lottie's leek and bacon tart out of his reach. "Sorry, I don't speak greedyguts-ish," I said as Grayson grunted in protest.

It was Tuesday evening, and at Grayson's own suggestion, he, Henry, and I had broken with our usual habit and were holding a crisis meeting in real time instead of in Mrs. Honeycutt's dreams. I'd had no objection; I really did need a break from all those nocturnal meetings. No one could dissolve into thin air here, and we weren't likely to be disturbed by murderers armed with flowered cushions stepping through invisible doors in the wallpaper when we least wanted them. However, there was plenty of good food in the house, and as Grayson had skipped supper because of the research he'd told us he was doing, for the last fifteen minutes he had been stuffing himself with everything he could find in the fridge.

"No more tart until we know what you've found out," I said sternly. "And please say it's some way of thwarting Arthur."

"That would be really good." Henry balanced a mini-basketball on his finger, rotating it. He had been very nervous all evening. "Arthur . . ." He cleared his throat. "Arthur is obviously planning something. And I hate to admit it, but the thought of him sends cold shivers down my spine."

Arthur had indeed been back in school that day with his bandaged arm, accepting congratulations like a war hero coming home. Which he obviously was, in the eyes of the other students. After all, when Persephone was running amok, he'd stopped her in her tracks, and then he'd survived the bite of a dangerous venomous snake—by this time they all thought he was the bravest person in the world. They acted as if he had self-sacrificingly thrown himself in front of the snake to save all the students of Frognal Academy from certain death.

Many of the girls, particularly the younger ones, had already been close to fainting away when Arthur came near them, but since last weekend, there'd been an official Arthur Hamilton fan club, with its own Internet page and cards to print out and collect. I was sure that, in secret, Persephone was already a signed-up member.

I'd seen Arthur only once today, and then he'd been besieged by girls wanting him to autograph the cards they were collecting. He didn't look exactly enthusiastic, more as if he thought it was all a terrible nuisance, but any private satisfaction I felt about that was short-lived. In fact, it lasted only until I imagined a horror scenario in which I saw forty giggling girl zombies rushing toward me with the cards they'd collected and tearing me to pieces. I was sure Arthur would really like that.

But in spite of the stress of dealing with all the hero worship, he'd somehow managed to get Henry and Grayson on their own. It annoyed me that I'd not been there to hear the conversation, particularly as neither of them would tell me exactly what was said.

"Only the usual," Grayson had told me when I pressed him. "How he can make dreadful things happen anytime he likes, and he wouldn't spare even those who had once been his best friends, blah, blah, blah."

The longer our meeting went on this evening, the more certain I felt that they were keeping the details from me on purpose, probably because my name had come up in connection with a particularly nasty kind of death. Or it could have been something else, but hard as they were trying to be as casual as usual, whatever Arthur said to them had clearly scared both Henry and Grayson.

"I've found out a good deal more about the demon business." Grayson could speak more clearly without a mouthful of tart, so now we finally got to hear about the latest stage of his research.

First of all, he held up the plastic bag of feathers. "Marabou. Down feathers dyed black. They cost twenty-five pounds per hundred grams in the handicrafts trade, considerably less wholesale. But I can tell you, a hundred grams of feathers comes to a good many."

Marabou. Aha. Okay, so that didn't explain how the darn things got into Grayson's room, but it was reassuring to know that they hadn't come wafting down on us from another world. Demons who had to buy the feathers for their terrifying wings in crafts shops couldn't really be taken seriously.

And that wasn't all that Grayson had found out.

"I won't bore you with the details, but it looks like I have a date tomorrow to meet BloodySword66," he said, looking obviously pleased when our jaws dropped. "Don't worry, it's not dangerous. The guy works as an aide in a senior citizens residential home in Islington, and he sounds pleasant enough on the phone."

"What on earth did you say to get him to agree to meet you?" I stared at Grayson.

"Like I said, I don't want to bore you with details." Grayson smiled with becoming modesty. "I can only repeat that with a little psychological empathy, much can be done without trespassing on other people's dreams." He paused for a moment, and then sighed and said, "Well, either that, or I just struck lucky. Sometimes it's an advantage to have a life-size battle droid robot from *Star Wars: Episode I* . . . Anyway, tomorrow I hope I'll be able to tell you how BloodySword66's novel connects up with Anabel's demon. By the way, BloodySword66's real name is Harry Triggs, and he comes from—wait for it!—Liverpool!"

"Like the roofer who founded that sect." This sounded good. At least one of his discoveries was getting us somewhere.

But Henry wasn't so optimistic. "I'm afraid it's far too late for Anabel," he said, frowning. "We'd better work out how to deal with Arthur without her support. She's sure that the demon has forgiven him because he survived the snakebite—

and I'm afraid she's going to try out that theory on the three of us next."

"Are you still sure it was Anabel who left the snake in Arthur's locker?" I asked.

Henry shrugged. "Who else would it have been? I don't know any other person who'd be crazy enough to do such a thing."

He had a good point there.

"As long as she thinks that the demon wants to punish us, Anabel is as much of a danger as Arthur," Henry went on gloomily. "Who knows what the voices in her head will be whispering to her next?"

"Nothing to do with snakes, I hope," I murmured.

"But we need Anabel," said Grayson. "And I'm sure that once she realizes all that demon stuff has no foundation at all—"

Henry didn't let him finish what he was saying. "I know you still believe that Anabel can see reason, and you think she'd be free of her delusions if you can show her firm evidence that she's wrong. But I don't." He looked down at his shoes. "I can still see her before me in that mausoleum in the cemetery, with the dagger in her hand, about to cut Liv's carotid artery. . . ." He stopped and said no more for a moment. Then he raised his head and looked straight at Grayson. "I don't mind all that much what Anabel does in her dreams, but I'd feel a lot safer if she was still having psychiatric treatment."

Grayson shook his head. "I've gone so far that I'm not giving up now."

"But suppose it turns out impossible to cure Anabel?" Henry folded his arms, and for the first time I realized that for Grayson the whole operation wasn't so much designed to get Anabel's support against Arthur, but to save her from herself. Henry, who knew Grayson much better than I did, had seen that all along.

For a while they looked at one another in silence.

"I think it's worth a try," said Grayson at last. "And it's the only thing I can do. You two are welcome to work out a plan B. So that we don't have to embark on plan C."

"What's plan C?" I asked.

"Plan C is dealing with Arthur before he can deal with us," said Grayson vaguely, and there was a small growl from Henry.

I looked from one to the other. They *were* keeping something from me.

"What did Arthur really say, damn him?" I asked, trying for the last time as Henry said good-bye to me at the front door later. I had to whisper because Florence was looking for something in the cupboard on the wall only a few feet away—something that she had obviously hidden well. "You don't have to spare my feelings, if that's what you were thinking."

"No, I know you have nerves of steel." Henry kissed me, although Florence promptly cleared her throat, even though she was really searching the cupboard. "Yes, damn Arthur— he's spoiling everything," Henry whispered. "Can't we just talk about something else? Next Saturday, for instance, when I've taken my mother, Milo, and Amy to the airport." His breath was tickling the skin behind my ear. "I can't tell you how much I'm looking forward to it. And then, I promise, I'll make sure you forget Arthur and the whole wretched thing."

Yes, I certainly would if my whole structure of lies collapsed around me. Henry didn't notice me stiffening in his arms, because at that moment Florence triumphantly held up a perfumed sachet, with a triumphant cry of, "I knew it was here somewhere!" When Henry looked at her inquiringly, she embarked on an explanation, but to be honest I didn't hear a word of it, I was so busy worrying about Saturday. (So to this day I don't know why the perfumed sachet was so important.) Henry kissed me good-bye and left me, rigid with shock, in the front hall, where it became clear to me again that there was only one thing for it: tonight I must try getting together with Matt again, and this time I wouldn't let my subconscious mind kit me out in flesh-colored horror underwear. This time I must go through with it.

Crazily, Matt turned out to be dreaming of flying when I entered his dream. I hadn't stepped into a flight simulator, however, but the cabin of a fully occupied airbus, ten seats to each row, three by each window side and four in the central aisle. A glance out of the plane, and the soft drone of engines, told me that we were airborne and far above the clouds. And Matt wasn't the pilot but obviously a passenger. I saw him farther forward in a seat by the aisle, this time in casual clothes and with a beard at least a week old, scribbling something on a newspaper. His red dream door had planted itself right by the door to the toilets, where it fitted in well in spite of its bright color. At least if, like Matt, you didn't have it right in your line of vision.

To get my first idea of what kind of dream this was, I made a fat woman disappear from the seat by the aisle in the central row, diagonally behind Matt, and sat down in it myself without attracting any attention. Ah, so Matt was dreaming of sitting in a plane and solving a crossword puzzle. Well, why not? I'd once dreamed all night of clearing out a bookcase. In principle, this wasn't a bad starting point, even if I didn't necessarily want my first time to be in a crowded aircraft. But I could always change the location once Matt had taken my bait. It might be best to get myself a flight attendant's uniform and serve him a glass of champagne that he hadn't asked for. It was a terrible cliché, but I was sure that it wouldn't bother Matt in a dream.

A flight attendant happened to be coming down the aisle at that moment with a serving cart, and Matt was still concentrating on his newspaper, so I didn't stop to think for long. A second later, I was the one pushing the cart, and I was a little proud of myself, because no one had noticed me taking over. In fact, I looked a good deal better than the attendant I'd replaced. Not only was I wearing about four kilos less makeup, I had also modified the uniform a bit. It was shorter now, it fitted more closely, and it had a plunging neckline— if those were more clichés, I hoped they were the right ones. I'd added to the contents of the serving cart a bucket of ice with a bottle of champagne in it, as usually reserved for passengers in first and business class, and before I stopped next to Matt and bent down to him, I looked down my own neckline to make sure I was wearing a dark-blue lace bra, and not armored flesh-colored underwear like last time.

"A glass of champagne, sir?" I said in dulcet tones, giving Matt my most charming smile. "Or perhaps something from our exquisite whiskey collection?" I added, when he didn't reply at once. "We have this twenty-five-year-old single malt, aged in a silver-oak cask . . . oh!"

Matt had grabbed my wrist and drew me down on the

empty seat beside him. He put a finger to his lips. "Psst! Don't say a word, don't let anyone notice anything, just listen to me. This is a matter of life and death."

I stared at him with my eyes wide open. Obviously he didn't recognize me.

"There are terrorists on board this aircraft," he went on in a whisper. "They are armed, and they are probably carrying explosives."

"But that's impossible," I whispered back, forgetting for a moment that I wasn't a real flight attendant. "Our security checks are very rigorous, and . . ."

Matt shook his head impatiently. "Security men can be bought, and it's too late for such discussions. Here!" He tore a page out of his paper, and I saw that he hadn't been solving a crossword but noting down numbers and letters. "These are the numbers of the seats occupied by the terrorists that I've spotted so far. But we can assume there are more of them on the upper deck too. It's up to you to inform the captain. I hope there's more than one sky marshal on board."

"Er . . ." At something of a loss, I took the piece of paper and rolled it up. I didn't really know my way around this kind of dream. In feature films where terrorists hijack planes, I either went to sleep or changed to another channel. But I knew it wasn't usually the sky marshal who saved everyone in the end (or everyone who had survived that long), but a brave civilian, a retired police officer, or a recently traumatized FBI agent who just happened to be on the plane. And generally there was a courageous girl flight attendant as well, but she often didn't believe in the plot and was either flung out of the plane or bled to death from a gunshot wound. Maybe I'd do better to turn into the pregnant woman who was guaranteed to go into premature labor during the movie and had her baby in the midst of the chaos—she usually survived. . . .

"What are you waiting for?" Matt looked at me impatiently. "The captain must summon help. And I need something I can use as a weapon." He picked up a bottle of whiskey from my serving cart.

I stood up, smiling as naturally as I could at the rows of seats. Hmm, the guy in 64D did look suspicious.

"Okay," I murmured, while I wondered how to give this dream a new turn, make it a love story instead of a disaster action thriller. Or even a romantic comedy; that would be okay too. "One more thing: who are you, and how come you know all this?"

"Never mind," said Matt roughly. "We must get out of here alive, that's all that matters."

"And it could be tricky," the passenger in the seat behind Matt intervened. My heart missed a beat when I recognized Henry. I was sure he hadn't been there just now. The seat had been occupied by a little boy stuffing himself with M&M's . . . aaaarrgh!

"Keep calm, or you'll endanger the whole operation," Matt told Henry.

"You don't understand," said Henry, winking at me. He looked so damn good that, if this had been a real movie, he'd surely have been the leading man. "Our Liv, in that wildly sexy outfit, is really an undercover agent from MI6, and I'm her colleague. So you're not on your own."

I hadn't recovered from my fright yet, but I was able to breathe again. I wondered feverishly how I could get out of this without giving myself away. The main thing was to keep calm. Henry couldn't be sure it was the real me—it was equally possible for Matt to be simply dreaming about me. So I stared at him, frowning. "What are you talking about? My name is Marianne Dashwood, and I'm not an agent. And you are clearly mentally disturbed."

"Let the girl go and see the captain," hissed Matt. "We don't know how much time we have left."

"Liv, Marianne Dashwood is a character in a Jane Austen novel." Henry stood up and looked straight at me. I was glad we had the serving cart between us. And annoyed that I hadn't had the presence of mind to give myself a large mole on my cheek or a gap in my teeth—such little details changed your appearance no end and would have made me look much less like myself.

"What kind of sick person are you?" Matt's subconscious mind could just as well have invented the name, so I looked as haughty as possible. "I don't know any Jenny Auster, and now kindly let me go to the cockpit!" I turned on my heel and stalked away along the aisle, leaving the serving cart to bar Henry's way. All the same, he followed me.

"Wait, Liv!"

"Stop calling me that!" Damn it, how could I persuade him that he wasn't looking at me but only at a Dream-Liv dressed by Matt in this embarrassingly seductive outfit?

The only solution that occurred to me in a hurry was diversion. My first thought was to blow a hole in the side of the plane, but I was afraid it might be beyond me to imagine the following scenario (if only I'd paid more attention to those disaster movies!). So I did the next best thing. I stopped and, with my eyes wide in alarm, pointed at one of the passengers.

"He has a bomb!" I cried as loud as I could, and a few

people kindly began screeching and jumped up from their seats, including the poor man I'd pointed out. Anyone not yet panicking caught up with the situation, at latest, when the oxygen masks dropped from the flaps above the passengers two seconds later. Henry himself looked away from me briefly, and I used that moment to sit down in an empty seat at the side of the plane, where I swiftly turned into my great-aunt Gertrude, pearl earrings, green eye shadow, Queen Elizabeth II hairstyle, and all.

Henry looked around inquiringly and went on making his way forward.

Great-Aunt Gertrude, on the other hand, marched past the central seats on her way to the toilets (there were certain advantages, I decided, in weighing about a hundred kilos). Just before I reached the red door, I looked around once again. No sign of Henry. But I did see Matt, who had climbed up on his seat and was shouting, "Keep calm! Don't panic!" It probably wasn't particularly helpful that he was brandishing the sharp neck of a broken whiskey bottle. But he provided the perfect diversion. I snatched the door open quickly, slipped out into the corridor, and slammed the door again behind me.

I waddled around the next corner as fast as I could—or rather, as fast as Great-Aunt Gertrude's body would let me—and then leaned back against the wall. That had been close!

What the hell had Henry been doing in Matt's dream? Had he followed me there? As I slowly slid down the wall to sit on the floor, I changed back into myself and buried my face in my hands. Had I really thought I couldn't make things any worse? Well, I'd been dead wrong there. My only hope was that Henry wouldn't . . .

"Nice try," he said, and there went my only hope. I didn't even ask how he had managed to appear beside me out of nowhere. As I made no move to stand up, he sat down beside me.

"Hi," I whispered.

"Hi." It was hard to read the expression on his face—even though he was smiling, he looked anything but amused. His gray eyes were inspecting me from head to foot. When I turned back into myself, I hadn't paid much attention to styling, so I was wearing the same clothes as last night, jeans and a white statement T-shirt. Mom had recently thrown it out, and I'd decided to have it. The statement said *Feminism is not a dirty word*.

Of course it caught Henry's eye. "Interesting. Especially on someone who was in a flight attendant's uniform that could have graced any porn just now."

"I can't say I know my way around that subject. But I'm glad you liked it." I didn't mean to sound so snide; I'd have liked to put my head against his chest and start crying, but obviously my pride wouldn't allow it.

Henry sighed. "Would you mind telling me what that was all about?"

I looked at him unhappily. If only it was that simple! "It . . . it's a long story."

"I have time," said Henry, stretching one leg out.

"Yes, obviously. Enough time to go spying on me." Strange how many emotions you could feel at the same time. Guilt, shame, now anger . . .

"I didn't—"

"Yes, you did." I didn't let him finish. "You did exactly what you blamed me for doing when I followed you into that whirlpool dream!" I managed to cling to my anger a moment longer by remembering how Henry had gone into the water to join B. "And later you said I must learn to distinguish dreams from reality, or something like that."

"Yes, right." Henry's voice sounded a little hoarse, and my anger went away as quickly as it had come. Lost in thought, he looked at his hands. "That was about the worst moment of my life. I talked all that nonsense because I couldn't admit, even to myself, that I'd gone too far. That to solve the problem of my father I'd done things that . . . that you don't do when you love someone. Even in a dream. But I was so stubborn that I preferred to risk losing you. And I'm so sorry." He almost whispered those last words.

I was fighting back tears. I'd forgiven him for that silly scene with B ages ago. It was so cheap of me to bring it up again now. Particularly as the situations couldn't really be compared. Henry had been concerned with the welfare of his little brother and sister, whereas I was thinking only of my wounded pride.

"I'm sorry too," I managed to say.

"What for, exactly?" asked Henry in his normal voice again. "Please just tell me what you were doing in that guy's dream, Liv. Do you think he's so great? Because it looked to me as if you were trying to seduce him."

"I was." My voice failed me. I swallowed hard, but the big lump in my throat simply wouldn't go away.

Henry's eyes had darkened. "That wasn't your first visit to his dreams, was it?"

I shook my head, and then he looked away and stared past me into space.

"No. But not because I think Matt is great or anything like that," I managed to say. "In fact, I think he's a bit of a show-off." My voice sounded like a chipmunk's, but I didn't care about that. I couldn't bear the painful expression of Henry's eyes a moment longer. At least he was looking at me again now.

"It was only because I had his copy of *The Hotel New Hampshire*, and you can learn to fly in a flight simulator, and that way I thought you might not notice that I'm not a pilot." It all came out in a rush.

Henry, obviously confused, drew his eyebrows together.

"I never did have a boyfriend in South Africa," I said, trying to make rather more sense but still talking at double speed (at least). "I didn't have a boyfriend at all before. We always moved before I had time to get to know any boys, and to be honest, I wasn't much interested in them until I came here—I think it has to be mutual. Until I met you I was like Mia. I didn't know anything about inferiority complexes and self-doubts. So they've kind of steamrollered me . . . like aliens taking over a larva and then controlling it. You always looked so sorry for me, so I invented Rasmus. Well, not me, the aliens did it. But I hated not knowing anything, while you can always compare me with other girls. I thought maybe you wouldn't feel so superior if you thought I could compare you with someone else too. And once I'd thought up Rasmus I couldn't—"

"Stop!" said Henry, which was just as well, because I badly needed to get my breath back. I was probably blue in the face by this time. But in a funny way, I was feeling relieved.

Even though Henry didn't make a sound. He simply

looked at me with his gray eyes shining, and I stared back and waited for him to say something. But he didn't. Only the muscles in his jaw were moving as if he was chewing something.

"I did some dog-sitting in Pretoria," I said, finally breaking the silence. "Our neighbors the Wakefields had a chow called Rasmus. It was the first name that occurred to me."

Henry bit his lower lip.

"The other dog I took for walks was called Sir Barksalot," I added, and that was too much for Henry's self-control. He spluttered with laughter.

"Oh God, Livvy, you'll be the death of me!" he said when he was able to speak again.

"Not intentionally." Now I'd told him all about it, I'd have liked to cry buckets. But oddly enough, the lump in my throat had gone away.

Henry looked at me, shaking his head. "What on earth gave you the idea that I might feel somehow superior to you? Of the two of us, I'm the one who has those complexes, problems with trusting people, fears of losing them. I'm the screwed-up person in our relationship."

"But a screwed-up person who's had any amount of sex."

"Any amount of it?" Henry snorted. "What does that sound like? Anyway, it's not true. If I had a couple of relationships before I met you, that doesn't make me an expert on the subject. And I don't draw comparisons, because compared to you, no other girl would come off well, anyway." His voice was softer, and he put out his hand to touch my cheek. "I always thought it was kind of a miracle that you waited for me, of all people, and I was eaten up by jealousy of that Rasmus."

"You had a point. I used to tickle his tummy." I was

positively bubbling over inside with relief. And happiness. "I do love you, Henry. And I'm sorry I was so silly."

Henry's eyes were shining again. "Yes, so you should be," he said, frowning. "I guess I won't ever forgive you for wanting your first time to be with stupid Matt."

But when he leaned over to kiss me, I knew he'd forgiven me already.

TITTLE-TATTLE BLOG

**The Frognal Academy Tittle-Tattle Blog,
with all the latest gossip, the best rumors, and
the hottest scandals from our school.**

ABOUT ME:

My name is Secrecy—I'm right here among
you, and I know *all* your secrets.

26 March

Today, for a change, a little collection of quotes for your
edification. Things that certainly weren't intended for all and
sundry to hear, but you can read them now in Secrecy's blog.
Oops. Some of them date from quite far back, but they've
lost none of their interest.

"Gabriel's tongue feels like a slug." (Persephone Porter-
Peregrin)

"Under that push-up bra there are only two peas on a flat
board." (Gabriel Cobb on Persephone's bust measurement)

"I've eaten tuna sandwiches with a higher IQ than that boy
has." (Mr. Daniels on Jasper Grant)

"I bet even his bum smells better than his breath." (Jasper
Grant on Mr. Daniels)

"You might not think it, because he always acts so nice and modest, but Grayson Spencer's ego is as enormous as Hazel Pritchard's behind." (Emily Clark)

"I wouldn't have said no to sleeping with her when she was ten years younger." (Mr. Vanhagen on Mrs. Cook)

"Our colleague has that certain . . . nothing." (Mrs. Cook on Mr. Vanhagen)

"They're crazy! All that fuss about a silly clipped box hedge!" (Liv Silver on the British)

"Yank, go home!" (the British on Liv Silver)

Oh yes, and finally this one, overheard in the school toilets yesterday: "I wish that damn snake had bitten your balls." (Grayson Spencer to Arthur Hamilton)

Okay, have fun!

See you soon!

Love from Secrecy

PS—I don't want to frighten anyone, but suppose the snake in Arthur Hamilton's locker wasn't just a silly prank, as the police and Mrs. Cook are trying to make us think. Wouldn't that mean there's still a murderer on the loose somewhere here? And who will be the next victim? You're welcome to post your preferences here.

22

LOTTIE WAS PREENING in front of Florence's mirror. The green dress fit her perfectly.

"I don't know—isn't it a bit short?" Lottie stared doubt-fully at her legs.

"Nonsense. If you wear your black boots instead of pumps, it'll be just right," said Florence. She was lying on her stomach on her bed and had not protested when Mia and I dropped on the white bedspread on each side of her. Now we were all three of us in exactly the same attitude: propped on our elbows, chins on our right hands, our eyes on Lottie. "It'll look superchic with boots, but not overdressed."

"You're a real fashion expert." Lottie gave Florence an appreciative smile. Then she put a hand to her breast and looked at us, delighted. "Oh, you should see yourselves! Lying there side by side, like real sisters! You've no idea how glad I am that you're getting on so well at last."

Hello? While Lottie wiped away a tear of emotion from the corner of her eye, we could only stare at her, baffled.

"Then I'll get my boots," she said in high spirits. "And

pantyhose. Do you think black or natural? Oh, I'll bring both, and then you can tell me which looks better, all right? Don't move from that spot! I'll be right back." She turned again at the door. "I must just make the icing for the carrot cake first, but it won't take long."

Florence was the first to recover. "Well, your former au pair doesn't seem to know all that much about human nature," she said.

"Hear that, Liv?" Mia tossed one of Florence's embroidered cushions off the bed to make more room for Lottie's iPad, which she had more or less monopolized for the last few days. "The real fashion expert doesn't like to admit that she's come to like us, even though we're guilty of murdering her great-uncle the topiary peacock."

I chuckled. "No need to be embarrassed, Florence. It's no use people denying their feelings. And it all depends on the feeling being mutual." I genuinely meant it at that moment. Since last night, when the Rasmus problem had been disposed of, I'd felt so good that I loved everyone and anyone. Including Florence. Well, particularly Florence, lying there with one hand in her caramel-colored ringlets and trying to look fierce. I gave her a big kiss on the cheek. "I'd feel I was missing something without our morning fight for the bathroom."

"Although you'd be better made up," said Florence, unable to stay serious herself. The dimples in her cheeks were showing. "Don't fool yourselves. I still think you're the worst nuisances who ever set foot in this house. Pick that cushion up at once, Mia."

"In a minute," said Mia. "I'm just writing a quick e-mail to Secrecy. So she'll know that I've unmasked her."

"What?" I cried. I couldn't believe it! She had such

sensational news, but here she was lying quietly on Florence's bed. "Since when? Tell us!"

"Dear Sec-re-cy. Thanks for post-ing this mor-ning's blog," Mia read as she typed. *"It was the missing piece in the jigsaw that I needed to tell me who you are."*

"Really and truly, Mia?" I reached over Florence's back and tugged Mia's sweater. "You actually know who Secrecy is? Come on, let us know too!"

"Nonsense, she's just bluffing." Florence snorted scornfully.

Mia just went on typing. *"Solving this case was fun. I'm not necessarily one of your fans, so I'm afraid there will be consequences for you. I'll mail you later with the details. Sincerely, Mia Silver, Private Detective,"* she concluded. "Here we go—send!"

"Mia!" I wriggled a little way forward so that I could see past Florence and look at my sister's face. She seemed very pleased with herself. "If you don't tell me what you know this minute, I'm going to tickle you until you wet yourself."

"Leave her alone. She can't tell you anything." Florence sat up. Her dimples had disappeared. "No one knows who Secrecy is. Your little sister is only showing off." She clicked her tongue, and for a split second that made her so like the Boker that it was almost uncanny. "It's obvious that you're still a child, Mia, but all the same, I think you're too old for these silly detective games."

"There are some things you're never too old for." Mia closed the cover of the iPad and sat up too. "Although I don't think that applies to writing an anonymous blog saying nasty things." She sighed. "I guess nastiness is more to do with a person's character than her age. Isn't that so—*Secrecy?*"

For a moment there was total silence in the room.

Then Florence yawned ostentatiously. "Is that supposed to be something I wrote?" She leaned back and closed her eyes. "Dream on."

"Oh, you misunderstand me, Florence," said Mia in friendly tones. "I didn't say you wrote that particular post on the blog, only that it gave me the last piece in the puzzle today."

I frowned. "So what about it?"

Mia adjusted her glasses. She was playing her part as Private Detective Silver brilliantly.

"Spit it out," I said, annoyed.

Mia gave me a broad grin. "Florence isn't *the* Secrecy. She's only Se. Or Cre. Or Cy. Take your pick."

I gasped for air. "You mean there are several of them?"

"Not several; exactly three." At this point, Mia gave up keeping her cool. "Crazy, right? I set out, quite early on, by assuming there were several bloggers, simply because Secrecy can't always be everywhere. But narrowing down the circle was really hard. And I can't tell you how tiring it was, sounding out all the suspects. All the same, the evidence was clear as well." She looked at Florence. "Did you notice how many trendy allusions there are in your own posts? Your colleagues' style is far less figurative."

I was amazed. Mia really did seem to have solved probably the greatest puzzle of human nature. I felt a surge of pride in my sister. And now I, too, understood some things.

"That's why Secrecy changed her mind so often," I said. I looked from Mia to Florence, who was still lying on the bed, on her back now, and was amazingly relaxed, in view of the situation. "And that's why the blog was always attacking everyone and anyone. I suppose the three of you were always pulling one another to pieces. How clever! Who are the other two?"

"Why ask *me*? Do you believe her?" Florence began braiding her ringlets. "Just because she says so?"

I kept my eyes fixed on her. How did she manage to keep so calm? "Yes, I do believe her. And yes, just because she says so."

"And because she knows I'd never make a claim like that if I didn't have conclusive evidence," added Mia.

"Well, I'd like to see this evidence of yours," said Florence sarcastically.

"Wouldn't you rather see if my e-mail has arrived yet?" asked Mia.

"I expect Secrecy gets e-mails like that every day." Florence stretched comfortably as she sat up, as if she'd just had a nice, refreshing nap. She really was incredibly cool, you had to give her that. In other circumstances, I'd surely have doubted Mia's theory now at the latest. "I expect she's laughing herself silly about it."

"Well, if you're too lazy to read your e-mails, I can do it for you." Mia opened the iPad again. "Wait a moment, here we are. The messages that arrive in Secrecy's inbox are automatically sent on to three other addresses, right? And your own secret account for Secrecy is in the name of Adelaide Hanley. Which I think is very sweet because it's your grandmother's maiden name."

Florence didn't jump or flinch, but the relaxed expression slowly left her face. Well, well.

"But of course it's not too clever—one should never use such personal details in fake e-mail addresses," Mia went on.

Her fingers flew over the keyboard on the screen, and I didn't know what I thought more fascinating, that or the change on Florence's face. "The same applies to passwords, even if you change them every week. It's inadvisable to use combinations with the names of pets, birth dates, house number and so on, but okay, here we have 172Spot97, so—"

"That's enough!" Florence snatched the iPad away from her, and for a moment I was afraid she'd throw it at the wall. But then she simply put it on her lap. There was anger, annoyance, and maybe a trace of shame in her face.

So Florence was Secrecy! I was slowly beginning to see what that meant. Which of the many catty remarks on the Tittle-Tattle blog had come from Florence? Was she the one who had written all those horrible things about me?

Oh, hell. So much for being lighthearted, full of good humor, and ready to like everyone.

"And I was just beginning to like you a little," I said quietly.

"Well, all I wanted was for you two to go away again." Florence sprang to her feet so suddenly that Mia and I jumped nervously. With great presence of mind, Mia managed to catch the iPad.

"So what? Suppose I am Secrecy?" Florence was looking daggers at us. "Do I always have to be perfect, while you can get your hands on anything you like, just because you're blondes and a little younger? Are you the only ones in this house who can get away with behaving badly? But sure, when it comes to you, everyone thinks it's cute and charming and you didn't mean it that way. Whatever you do. Dad and Grayson always have excuses for you. Everything revolves around the pair of you!" Up to now she'd sounded angry, but at this point, her mood changed. She looked at me accusingly, and her eyes filled with tears. "It's bad enough that Dad has eyes only for your mother, but even Grayson spends more time with you than with his own sister, and with his friends, it's Liv this, Liv that—they've forgotten I even exist."

"When they find out that you're Secrecy, who's always writing such delightful things about them, I'm sure they'll remember you exist," said Mia, and Florence shuddered.

Grayson and his friends—well, well. I narrowed my eyes as I looked at my future stepsister. Arthur had once been one of Grayson's friends. Arthur, who had admitted giving Secrecy information. Did that mean Florence and Arthur were hand in glove?

Mia unsympathetically folded her arms. "You were writing the Tittle-Tattle blog way before we came to London, so don't go holding us responsible for the nasty, sly way you behave!"

"Mia!" gasped Lottie, horrified. She was standing in the doorway, carrying her boots and pantyhose, and she looked as if she couldn't believe her ears. "What's the matter? And you were all getting on so well just now!"

"She's Secrecy!" Mia pointed to Florence. "She just this minute admitted it."

Lottie knew the Tittle-Tattle blog. Ever since there'd first been something about us in it, she read every entry posted— sometimes she even read it aloud to us. And if it was something unpleasant, she used to get much more indignant than we did. So she laughed incredulously now. "This is no laughing matter, you silly girls. Florence has nothing to do with that nasty, horrible person who writes such wounding things."

Florence interrupted. "Yes, I do, damn it! I *am* that nasty, horrible person. And I did write all those wounding things." At this point, she really did burst into tears.

"Not all of them. You're only one of three nasty, horrible people," Mia corrected her, while Lottie was staring at Florence, unable to take it in.

"But . . . but you're an *angel*," she protested. "You do all that good work for charity in the soup kitchen, and you sign petitions against breaches of human rights, you give Buttercup little treats, you tickle her behind the ears when you think no one's looking." It almost looked as if Lottie herself was going to start crying. "I know for a fact that you're so prickly with Ann only because you're afraid she might break your father's heart. You seem so tough only because you lost your mother when you were a little girl, and I'm sure there's a soft heart under the tough exterior."

While Mia was rolling her eyes and muttering something about "karma, cause and effect," the blood rose to Florence's face. I'd never seen her go red like that, and all at once I was almost sorry for her.

"You only think that, Lottie, because on principle you believe the best of everyone," she said, suppressing a sob. "I was so horrid to you, but you always made out you didn't notice. You always understand everyone, and then you bake those wonderful tarts and cakes, and although you adore Liv and Mia, you tried to be nice to me . . . and all the time I was . . ."

"Secrecy," said Mia, finishing her sentence for her. "But if it's any consolation, you had by far the best literary style of any Secrecy. And you were much the funniest." After a moment's hesitation, she added, "And no, you weren't the nastiest of them—at least, not about Liv and me. Except maybe over Mr. Snuggles the topiary peacock."

Florence dropped on her bed again. "I'm not proud of what I did, okay? But it felt so cool when Secrecy came to me last summer and made me her successor, if you can understand that. I mean, *me*, out of all the people she could have picked, and when Emily and Grayson didn't want me to have anything to do with their silly school magazine. Secrecy said she could imagine me being better than she was, and then—"

"Wait a minute," I interrupted. "So there was another Secrecy last year?"

"Yes, I knew that," said Mia at once. "Until last year, all the posts were by the same person—it was only after that I could see the differences. Why did the first Secrecy give up the blog?"

"She left school." Florence had herself under control again. "But she didn't want to let the Tittle-Tattle blog die—it was kind of her baby, and she wanted someone else to go on with it. So we took the blog over, with all sorts of technical know-how—Secrecy's father set it up for us on a server that can't be hacked into, it's in Latvia or somewhere. Did you know that the website gets over eleven thousand hits a day?" I couldn't help seeing that she was really proud of that. "First only the students at Frognal read it, then the teachers, and then other schools in our part of town found out about it, but now we're known all over London—all over the world, really."

Oh God, now I really was sorry for her. I hadn't realized how much Florence had needed the blog for her ego. But she couldn't talk to anyone about it. Except . . .

"Who are *we*?" I inquired.

"Who's the first Secrecy?" asked Mia at the same time. "The original Secrecy?"

Florence looked up and managed a wry smile. "I thought you knew that, Private Detective Silver."

"No, I hadn't reached that part yet," Mia reluctantly admitted. "My inquiries were concentrated on the present Secrecy."

"And who's doing it now?" I was beginning to get impatient.

"There are two others, and I know only one of them," said Florence. "Pandora Porter-Peregrin. We often exchanged information and discussed subjects."

Mia nodded. "Pandora is the Secrecy who has something against Hazel Pritchard and her mother. She likes to criticize people's appearance. And best of all she liked writing intimate things about Persephone."

"Her own sister!" Poor Persephone! How awful to live under the same roof as someone who betrays your trust like . . . Hang on a moment! It was the same with me. I gave Florence a dark glance.

She looked down.

Lottie, still all confused, looked at her watch. "I think it's time we had that carrot cake. Carbohydrates are good for the nerves." As she left the room, we heard her murmuring, "If only I'd known, of course I'd have baked vanilla crescents."

"We ourselves don't know who the third Secrecy is," Florence went on before we could ask her. It was obviously doing her good to unburden herself like this at last. As if a dam had broken. And somehow or other the situation struck me as only too familiar.

"I even suspected Emily of leading a kind of journalistic double life, because the third Secrecy writes the fewest articles, but at the same time she's in charge in a way," Florence told us. It was all coming to light now. "She's the one who actually posts them online—and often she's made changes or added something, which would be typical of Emily, but that doesn't fit, because she'd never criticize herself like that. And that Secrecy was the one who first tracked down the scandals and affairs among the teaching staff, and Emily wouldn't have a clue about that kind of thing. No, she must be someone else."

"He," said Mia, relishing the look of astonishment in our eyes. "The third Secrecy is a he. And you were getting close to it, Florence. I had Emily on my own list of suspects for quite a while. But it's her brother, Sam."

"Oh no!" Sam, who was always telling people they should be ashamed of themselves—was Sam, the school's self-appointed guardian of morality, really Secrecy? Impossible! Yet when you thought about it, it fit. Sometimes Secrecy had sounded really priggish.

"Sam, is it?" growled Florence. "That little horror! I ought to have known—he was always pestering Emily and me. I was furious with the way he talked about poor Mrs. Lawrence." She glanced at me sideways. "And a few of the nasty things about you were his work, Liv. I swear they weren't all mine."

The door swung open, and Lottie tottered in with a tray of plates and cups, as well as a steaming teapot. The carrot cake took pride of place in the middle of the tray, and Lottie had quickly put the marzipan carrots she'd made in advance on the icing, which was still soft.

"Wait a minute," she said when she had put the tray down on the desk. "It's not usual with carrot cake, but I have some whipped cream downstairs, and it'll do us all good. Mia, you cut up the cake and share it out, Liv can pour the tea, and, Florence, blow your nose. I'll be back in a minute."

"She really does think her magic baking will solve all the world's problems," said Florence as Lottie went downstairs again. But she obediently took a tissue off her bedside table.

Mia stood up. "She's right. Her carrot cake has saved the day for me goodness knows how often." On her way to the desk, she accidentally kicked the cushion that she had swept to the floor under the bed.

"Watch out," said Florence in her best Boker-like voice, probably an inborn reflex. She seemed to feel embarrassed about it herself, because by way of explanation she added, "My mother embroidered that cushion. It's my favorite."

Mia knelt down and felt under the bedspread. "Yuck, it's ages since anyone swept up under here . . . oh." There was a soft rustle as she emerged again, holding two empty, transparent plastic bags.

"Do you . . . what are those?" asked Florence.

In silence, Mia handed me one of the bags and gave the other to Florence, who gazed at it, totally at a loss.

Marabou, sorted, black, six to ten centimeters. 100 g. Product of India, said the white sticker on the bag I was holding. I suddenly felt as if someone had grabbed me by the throat. "*Keep away from children under three years old*. Oh my God, Florence . . ."

"It was you in Grayson's room with the feathers," said Mia, and she sounded like a shocked little girl, not a bit like Private Detective Silver, who had just brought clear evidence to the light of day.

"What are you talking about? I've never seen these bags

before!" Florence was staring alternately at the plastic bags and Mia. Stammering, she tried to find an explanation. "It . . . it's someone from school trying to make me look as if I did that scary thing with the feathers." She looked at Mia. "Was it you? Did you put them under my bed so no one would suspect you?" She looked upset. "My father thought it was you at once. And you kicked my cushion under the bed yourself so that we'd find the plastic bags."

"Have you lost your marbles?" Mia tapped her forehead. "And I suppose I'm Secrecy too, am I?"

"No! I mean yes. Oh, shit!" Florence ran her fingers through her hair. "Why in heaven's name would I go scattering feathers around Grayson's room?"

"Well, to make it look like I'd been playing a stupid prank again," said Mia. "And because you're an underhand—"

I put a hand on her arm to keep her from going on. Okay, so it had taken me a full minute, but now I knew exactly what had happened. How could we have been so blind? It wasn't as if this was the first time!

"Livvy?" Mia was looking at me sideways. "What's the matter? Why have you suddenly gone so pale?"

"Florence can't help it. She doesn't remember scattering those feathers around—she did it in her sleep." I crumpled up the two plastic bags and got to my feet. And now, of all times, neither of the people I needed was here. Grayson was on his way to meet that Bloody Sword character in Islington, and on Wednesdays Henry always took Amy to little kids' swimming. "Please can I borrow your cell phone, Florence?" I looked around for it.

"No, you can't." Florence's lower lip was beginning to

tremble. "And I didn't do anything in my sleep. This is all nonsense. What are you getting at with—"

"Oh, for heaven's sake, let me use your damn phone!" I snapped at her. Ideas were whirling around in my mind, all mixed up, confused, and biting each other's tails. It was so logical, and yet . . . no . . . and how did the snake come into the picture? I really had to talk to Henry and Grayson, urgently. Together, maybe we could assemble the separate parts of the jigsaw puzzle into a pattern that made some kind of sense.

Florence seemed to realize that I was serious. She gave me her phone and looked at me uncertainly. "You have to believe me. I . . . ."

I brusquely waved her explanations away and looked for Henry's number in the contacts.

As the phone rang, something else occurred to me— something that we had entirely forgotten in all the uncertainty. "Who was the first Secrecy, Florence? The one who originally began the blog?"

Florence shrugged her shoulders. "I don't know if the name will mean anything to you. She took her final exams and left before you and Mia came to London. The girl who ended up in a psychiatric hospital." She sighed. "Anabel Scott. Arthur Hamilton's ex-girlfriend."

Anabel, then. Well, of all today's surprises, that was maybe the least surprising.

At the other end of the connection, I got not Henry himself but his voice mail. Damn it!

23

THE FIRST PERSON I saw when I stepped out into the corridor was Emily, and as usual, she was about the last person I wanted to meet. But today the sight of her made me really furious. She had the nerve to sit right beside Frightful Freddy as he guarded Grayson's dream door, and she was chewing a pencil and staring at a notepad on her knees with such concentration that she didn't notice my door, with the lizard knocker, closing behind me as I slowly came closer.

"Okay, the root of three million nine hundred and twelve thousand four hundred and eighty-four," she was muttering. "That would be one thousand nine hundred and seventy-eight. Correct?"

"I'm afraid I can't give you any information about that," squeaked Frightful Freddy.

I let my eyes wander down the corridor. Neither of the other two seemed to be here, although Grayson had actually gone to bed before me. After such a strenuous day, however, when so much had come to light, he would probably be in a phase of deep sleep for now, however anxious he felt on behalf of Florence. And to be honest, I didn't mind that; he had never been all that helpful to us in the dream corridors. His strengths lay elsewhere. Although I still doubted whether the admittedly sensational results of his dogged research could really save us, now that we knew Arthur was more than just a few steps ahead.

I couldn't find Florence's elegant reed-green door at once because it was no longer in its old place. But then I saw that it had moved closer to our doors, in fact much closer; it was now beside Mia's door, and right opposite Grayson's.

All the better: it would be easier to keep watch on her here. But I secretly hoped that at least tonight there'd be no need for that. After all that had happened today, surely Florence wouldn't get a wink of sleep and would be tossing and turning restlessly in bed. And if she wasn't asleep, then no one could get into her dreams and wreak havoc there.

Always supposing it wasn't far too late to stop that already.

We really should have known better—after all, as I had told myself before, it wasn't the first time. Or as Henry put it, "Still Arthur, then."

Yet again, Arthur had used his unpleasant tricks to get someone close to us under his control. Last winter it had been Mia—he had manipulated her in her sleep, and in the end he almost killed her—and this time he had picked Florence as his nocturnal puppet. Until now all she had done, at least so far as we could reconstruct it, was to put a feather in my hair, scatter two packets of them around Grayson's room, and switch on his ventilator, but she could just as well have been standing beside my bed armed with a knife instead of a feather, and anyone who knew Arthur was aware that he wasn't going to stop at harmless terrorist games with feathers.

Especially as he now had very different methods at his disposal. We'd been able to see what he was capable of in the cases of Mrs. Lawrence, Persephone, and poor Theo Ellis. For safety's sake, I had double-locked my bedroom door before I went to sleep.

I'd advised Mia to do the same, and for once she hadn't asked me why. She had been unusually quiet altogether after our discovery. Unlike Florence, who was understandably much upset by the idea that she'd done extraordinary things in her sleep. Once she had overcome the denial phase ("I'd never do a thing like that!"), she had burst into tears again—and not even Lottie's whipped cream could cheer her up.

"It's true!" Florence had sobbed with her face buried in her hands. "I had those strange dreams . . . and the soles of my feet were dirty the next morning. Does that mean I'm losing my mind? Scattering feathers—who'd think up a thing like that?"

I could have told her, of course, but it would only have confused her even more. And it would have scared her to death. As things were, she was absolutely shattered, and she'd let Lottie take her in her arms without resisting.

"Is this burnout or something? Have I been studying too hard?" she said between two sobs. "I don't want to end up in a psychiatric hospital."

"You won't." Lottie had stroked her hair comfortingly. "A lot of people walk in their sleep—maybe there's a water vein under this house, or something. Remember the odd way Mia behaved in January. She nearly jumped out of the window of my room! And I assure you she's not lost her mind, not a bit of it!"

In fact, Florence had cast Mia a glance suggesting that she wasn't so sure of that, but at least she had stopped crying.

I envied her a little because believing you had burnout was a thousand times better than being confronted with the truth, as Henry, Grayson, and I had been. While you could deal with burnout by going for a nice healthy stay by the seaside, there was obviously no anti-Arthur treatment. He had fooled us as easily as if we'd been in elementary school, which made us feel furious and helpless at the same time. Grayson, in particular, was bitterly disappointed.

Yet his meeting with BloodySword66, a.k.a. Harry Triggs, had exceeded all his expectations. True, Grayson had had to sacrifice his life-size battle droid robot from *Star Wars: Episode I* (the way he talked about it, you'd have thought it was his own child), but in exchange he had the ultimate proof that Anabel's demon didn't exist: an old, rather dusty notebook, its pages scribbled all over in ballpoint pen, and bearing bloodred seals. It didn't look exactly like Anabel's alleged heirloom, the notebook that went up in flames in the cemetery, but it was extremely like it.

And as Grayson informed us, it came into the same category as the long Celtic knife (handmade carbon steel, with the blade riveted to a hardwood handle), and the drinking horn, real horn with a leather holder; they were only stage props. The book was one of several that were supposed to be collections of spells and incantations, laboriously handwritten by two unemployed nerds with bad breath and a peculiar hobby. Grayson had borne it bravely when BloodySword66 took accessory after accessory out of a chest of drawers, while he indulged in reminiscences of the old and evidently glorious role-playing days he had spent in Liverpool with his friend Timothy, the roofer and later demon-hunting guru of a sect.

Swordy wasn't so keen to talk about the breakup of their friendship or how he had discovered from the newspapers that his former role-playing buddy had the deaths of several people on his conscience. But it was a fact that the two of them had thought up violent fantasy stories together and imagined playing them out. Then their ways parted. Harry Triggs began writing the stories down in the form of novels, but after his *Night of the Bloody Something-or-other* and three other pioneering works had been turned down by twenty-seven publishing firms, and then met with only a lukewarm response on the Internet, he abandoned his literary ambitions and had been working as an aide in a residential home ever since.

His friend the roofer, on the other hand, had started hearing voices and thinking he was one of the Elect. He'd hopelessly confused fantasy and reality, gathered some people around him, and then obviously presented one of those old notebooks based on role-playing as an ancient work of wisdom.

We didn't know exactly how the guru's notebook had ended up in Anabel's hands. But it was certain that we could finally prove to Anabel that BloodySword66's version, for which Grayson had sacrificed his droid (and the author had insisted on signing his book in return), was clear evidence that her notion of conjuring up demons was all smoke and mirrors, and she owed her childhood trauma to a crazy roofer.

The stupid thing was that we hadn't yet been able to show Anabel the notebook and thus prove that she was deluded, because today of all days she wasn't at home. Grayson had put the notebook through her door and had left her several messages by e-mail, but she hadn't replied by the time he went to sleep. Now it was up to her to draw her own conclusions. If she was in any position to do so.

So far as the details went, we ourselves were groping in the dark. Even now, as I stared alternately at Florence's door and Emily, ideas were going around and around in my head. Had Arthur staged the shower of feathers in our house just to make us think that Anabel's demon really existed again? Or had he wanted to cast suspicion on Anabel herself with what he did?

The feathers had always turned up after we met Anabel in the corridor. Along with the darkness and the cold. Had Arthur been following Anabel in secret and providing special effects? It wouldn't have been difficult for him to act the demon for Anabel in the corridor.

But why? Well, of course, so that Anabel would put her outstanding abilities in—well, let's call it dream magic—at the disposal of the demon, in other words Arthur. There were a few loopholes in that theory, however. One was the snake. If it was Arthur who was acting as the demon for Anabel's benefit, he would hardly have told her to leave a venomous snake in his own locker, would he?

"You horrible, wretched creature!" Emily's voice brought me out of my thoughts. At first I thought she meant me, but it was just that she had lost patience with Frightful Freddy. "Tell me the whole mathematical problem now," she demanded angrily. "Slowly and clearly, you great fat brute."

Freddy politely lowered his beak. I didn't understand why Grayson hadn't at least made him look a little more ferocious. "Add the year of Prince William's birth to five thousand and thirty-nine, and the root of zero point six two five, the root of three million nine hundred and twelve thousand, four hundred and eighty-four, plus the root of one hundred and eleven thousand five hundred and fifty-six, and multiply the result by four. Reverse it, and you will find what you have lost."

"Prince William's birthday." Emily scribbled something on her notepad. "I expect Grayson thinks I won't know that because I'm not interested in all that royalty stuff, but as it happens I have a memory like a . . ."

"Horse?" I suggested.

Emily looked up but didn't seem particularly surprised. "You again" was all she said, groaning.

Well, if anyone had a right to be here, it was me.

"Having a nice dream?" I asked.

"Push off, and maybe I will," said Emily. "And for your information, horses have an excellent memory. I bet my horse, Conquest of Paradise, has a higher IQ than you." She bent over her notepad again. "I bet *you* couldn't work out the root of one hundred and eleven thousand five hundred and fifty-five in your head."

"Why doesn't your horse use a calculator?"

"Because calculators don't work here," said Emily without looking up. "Or at least, only as well as I can work things out for myself. Because this labyrinth of doors is in my head! Everything you see here, everything that goes on here is part of my subconscious mind."

Well, an interesting theory, anyway. "So right now we are in *your* head?"

Emily nodded. "In my dream, to be more precise." Now she looked at me again. "You're a projection of my subconscious."

"Right. Okay," I said. "Then ask your subconscious if you're going to sit around here much longer."

Emily shrugged. "Anyway, what does time mean here?"

"Has anyone gone in there, or come out?" I pointed to Florence's door.

"There? No," said Emily.

That was all right, then. "And the door didn't just open of its own accord?" I asked, to be on the safe side.

"Not that I know of," said Emily. "Now, be quiet. I have to work out this sum."

"I don't—" I cleared my throat. "I mean, your subconscious doesn't see why you keep trying to get into Grayson's dream if all this is just going on inside your head."

"Because I want to know what my subconscious has to tell me about Grayson and myself. . . . Oh, you can't follow that, it's on a high level of psychology. Now do go away and leave me to do my calculations in peace. We get eight thousand nine hundred and ninety-nine plus three hundred and thirty-four plus zero point seven five . . . times four . . ."

"If you want to know something about yourself and Grayson, why not just ask me?" I said. "First, the two of you aren't meant for each other. Second, he's delighted to be rid of you. Third—"

"Shut up!" said Emily.

I wasn't to be deterred. "But hey, your subconscious would like to tell you a few difficult truths. For instance, third, you need to put in some hard work on your own character if you—"

"I said shut up!" Obviously she didn't seem to think much

of the advice of her own subconscious. She tried to concentrate on her arithmetic again.

Okay, then she could have it straight.

"Your horrible little brother is Secrecy," I said.

"What?" Emily lowered her pencil and looked at me, frowning. "Sam is Secrecy?"

"Didn't you know?"

Emily shook her head. "No. Of course not. Or well . . . somehow I did, or you wouldn't be able to say so to me now."

"Exactly! Seeing that we're here in your head, and you subconsciously realized ages ago that it was your brother writing all those nasty comments, not stopping short even at you." Here I quoted from memory. "*Reflexx!* The school magazine that should really be called *Reflux*, because it's so boring and toffee-nosed, like the girl who's its editor in chief."

Emily looked genuinely shocked. Or more precisely, totally shattered. "Sam is Secrecy?" she repeated quietly. "My little Sam? But he would never say I was . . . I wish you hadn't told me that."

"And I wish you'd stop poking around in your subconscious," I retorted. I couldn't stop it now, even if I did feel sorry for Emily. I wanted her to leave this corridor once and for all. "Or I'll be revealing more unedifying truths every day. Truths from which your subconscious would really like to protect you, but that's not going to work if you go rooting about so mercilessly in your own depths, bringing stuff to the light of day when it was meant to be forgotten in the darkness." Hmm, I didn't think much of my own metaphors. I hoped Emily's inner editor in chief would let them pass. "Why do you think there are all these doors? Only to keep you from seeing what might endanger your physical and psychological well-being." I was laying it on quite thick now. "You should never have come into this corridor . . . into the labyrinth of your brain. And deep down inside, you know that."

Emily looked a little unsure of herself. "But the truth never hurt anyone," she murmured.

"Oh, didn't it, though!" I tried to lend my words a little more emphasis by sending a strong gust of wind blowing down the corridor and sweeping the hair back from Emily's forehead. Now I had her full attention.

"All the truths you're going to dig up here will not only make you unhappy and lonely, they will slowly but surely drive you to madness," I said firmly. Leaning a little way forward, I whispered in a confidential tone, "Admit it—right now you feel you're on the verge of a nervous breakdown, because everything here is more than you can grasp. You're starting to doubt your own reason, and that's only the beginning. The end will be a psychiatric hospital," I added in a sepulchral voice.

To my relief, Emily had stopped contradicting me. "I really do sometimes feel afraid of losing my mind. Because I know for a fact that I'm only dreaming this, but all the same it feels so real . . . that's to say, it can all be logically explained, but never mind how much I read about it and think about it, new puzzles are always coming up, if you see what I mean."

Oh yes, I saw what she meant very well. She had no idea how well. "The brain is a complex organ," I said. "And if you want to save yours from collapsing because you'd like to take your final exams, study at university, and start a family, instead of moldering away in a nuthouse, go back through your door and never come here again."

"People don't use terms like nuthouse anymore," Emily primly put me right.

I shrugged. "Sorry, I'm only a part of your subconscious."

"I know, I know," said Emily. "And I'm afraid you're right." She stood up. "I'd better not come here anymore. I never liked it much, anyway. My brain has kept presenting me with people and animals here that I can't stand in real life. Apart from Grayson, that is. I hate leopards, I hate you, and I hate bats. I can't abide your know-it-all little sister, and Arthur Hamilton is the greatest show-off in the world. Closely followed by Henry Harper, who's shockingly lazy but always gets top grades because the teachers think he's some kind of genius, and they fall for the unfortunate-childhood line."

Looking past me, she made a face and added, "I could puke when I see him strolling along like that, so casually, with a pseudo-cool grin, and his hands in his pockets."

I turned abruptly.

"Always nice to see you, Emily," said Henry. For he was indeed strolling along, hands in his jeans pockets, and so casually that it made my heart beat a little faster. Not that his grin was pseudo-cool; it looked rather strained.

"Weren't you going to keep watch on Florence's door?" he asked me.

"I have been. While Emily and I had a little conversation," I said, entirely forgetting that Emily had said something that I wanted to ask about. Something to do with bats.

"I was just going." Emily put her pencil behind her ear.

"Forever," I said. And because Henry frowned instead of congratulating me on getting Emily out of our corridor, I added quickly, "Florence is okay, don't worry. She'll prob-

ably have a sleepless night. And Arthur himself may have better things to do than—"

"Stop!" Henry put a finger to his lips. "Look, before you
tell me anything at all here that isn't meant for all and sundry, you'd better check that I'm the person I say I am."

"The person you say you . . . Oh, I get it. You mean
Arthur could be up to his shape-changing tricks again." It was
true, I hadn't thought of that. "Then maybe this isn't Emily
after all. . . . Oh, no, she is. Even Arthur couldn't have imi-
tated her so well." I grinned, while Emily looked at us disapprovingly. Her unconscious was obviously giving her a hard
time.

"That's not very funny, Liv," said Henry, unusually serious. "I thought you saw how serious this situation is."

Yes, I did. But it wasn't going to help us against Arthur
if we all panicked.

"Ask me something that only Henry can know," Henry
told me.

"Okay." I sighed. "What was the name of the dog—not
the chow, the other one—that I used to take for walks in
South Africa?"

"Sir Barksalot." Reluctantly, Henry shook his head. "But
Arthur could know that, too, if he'd been eavesdropping
on us last night."

"Right . . . but if you think of it, then he could have eaves-
dropped on just about anything. . . . So kiss me! Then I'll
know at once if it's you."

"Hmm," said Henry, and his features relaxed a little. "That
really is a clever method. And at the same time I can check
if you're really you."

But before we could start finding out, Emily put her oar

in, obviously feeling neglected. "I hope you're not about to start kissing here! What's my subconscious going to say about that?" She went on fretfully, "And what was all that about Arthur and Florence? I mean, what do all these characters stand for? I see them walking around, but I don't get the point. Is there some symbolic significance for that damn vulture letting Arthur into Grayson's dream, for instance, but keeping me out? And can't you explain it simply? I'm much more sensitive to words than images."

What had she just said? My mouth was suddenly dry as dust.

Henry was obviously thinking the same as me. He grabbed Emily's arm. "Hang on a moment—you mean Arthur went into Grayson's dream? Can you remember roughly when that was?"

Emily shrugged again and shook off Henry's hand. "Not long ago," she said. "Before you two turned up. And he didn't wait for that stupid stone vulture to ask his mathematical question, he just whispered the answer straight into its ear. Giving me a dirty grin. Whatever that means—from the symbolic viewpoint."

She was going on, but Henry and I had stopped listening. We were staring at each other, horrified.

"So it's begun," whispered Henry.

24

OKAY. DON'T PANIC. I thought. Right now the most important thing was to keep calm and . . .

"We have to get in there!" I shouted at Henry.

He seemed to be in as much of a panic as I was. "You could wake, and then wake Grayson . . . but maybe it's too late already, and he . . . Did you lock your door as I suggested?"

"Yes." I was near tears. "What are we going to do now?"

Henry was rattling Grayson's door. "Do you have some personal item of Grayson's with you? Because today, of all days, it so happens that I don't."

"Add the year of Prince William's birth to five thousand and thirty-nine, and the root of zero point six two five . . . ," Freddy began reciting.

"I'm wearing one of his old T-shirts," I shouted. "But damn it, I can't do this sort of mental arithmetic in my head!"

"Too bad," said Emily with a touch of malice. "If you'd only left me alone, I might be able to tell you the answer now."

". . . and multiply the result by four. Reverse it, and you will find what you have lost," Freddy finished.

"LOVE!" I shouted. "I mean *LIEBE*!"

Freddy shook his head. Henry looked inquiringly at me.

"It's a word made up of the letters on a calculator," I hastily explained.

"Er—Liv, calculators are those things with numbers on them," said Emily. "You're more likely to find letters in books."

"Oh, shut up and push off!" I hissed at her, flinging a few more random words at Freddy. "SEE! SILL! LIES."

"What on earth?" murmured Emily, but when we both looked angrily at her, she finally went off down the corridor, holding her notepad, and disappeared around the corner, where we heard her door latch. I had no time to call, "See you soon—I don't hope!" after her, I was feverishly trying to make words out of numbers that look a bit like letters if you turn them upside down. But Freddy kept shaking his head at all my suggestions. "Oh, hell, I forgot *G*—that looks a bit like a nine upside down. *Sigil* . . . and I left out *O* entirely, *igloo* . . ."

"Soul," said Henry. "*Seele* in German."

And as I stared at him in surprise, Freddy solemnly squeaked, "You may both enter."

I turned the doorknob left. This time it worked. I gave Henry an admiring look. "Fantastic! How did you jump to it so quickly?"

"Because of *you will find what you have lost*," he said, quoting Frightful Freddy.

"You're a genius, never mind what Emily—"

"Shh." Henry put a finger to his lips. He had cautiously opened the door a little wider, but now he hesitated. "Do we have an actual plan?" he whispered.

No, we didn't. But now it simply had to work without one. I straightened my shoulders and stood tall. To give us courage, I picked the first proverb from Mr. Wu's large collection that came to mind. "Even the darkest cloud has a silver lining," I said firmly. It suited the situation rather well—I hoped.

We stole through the doorway as quietly as possible and cautiously closed the door behind us.

I saw at once that we had landed in the school library, between two bookcases in the Natural Sciences section. That was typical of Grayson—he often dreamed of school, usually only too realistically. We found him farther away, at one of the tables, where he had a whole pile of books stacked up in front of him and was leafing through one of them. Miss Cooper, the friendly little librarian, was busy right beside us sorting books on a trolley full of them and putting them back on the shelves. The peaceful, contemplative silence that I liked so much in libraries reigned, and I imagined that I could even pick up the smell of books. The only thing to show that this was a dream was the parrot in a cage standing beside Grayson, and looking very like the parrot in Mrs. Honeycutt's room.

There weren't many other people using the library, but one of them was—Mia. She was sitting cross-legged at the next table, with a little silver princess coronet on her head, and seemed to be watching Grayson as he read.

Henry and I exchanged a quick glance. "Do you think that's Arthur?" asked Henry in an undertone, and I nodded. Arthur liked to shelter behind someone familiar—and somehow the coronet fitted, too, from a symbolic viewpoint.

"Shh! Whispering makes a noise too," Miss Cooper told us, just as she always did in real life. "If you want to talk, go somewhere else. People come here to study." She put a copy of *The Molecular Basis of Genetics* back on its shelf, looked past us to the door that we had just come through, and a smile briefly crossed her face.

"We must do away with that, of course," she said, waving her hand and making a bookshelf in front of the door disappear. "Remember, the first rule of fully functioning BPID is the dream door must not be in the dreamer's field of vision." Her smile was wider. "Not that it would make any difference now—I fixed it some time back. You're too late!"

And then, all of a sudden, it wasn't dark-haired little Miss Cooper standing in front of us, but Arthur, tall and blond and in a horrible way extremely handsome. I felt my heart sink. Arthur. As usual, it was Arthur.

"So what's BPID?" asked Henry. I could hear the frustration in his voice.

"Behavioral Programming in Dreams, Arthur Hamilton's patent method," Arthur willingly replied. "At least until I can think of a better name for it." He followed my glance over to Grayson and Mia, and grinned. "Don't worry, he can't hear us. I installed an energy field over there to be on the safe side. So you can shout at me if you feel like it."

When we didn't, he went on, in high good humor, "Like I said, the exciting part of this dream is over. When I arrived, Mr. Fourley was just telling Grayson that he'd failed his chemistry exam—isn't it funny that he's always failing in his dreams? Anyway, I've programmed something nice into him, which will make him—well, I'd rather not tell you yet. Let's keep it as a surprise for you too." He looked at me with his head to one side. "Although for you, Liv, it will be a short and rather painful surprise."

Something flashed in Henry's eyes. His hands clenched into fists, and for a moment I imagined I saw the air between us flickering. Then, however, he only asked wearily, and sounding as resigned as I felt, "Why, Arthur? Why?"

"Why?" Arthur repeated. The good humor left his face like a mask slipping off. Sheer fury took its place. "Are you seriously asking that? After all these weeks when you had nothing but hatred and contempt for me, all these weeks when I was positively begging you to think of our old friendship! Weeks when I was sparing you all out of pure sentimentality . . . it took me far too long to realize that you're just not worth it. But when I nearly died, when I was lying in the hospital pumped full of snake venom and the serum of the antidote, the scales finally fell from my eyes." They were certainly looking daggers at us.

"But the snake wasn't our doing," I said.

"I know that," he snapped. "All the same, I could have died, and neither Henry nor Grayson was interested. They didn't even send a message to ask how I was doing."

"And they'd have been dancing on your grave if that snake had done a better job," said Henry.

Arthur's nostrils distended. He was about to say something, but at that moment Mrs. Honeycutt's parrot screeched, "Nothing is for free, not even death."

"Oh, you've done away with my energy field." Arthur turned to Grayson and Mia, who hadn't moved from the spot. Only the parrot seemed to be rather restless. It was beating its wings and squawking "Death! Death!" as if Grayson's subconscious mind was trying to say something to him, to deliver a message. It almost broke my heart.

"Grayson!" I pushed past Arthur, expecting to come up against a new energy field at any moment. Henry followed me.

"It's sweet that you're so full of concern for Liv's future murderer," was all Arthur said. "I already told you, you're too late. So far as I'm concerned, you're welcome to tell Grayson that he's dreaming, and he's a victim of BPID. Wake him and tell him everything—it won't make any difference. I can activate him anytime I like."

"Not if I kill you first," growled Henry, but it sounded desperate rather than really threatening.

Reluctantly, Grayson looked up from his book. "You lot—this is a library! And I have to study. I've already failed chemistry, so at least I must get a good grade in biology."

"Yes," Mia agreed. "Or he can say good-bye to studying medicine at Oxford."

And the parrot squawked, "Without hard work you're just a jerk!"

"Exactly. And life won't reward you if you can't keep up." Arthur leaned back against a bookcase, making a volume fall out on the floor. "Sweet dreams, eh? Very laudable, like Grayson himself. How astonished everyone will be to hear that he's killed his own stepsister. And in such a monstrous way at that." He gurgled with amusement, while the book that had dropped from the shelf, in defiance of all the laws of gravity, slid slowly over the floor until it came to rest in front of the toes of my shoes.

I dropped on the chair beside Grayson, feeling more helpless than ever before in my life. Henry was still standing beside the table, staring indecisively at Arthur. A kind of globe of light was flickering back and forth between the palms of his hands, made of the same material as he used to install glittering energy fields in the corridor. But what use would it be to fire off energy light at Arthur? However much Henry drew on the power of his imagination, it was too late.

Arthur had won long ago.

"Like I said—you can't do anything now," he confirmed, as if he had read my thoughts. "BPID can't be reversed. Grayson can be prevented from becoming a murderer only if—well, if he kills himself first. It would still make him a suicide, a murderer of himself." He favored Grayson with an almost affectionate smile. "It would be just like him to do a thing like that."

Oh God, yes. It really would. "You . . . you . . . ," I stammered, and then fell silent again. There wasn't even a term of abuse bad enough for Arthur.

"Brilliant bastard?" he prompted me, with a broad grin.

"Keep quiet," said Grayson, annoyed. "Can't you quarrel somewhere else?"

"That's right. The chandelier is beginning to clink with all your noise," said Mia, pointing to the ceiling. The real school library had only plain neon tube lighting, but here there was an opulent chandelier that looked somehow familiar to me. Mia uncrossed her legs and let them dangle. "I think your hair looks great," she told Arthur.

"Thanks, princess." He made that gurgling sound again. Another book came off the shelf close to his head. This time it didn't drop to the floor but turned in the air to show us its cover. The title stood out, in huge letters, against a black background. It said *Don't Worry*, which in view of the situation I thought especially cynical.

Arthur took no notice of the way the bookshelf behind

him had come to life. He had dug his hands into his jeans pockets in a relaxed way and was watching a flock of blue butterflies that had emerged from nowhere and were disappearing into the Historical Novels section again, leaving no trace behind. "Then I'll leave you alone in your misery," he said with satisfaction. "You don't have much time left to spend together, and I have a date with my ex-girlfriend. I wouldn't like to keep her waiting. Unlike you, she's still an important part of my plans."

"Arthur, please! Let's talk." Henry took a step forward. "Surely you can't really want—"

"My former best friend Grayson to kill the girl my former best friend Henry loves?" Arthur interrupted him. The book beside his head changed the color of its cover, and the title also changed. It now said *Let Him Go*.

"Do I want to ruin your lives forever?" asked Arthur again, looking Henry's way. "Yes, I do, old friend. That's exactly what I want. So spare yourself begging and pleading. We could have conquered the world together, but you declared war on me, and now you must live with the consequences."

There was more clinking up in the chandelier, and when I looked, I saw a monkey swinging from it. It was playing with a pearl necklace and put its tongue out at me. I was getting irritated. And suddenly I knew why that chandelier seemed so familiar to me. Its exact counterpart hung in Great-Aunt Gertrude's living room. But minus the monkey. What in heaven's name . . . ?

"If we promise—" Henry began, but Arthur didn't let him say any more.

"You want to negotiate?" he asked coldly. "Too bad. No

luck. You have nothing left to offer me—because now I know what your friendship is worth. Absolutely nothing. So sorry, but I'll be conquering the world without you." He took his hands out of his pockets and strolled over to the bookshelf behind which the door to the corridor was hidden.

"Don't hold up a traveler," screeched the parrot, but neither Henry nor Arthur took any notice of it. Grayson was staring at his book as if hypnotized, anyway.

"I'll kill you first," said Henry.

"You're repeating yourself, old friend." Arthur yawned. "Go on, then, kill me. Run me down in a car, burn the roof over my head, slit my throat. That won't change anything, except of course that you'll spend the rest of your life behind bars." He waved the bookshelf away, and Grayson's door came into view behind it. "It's like this: the phrase I've programmed to activate Grayson isn't the most unusual one in the world. To be precise, it's very common indeed. Sooner or later—and my bet is that it will be sooner—someone will say it in front of Grayson, whether I'm still alive or not, and then . . ." He spread his arms regretfully, and the next moment he disappeared through the doorway without another word to us.

25

"OH GOD. I thought he was never going to leave!" Mia snatched the coronet off her head and jumped up from the table.

Grayson groaned. "And I thought he was going to notice something any moment. There aren't normally any butterflies flying around in my dreams, and no monkeys either."

"But the parrot needed a bit of company." Mia was grinning. Then she looked at Henry and me, shaking her head. "All that everlasting talking! Didn't you understand our messages?"

Henry and I were staring at each other, and for once Henry seemed as slow to catch on as I was. "What messages?" he asked, while I took Grayson's arm and shook it hard.

"Are you by any chance *awake*?"

"No, Liv, I'm not awake, I'm dreaming," he replied, sounding annoyed. "But I'm well aware that I'm dreaming, if that's what you meant."

"Oh my God." I burst into tears. Only now did I realize

that I'd been wanting to do that very thing all the time. "Arthur has programmed you, Grayson. He's—"

"No, he hasn't," Grayson interrupted me. "I mean, yes, he tried, but when he came in, I was already on my way out to the corridor. It was quite a strain making him think he'd landed in one of my dreams. But Mia helped." He smiled at her. "You were terrific. Thanks!"

"You're welcome," said Mia, smiling back. "It was pure luck that I know my way around the school library so well. And that tonight I just happened to . . . er, have borrowed your watch by chance. That way I could follow Arthur inconspicuously when I saw him disappear into your dream."

"But . . ." I didn't understand any of this.

"Are you sure Arthur's programming didn't work?" Henry was shaking Grayson's other arm. "He said it couldn't be reversed."

"I'm fine." Grayson shook off our hands and stood up. "Arthur's patent method of ruining people's lives works only in the genuine REM phase, when his victim has no idea what's going on. But try it if you like, and see what happens when you say what's supposed to set my programming off. The phrase is: *Have you had your hair cut?*" He snorted scornfully.

"Oh my God," I whispered. It was true—sooner or later someone was bound to ask Grayson that. "And then what would have happened?"

He exchanged a quick look with Henry. "Believe me, Liv, you don't want to know."

"He's right," said Mia, shuddering. "Arthur has a really evil imagination." She turned to me. "Livvy, stop crying." She handed me a tissue, and I blew my nose, although that's not really necessary in a dream. But it felt kind of comforting.

The monkey was swinging back and forth from the chandelier overhead, squealing excitedly.

"Is that Shiva?" I asked. That was the name we'd given the monkey that we used to feed on our terrace in Hyderabad.

"Of course it's Shiva!" Mia looked reproachfully at me. "And you haven't even noticed that he's wearing the pearl necklace Mom lost in South Africa. There's a photo of Papa on the book at your feet, and the title of the book is *All's Well*. How much clearer did I have to be? Great-Aunt Gertrude's chandelier, the Californian butterflies, the picture of our old Nissan Pathfinder . . . how could Grayson be dreaming of things he's never seen?"

My head was in confusion. "Mia—how come you know about all this? Who told you about this place, and everything? I always thought . . ."

Mia was looking almost insulted. "Oh, honestly—as if I hadn't noticed something fishy about your story of my sleepwalking!" She shook her head. "And that night in the kitchen, after I nearly jumped through the open window, and Lottie baked vanilla crescents—even a deaf person would have overheard what you were whispering. So I knew Arthur was behind it, and from then on it was pure research work."

Henry dropped a kiss on Mia's cheek. "I was in favor of telling you," he said, "but Grayson and Livvy wanted to protect you. Seems like you have a natural talent."

Mia tried to look modest and failed miserably. "Well, yes! It did take me a little time to catch on to the bit about personal items but then . . ." She lightly punched my arm. "Where do you think I found all those clues to the identity of Secrecy?

The e-mail addresses, the passwords—did you think I'd joined the ranks of computer hackers, Livvy?"

For once, I was left speechless.

"You know who Secrecy is?" asked Henry, taken aback, and it occurred to me that in all the excitement about Florence and the feathers, I'd forgotten to tell Grayson and Henry about the Secrecy developments. But maybe it would be better for Florence to do that herself. After all, there'd been equally intimate comments on Grayson and Henry in the Tittle-Tattle blog—she certainly had some explaining to do.

"I know a good deal," said Mia evasively. "But there are still a few gaps I have to fill in. For instance, what exactly was going on between you, Arthur, Anabel, and her demon? And was Arthur behind what Theo Ellis did? And why is Emily always hanging around outside Grayson's door in the corridor, as if the whole place belongs to her? Sometimes she'd only let me go past if I sent a flock of bats to pester her. . . ."

Henry and I laughed, and so did Mia. Even the parrot joined in.

"Listen, everyone!" Grayson, who had been wandering up and down between the library tables, looked at us, frowning. Our laughter died away. "To hear you, anyone would think it was all behind us. This isn't a victory celebration! Next time we may not be so lucky, don't you realize that? Arthur's not about to let go, and we now know that he won't shrink from anything."

I swallowed. Quite right. There was nothing to laugh about.

Henry also bit his lip. "I was just so relieved that . . . ," he murmured. He turned to Grayson's door for a moment and then looked at me. "Grayson is right. It's not over yet."

"But over for tonight at least?" I asked hopefully. "We can think again tomorrow. An idea will occur to us, we'll make a plan, and . . ."

Henry shook his head. "It will never be over. At this moment, Arthur is out there meeting Anabel."

"And heaven help us if those two are working together." Grayson hit a bookshelf with his fist. "It's not fair! I found out so much, and will it all have been for nothing?"

"No. No, it won't." Henry was suddenly looking very determined. A few steps took him to the door. "I'm going out there now to end it once and for all!"

"Wait!" I jumped up. "I'm coming with you. You have a plan, don't you?"

Henry smiled at me. "More of an idea, and I'm not sure it will work. But you can't come with me, Liv," he added immediately. "Not this time. I can only do it without you if . . ."

His sentence hung in the air, unfinished, and then, without more warning, he pushed the door open and strode out into the corridor.

I sprinted straight after him, but the door closed right in front of my face and I collided with a sparkling energy field.

"I don't believe it!" I stamped my foot. Henry was certainly on a learning curve. This time he had tricked me. Furiously, I turned to the other two. "Do you understand what this is all about? What's he going to do that he says can only be done on his own? And why doesn't he simply tell us what his idea is? Why this ego trip all of a sudden?"

Grayson just shook his head, baffled, and Mia said, "It'll be something dangerous, anyway."

Exactly. That's why I was so annoyed.

"I hate it when he does this!" I tried reaching for the

doorknob through the energy field, but I was flung a couple feet back. "This obsession with protecting me really gets me down. I've saved him at least as often as he's saved me, and he ought to know me better by now. And I didn't leave him alone in Mrs. Honeycutt's sister's dream . . . Oh!" Realization went through me like lightning, and all at once I knew what Henry was trying to do.

And yes, it was only an idea—but a brilliant one.

If we could somehow lure Arthur into Muriel's dream and make sure he couldn't get out again, he was bound to wake up while he was still in it. And next time he fell asleep and dreamed he would land right back there, just as I had done. Then, because he'd have no idea whose dream it was, he would be stuck—again, just as I had been stuck. He'd be visiting it night after night for the rest of his life. He would never again . . .

"Livvy?" Mia and Grayson were looking at me with a question in their eyes, and I tried to tell them, in as few words as possible, about Muriel's dream. Neither of them looked as if they understood much of what I was saying, although when I had finished, Henry's energy field was considerably weaker than before. But then it wouldn't have stood up to my determination, anyway.

"I'm going out there now." Without even looking at it, I made the energy field of glittering dust motes collapse. "I'm going after him. And I want you to keep watch and look out for Florence—only to be on the safe side."

Mia had risen to her feet, and she clicked her tongue in annoyance. "Oh, sure, we'll look after the old folk, the women, and the children, while you and Henry save the world—you're in the wrong movie, big sister! If you think

I'm going to sit around all night biting my nails and waiting for you, you have another think coming."

"Take her with you," said Grayson too. "She's really good. The mere way she imagines that boy . . ." He pointed to a student sitting at the back of the library, alternately chewing his pencil and scribbling something in an exercise book. Unless I was much mistaken, it was Gil Walker. Like the other visitors to the library with walk-on parts in this dream, he hadn't noticed any of what had gone on. "She kitted him out with amazing authenticity, and even though she was sitting with her back to him, he put his pencil up his nostril and picked his nose. . . ."

"At least one person appreciates my skills." Mia joined me at the door and linked arms with me. "Come on, Livvy, pull yourself together! We're going to help Henry! We're going to save the world!"

"But we don't know . . ." I sighed. "All right. But you must promise me, whatever you do, don't go into Muriel's wool shop."

"It doesn't sound all that interesting. I promise." Mia raised her free hand as if swearing an oath.

"And then I'll wake up," said Grayson.

I was on the point of running back to give him a hug, but instead I just said, "I'm glad you're not going to be my murderer."

He smiled. "Me too," he said. "I'd never have dared to have my hair cut again."

All was quiet out in the corridor, which stretched ahead in the twilight to infinity, door beside door beside door, and every time it branched off, it led to another endless corridor, crisscrossed in its own turn by countless other corridors, branching off into more endless corridors. . . . All of a sudden our prospects of tracking Arthur down anywhere here seemed hopeless. When he'd said he had a date with Anabel, had he meant a real meeting, or was he only going to lie in wait for her pretending to be the demon again? He'd probably often done that before; he must have enjoyed whispering things to her in his demonic voice, making winged shapes appear on the walls, and slowly but surely driving her back into her delusions.

Where were we to start searching? At Anabel's Hello Kitty door? Where had Henry gone in looking for the two of them?

At that moment the light in the corridor turned very bright, and at almost the same time we heard the echo of an explosion some way off. Or at least, that was what it sounded like. We even felt the blast.

"It came from over there." Mia pointed down the corridor to where it turned just after Mrs. Cook's door, and without any more discussion, we set off. Mia had turned into a bat and shot around the corner fast as an arrow.

In my jaguar shape, I could hardly keep up with her.

Another flash of light showed us the way, and it looked as if it were leading us straight into the corridor with Mrs. Honeycutt's door in it. We heard voices from that direction, and when we were nearly there, we could also hear Arthur's mocking laughter.

I slowed down before reaching the last turn and peered cautiously around the corner. Mia was fluttering somewhere overhead.

Arthur, with his hair very untidy, was standing in the middle of the corridor, right in front of Mrs. Honeycutt's door.

There was no sign of Henry. But obviously he was somewhere here, because Arthur, his arms outspread, was turning on his own axis, looking for him. "Henry!" he called. "What's the idea?" His face and the palms of his hands looked sooty, as if he'd just been fighting his way out of a burning house. "Stop it. Are we going to spend all night showing each other how good at this we are? Or is that why you lured me here?" He pointed to Mrs. Honeycutt's door. "Is there something in your dream of private meetings that you think might somehow help you?"

Of course—Arthur knew we had been meeting here. He'd probably observed us in secret all this time. And it must have been Arthur who recently created that sinister darkness to haunt me.

My heart sank. Was he really still a step ahead of us?

"*Lured* you here?" said Henry sarcastically. He had materialized out of nowhere and was leaning back against Mrs. Honeycutt's door. Unlike Arthur, he didn't look at all the worse for wear. "I'd say I *forced* you to come here, wouldn't you?"

Arthur shrugged. "Whatever you like. Yes, yes, you're really good, Henry. Go on, blow everything here sky-high if that's what you need for your ego trip. But that doesn't alter the outcome as a whole." He stared at Henry with narrowed eyes. "Why don't you understand? If what I can do to Liv isn't enough for you, I'll sort someone else out next time. Your little sister, for inst—"

But in the middle of what he was saying, he was catapulted backward by an invisible pressure wave and crashed into the wall. He stared furiously at Henry, who hadn't so much as lifted a finger. Because it hadn't been Henry but me who set the pressure wave going. I moved into the light, growling softly. A small smile passed over Henry's face.

Rolling his eyes, Arthur scrambled up. "Of course," he said. "I might have known it. Do you two know something? You bore me to death! I'm off!"

"Oh yes? Off to where?" asked Henry.

Arthur laughed, but it didn't sound like genuine amusement. "Don't fool yourself that you can really hold me up with your stupid energy fields! I can always come awake. Any time I like!"

"But then you'll never know why I wanted you exactly here," said Henry. "Because it's not about that door, but this one." He pointed to Muriel's wool shop opposite, and for a moment I held my breath. A bat was fluttering around the sign above the door and ended up hanging head down from the lintel.

"Besides," added Henry, "if you wake now, you'll miss your date with Anabel."

Arthur shrugged again. "So? Once and for all, unlike you two I have all the time in the world. Ever since that business with the snake, Anabel thinks the demon has forgiven me. So we're fighting on the same side. If I can't convince Anabel to tell me about your diabolical tricks with the secrets of dreams today, tomorrow will do. Or the day after tomorrow. Or after Liv's funeral. A few more days won't bother me one way or another."

Of course every word he said was true, and unfortunately Henry and I knew it ourselves. I was sitting beside Henry, leaning my jaguar head on his thigh. Somehow I couldn't bring myself to change back. Absentmindedly, Henry stroked my furry ears.

"Did Anabel put the snake in your locker?" he asked.

Arthur laughed, and this time he did sound genuinely amused. "No, idiot, the demon had to do it himself." A black feather floated to the floor right in front of him. "So that Anabel would see how vast his power is in the real world." More feathers followed, swirling around his head like a flock of tiny birds.

"You put the snake in the locker yourself?" said Henry.

Arthur nodded. "My father is friends with a hedge fund manager who's always showing off about his terrariums and the snakes he breeds. That gave me the idea. Is there a more demonic creature than a snake? I knew it would make everyone's hair stand on end. So I programmed the hedge fund guy to give me one of his snakes, preferably a venomous one so that it would all look very dramatic." He snorted. "Not that I planned for the idiot to choose the most venomous snake of all. It nearly did for me." He looked at his hand, which in waking life was still bandaged. "Never mind—it did what it was meant to do. Now, tell me what's so special about that yellow door. Or don't if you'd rather not. It makes no difference."

For a while he and Henry stared into each other's eyes in silence.

"The door," Henry finally began, "is very unusual. But I'm afraid you'll never find out in what way. Because I've just changed my mind."

"How will I ever survive?" said Arthur sarcastically. "Those crochet patterns look so wildly exciting."

"He's not entirely wrong about the door," said a sugar-sweet voice. Arthur's eyebrows rose as Anabel materialized beside him, like an evil blond genie coming out of its bottle.

She smiled at Arthur. "Sorry I'm a little late, darling, but his energy fields"—she pointed to Henry—"held me up a bit."

Damn it, how did Anabel know about Muriel's door? And why did she have to turn up now and tell Arthur? We'd been so close to tricking him. I'd seen just how curious he was already feeling, even if he'd tried not to show it.

"Now what?" I whispered to Henry. I'd returned to human form without noticing it myself. Henry didn't reply. He was grinding his teeth.

Pleased, Arthur smiled at his supporter, and at the sight of her, my heart sank even further. Anabel had placed herself at Arthur's side like a queen next to her king.

"You've arrived at just the right moment, Bella," said Arthur.

"So she has!" I took a step toward her. "If you'd come a little earlier, you'd have heard Arthur admit to putting the snake in his locker himself," I said urgently. "He's been fooling you the whole time, Anabel! Did you listen to the message Grayson left for you? And did you find the notebook that came through your real-life door? Because if so, you'd know that—"

Anabel cut me short with a wave of her hand—so effectively that I literally couldn't say another word. It was as if an invisible hand were holding my mouth shut.

Arthur grinned. "You must show me that trick!"

"Later," said Anabel. She turned to Henry, who so far hadn't moved. "Open the door," she told him coolly.

"No, I will not," said Henry. But all the same, as if moved by invisible forces, he slid over the floor until he stopped in front of Muriel's door. The bat was flapping its wings restlessly, and now I was immobilized by not just one hand but many, holding me back against the wall and keeping me there. All I could do was breathe in and out, and watch Anabel go over to Henry and destroy our last hope. If she revealed the secret of Muriel's dream to Arthur now, we'd never be able to put our plan into practice.

"Open the door," she repeated quietly.

Henry shook his head.

Arthur came closer. "What's behind it?" he asked, sounding positively avid to know.

"You'll see in a minute." Anabel turned the palm of her hand to Henry. The bat began to dive in the air, but Anabel just snapped her fingers and it flew in a circle. And then another.

"You are not authorized to use this door, Henry," said Anabel in the dramatic tone of voice she always used for anything to do with the demon. "Only the Lord of Shadows and Darkness may do that."

As if in slow motion, Henry raised his hand and pressed down the handle of the door. I tried to scream, but no sound came out. The bat was still caught in its circular flight, squeaking furiously.

When the door swung open, Arthur let out a cry of triumph. "You're the best of us all, Anabel. I bow to you! To think you can even pull the strings of the great Henry Harper like a puppet's . . . We'll be able to learn a lot from each other."

"So we will." I couldn't see her face, because her back was turned to me, but I was sure that Anabel was smiling. No wonder. As long as she had Henry under control, she and Arthur could walk in and out of Muriel's dream whenever they liked. I tried to free myself one last time and then gave up.

Anabel made an inviting gesture. "After you," she said to Arthur.

He turned to me again. "I hope you'll console Henry a bit tomorrow. He hates to be a loser. And maybe you'd like to discuss the arrangements for your funeral. For instance, Henry could play something on his guitar. . . ."

He gloated over my helplessly wide eyes for a moment longer, then took a self-confident step through the doorway and disappeared into Muriel's dream.

At lightning speed, Anabel closed the door behind him and clung to the handle. "Go on!" she shouted at Henry. "Seal it!"

Only now did I realize that the invisible hands pinning me to the wall had also gone away. In spite of that, it was some time before I could move. I was staring incredulously at Anabel. The air around her had begun to flicker, and Henry turned to me with a broad smile on his face.

"She—she lured Arthur into the trap," I stammered.

"So she did." Henry put a hand on Anabel's shoulder. "You were simply amazing, Anabel," he said. "I thought we'd lost you to Arthur until almost the last minute."

Anabel was still clinging to the handle. "Are you sure the energy field will hold?" she asked. "It didn't keep me away for long."

"I don't think any energy field will be necessary," said Henry. "If everything works the way it should, Arthur won't be able to see the door from inside without a personal item belonging to the lady whose dream he is in. But even if he can,

I guess he'd think it beneath his dignity to rattle the handle. I bet you anything he'll prefer to wake up at once."

Anabel let go of the door handle and leaned over with her hands on her knees, as if she had been out for a long run. She was breathing heavily, and at that moment her usually doll-like face, with its perfectly regular features, looked positively human. It showed one emotion above all: relief. "I hope you're right," she said to Henry. "But for safety's sake, we ought to stand guard here all night."

I slowly went closer to her. "Anabel . . ." I was trying to find the right words. "You . . . were you on our side all along?"

She searched the corridor with her eyes before turning them on me, as if it took her some time to get control of herself, and then slowly shook her head. "Not the whole time. Yes, I listened to Grayson's message, and the notebook came through the door, but . . ." She hesitated. "But most of all, I heard what Arthur said just now. What he said about me. And how he'd deceived me." She pointed at the opposite wall. "I was up there—you were staring at me all the time, but your eyes were full of tears."

The letter box. Of course. Mia was right: I really did need to work on my powers of perception.

Where was my little sister, anyway? I turned around, looking for her.

The bat was still flying in circles overhead.

"I think I'd better be going." Anabel looked at the floor. "I've a feeling there are a few urgent things for me to put right. Someone who's been dreaming for a little too long."

I thought of Senator Tod and nodded.

"Off you go, then," said Henry. "Arthur's never going to set foot in this corridor again."

Anabel swallowed. "Maybe I won't either. Or not for a while, anyway. Not until . . ." She cleared her throat. "Not until I've straightened myself out properly."

I very much hoped she'd find a better psychiatrist than Senator Tod this time.

Anabel looked up at the bat, still describing circles in the air, snapped her fingers twice, like Mary Poppins, and then simply disappeared.

Mia landed on the floor in front of us with a thump. "Ouch," she said. Her face looked slightly green. "I feel sick to my stomach. I need a slice of Lottie's carrot cake with whipped cream this minute."

"Then there's only one thing to do," I said. "Wake up."

Henry grinned. "I can be with you girls in ten minutes' time," he said. "Even five minutes' time, if I come on my bike and don't change out of my pajamas."

TITTLE-TATTLE BLOG

**The Frognal Academy Tittle-Tattle Blog,
with all the latest gossip, the best rumors, and
the hottest scandals from our school.**

ABOUT ME:
My name is Secrecy—I'm right here among
you, and I know *all* your secrets.

27 March

An era is ending. Or should I call it a social experiment?

This blog is a perfect example of how to provide a large
quota of nasty comments, unjust statements, and distorted
truths, and I am truly sorry for what I've done with it.

This is the last blog that Secrecy will be posting. The site is
closing down and will be taken off the Internet this
afternoon.

First, however, I'd like to apologize wholeheartedly to all the
people whose secrets I've exposed, holding them up to
ridicule, and to everyone I've injured, wounded, and robbed
of their dignity—I'm ashamed of myself, really ashamed,
more than you can guess.

But I'm not the only one; the rest of you ought to be
ashamed too. All of you who have read this blog, greedily

taking in all the latest news, all of you who have e-mailed me information and cell-phone photos, all of you who were glad when you yourselves were spared, and instead you could revel in the misfortunes and embarrassment of others. The Tittle-Tattle blog could never have worked if it had attracted the attention it deserved—none at all. Secrecy would never have been so powerful if you hadn't been so malicious and eager for sensational news, if you hadn't encouraged Secrecy's own intolerance, nastiness, and false morality so much.

Now it's up to you to decide what that says about yourselves. And to decide whether an attitude like that doesn't promote everything that's wrong in the world today.

I for one don't want to go on being one of those irresponsible people who hide behind their superficiality and cowardice, and let bad things happen in the first place. From now on, I want to be one of those who make the world a little bit better.

Amen.

See you—but from now on I won't be looking at you quite so closely.

Love from Secrecy

PS—This is a message for Gil Walker. Stop wasting your outstanding poetic talent on Mia Silver. She isn't worthy of your poetry.

TITTLE-TATTLE BLOG

**The Frognal Academy Tittle-Tattle Blog reloaded.
Without all the latest gossip, the best rumors, and the
hottest scandals of Hampstead, but with lots of love.**

ABOUT ME:
My name is Secrecy—I'm right here among
you, and I know *all* your secrets.

21 June

Okay, okay, so it's me again. I did try, honestly. I wanted
to take the blog off the Internet. But I gather from your
comments that you need me. You love me. You can't live
without me.

So I've decided to revive it, but in a different way. Do
something good with it. The subject is obvious—there's a
lot of it about.

Love.

Wherever you look these days—love all over the place. And
peace and joy. It would be downright unbearable if I was still
the old Secrecy.

Take Liv Silver and Henry Harper, for instance. A match
made in heaven if ever there was one! It's even rumored that

they keep on smiling at each other in their sleep. The whole time, at that!

Or there's Pandora Porter-Peregrin and her little sister—so touching, don't you agree? Not only does Pandora help Persephone with her homework, she also offers to lend her clothes to her sister. And she wasn't cross even when Persephone recently trod in some dog mess with Pandora's pumps on. That's what I call real love between sisters. Pandora is going to Canada for a gap year after A levels, and she's offered to let Persephone have her room while she's away.

In fact, a good many students in the top class are having a gap year abroad after the exams, but luckily a few of them—and the nicest, if you ask me—will be left.

Jasper Grant, for instance, who surprised everyone by passing his A levels, doesn't want the year abroad that his parents were going to give him as a reward. He'd already matured from a boy to a man in France, he said, and if possible, he'd rather spend the next few years in the parental home, recovering from that experience. Persephone In particular will be glad of it. The two of them were spotted holding hands at the cinema on Monday.

Of course Grayson Spencer is staying here—otherwise Great Britain would have lost its last Knight of the Round Table (and he's starting his studies of medicine this fall). When he isn't helping old people cross the road or looking after orphaned children, he visits Anabel Scott in the psychiatric hospital to which she's committed herself. Apart from that, he spends a lot of time with Mia Silver—give that girl another year or two, and I'm not guaranteeing anything.

Emily Clark is looking much healthier than before the spring vacation, and as if she's getting more sleep. Maybe because she's finally given up stalking Grayson and has more time for her true love—her horse, Conquest of Paradise. They won at two gymkhanas only last weekend. And her A-level results were the third best in the entire country, just after Theo Ellis, by the way. It's only her relationship with her brother, Sam, that has cooled off—no one knows why.

Have you noticed something? Love has many faces, and here we have them all. Love between sisters, love of animals, love of your neighbor, love between parents and children, love of yourself, and, of course the staple of a gossip blog, romantic love.

The latest fine example: Ann Matthews (Liv and Mia Silver's mother) and Ernest Spencer, with the understated wedding of the year (not my own phrasing, the tabloids had that and even better headlines). It was preceded by a really juicy scandal, leading to symptoms of heart disease in Mrs. Spencer Senior, who I'm glad to say is responding to treatment, and a splendid crime story.

Here are the details: Pascal de Gobineau isn't a wedding planner after all (or even a Frenchman) but a con man who was recently seen boarding a ferry to Calais with his Mercedes convertible, also taking the advance payments already made to him for no less than five society weddings. Interpol is investigating, a number of brides are weeping into their pillows, and Charles Spencer is laughing. Because it was he who (for other reasons, but also to do with love) engaged the private detective who got on the trail of Pascal de Gobineau, a.k.a. Peter Pickering, a gambling addict.

The only ones affected by this revelation who aren't crying are Ann and Ernest Spencer. Last weekend they simply went off and got married in the morning sunlight at a nature reserve on the Kentish coast. Barefoot. With a small family party. It sounds terribly kitschy, almost like a hippie wedding, but anyone who saw their faces would want to get married the same way. Particularly as the picnic on the beach after the wedding was so delicious that even Granny Spencer overcame her dislike of just about everything, and ate heartily.

Or so I've heard.

It's said that the tarts and cakes in particular were really special, and amateur baker Lottie Wastlhuber became famous almost overnight as *the* caterer to engage for society parties. I guess you could call it cupboard love—yet another variation on the love theme. It's also rumored that Lottie will soon be marrying into the Spencer family herself. We can't wait to hear more.

The only one who doesn't seem to have access to all this enjoyable love at the moment is Arthur Hamilton. At least, he goes about looking glum, almost as if he were behind bars. When he thinks he's unobserved, he talks to himself. "Bloody stupid sand. Bloody stupid seagulls. Bloody stupid sunset," I heard him muttering the other day. Anyway, here are the results of his latest search when he was last on one of the library computers—maybe one of you can help him? *Pier. List of piers. Women's names beginning with M. Mandy's Crochet Basket. Melanie's Crochet Basket. Wool shops in Clevedon.* Oh dear. Let's hope Australia will take his mind off all that—that's where he's going for a year in August.

Well, that's it for today—I hope you've been inspired by all the love around here to go out and make someone happy!

See you soon!

Love from Secrecy

PS—Hazel Pritchard: I just LOVE your yellow dress for the end-of-year ball. It suits you perfectly.

HENRY WAS ALREADY waiting for me when I stepped out into the corridor. I smiled at him. "Hello, cheese girl!" he said affectionately. "About time too." He took my hand. "Well, where are we going today?"

"We could pay Mrs. Honeycutt a visit," I suggested.

Henry grinned. "I did that only the day before yesterday—for real. She's knitted me a scarf. A mohair scarf."

I chuckled. "Great! Just what you most need in June! Oh—look!" I stopped, feeling much moved.

On the door handle of Matthews's Moonshine Antiquarian Books, a notice was hanging slightly askew. Someone had scrawled on it, obviously in a hurry: JUST MARRIED—CLOSED FOR NOW ON ACCOUNT OF HAPPINESS.

It had really been a perfect wedding—aside from that moment of horror when Charles had looked at Grayson and asked, "Have you had your hair cut?" For a split second we had stared at each other as if petrified and then had the most unstoppable fit of laughter ever.

"There ought to be a notice like that on my own door." I beamed at Henry. "Any more happiness and I'd burst."

Henry put his arm around my waist and drew me close. "Then we must go very carefully," he said, kissing me. But only to push me away about ten seconds later and look at me with mock disappointment. "Damn it, that doesn't work. You didn't burst."

No, but I had melted a tiny little bit. As usual when Henry touched me. "Forget what I said." I heaved a sigh. "One can never have enough happiness."

"Just like the love Secrecy was blogging about the other day," said Henry mockingly.

"Or enough mysteries," I said.

"Oh, I don't know." Henry made a face. "Mysteries are much overrated. We've solved enough of them these last few months. I'd be satisfied with exploring just one mystery for the rest of my life, and that's you."

"That's so sentimental!" I couldn't help laughing. "I bet you got it from a movie. Apart from the fact that I'm about as mysterious as an open book."

"You've no idea." Henry brushed a strand of hair back from my forehead. And then he kissed me again, and I forgot what I had really been going to say. Which was that we still didn't understand the real mystery—the nature of this corridor, why we of all people had found it, and how it could be scientifically explained. But why did there have to be a scientific explanation for everything?

When we let go of each other, I glanced around.

"What are you looking for?" asked Henry.

"I'm waiting for Anabel to come around the corner and whisper mysteriously that it isn't over yet, it's only just begun."

Henry smiled. "Exactly right. It's only just begun."

Cast of Characters

Liv Silver, has so many dreams

Mia Silver, Liv's younger sister, known in some circles as "the new Miss Marple," unmasks Secrecy

Ann Matthews, Liv's mother

Ernest Spencer, Ann's fiancé, has a weakness for irises

Lottie Wastlhuber, Liv and Mia's former au pair, believes there's good in everyone

Grayson Spencer, Ernest's son, former owner of a life-size battle droid robot from *Star Wars: Episode I*

Florence Spencer, Ernest's daughter, twin sister of Grayson

Charles Spencer, Ernest's brother, dentist

The Boker, also known as Mrs. Spencer Senior, Ernest's mother, mourning a topiary peacock known as Mr. Snuggles

Henry Harper, likes dreaming with Liv

Arthur Hamilton, ex-friend of Anabel Scott, in fact ex-friend of everyone but Jasper

Jasper Grant, a friend of Henry, Grayson, and Arthur, ex-dreamer, has finished with "dreams and demons and all that garbage"

Anabel Scott, Arthur's ex-girlfriend, unfortunately has lost her marbles

Emily Clark, Grayson's ex-girlfriend, has a horse called Conquest of Paradise

Persephone Porter-Peregrin, Liv's friend, likes lipstick, hates guns. Honestly.

Mrs. Lawrence, Liv's ex–French teacher after an unfortunate incident in the school cafeteria

Sam Clark, Emily's little brother, has dubious ideas of morality

Dr. Otto Anderson, also known as *Senator Tod Nord*, in a coma and dreaming that he is still Anabel's psychiatrist

Mrs. Honeycutt, eighty-year-old superknitter, shelters Liv, Grayson, and Henry in her dream

Muriel Honeycutt, Mrs. Honeycutt's sister, also a great knitter, was murdered by her husband, Alfred, in 1977

Matt next door, good-looking law student, is sometimes surprised by his vivid dreams

Pascal de Gobineau, wedding planner for the rich and beautiful

Harry Triggs a.k.a. *BloodySword66*, role-player, aide in a home for senior citizens, unappreciated literary genius, and the new owner of a life-size battle droid robot from *Star Wars: Episode I*

Timothy Donnelly, first a role-playing friend of Harry, then an unemployed roofer, later on guru of a sect, even later on dead

Rasmus Wakefield, an imaginary person called after an overweight chow

And not forgetting *Secrecy*. Se. Cre. Cy.

In minor parts, also:

Princess Buttercup, the family dog

Spot, the Spencers' cat

Ben Ryan, pees in umbrella stands when he thinks no one is looking

Maisie Brown, sometimes spills things, but honestly, it really was just lemonade on her dress

Mr. Vanhagen, tore Mrs. Lawrence's heart out, figuratively speaking

Gil Walker the Stalker, writes love poems to Mia

Molly, the donkey, and *Herby*, the amorous crocodile;

Alfred, the murderer with a flowered cushion; a blackbird; several bottles of 1972 Château Margaux; a great many feathers, tarts, cakes, quiches, some whipped cream, and of course . . . THE SNAKE!

AUTHOR'S NOTE

I wasn't really going to write any afterword for this third and last volume. Time is short. As I write this, the final showdown still has to be written. It's already late May (I was really meant to deliver the manuscript in March), and no one ever reads all the acknowledgments. Just to make it more exciting, I somehow stuck a bamboo cane in my eye the day before yesterday—and in the ambulance on the way to the emergency room I had plenty of time to reconsider the afterword question. It's really a good opportunity to say thank you. Particularly to those to whom I can't send e-mails, cards, boxes of wine, and so on: my readers. Thank you for immersing yourselves in my books, feeling for my characters, and always wanting to know what happens next. It's for you that I rethink every sentence fifteen times until it finally seems to be right, and there are days—there truly are—when it's only for you that I get up at all. This book is for you.

Anyone who has read my books will know that I have a weakness for secret societies (right now I am toying with the idea of founding the Lodge of the One-Eyed Lady, if you ever happen to hear of it . . .), and sometimes I imagine that the people who like my books are at heart a kind of secret society, a community in which they can all laugh at the same things and exchange insider remarks that no one who hasn't read the same books will understand, such as "He's more of a Grayson than a Henry, if you see what I mean." (And of course the others will know just what you mean ☺.)

I'm sometimes a little sorry for those not in the society. But there we are: one of the good things about secret societies is that not everyone can belong. We're an exclusive, elite club of dreamers, night owls, romantics, and bookworms, and I am glad, proud, and thankful that we can dream together.

Whether it's by night in the endless labyrinth of dream corridors, virtually online at thesilvertrilogy.com, or in the next story—see you again soon!

Love from

Kerstin Gier